ROGUE WOLF
HUNTER

KAIT BALLENGER

KB

To my mom,
for helping make this possible

1

JACE MCCANNON PALMED the Mateba and clicked back the gun's hammer. The cold grip panels of the modified revolver sat comfortably in his hand. Six silver bullets for a rogue werewolf. Limited shots. But he was feeling lucky.

Jace gripped the gun with both hands, lowering it to his side as he slipped in and out of the shadows. The rank scents of garbage, car exhaust and piss wafted into his nose. Ah, the sweet aroma of Rochester's backstreets. Something about this godforsaken city he *hadn't* missed.

He ran his tongue over his teeth, jonesing for a cigarette to drown out the smell and steady the adrenaline buzz creeping through his veins.

Damn, he wanted to find this son of a bitch.

Resting his back against a brick building, he paused and glanced up. The white moon stared down at the city streets, calling to him. Heat prickled beneath his skin. He needed to find this monster yesterday. Hell, weeks ago.

He wrenched his gaze from the tempting sky and forced himself into the moment.

Inhaling a deep breath, he rushed around the corner and scanned the area, pointing his gun into the darkness.

No one. No wolves, no suspects. Damn, not even the working girls were roaming tonight. Not that he blamed them. Rochester wasn't exactly known for being the safest of cities.

Unfortunately, street violence wasn't anything to call home about—happened all the time. But this was different. Innocent women being found with their organs slung around their corpses, Jack-the-Ripper style. The worst part? Jace had no idea where to find the sick fuck responsible, and the thought of the young women's pain sent his blood boiling.

Steadying his focus, he explored the alley, gun still at the ready and eyes searching for any sign of movement. A rustling noise hissed from around the next corner. Jace held his gun tight and slipped down the narrow passage toward it.

Showtime.

The sound grew louder, and he quickened his pace. When he reached the bend, he stopped, listening closely.

Now or never.

He threw himself around the corner, gun ready and finger on the trigger.

A plastic bag caught on a dumpster swished in the light wind.

"Shit." He cursed under his breath, before he pushed his fingers through his hair.

Maybe he wasn't so lucky tonight.

As if on cue, the cell phone jammed in the pocket of his jeans vibrated. Of course. He hadn't put up with enough bullshit for one evening. Life clearly hadn't stuck it to him enough...yet. He pulled out the annoying piece of shit and read the screen: restricted. Likely David. Headquarters insisted on nothing more than burner phones.

It made hunters like them harder to track.

Jace jabbed his thumb into one of the buttons and shoved the phone to his ear. "Yeah?"

"Meeting in an hour." David's deep voice rumbled over the line.

Aw, hell. If that wasn't the last thing he wanted to hear. He shook his head. "Don't toy with me. I've got business."

"I'm not shittin' you, J. One hour, and you better show or Damon's gonna rip my head off. I told him I'd get you here."

Jace frowned. Damn, he hated being forced to carry a cell phone, even the low-tech burner kind. He didn't enjoy people contacting him whenever they pleased. Period. Meetings with HQ were exactly why he hadn't stuck around out west. Settling in one place for so long had caused questions, raised suspicions.

"It's nearly the full moon, David. This is my prime time. You know that."

"You don't have to preach to me. Damon's the one riding your ass like a Grand Canyon donkey, not me." David paused for a moment. "He's gonna want a report tonight."

"Yeah, yeah, I hear ya. I'll have something."

"Sure you hear me, and I like to dress up in tutus while my girl spanks me and calls me Big Daddy."

Jace smirked. "Hey, if that's what gets you off..."

"Shut it," David said. "You've gotta report tonight or Damon will go postal. So what are you gonna tell him?"

Jace glanced into the empty darkness surrounding him. Maybe he was getting too old for this shit—or too tired. Hell, both? "Same thing I told him last time—jack shit. I'm not opening my damn mouth until I've got their packmaster bound and chained, or, preferably, I'm carrying this perp's head on a silver platter courtesy of my bare hands."

David let out a frustrated sigh. "I thought you said you had something."

"I do." Jace lowered his voice. It didn't matter that he was alone; some things he couldn't say aloud if he wanted to keep his sanity. "I've got a scent, and it's...different." He hesitated. "Trailing this monster's stink is about as much fun as shooting myself in the foot."

"It's something."

Jace nearly swore. "You better believe it's something. But what do you expect me to do, David? Tell the whole damn division their wolf hunter happens to be so good at his job because he's a friggin' half-breed? That'll go over real well."

Silence answered him from the other end of the line. Another rustling sound blew through the alley, but this time, Jace ignored it. David was only in the know, because they'd been friends before. Helluva word: before. Before their roles as hunters had been official, before life had gotten complicated, fast, before all the shit they'd been stupid enough to dream of became too real. These days Jace was over it.

"Look, I'll deal with this, all right? Forget about it. I'll be at the damn meeting with bells on and a smiling face, but let me do it on my own terms."

"Yeah, fine. I better see you there or the next time I'm around, I'll have a dog collar and it'll be coming straight for your neck."

Jace huffed. "Talk to you later, Big Daddy."

David snorted. "Yeah, you too, Sugar."

The line went dead.

Jace shoved the phone in his pocket again, welcoming the noises of the city over David's nagging. Maybe he really *was* getting too old for this shit. A siren sounded in the distance. The occasional honk from busy traffic. The thumping vibration of someone's overstressed speakers.

But damn, he'd missed this place.

The constant din.

Montana, then Idaho, hell the whole western tour had been quiet. Too quiet.

Nine years and he was finally home again.

Yet he was still hiding...

Releasing a long breath, he shook the thought off. He'd missed the city, but he hadn't missed this. He kicked at an empty Budweiser can. The backdrop of littered city garbage everywhere. Covering his tracks.

Through the din, the swishing sound continued, the noise growing. Jace rolled his eyes, ready to ball up the grocery bag and pitch it. He eyed the plastic.

Shit. The wind had stopped. The bag wasn't blowing.

The faint sound of footsteps echoed, and the rustling quieted. Jace lifted the revolver from his side, launching himself down the alley and around the corner. He held his gun steady, prepared to shoot. Only to stop mid-run.

He stared in horror.

The streetlights overhead illuminated what lay in front of him as all the breath escaped from his lungs in one fell swoop. "Shit."

Anonymous tip his ass.

Blood. There was so much blood. Everywhere. The dim orange light from the street lamps framed the corpse like spotlights at a macabre play starring an innocent, mutilated victim. The girl's head hung crooked, touching her shoulder, mouth open and eyes lifeless. Her features were contorted in a look of pure terror. Pale arms lay limp at what had once been her sides, her legs spread wide, with her pants and underwear wrapped around one ankle. The middle of her body had ceased to exist, ripped to shreds by what Jace knew were large canine teeth.

Anyone with a weak stomach would have tossed their cookies at first glance. Despite all the crazy shit Jace had seen in his years as a hunter for the Execution Underground, even *his* gut did a flip. What the hell was wrong with this guy? *Guy?* No, this killer wasn't a person. This sicko was subhuman, and not because he was a werewolf.

Jace fought the urge to punch his fist into the brick wall beside him. Rage overcame him as he thought of the woman's pain, causing his hands to clench into fists. The beast inside him stirred, longing to emerge. He didn't know her, but that didn't matter. She'd been someone, and that someone mattered damn it.

He growled, releasing the tension, and tried to calm himself. He needed to examine the body, and fast. If the police got here, he was screwed six ways to Sunday. Headquarters would have to bail him out. Damon would go apeshit.

Carefully, he knelt by the corpse. Bruises marred her forearms and neck. Based on their colors, they had definitely been made pre-mortem. She'd been dead at least thirty minutes. Long before he'd been nearby. He swore under his breath again. He was always two steps behind this bastard. Leaning over her, he made the mistake of breathing in, and underneath the overpowering smell of blood, the distinct scent of sex lingered. She'd been raped before her death.

A snarl ripped through him.

Power. That was what this freak was all about—power. He attacked young women, humans in their early twenties, who were no match for his supernatural strength. This monster preyed on victims he knew he could take with ease, because deep down, he was a coward. And from the carnage of his attacks, this wasn't just about overpowering his victims. With this kind of blood display, these attacks were either personal or passionate, and Jace would bet on the later.

A sexual sadist. Anger excitation. It wasn't the sex that got this bastard off. It was the pain these innocent women endured. Intestinal damage and blood loss: a slow death, so his victims suffered in front of his eyes. He likely attacked them as a wolf and then assaulted them in human form. The even more gruesome perversions came after. A familiar anger built inside Jace again.

He pulled the old, unopened pack of Marlboro Reds from his leather trench coat, smacking the box against his hand as he contemplated opening it, lighting up. The smoke would rush into his lungs, the nicotine calming him instantly. He shook his head, slipping the pack back inside his coat. This shit was going to kill him, more than the cigarettes ever would, but most days he didn't care.

Guilt twisted knots inside his stomach as he stared down at the victim. Here he was, clearly not giving little more than a rat's ass about his health or his life, with no family left to care if he lived or died. But he was living and breathing, while this innocent girl, who'd had a full life ahead of her, lay at his feet. She'd likely had something to lose, people who would miss her.

She'd been someone.

He stared into the open cavity that had once been her chest. No heart. It wasn't like shifters to eat humans, or even attack them out in the open, but this sicko did. *Consumption shows a desire to keep part of the victim with him. No remorse.*

And that's if this monster was even a true wolf shifter to begin with.

There was something...off about the scent. It was similar to a wolf, familiar, but not quite...right...in a way Jace couldn't put his finger on.

Different.

His explanation to David echoed in his head again.

Different was putting it lightly.

Jace grabbed the flask that always resided in his pocket, unscrewing the cap and downing a long gulp of Bushmills Irish Whiskey. The liquor trickled down his throat in a warm rush. If this was any sign of how the night was going to go, he'd need a helluva lot more than the contents of the flask to keep his demons at bay.

He glanced at the victim again as he crouched at her side, wracking his brain for any possible clues he could have missed. Careful to use only his sleeve and not leave a fingerprint, he lifted her hands and peered underneath her fingernails. No skin or fur. She hadn't put up much of a fight. Maybe the killer took her by surprise? Jace wouldn't doubt it.

Or maybe she'd known her attacker...

There'd be no way to tell for certain. He'd report to Damon, his division leader, and Execution Underground Headquarters and then leave the details to his fellow hunters. Shane could use the voice distorter he'd rigged up to report the crime from an untraceable number, and Headquarters would have the local police and coroner reports in their database as soon as they were available. Jace had what he needed for his own report, but he couldn't notify the beat cops himself, not until he was far from here. Though it would take them a while to find her in the back alley like this, if they ever did. It was more likely some poor civilian would stumble upon her.

As he stood, less-than-ready to go to the damn meeting, another scent came to him on the wind. A sudden sense of awareness prickled over his skin. Tucking his flask away, he paused for a long moment.

What the...?

Spinning so fast his vision blurred, he had his gun out and his finger on the trigger within seconds. A wolf shifter emerged from the darkness.

"Don't move," he warned.

The wolf froze, the lucidum of its golden eyes flashing in the streetlights. With an irreverent snarl, the beast bared its canines, its eyes darting to the gun in his hand. He knew what that look meant.

He cocked back the hammer, the sound audible against the cold winter winds. "You put the teeth away. I put the piece away," he offered. "Fair enough?"

The wolf snapped its feral jaws. *You first,* it seemed to say.

He snorted a near laugh. "Like hell."

For a moment, they lingered like this, both refusing to yield, until the piercing sound of a car alarm went off in the distance, drawing both their attention. Seizing the split second of distraction, the shifter turned tail and bolted from the alley.

Shit.

Jace dashed after his target, his boots clashing against the pavement as he tailed the beast. A werewolf's speed outranked a regular human's any day, but he tailed the shifter with ease. The shifter skidded sharply to the left with Jace on its heels, his pace never faltering. Adrenaline shot through his veins, charging him like a live wire.

He tapped the trigger of the Mateba and, aiming while he ran, fired wide with purpose in mind, intentionally missing and using his silver bullets to herd the wolf. If he fired right, it turned left. He was careful, making each bullet count and ensuring he had one left for his own defense. He'd need to make this fast. The sounds would draw the local PD.

One of Jace's shots ricocheted off the ground near the wolf's feet. It jumped with a loud yelp and bounded into another alleyway. But he was prepared; he knew these back streets better than his own damn hand. He sprinted after the wolf. A smirk spread across his face as the monster ran into a dead end. It spun toward him and growled.

Right hand bracing his gun, he reached with his left and removed his silver dagger. When the wolf's golden eyes locked on the weapons, it backed into a corner, and Jace swore he heard it keen before its growling continued. Stalking like a predator, he moved forward. All his muscles tensed as he prepared for the animal to lunge at him. The wolf was primed for a fight.

And damned if he wouldn't give this monster the fight of its life.

2

FROM THE MOMENT he pulled his gun, Frankie Amato knew what he was. A hunter. She'd stumbled onto a hunter. She stared down the barrel of his gun with fear and adrenaline pumping through her veins. A large lump crawled into her throat.

The rumors are true.

Shit. She hadn't expected this. A hunter in Rochester— on her turf. There hadn't been a wolf hunter for the Execution Underground this far east in years.

Damn it, she should've known better. Been on higher alert, all things considered.

In the past few months, several rogue wolves had been murdered in her territory. As alpha of Rochester pack, one of the few, remaining packs not under the protection of The Grey Wolves and their Seven Range Pact out west, it was her job alone to keep her packmates out of harm's way. But the protection she guaranteed didn't extend to the rogue wolves who'd refused to join her pack, and she'd given no more than a fleeting thought to the rumors that they'd died at the hands of a hunter. Rogues weren't known for living the most peaceful of lives.

But now the voices of gossip and the murmurs of trouble, which had spread like wildfire throughout her pack, smacked her in the face with a major reality check. And son of a bitch, he'd backed her into a dead end. She'd let down her guard, and the bastard had cornered her.

She bared her canines, growling from deep within, but still, the hunter strode closer. Shadows covered his face, and his gun pointed straight at her head. The silver dagger he'd pulled from his coat flashed in the moonlight. Her heart pounded, knowing the fate she would be subjected to if she didn't fight fast.

Frankie's tail hit the wall. Even if she lunged, his dagger would pierce right through her chest, but considering how her kind healed, she'd likely recover in a few days. He'd bleed out long before that. Humans were weak creatures. Granted, the injections the Execution Underground gave their human hunters which gifted them increased strength and agility made them tougher than most. Still, by her estimation, huge monster of a man or not, she could take this asshole out with ease.

But she couldn't, because he was a hunter.

That single fact froze her in place.

Frustration filled her, and she snarled as logic prevailed. Where would that leave her pack? The Execution Underground wouldn't allow any of them to live if she killed even one of their own. It'd be akin to a declaration of war with his division, not to mention Execution Underground Headquarters.

But no way in hell was she going down without a fight.

Frankie lunged for the hunter's ankles, hitting lower than he expected. He crumpled to the ground, his elbow jabbing into her side as he fell. She yelped in surprise before sinking her canines into his forearm.

"Fuck!" The guttural curse tore from his lips as his weapon fell from his hand.

Satisfaction filled her. If he was temporarily disarmed, he'd lost his advantage and the asshole deserved to be torn to shreds for killing her kind. Hell, at least roughed up a bit. Even if the wolves he'd killed were reckless brutes she'd intended to take care of anyway.

This was *her* city. Her turf.

And she'd make sure he remembered.

Shaking her head side-to-side, she ripped at the hunter's arm. Without warning, he rolled onto his side and slashed his knife in defense. The blade cut across her belly. With a yelp, she released him. Scrambling across the pavement, she bolted down the alley. But within seconds he was on his feet again and sprinting after her. She needed to gain some distance, so she could get a running start, get her momentum going. But he was fast for a human, even for a hunter.

Too fast.

He threw himself at her, landing on her hind legs and pinning her. The soft pads of her paws scraped the pavement, struggling to gain traction as she clawed her way free. Turning on her attacker, she jumped for his throat. Her paws hit his chest, and he slammed to the ground from the weight of the blow. She snarled and snapped at his neck, but he caught her by her scruff and tossed her aside as if she weighed nothing. She skidded across the pavement.

What the—?

His strength was off-the-charts.

Before she could process what was happening, he was on top of her again, lifting her by her scruff as if she were no more than a petulant pup. With superior strength, he pinned her to the brick wall. He shoved the blade of his knife against her throat as she struggled to breathe.

She growled. What the hell?

He'd bested her.

He'd actually bested her.

Impressive...and infuriating.

His knife held steady as she dangled by her scruff, teeth bared. A quick glance down to his belt showed he'd somehow managed to reclaim his gun. An uncharacteristic streak of fear rushed through her and her hackles raised.

Agile and strong as she was, even if she managed to wiggle away this time, she couldn't outrun a bullet. Not at this close range. Her heart pounded, knowing the fate she might be subjected to if she didn't think fast. Hunters like him weren't supposed to kill her kind unless they broke one of the three rules set out by the North American Free Species Agreement, but she knew firsthand many often shot first and asked questions later.

Her uncle had learned that grim reality all too well.

She could still hear his keening in her ears.

A shiver ran down her spine. Limbs and muscles contorted as she started to shift. Pleading wasn't her style; she was a packmaster, an alpha, after all—and one of the few females of her kind to claim the title—but if it would protect her pack and keep them off this hunter's radar, she'd do whatever it took.

A low growl escaped her lips, slowly transitioning into the battle cry of a woman. He shoved off her as she slumped back onto the brick wall behind her in human form, bare flesh scraping. But he remained close, leaving her no chance of lunging for him or escaping his bullet again. A streak of rage rushed through her.

She scanned the alley. All brick walls, a couple of dumpsters that were too far off to offer protection, and nothing amongst the garbage she could use as a weapon. Nothing that would help her escape, and there was no way in hell she could dodge around him when she was cornered like this. He'd proven he was a good shot when he'd oh-so-successfully corralled her into a dead end.

She lifted her hands and held them up, palms out.

Draw him in. Pretend you're weak. Then shift, and get the hell outta Dodge, she tried to reassure herself.

But within seconds, he was on her again, pinning her between the brick wall and his body as his blade pressed against her throat. She let out a small whimper of panic. She wasn't below milking the helpless-female card. Not if it saved her.

Face obscured in shadow, he hovered over her, a massive black silhouette, nothing visible but the width of his body and his knife still trained on her. Yeah, there was no missing that.

"I'm not your enemy," she said.

A rough sound escaped him.

Had he just scoffed at her?

She guessed she *had* just ripped into his arm like it was a chew-toy...

"I'm serious," she insisted. "Look at the evidence. That woman was more than mutilated." She gestured to her own nude body pressed against his fully clothed one. "I'm not covered in blood. I'm weaponless, and I don't have the right...equipment to do what was done to that poor girl."

Frankie held her breath as she waited for him to reply.

Blood rushed to her head, pounding in her ears.

"Don't make any sudden moves." His deep voice washed over her.

A chill rushed down her spine as the night clouds drifted, bringing him into focus in a pool of light. Her gaze traveled up his frame as the moonlight illuminated his face and for a moment, Frankie struggled to breathe.

Alpha wolf or not, she was suddenly aware of how very naked and vulnerable she was as she stared up at the hunter before her. She recognized this man, and he wasn't just any hunter. He was *the* hunter—or at least, one of a legendary few her kind knew by name.

Jace McCannon, wolf hunter for the Execution Underground, a man who, in the words of her own people, was both a fiercely protective warrior for humanity and a lethal killer of any wolf who dared cross him. She'd seen the photos. Heard the rumors.

And yet she'd bitten him.

Shit.

She swallowed hard. Even as an independent packmaster, Frankie made it her business to keep tabs on the politics of the larger packs out west. The Grey Wolves, a pack that outnumbered her own nearly a hundred to one ruled supreme over both the Seven Range Pact and the North American west, and this man who stood before her along with Quinn Harper, Reid Murphy, and a handful of other hunters were singularly responsible for bringing the Grey Wolves' attempt to expand east of the Montana mountains to a halt.

It didn't matter that it'd been years since that conflict, and the Execution Underground and the Seven Range Pact had now come to a tenuous mutual agreement—the Wolves of the West now helped the Execution Underground protect humanity from their mutual bloodsucking enemies in exchange for being left alone by the human organization.

But during their fighting years, this man, this hunter, had been a verifiable killer.

As she understood it, Quinn Harper, the Execution Underground division leader in Billings, Montana, where the Grey Wolves made their home, had been the negotiator, but *this* man had been his enforcer, the weapon to back them up.

Few of her kind crossed his path and lived to tell the tale.

So what on God's green earth was he doing here? In Rochester, of all places?

At *her* crime scene?

Abruptly, he shoved away from her, unpinning her from the wall as he traded his knife for his gun. At the sudden release, she slumped against the brick of the building, her legs weak post-shift. She was crashing hard from the adrenaline. Not to mention, her side was still bleeding.

"You alright?" he asked, gesturing to the wound.

Alright?

The blood had already slowed to a trickle. It'd barely scratched the surface. He'd only cut enough to defend himself without actually hurting her.

She nodded. "It'll heal." At the rate her kind mended, it'd be closed within an hour. Already she could feel the skin knitting back together.

He nodded, but didn't offer her any reprieve. Not that she'd expected as much.

"Good." His voice was like a low growl in his chest. "Get up." The gruff, deep vibrato hummed through her, even as his gun remained still.

Frankie didn't dare move.

"That was an order, not a request," he growled.

Slowly, she inhaled a deep breath. She didn't respond

kindly to orders, but for the sake of her pack, she found her footing and rose to her feet. Her hands remained steady, palms out. She wasn't afraid of this bastard, and she intended to show it. His gaze raked over her, slow and assessing, like he was sizing up her strength and nothing more, yet heat flooded her cheeks. She was far too naked to be standing before this man.

"What's your name, she-wolf?"

She-wolf? She bristled. On his lips she didn't like the term.

Not in the least.

For a moment, her stomach churned. If she told him her name, he would know exactly who she was. No doubt he'd come across her name in the E.U's records whenever he'd scoped out the packs in this area. Though she'd worked hard to keep her face off the Execution Underground's radar, helping give her pack a low profile. She wasn't about to throw that away by being honest, especially not with this particular hunter.

She didn't think his division would likely want a war with her pack, but she couldn't be certain. His kind wasn't supposed to hurt innocents, but killing the Rochester pack-master and dispersing one of the last small packs this far east might be too sweet a temptation for an ambitious hunter to resist.

She swallowed hard.

He eased nearer, waiting for her response. Too near for her tastes.

"Come any closer again and I'll tear into more than your arm tonight," she growled.

A smirk quirked his lips. "Is that a promise?"

She didn't answer.

His wry grin widened. "Let's get something clear. You're at my crime scene. I call the shots here."

"Your crime scene?"

Ignoring her outrage, he lowered his gun. "Yeah, my crime scene," he said as if it were a matter of fact, rather than a debatable point. "Now, you got a name or not, Princess?"

Princess? She snarled. "Francesca." Her mother's name, from which her shortened version originated. The half lie would save her.

For now.

"Francesca." Slowly, he nodded his head. He chewed on the name as if he didn't believe her for a second. This hunter was good. Too good.

"How about you?" she asked, deflecting the attention from herself. "You got a name?"

He smiled that smug grin again. "Sure," he drawled. That wide smirk reminded her far too much of a hardened cowboy to be this far east, though his accent was pure upstate.

She quirked a brow. "Care to share?"

That grin widened. "Don't need to. You already know it."

She frowned. He was reading her like a damn book, and she didn't like it.

To her relief, he gave her a quick once over and whatever aggression he saw there, he must have realized he needed to reconcile, because he smiled that damn grin again whilst he made a show of clicking on his gun's safety and holstering it. When he was finished, he quirked a brow as if to say, *See, friends now?*

She growled again. Friends her ass.

His smile faded before he cleared his throat. "Fair enough, down to business then. So here's what's going to happen, sweetheart. You're going to march that sweet little ass to my car, and we're going to take a ride to division headquarters," his voice dropped low as he drew closer, "and then you're going to explain to me what the fuck you've been doing sniffing around my crime scenes. Understood?"

"Crime scene," she corrected. "Singular."

He gave a derisive huff. "You'll learn fast I'm not one for games." The cold, knowing look in his eye froze her in place.

A chill shivered down her spine. She *had* been sniffing out all the crime scenes for the past several weeks. But how could he possibly know that she'd been—?

In an instant, that threatening look was gone, cutting her thoughts short. Instead, a look of pure business took its place. "Now beat feet." He nodded toward the mouth of the alley.

Her jaw clenched, and she lifted her chin. "And if I don't?"

He chuckled like he half-hoped she would. "Why don't you try and find out?"

They stood like this for a long beat, at a standoff once again, both too stubborn to move, before she finally let out a long huff.

Fine. For the sake of her pack, she'd cooperate. She could already tell there would be no negotiating with this prick. She stepped forward, opening her mouth to come back with a snarky retort, but before she could get a word out, within seconds her back was pressed against the brick wall once again; his body pushed against hers as his giant hand clapped over her mouth. She screamed, but the sound muffled against his hand.

"Listen," he hissed. His hot breath fanned over her ear.

She stilled, not at his words, but because she heard the only thing that could possibly have united her in a common goal with this massive intrusion of a man—footsteps. Likely human, a beat cop by her guess, considering how loudly the idiot's boots were clomping. But it was still too quiet for human ears.

Her gaze locked with his, and he lowered his hand. "How did you—?"

He hushed her again, his expression dead serious. A hunter would never allow a shifter like her to expose what she truly was to a human. Ever. And his gaze said as much.

It was an offense punishable by death.

This close to her, his raw gaze penetrated her, the calm fury in his green eyes causing her to still. Eyes that vibrant didn't belong on a human. They were fit for something more. More daring. More lethal. Just more...

"I don't want to hurt you." His voice was gruff, strained. Not gentle.

But for some reason, she believed him.

He quickly wrapped the flaps of his coat around her, and pulled her flush against him by the small curve of her waist to shield her nudity from view. His hands were purposeful, not exploratory. All business. The last thing either of them needed was a charge from the human police for her indecent exposure.

As he worked to position her against him, strands of his auburn hair fell into his face, accenting his sharp features. A strong jaw, a regal blade of a nose that looked like it'd been broken one too many times and a sharp, harsh line of a mouth stood out on a gruff, handsome face. Everything about this man screamed danger, from the brutal scars on his hands to his massive steel-toed boots and that dark fury in his eyes, but somehow, she felt...safe here, pinned beneath him, like he was truthful and not only would he not hurt her, he'd protect her.

For now.

Safe in a killer's arms? She quirked a brow.

Clearly, her instincts were failing her.

He towered over her, well over six feet, and his physique matched his height in enormity. She could feel that much from where he pinned her, dwarfing her in both height and width. Muscles strained against the sleeves of his trench coat, and considering how he'd bested her with such ease, she had no doubt he had the strength to hurt her.

But he wouldn't. At least not this time. She saw it in his eyes.

She'd figured out his endgame here, pretending they were lovers, ducked into an alley for some kind of romantic tryst. To a human, what else would explain her nakedness? Humans were so weirdly uncomfortable with nude bodies. She'd never understand it.

"So I'm just supposed to pretend and go along this?" Her whisper was sharp, angry.

There was that sound of amusement again. "You won't need to pretend, sweetheart."

He pressed her flush against him, one arm cradling her nude waist, the flap of his coat shielding her body from view as his other hand settled at the base of her throat. But he didn't kiss her. Instead, he lingered there, his lips no more than a hairsbreadth away, the warm, welcome heat of his breath tickling her face peppered with the scent of mint.

His fingers gently clutched the nape of her neck.

And still, he didn't kiss her.

Gasping for breath, she wanted to tell him he was full of himself, that she wouldn't go along with his game, even to save her own skin. Ridiculous as it was, she wanted to tell him that she wouldn't even pretend to kiss him if he was the last man on earth because he was her enemy, goddamnit, and she didn't know him. Not to mention, she was engaged to be married to someone else—even if that someone was a packmaster not of her own choosing. A man she barely knew. She wanted to tell him that no matter what, she wouldn't allow it.

But somehow, she couldn't find the words.

An echo of desire thrummed deep within her, distant, yet hot and wicked from the feel of his rough fingers at her throat and the hard, surprising ridge of his arousal against her. As if the very air she breathed wanted to betray her, the cold breeze between them seemed to crackle with tension, charged with electricity, and for a moment, the ludicrous thought that perhaps they'd been meant to meet each other tonight passed through her mind.

Still, he didn't kiss her.

He held every ounce of power to do so, yet he didn't dare use it. Even though he could. His lips could be on hers even though he only had a small amount of breath. Even though part of her wanted him to.

It wouldn't be a real kiss. It would be a fake kiss to save her and nothing more. That's the only reason she wanted him to.

She knew that. He knew that. They both did. They were strangers, after all. She couldn't help that it *felt* real. Her eyes flashed to her wolf.

"Kiss me or I'll die." The words fell from her lips before she could stop them.

He chuckled and the deep sound twisted something low in her belly. "Not tonight."

Whether he meant her death or his kiss, she couldn't be certain.

The human beat cop rounded the corner then, drawing their whispers to a halt as his gaze immediately found them, tangled together in the orange glow of the streetlights and now the high beam of his Maglite. Frankie flinched against the searing glow. In an instant, the tension between them dissipated.

"Evenin', Officer." The hunter nodded toward the beat cop as he held her steady against him. He cast the cop that disgustingly charming grin as if he had all the right in the world to be in that alley. She could practically imagine him out west in Montana Grey Wolf territory, tipping his Stetson low over his brow, upstate accent or not.

The beat cop adjusted his too-tight belt buckle as he held his Maglite high. "You two see anyone come through here? Someone called in gunshots."

"Gunshots?" The hunter quirked a brow, his eyes wide with mock fear.

The ease with which humans could lie to one another never ceased to stun her. Her kind never bothered with false pretenses. They could practically smell it on each another.

And he *was* human. She glanced up toward those vibrant eyes again.

Wasn't he?

"No, sir," the hunter continued, shaking his head. "Though we saw someone run that way a few minutes ago." He gave a nod in the opposite direction toward where the victim's body lay several alleys beyond.

Clearly, he was hoping to lead the beat cop in the right direction—and more importantly, away from them.

The cop nodded. "Thanks." He turned to walk away, then paused mid-stride. He gestured between them with a dismissive wave. "And you two do me a favor and go get a room, would ya?"

A wave of embarrassed heat rushed to her cheeks, even as the hunter nodded. "Yes, sir."

A moment later, the cop was gone, disappeared into the darkness and the din of the city, leaving her and the hunter alone once again. For a long beat, neither of them moved. Frankie's breath rose and fell in ragged pants, the heat of it swirling about her face in the freezing night air, both of them filled with awareness of human fragility, yet...the danger those same humans posed to their existence—her existence.

Pushing off her, the hunter stripped off his trench coat, passing it toward her. "Put this on."

She didn't question it. She slipped on the coat and pulled it tight around her in case the cop rounded back again. As she did, she met the hunter's haunting emerald gaze, this man who for all purposes was somehow both legendary and mysterious, as she breathed out the question which his nearness seemed to have burned into her lips.

"What are you?"

3

_____

"What am I?" Jace shook his head. "Hell of a question for a woman who was a wolf five minutes ago." He let out a frustrated grumble, and stepped away from her. He needed to place some distance between them, because moments earlier, despite the fact that he'd been staring down an offense with the local PD for an illegal weapons discharge or solicitation at best and a murder he hadn't committed at worst, he hadn't been desperate for distance.

He'd been desperate for _her_. A woman, a wolf he didn't even know, and shit if that didn't take this situation to a whole new level of clusterfuck.

Jace was screwed. He was so totally, and completely, screwed.

She pulled his coat around her, shielding her nudity from him, though he was still keenly aware of it. It'd been necessity, survival. Period. There was nothing real to the way she'd felt pressed against him. Her sharp intake of breath as he'd drawn close. The look of longing in her eyes. Or her words.

Kiss me or I'll die.

Her words had been a plea for him to protect her. Nothing more.

Hadn't it?

Christ.

He moved to draw the burner cell from his pocket and phone division HQ, only to realize his coat was now covering the same nude woman who was making him need backup in the first place. Son-of-a-bitch.

"Hands behind your back," he grumbled the first thing that came to mind. He gave a wave to cue her to spin around. He needed to gain control of this situation and fast.

"What?" Her eyes grew wide with fear.

No way. He wouldn't relent. Not even for those big, brown doe-eyes.

She was far too dangerous.

"You heard me. Turn around. Hands behind your back."

From the jut of that heart shaped chin, there no way was she going quietly. "I didn't do anything wrong."

"We'll leave that for Headquarters to decide." They both needed to book it before that beat cop stumbled across the victim. He reached to his belt clip and pulled out a pair of silver cuffs. "Now unless you want to wait for that cop to come back and do you one worse, you know the drill."

"You're lucky I didn't rip your throat out, asshole." She thrust her hands behind her.

Despite her words, his cock jerked as her smooth, feminine voice hit his ears like the call of a siren. What was wrong with him?

"This is ridiculous," she growled.

No argument there. Ridiculous didn't cover it. Fucked up beyond comprehension was more like it.

He slapped the cuffs on.

A few minutes later, he was slamming the door to his blue 1970 Chevelle SS and moved to the driver's side while the she-wolf sat in the backseat. Reaching for the handle, he silently cursed himself and wondered what the hell his problem was.

Mercy was one thing. Kissing was another.

Though he hadn't kissed her, had he? He'd only wanted to.

Damn it.

He muttered a string of curses under his breath as he climbed into the car and closed the door behind him. Glancing in the rearview mirror, he saw her in the backseat, his coat she wore open and naked breasts exposed. It was like she had no sense of her own nudity; he knew from experience most shifters didn't.

She was wild. Free.

He shifted his weight, his hard cock still pressing against his jeans.

She was right about the evidence. With no blood on her, no weapons and a different scent, there was no question she hadn't killed that girl. But he had scented her at more than one of the crime scenes and as far as he was concerned that was more than enough of a reason to haul her in. He needed answers and with any luck, she'd be able to provide them.

He revved the engine and glanced in the mirror one more time. Her jaw clenched, pure frustration evident on her face as she continued to struggle with the handcuffs. Princess was seriously pissed off.

Ripping his gaze away, he pulled away from the curb and floored the gas pedal. Damn meeting started in half-an-hour.

As he drove, a feminine grumble sounded from the

backseat. "Just because I'm a wolf doesn't mean I'm a monster. You didn't have to be so rough with me."

"Old habits die hard." Jace glanced toward the rearview. "Rather demanding for a suspect, don't you think? Besides, we both know a fight like that isn't going to kill you. You wolves are pretty damn indestructible." He fought back a near laugh. He knew that all too well, didn't he?

And for what? To prove that he could? He scoffed.

"I'm no one's suspect." She glared at him in the rearview mirror.

Jace raised a single eyebrow. "Then what do you call those cuffs there?"

A deep scowl crossed her face, but even with an angry frown, she was still beautiful. "I'll get out of here, and the first thing on my to-do list will be ripping your throat out with my teeth."

"Feisty much?" One side of his mouth lifted into a half grin.

"Kiss my ass."

"Gladly." He smirked.

He checked the mirror; a blush bloomed across her high cheekbones, strong enough to show through her golden skin. She was likely some kind of Mediterranean descent by his guess, despite the fiery red undertones in her dark hair. His heart jumped, revving to life like his car's engine. His knuckles whitened where he gripped the steering wheel before he bumped his fist against it again. He needed to focus.

Damn it. She was killing him. She'd been around maybe twenty minutes, and already he regretted every decision he'd made thus far.

"What's your problem with my kind, huh?"

An electric shock zoomed down his spine at the sound

of her voice. Why? It was just a voice? He grumbled. "Suspect, remember? That means you're supposed to be quiet."

"I won't shut up until you gag me."

His eyes shot to the rearview. "That can be arranged."

"Try it," she taunted.

From the growl in her tone, he'd likely lose a finger or two.

She smiled, and in the mirror's reflection, he saw her long canines. He ran his tongue across his teeth—he had a pair of his own.

Sexy.

The word rang through his mind before he could stop it, and he instantly hated himself all the more. He thought of his mother's face: the purple and yellow bruises that marred her porcelain skin and the wrinkles around her eyes as she sobbed. That was the night his sorry excuse for a father had walked out, leaving her unable to provide for her rapidly growing son, and slamming Jace with a lifelong curse. Damn. He wasn't right in the head, fantasizing about one of those monsters.

And as if his self-hate wasn't enough, the sound of the she-wolf's voice coming from the back seat taunted him, poking fun at his agony by driving him wild.

Kiss me or I'll die.

"You know, I—"

He stomped on the Chevelle's brakes, and the car jerked. Princess toppled halfway into the front seat, and only his death grip on the steering wheel stopped his forehead from colliding with the dashboard.

"Ow! What the—"

He turned to her, eyes narrowed. Her mouth snapped shut when she met his gaze. His wolf stirred beneath his skin.

"Enough. Let's get something straight. Unless you want a forty-caliber lodged in your skull, I suggest you keep your mouth zipped up nice and tight. Got it?"

She shook her head, the movement almost imperceptible, so much so that it looked like she was trembling. Maybe she was. Shit. She peeled herself off the floorboard and retreated to her spot without another word. He hit the gas again and sped toward the division's warehouse four blocks away.

The small sniffle he heard behind him ripped at his heart. He tried to ignore it and focus on driving. Another sniffle. He couldn't help himself. He checked the mirror.

Angry tears streamed down her cheeks, staining her perfect face. Her legs were hunched up to her breasts, and she stared at the floor. She was naked and vulnerable, and he'd just issued her a death threat, but...something told him the emotion wasn't real.

"You expect me to believe those crocodile tears?"

Her crying stopped in an instant, as she dropped her ploy. "Worth a try."

She glared at him in the mirror. Her reflection every bit the vicious she-wolf she'd shown herself to be. And yet...

There was something almost...vulnerable beneath her gaze. Something real he was certain she wouldn't want him to see. Something she worked hard to hide.

He tore his gaze away from her. A wave of guilt shot through him as he thought of how he'd roughed her up in the alley. He really was a worthless bastard. He'd sworn to himself that he would never be like his father, never hurt a woman, but in the end, he was no better than his asshole dad. Did it matter that she was a shifter? She was still a woman.

The angel and devil on his shoulders duked it out. He

wasn't sure which one was calling him a jackass. Maybe both.

Speeding around a final corner, he spotted the warehouse that was the cover for Headquarters local offices—an old abandoned Kodak building now surrounded by a gated fence with barbed wire. He drove up to the gate, pressed in the code to enter and parked the Chevelle inside the nearly empty lot, glad he had tinted windows.

Before he chanced doing something stupid, he twisted the rearview mirror away from him, so her reflection wouldn't tear him apart.

"The guards will be out in a minute to escort you to an interview room." He stepped out of the car. "She may be old and refurbished, but this car is alarmed. Open a door, shatter the glass, fuck with the wiring, and the noise will wake the dead. That'll bring me and three other supernatural-hating sons of bitches running." He dared to glance back at her as he raked over her nude form beneath the open coat. "Unless you want that kind of attention..."

She curled a lip at him, holding in a snarl.

Without another glance, he slammed the door and walked toward the warehouse, refusing to let her faze him.

Never in his whole goddamn life had he hurried faster to a division meeting.

~

JACE STRODE INTO THE RUSTED, run-down warehouse, the scent of must and old wooden crates renting the air. He couldn't catch a break tonight. That was for damn sure.

Once he'd descended the staircase to the basement entrance, a door that to the naked eye appeared to be an entrance to a boiler room, he keyed in. At quick glance, someone would be hard-pressed to find the security pad that opened the door to the hidden maze of halls and rooms which housed the Rochester division's local branch of Headquarters, unless they moved a hell of a lot of wooden crates. Even if they located the keypad, they would still be faced with the code and the body scanner.

Once inside, after tossing his keys to the guard and giving a few barked orders to retrieve the waiting she-wolf from his vehicle and leave her on ice in an interview room, he was half-way through the maze of the white-walled cinderblock facility.

When he reached the meeting room, he threw open the door only to find three other hunters waiting for him. Damon sat at the far end of the table, his hands folded together on his lap as he shot daggers at Jace with his ice-blue eyes. The usual warm fuzzy welcome.

Save for its occupants, the large room contained no more than a single conference table, an old hot plate coffee machine with a peeling sticker emblazoned with the words Liquid Sanity which produced barely drinkable—yet thankfully still caffeinated—sludge and several old, flickering florescent lights.

Damon spoke first. "You're la—"

"No." Jace held up one finger, cutting Damon off. He took a long inhale, exhaled through his nose, then glanced down at his watch with a smug grin on his face. The minute hand ticked past. "Now I'm late."

Damon's face hardened into a frozen mask, but Jace knew the anger that lay beneath that cold, impassive stare. Jace felt rage—it was in his blood—but Damon took angst and made it into a lifestyle. Head of the division and the fiercest vampire slayer Jace had ever met, Damon Brock never smiled, and he sure as hell couldn't take a joke.

"Sit down," Damon ordered.

Jace flopped into one of the hard, metal chairs and propped his dirt-covered boots on the table. Shane, the brains of the group, sat to Damon's left, obliviously pouring over a stack of paperwork while David sat to the right with his large hand covering his black goatee to stifle a laugh. David may have kept Jace in check and coming to meetings, but he wasn't beyond goofing off a bit to grate on Damon's nerves.

Jace nodded in his direction. "How's it going, Big Daddy?"

"Not too bad, Sugar Plum." A conspiratorial smirk crept across his David's face, reaching all the way to his dark eyes. "What the hell happened to your arm?"

Jace was so used to the job, he'd damn near forgotten that the she-wolf had nearly torn his arm in two. He glanced down to where the plethora of bite marks had broken the skin. He'd duck into medical once this was over and get it stitched up and bandaged to cover his tracks.

"Don't ask. Where's Ash and Trent?" Jace gestured to the empty chairs at the table.

"Down in the city. They're still assisting on that Brooklyn case," Shane answered without glancing up from his papers.

David and Jace exchanged knowing smirks. Ash and Trent had already been down there a week and were due back today. In other words, their fellow hunters were likely taking their sweet old time to avoid coming back to this very meeting. Jace didn't blame them. If Damon was a splinter in his ass, their region lead, Chet, was a Godzilla-sized thorn.

A grim look crossed Damon's face as he caught Jace and David's exchange. "Whatever you idiots are cooking up, can it before Chet gets here."

So that's what they were all sitting around waiting for: the arrival of the Big Kahuna of Assholes himself.

Jace struggled not to roll his eyes. Damon was always suspecting him and David of conspiring over something. "Can't a man grin without being suspicious?"

Damon gave only a mild grunt in acknowledgement.

Jace pointed a finger at him and clicked his tongue with a wink. "That mean mug is how I know I'm getting a hell of a lot more action than you, that's for sure."

In fact, torn arm or not, he could think of one very naked, gorgeous she-wolf he'd like to get some action with. The passing thought instantly soured his mood.

Now was definitely not the time or place. Hell, there *never* would be a time and place. Human-shifter relationships were forbidden, and hunter-shifter relations? Ha, not in this life. Not to mention, that didn't even account for his own hang ups. He had bigger problems than attraction to some random she-wolf.

"There something extra interesting in that paperwork, kid?" Jace nudged the edge of Shane's chair leg underneath the table, casting all thought of the night's less-than-desirable turn of events from his mind.

Shane grinned, finally abandoning what he was reading. He straightened his gold rimmed glasses and smoothed a hand over the buttons on his dress shirt. "Call me kid again and see what happens." A religious studies professor by day and the division's occult specialist by night, Dr. Shane Gray may have looked the part of the buttoned-down academic, but he was anything but. On the street, he went full-blown Indiana Jones with a blade instead of a whip.

Of course, that didn't stop Jace from ribbing him on the regular for being several years the rest of the group's junior.

"In your dreams." Jace chuckled.

Damon frowned. "If all of you would quit screwing around, we've got a bunch of mutilated victims and we'd best get the details straight before Chet's here."

Like Jace would ever forget that viscous mess he'd encountered in the alley. "Mutilated victims—way to spoil the mood."

"Get your head out of your ass and focus," Damon barked. "This concerns you more than anyone." Jace scowled, but managed to keep his mouth shut while Damon addressed the group. "It's been three weeks, and the frequency is escalating, which means we've got to end this, and soon. Four young women, mutilated and dead, means—"

"Five." Jace sighed.

Damon closed his mouth, and the room fell still.

Jace pushed back his chair and stood, before he leaned against the nearest wall. "Right after David called me about the meeting, I found another victim in an alley. Same M.O. That monster called in his own crime this time."

A string of curses came from his fellow hunters.

Damon pegged him with a hard stare. "You've had three weeks. Three weeks to find this son of a bitch, and yet innocent girls are still being murdered on your watch."

The anger Jace directed toward himself and his rage at the killer combined. His frustration bubbled beneath his skin. He pointed straight at Damon. "Talk to me when you're the one out there every night, trying to track this monster down. I'm the only one working this damn assignment."

"Because it's your area of expertise," Damon shot back.

Jace pushed away from the wall and straightened to his full height. "Just because the guy's a wolf, that doesn't make it solely my problem. What's so pressing on your docket?"

Damon snarled, opening his mouth to speak, before Shane interjected.

"What if he isn't a shifter?"

Jace's head whipped in Shane's direction. "What are you getting at?"

Shane ignored his pissed-off tone and continued. Sometimes the kid had more guts than anyone gave him credit for. Not to mention, an effortlessly calm, level head. "What if the killer's something else? Maybe that's why we've had such difficulty catching him?"

"Shane has a point," David said, pawing a large hand over his five o'clock shadow. "For all we know, it could be some bastard who likes to pretend he's the new and improved Ted Bundy. He could be human."

Jace slammed his fist against table with an exasperated sigh. "I know this is a wolf shifter, all right?"

Shane piped in again. "How can you be certain?"

Jace frowned at the challenge. "Because I've got a she-wolf sitting in the interview room whose been sniffing around the crime scenes enough that she'll confirm as much."

Damon's glower faded into a neutral line at this new break in the case, the closest Jace had seen him to a grin in weeks. "You think she's good for it?"

Jace shook his head. "I don't think she's involved, but she's hiding something."

"And you're certain it's a wolf shifter?" David challenged.

Jace nodded. "I've never been so certain in my damn life. The way this shithead rips open his victims isn't possible with human hands or weapons—or human teeth. So unless he's siccing a pack of rabid dogs on his victims, then there is no damn way this is anything other than a wolf shifter. Everybody got that?"

David moved to stand at Jace's side and slapped a hand on his friend's shoulder. "Can't hurt to work it more than one way, J. Why don't you call Trent tonight and see if he'll check it out? Maybe it's some other kind of shifter. We can update him and Ash when they get back from Brooklyn."

Jace gritted his teeth together and kept his jaw clamped shut.

Damon nodded in approval. "While you're at it, you and Shane look, too."

"Maybe hellhounds?" David offered.

"Or voodoo," Shane added.

Jace let out a low growl. "Even the beat cops avoid those back alleys, so who knows, maybe you'll get lucky and find her the way I did—legs spread, heart missing, and organs thrown around like fucking confetti over the asphalt. So once you've all taken a good long look and made a spectacle of this poor girl's corpse, why don't you give me a holler so I can say I told you so?"

"Cool it." Damon glared at Jace, his high cheekbones casting shadows across his features, hollowing him out like a dead man. "If this is a werewolf, you have one week from tomorrow before HQ takes over the investigation. They're breathing down my neck as it is, and they're not going to sit back and do nothing if civilians keep dying."

"That isn't gonna happen. I'm the best this organization's got and you know it, Damon. Don't give me that shit." Jace could run this whole damn operation if he wanted, but he didn't care for leadership. Nor did he have the patience for it.

It wasn't a matter of pride. It was a fact.

As one of the original hunters of the Execution Underground, Jace held more seniority than most. Damon included, though he was a lifer as well. They'd both been around since long before the organization had been bought out, restructured and corporatized by Cronos, Inc. Everything had changed within the past ten years.

He still remembered back when they'd been only a handful of rag-tag, self-trained vigilante fools driving across the country with a hope and prayer of protecting humanity from the supernaturals that'd stolen the lives of their loved ones.

God, they'd been young. But they'd had justice on their side and America's best all-night diners to fuel them. Always.

"Please, Jace, no reason to use so much humility." Damon wrenched open the drawer to the file cabinet on which the coffee pot sat. The dark, sludgy contents sloshed as he pulled out a large stack of papers. Damon glued his gaze to the pages. "I'll deal with Chet. All of you fill out your damn paperwork, so HQ can have their signatures, then scan it into the database and get out. David, I need the updated report on that Vetis demon possession, and someone call Trent and tell him to get his shit together and give me some notes on the influx of non-wolf shifters. I want to know why the hell, on a regular basis, we're being overrun with freaks who shift into alley cats and squirrels. And while you're at it, tell Ash I need a report from him on the haunting in that old psych ward."

David groaned, griping under his breath about the paperwork.

Jace shook his head as he snatched the coffeepot and poured some of the lukewarm liquid into a white Styrofoam cup. With all Cronos' resources, they should at least be able to get a decent cup of joe. State of the art weaponry? Check. Latest tech? Cleared. Half-way decent coffee, not so much. Man, he missed the beans at the late night diners, especially that place out in the middle of nowhere outside the Sioux Falls stretch of I-90. He was practically salivating at the thought.

"Why the hell did we have a damn meeting if it's only going to last ten minutes? You could've picked up a phone if all you wanted was to verbally ream my ass."

"Maybe it would have lasted longer if you hadn't pissed me off." Damon didn't look up though from the lack of a scowl on his face, he didn't really mean it. "Get in the interview room, Jace. The last thing I need is you and Chet butting heads."

Jace didn't need to be told twice. Poor excuse for coffee in hand, he strode out the door of the conference room. The large metal entrance to their haven slammed in its frame, cutting him off. The cold air of the unheated halls hit Jace hard. He exhaled and watched his breath swirl in the overhead light like steam. His thoughts flashed through the night's events, and he frowned.

Mutilated human victims, a pissed-off wolf hunter and a naked she-wolf. Not a good combination.

4

Frankie threw all her body weight against the Chevelle's window. Her shoulder hit the glass and sent pain surging through her torso. She maneuvered her hands onto the handle one more time and pulled. Nothing.

"Damn it."

She rested against the seat. The leather stuck to her naked skin despite the cold temperature. She let out a loud huff. Locked up in a hunter's car, and every escape route she'd tried thus far hadn't worked.

She willed her body to change. In her wolf form, these shackles would slide from her wrists, but she couldn't manage it, not with the silver cuffs singeing the skin of her wrists.

But damn, she had to do something.

Think, Frankie. Think.

Trying every handle and unlock button—no easy feat while handcuffed—hadn't yielded any luck either. The hunter hadn't lied—there was no way in hell she could get out of this gas-guzzler unless he allowed it.

She kicked the window out of sheer annoyance. Though it had proved impossible to break earlier, she had to keep trying. Her foot slammed into the glass. The release of tension calmed her, and she side-kicked harder, finally leaving a solid crack, but the window refused to shatter. It had to be bulletproof.

"Stupid. Handsome. Kidnapping. Psycho," she grumbled, timing a word with each blow. Cracks splintered across the glass, but it still refused to break.

Without warning, the door to the old car swung open. Frankie scrambled back. Two goons, who without a doubt from the stupid looks on their faces were EU security, beckoned her out of the car.

"Let's go," the larger one said.

She scooted her way to the edge of the bench seat. As she tried to stand, one of the guards moved to hold her arm, whether to assist her or restrain her, she couldn't be certain. Her eyes flashed to her wolf as she bared her teeth and snarled. No way was she letting these idiots lay a hand on her.

The guard's brow drew low, even as his hand dropped to his weapon. "Move it," he ordered again.

They led her through the abandoned warehouse facility, down a flight of stairs to a basement entrance door. The soles of her feet were freezing against the concrete thanks to the subzero temperatures outside and she regretted more than once not bothering to button the hunter's trench coat she was donning, but she allowed her rage and her wolf stirring inside her to keep her warm. How had she gotten herself into this mess?

A few minutes later she was deposited in a flimsy, metal folding chair in an interrogation room. The harsh florescent lights overhead seared her wolf's retinas. The lights, the creaky chair beneath her ass, and the cuffs still holding her hands behind her back were all meant to set her on edge, but she was too smart to fall for it.

Then, she waited.

And waited.

She knew the drill. They'd leave her here on ice as long as they could, making her sweat it out like she was some kind of criminal. She could practically feel his eyes on her through the two-way mirror, watching, judging, sizing her up. But she wasn't a criminal. Protecting her pack and eliminating rogues that broke her pack and the Execution Underground's laws wasn't a crime. Neither was sniffing around crimes scenes in her jurisdiction. It was her birthright as packmaster.

Then again, his kind had shown they didn't always follow policy, which was exactly why she needed to play her cards right.

Finally, the door to the interview room swung open and the hunter stepped inside. She frowned at the sight of him. He had a name, not that he'd cared to share it with her earlier. Even though she knew it in her head, she couldn't bring herself to use it, to humanize him.

Humanize.

She nearly scoffed at the cruel irony of that word. If only his kind could feel the same for hers as they did for their precious fellow humans. She wasn't certain what she'd been thinking back in the alley, wondering what he was. He was too single-minded to be anything but human.

He closed the door behind him, holding a thick manila folder of papers in one hand and a Styrofoam cup in the other. From the scent that followed him: black coffee. She sniffed harder, searching for his scent and finding none.

Normally, for a human like him, she could scent everything about them. Fear, rage, sadness.

Hell, she could have likely even told him what he'd had for breakfast if she really wanted to strain herself. Even for her own kind, her people held unique scents, allowing for increased awareness of one another. She'd heard rumors that the injections the Execution Underground gave their hunters masked their smell from supernaturals, but she'd never confirmed it until tonight. It was unnerving.

She gave him a quick once-over like he wasn't worth her time, which he wasn't. "So you going for good cop or bad cop?"

He set the coffee and the manila folder down on the table across from her but didn't say anything. Instead, he watched her with those intense green eyes as he rounded the table, only to lean against its edge next to where she sat. His gaze flicked over her, quick and assessing, impersonal, but still a flood of heat rushed to her cheeks.

Why hadn't she buttoned the damn coat when she had a chance?

Her thoughts turned to that trashed alley again.

Kiss me or I'll die.

The words she'd whispered against his lips echoed in her mind.

God, she'd sounded desperate, even to her own ears.

It was the adrenaline that had made her sound like that. Fear. Nothing more. She hadn't been able to help herself. She knew that.

Did he?

Pushing off the edge of the table, he stepped behind her. Even no longer in her line of sight and with no sense of smell to aid her, she could feel him there, lingering. A large imposing presence at her back. The air felt heavy with tension, even though she couldn't see him, couldn't move. When the rough, calloused skin of one of his hands brushed against her own, she startled, nearly coming out of her chair.

"Easy," he said, his voice a low rumble that vibrated through her chest.

Gruff yet somehow soothing.

She heard the quiet jingle of a set of keys being pulled from his belt clip before she felt the first cuff fall from her wrist. A sigh of relief tore from her. The cuffs. He was just removing the cuffs. She swallowed hard.

What are you?

Her question from the alleyway echoed through her. He hadn't answered her. Logically, she knew he was human. He had to be, considering his employer and the facility in which she was currently sitting in. So what was this tension between them? This electricity?

Attraction?

No. She pushed the word aside. It couldn't be.

When the last of the silver clattered into his hand, she groaned in relief, rolling her wrists and shoulders. She was grateful to move them freely again. Silver didn't sear her kind's skin in the way human movies showed, but it irritated and aggravated their flesh all the same, weakened their natural healing response.

Casting the cuffs onto the tabletop with a loud clatter, he rounded the table's other side and pulled out the metal chair as she made quick work of buttoning up his coat she still wore. The chair's metal screeched an echoing scrape across the concrete floor before he dropped into it, leaning back and watching her. He pawed at the five o'clock shadow on his cheeks.

She held his gaze for a long beat. He'd changed from the

black shirt he'd worn beneath the trench coat into a fitted white Henley that contoured a little too closely to his muscles for her tastes. The white color contrasted against the golden tan of his skin, and she briefly wondered if it was left over from his time out west. She could imagine him outside in the summer sun, Stetson on his head, working long hours without the shade of Rochester's few high-rises.

The sun hadn't shined here in months.

She was the first to speak. "Apparently we're going with good cop." She nodded to the cuffs on the table between them.

He leaned forward in his seat, drawing his chair closer as he set his elbows on the table. "I hear you did a number on my car."

She laughed. She couldn't help it. Of course, that's what he'd care about. Not her or her time, or the fact that she didn't deserve to be here.

To her surprise, her laugh didn't seem to faze him.

"I thought I told you there was no point in wasting your energy?" He took a sip of the coffee, before muttering, "Shit, that's too hot," and setting it back down.

She shrugged. "I had to try. You could've been lying."

"I could've been, but I wasn't." He blew on the steam from the cup before he drew a careful sip. "Better," he nodded at the cup contents, then he met her gaze again. "I'm no liar." His voice was low and graveled enough the words sounded like a growl.

"You want a trophy for that?"

He gave a short huff, like she'd amused him, and leaned back in his chair again. As he did, her eyes darted to where the sleeve of his Henley bunched at the wrist, revealing a wrap of bandages beneath. Right. Where she'd torn into him.

His gaze followed hers. "I'm alright. Thanks for asking."

"I didn't ask."

He nodded. "Of course." He paused for a long beat. "What was your name again?" He grabbed the manila folder off the table and flipped it open, glancing at the top page as if he actually had a rap sheet on her.

Maybe not a rap sheet, but information all the same. A chill shot down her spine.

He nodded as he scanned the page. "Oh, that's right. Francesca." Her mother's name dripped from his lips with more than a hint of sarcasm.

She didn't answer.

"Is that what your pack calls you?" He set the manila folder back down.

She didn't like what he was implying. "I don't know what you're talking about."

"I'll give it to you straight, then. Are you part of a pack?"

She stayed silent. Would he hate her more if she belonged to a pack or if she were a rogue? Considering the recent DOA rogues, she would bet on the latter.

"A rogue, huh?" He raised a brow at her.

Her heart pounded faster as she stared at that manila folder. She cleared her throat. "I'm in a pack."

Her pack. Even after functioning as packmaster for the last five years, she still struggled to absorb the idea. But through her blood, she had birthright, and since her mother's and father's deaths, she had fulfilled her duty. No brothers, no sisters, no cousins. Just her. She was the only one left, and now the first alpha female ever to run Rochester.

"Local, I assume?"

She didn't confirm or deny it. No way would she throw her pack under the bus.

He watched her face for a long moment, before nodding. "Local. Got it."

Damn him.

She knew she wasn't easy to read. Her pack lieutenants and packmates all said as much and she'd never had an enemy who could predict her, which made the ease with which he was doing so all the more disconcerting.

"Last name?" he asked.

She stared at him, refusing to answer. Maybe he had been bluffing about the information in the folder.

He leaned against the chair back like he had all the time in the world. "Look. You're going to have be to a little bit more forthcoming if you want to get out of here any time soon."

"I didn't do anything wrong."

"I don't know that. Not until you talk to me."

"If you wanted me to be more forthcoming, maybe you shouldn't have herded me around like a sheep dog with that revolver of yours."

"Maybe if you hadn't run like a sheep dog, I wouldn't have had to."

"Would you have run if you were me?" She lifted a brow.

He didn't say anything, but for a second, she thought she saw a hint of understanding in his eyes. However, brief. "This isn't about me."

"Isn't it?" She leaned forward. "You hunters roll into this city like you own this place, like you have jurisdiction when your kind hasn't set foot here in nearly a decade."

"Fair enough." He ran his fingers through his auburn hair and pursed his lips as he nodded. "But we do have jurisdiction. Thanks to the treaty your kind signed. A mutual agreement, if I remember right."

An agreement he had helped negotiate. She knew that much.

"That agreement is with the Grey Wolves. Not my pack."

He nodded. "Ah, I see. That's what this is about. Your pack's status as 'independent.'" He made air quotes with his fingers around independent, and she couldn't help the snarl that tore from her throat in response.

He didn't know a thing about her or her kind. "Independent means exactly that." Her wolf eyes flared.

"Right. So you mean to tell me that when Maverick Grey calls you don't pick up phone?"

Maverick Grey: the leader of the Grey Wolves. She didn't resent the Grey Wolves for their cooperation with the Execution Underground. In fact, she respected it.

Of course, she would pick up the phone if she'd been anywhere near powerful enough to be on Maverick Grey's radar. She'd be a fool not to. But that didn't mean she wanted to subject herself and her own pack to one size fits all leadership.

But apparently, to the humans of the Execution Underground, an agreement with the Wolves of the West meant an agreement with them all. As if her kind, her species were a monolith, rather than living, breathing, diverse creatures whose existence was as valid, complex, and varied as their own.

When she didn't answer, he gulped another swig of coffee. "That's what I thought."

He said it with such smug satisfaction she could have bitten off his face, if she wouldn't have had the repercussions against her pack to deal with.

All she was. Everything she had. She did for them.

The wolves, the family she loved.

Even dealing with this asshole.

He must have sensed he'd pushed her too far, because he threw his hands up in a sign of surrender. "Alright. So you don't think we have jurisdiction here. I get that. But explain to me why I shouldn't be suspicious of a she-wolf sniffing around a string of dead human bodies?"

Emphasis on the word human. She didn't miss that. "Because it's our jurisdiction, not yours. We're working toward the same end goal."

Maybe that's where she could lead this. Build common ground.

"Okay. For argument's sake, let's say you're right. That still doesn't explain to me who you are or why I should trust you."

"I could say the same."

He released a long sigh and shook his head, causing several strands of hair to fall into his harsh, handsome face. For a man so rough around the edges, he was oddly...beautiful. "I've got all the time in the world, sweetheart."

But she didn't. If enough hours passed with no word, her packmates would come looking for her. She couldn't risk their safety on something this insignificant. Wolves in the middle of Rochester's downtown streets weren't exactly inconspicuous. She needed to give him just enough to get him to let her go. "We don't want a rogue killing human women on our turf any more than you do. My packmaster ordered me to examine the scenes."

She held her poker face. This way she was throwing the heat back on herself and hopefully throwing him off identifying her in the process.

"You expect me to believe Frankie Amato ordered a she-wolf to prowl around looking for a killer for him?"

She stiffened. She didn't know what she took umbrage with more—the fact that he knew her name, that he automatically assumed that to be a packmaster and have a gender neutral name meant she was a man, or that a she-wolf couldn't get the job done.

"That's what I said." She crossed her arms over her chest.

"Okay." Abruptly, he shoved back his chair with a nasty scrape that grated against her wolf senses. He grabbed the manila folder from the desk before he downed the last of the coffee and tossed it in the trash bin. Then headed toward the interrogation room door.

"Where are you going?" A rush of panic shot through her.

He pulled the door open before he cast a glance over his shoulder. "What? You didn't think I'd have a way to check your story out?"

She tensed, but tried not to show it.

"Let's get one thing clear," he said. "You don't want to make an enemy out of me."

"Too late," she shot back.

He chuckled, low and deep in a way that caused her wolf to stir. "We'll see about that."

5

____

"What in the flying fuck was that?"

The door to the interrogation room slammed shut, and Jace let out a frustrated sigh. Scowling, he faced toward his region lead. "Hello to you, too, Chet."

Jace tossed the case folder onto a nearby filing cabinet, which Damon quickly retrieved. His division leader flipped through the pages, meanwhile shooting Jace a look that warned *play nice*. No doubt Damon had tried to keep Chet away, but whenever their region lead got a bright idea in his thick skull, there was little deterring him.

Ignoring Chet, Jace crossed the small space and parked himself in front of the two-way mirror. The viewing room's close quarters smelled of stale coffee, male sweat, and the mayonnaise-soaked paper from someone's half-eaten sandwich.

Disappointment and aggression all rolled into one.

Through the two-way, Jace stared into the interrogation room, watching where Francesca rolled her neck and shoulders, then adjusted her position atop her creaking chair. She was still glowering at the door where he'd exited moments ago, as if she could somehow see him there and wanted to tear into him. He shook his head. This part had always struck him as messed up.

Watching their suspects like they were goddamn lab rats. What point did it serve other than to screw with their heads?

Still, he couldn't bring himself to take his eyes off her.

What was with that?

"I said," Chet bellowed again. "What the fuck was that, McCannon?"

"Standard protocol?" Jace lifted a brow, though he didn't look toward the region lead. He was fighting too hard to keep his eyes even, steady. Colored to their human green.

If he expected to get through this little Headquarters inspection with his job intact, he'd need to play nice, like Damon said. Or at least something close to it. If there was one thing that'd goad their asshole of a region lead to fury faster than unfiled paperwork, it was disrespect.

Never mind that "superior" or not, Chet had never given an ounce of that same courtesy to anyone around him— Jace, Damon, or otherwise. Jace would do his job, whatever his team needed to make this go smoothly, but that didn't mean he'd kowtow to some pompous prick without even half his or Damon's experience. The whole Rochester division knew Chet had only gotten his job either from blatant nepotism or shameless ass-kissing.

Either way, he was calling *someone* among the higher ups Daddy.

And Jace wasn't enough of a pushover to play second fiddle to that.

"You want to explain why you walked out of there without so much as a last name?"

Jace shouldn't have had to explain himself to this dick. Not when any of his other hunters would have done the same. But he would. For his own sake.

If only to get Chet and Headquarters off his back.

"She's cornered and she's scared. If I push her, I'm only going to get bit in return." He resisted the urge to touch his still-healing forearm. Medical had dressed it up for him. But the skin knitting back together itched like mad. She'd torn into him good. "Metaphorically speaking," he added.

Chet grumbled. "We aren't paying you to play good cop."

"You aren't paying me to play bad cop either." Jace finally turned toward the other man.

Chet had the look of every puffed up, pencil pusher in middle management who'd ever came before him. Boring. Non-descript. A product of family money. And willing to use his privilege exactly like he'd earned all the benefits that came with that.

Jace cleared his throat. "I'm a hunter. There's a difference."

Despite how Francesca had ribbed him about playing good cop, bad cop in the interview, he still believed that. Still felt that as his truth.

Chet scoffed. "Keep telling yourself that."

Jace's lips pulled into a thin line. Of course some corporate flunky like Chet, who'd arrived as standard issue post buy-out, would think that. That's what the new Cronos hires like him were paid to do. Aim for results.

They were numbers guys. Nothing more.

They didn't give a rat's ass about humanity, about the protection of damaged communities and families Jace and so many others had founded the organization on. Nor the weight of responsibility that came with that. The oaths they'd all sworn.

In the early days, they'd been their own free agents, out to avenge their families and prove that there was something about humanity that was worth saving, worth the fight. Now it was all laws, treaties, arrest and investigate. No matter who it damaged.

How the hell had they gotten themselves here?

Jace hated it.

"If I push her, she'll be even less likely to talk. We need information."

"We need a *confession*," Chet countered.

"Only if she's culpable." Jace reached for the file Damon had returned to the top of the cabinet and shoved the now open folder at Chet. "You really think she did that?" He jabbed a finger at one of the crime scene photos, pointing to a particularly gruesome scene. "What evidence points toward her?"

"I'm in agreement with Jace on this," Damon said from where he leaned between the filing cabinet and the wall. "If Jace found her so close to a fresh scene, she wouldn't have had time to clean up, nor would she have hung around. She's not good for it."

"Not to mention the profile we've built is for a thirty-something white man," Jace said.

Francesca might not have an alibi, but she could be a powerful asset for information for them, and even his division lead could see that.

Jace and Damon didn't always see eye-to-eye—hell, their relationship was often more contentious than not, but unlike Chet, Damon had earned his place, helped forge this organization. A worthwhile hunter didn't need to wield power like a weapon against those who were powerless. He used his place to protect those who couldn't protect themselves, the defenseless among humanity. It was a collaboration that didn't apply to only one species or community. A message sent not *for* humanity, but on *behalf* of it.

Because there was something good in them. Something worth protecting and saving.

Jace had to believe that.

"You've had three weeks. Three weeks and no results," his region lead spit. "And now you find a wolf at the crime scene and want to let it off the hook?"

The words were so similar to Damon's warning about HQ, it was eerie. A corporate echo.

"I wasn't aware catching a rogue wolf serial killer had a standard timeline." Jace failed to keep the snark from his voice.

Chet's lip curled. "Shut your mouth now, McCannon."

Jace held his frustration in. It was only for the sake of the rest of his division that he fought to keep his voice even. "Pushing isn't going to work. We need to build trust."

"You want to build trust with these monsters? Do it on your own time." Chet stepped forward, pointing toward the interrogation room door. "Now get back in there and push that bitch harder, or I'll do it for you." Chet tossed the file back at Jace again, nearly spilling the contents all over the floor.

"I'd like to see you try," Jace mumbled under his breath.

"What was that?" Chet shot back.

Jace grit his teeth. Man, what he'd give to see Princess tear into Mr. High and Mighty Prick like she had him. Jace wasn't sure which pissed him off more, the threat toward him or Chet calling Francesca a bitch. It didn't matter whether she was a wolf.

It was uncalled for. Violent in its own perverse way.

Jace forced a pained smile onto his face. "I said, 'of course'. After all, Headquarters knows best." He shot a sarcastic glance toward Damon and grinned for Chet's sake. "The rest of us are mere peons by comparison."

Chet's lip curled.

Damon clapped Jace on the shoulder then, and Jace wasn't sure whether it was for his sake or the region lead's that the division leader whispered, "Just do what he says."

A moment later, Jace was back in the interrogation room, meeting Francesca's gaze head-on. She stared up at him, those large doe-eyes sparking with challenge. He didn't exactly have a plan for this interaction. He'd intended to keep her on ice a bit. Let her sweat it out, until finally she was ready to talk, because she wanted to get the hell outta there.

Best laid plans and all that shit. So much for that.

"Back so soon?" For a wolf shifter, her grin turned positively feline. "What happened? Did you miss me?" Her eyes flashed to her wolf momentarily. Gold and glowing.

Fuck, that was sexy in a way it shouldn't be.

"Don't flatter yourself, Princess." He closed the door behind him. At the very least, he was thankful to escape Chet. "Turns out your story checks out," he bluffed.

"That quickly?" She looked a little amused by that. From the way she was watching him, she was too clever for anything he'd concoct on the spot. If he was going to make any headway with her, he needed to play this straight. Earn her trust. Honest.

Exactly like he'd told Chet.

"Look," he said, leaning against the doorway as he hitched a thumb over his shoulder. "I've got my prick of a region lead from Headquarters riding my ass in there."

Francesca quirked a brow. "One who can hear what you just said about him, right?"

If it weren't for the interrogation room's sound proof

walls, Jace could have sworn he heard Chet losing his shit at that moment. Or maybe he'd simply imagined it for his own amusement. Damon would be pissed. But it'd be worth it if it got Chet off their backs, and also led to results. "It's said with lovable affection, of course." Jace grinned, placing a hand over his heart. "He wants me to push you hard for answers. But I don't wanna to do that."

She watched him for a beat, eyes shifting back to a human-like brown. "Okay, I'll play. Why not?"

"Because me and my division lead don't think you're good for this."

She nodded slowly. "Finally, some common sense. Can't say I disapprove." She nodded to the abandoned cuffs on the table. "That mean you're going to wise up and let me out of here?"

Jace faked a pained expression. "Unfortunately, it's not so simple."

"Because I'm a wolf shifter?" She lifted her brows defiantly. "We all know the Execution Underground doesn't take kindly to that. To any non-human species for that matter."

In other words, she thought he was some supernatural-hating ass.

Damn, if she only knew the half of it.

"I'm not some corporate flunkie," he shot back, a little too defensively. "I'm pre-buy out."

She grinned, clearly realizing she'd struck true. "Oh, I see." She blinked those large warm eyes at him. "A government-sanctioned vigilante then. That's *so* much better."

Princess could dish out the sarcasm. That's for sure.

Jace frowned. "Look, whatever you think of me. I promise you're not gonna take as kindly to that guy in there." Slowly, he made his way toward her, drawing near until he leaned over the interrogation table, close enough to whisper into her ear. "You'd rather kiss me than die, remember?" He felt a shiver run through her. "You can't hate me that bad. How do you think it'd go if your packmates heard about that?"

"You wouldn't dare."

"Wouldn't I?" He lifted a brow, pulling away from her.

"They wouldn't believe you," she shot back. "It was a survival strategy. Nothing more."

He grinned. "Keep telling yourself that." He rounded the table to the far side again, taking a seat. "So what's it going to be, Princess? You ready to give me some more information so you can get out of here? Or would you prefer to deal with Chet?"

She wrinkled her nose. "God, is that really his name?"

Jace nodded. "Unfortunate, isn't it?"

Princess eyed him for a long moment like she was trying to assess which was the bigger threat, him or the unknown behind the two-way mirror. "My pack is aware of these killings," she said finally, "and we know that if you don't find this monster soon, we're going to get the blowback. I was trying to help, to catch him myself. It's our jurisdiction. That's it."

"So that's still your story?"

She nodded. "And I'm sticking to it."

"Care to share a name to go with that statement?"

"I already told you. Francesca."

"Sure." He nodded. He didn't believe that was her real name for a second. It didn't suit her. But he'd go with it. For now. "And a last name?"

She shook her head. "I'm not going to give you that. Not today. Not tomorrow. Not anytime soon."

Jace blew out a long sigh. "You know that doesn't exactly look good, right?"

"You know what else doesn't exactly look good, that you're holding me with nothing to charge me on? How about I call Maverick Grey and tell him *that*?"

Jace shuffled the file folder. "Per the North American Free Species Agreement, we have twenty-four hours to do exactly that. And which do you think will matter more? A deal with us that keeps Maverick Grey's own protected or the fate of a she-wolf who's not even his pack?"

"You're the expert in wolf shifters," she quipped. "You tell me." She leaned back in her seat. "Better hope it's not species before treaties."

The way she said "tree-ties" it made the phrase rhyme.

It was a smart counter, and Jace would have said as much, but suddenly, the door to the interrogation room flew open and Chet stepped inside. His gaze fell toward Jace, his face beat red, and from the look of rage there, he hadn't exactly found the jokes about his name humorous.

Chet sneered. "Get out."

Jace glanced back toward the she-wolf. "Warned you it was going to come to that."

He stood then, reluctantly yielding his chair, only for Damon to poke his head inside the room with a sour-faced grumble. "Jace's stays." Chet opened his mouth to protest, but Damon cut him off. "Protocol."

In other words, Chet wasn't remotely qualified to be in on this interview, and they all knew that.

"Fuck protocol," Chet shot back. "Who do you think is in charge here, Brock?"

If Chet wasn't so full of overinflated ego, the icy look Damon gave the region lead would have made him shiver. For a long beat, Damon glared at Chet, refusing to close the door until finally he nodded for Jace to follow him out.

Jace shook his head. No way. He wouldn't buck the rules.

Not for Chet.

His region lead turned toward the she-wolf, ignoring Jace like he'd already been dismissed. The world seemed to still then, as if it were in slow motion. The moment Chet's eyes locked on Francesca, Jace watched as a flicker of dark amusement filled the other man's gaze, and for a moment, Jace was no longer in the interrogation room.

Instead, he was a child again. Alone and hiding in the shadows. Back in that too small dingy kitchen with the patterned linoleum tile that curled and cracked at the edges from age. Back to one of too many times when his asshole father had gripped his mother by her hair, until her cries shook through him. Filled him with fear.

His father had looked at his mother in that same way then. Like she was nothing. Like he could use her for his own twisted games. For his own fucked amusement. Jace had been too young, too weak and powerless to stop him then.

But he wasn't powerless now.

He was a monster in his own right. Exactly what his deadbeat dad had made him.

And this time, he intended to bite back.

FRANKIE KNEW Chet was bad news from the moment he stepped into the interrogation room. Sure, not bad news in the way Jace McCannon was bad news, or the brief, albeit lasting, impression she'd gotten of Jace's division lead, a notoriously lethal and stone-faced vampire hunter by the name of Damon Brock. Nor was Chet even as much bad news as she considered herself to be. She was a packmaster in her own right, after all. Highly trained. She had to be.

But Chet wasn't a threat in the *I have the ability to deliver a beat down* sense. No, the Execution Underground region lead was bad news in the way all bureaucrats and powerful men were bad news. In the fact that she was a woman, and a woman of a marginalized species to boot. Which meant he had institutional power she didn't.

And he intended to wield it against her.

"Chet," she said cheerily as Jace stalled in making his way toward to the door. "Your reputation as a Grade-A prick proceeds you."

She wasn't here to make friends, especially not with this asshole.

Chet stared down his patrician nose at her as if she were so far beneath him, she was barely worth addressing. He shot a glare toward Jace. "Is there a way to muzzle her?"

Frankie snarled.

To Jace's credit, he looked as disgusted by the inhumane suggestion as she did. He glanced between them then and for a moment, something in his eyes flickered.

But she didn't know him well enough to be able to read the emotion.

"No," he answered tersely. "No, it's against protocol." Chet opened his mouth to respond, but Jace cut him off with a shake of his head, abruptly closing the door. "Which is also why I'm staying." He met Chet's gaze head-on, refusing to break eye-contact. As if he dared the region lead to challenge him. "Damon observes and I stay. We follow the rules, or I'll remove you from this interview room myself."

It was a direct challenge to his superior.

On her behalf. Or so it seemed.

Frankie wasn't exactly certain what to make of that, or why she felt...surprised. Even...grateful? But she did.

It was the right thing to do. The decent thing, and yet...

How often did other men like Jace look away to protect their own asses?

Jace nodded toward the two-way mirror, as if reminding Chet that his division lead was also observing, doing his duty to keep them both accountable. Or so she hoped.

The tension between the two men thickened.

"Fine," Chet relented, before he sat down, claiming Jace's chair, though the look in his eyes promised Jace would pay for the defiance later.

Frankie almost felt sorry for it.

Once Chet was in Jace's seat, the look of hatred which settled on the region lead's face as he watched her sent a chill down her spine. "Here's what's going to happen," Chet said, as if he were a man used to being obeyed. "You're going to tell us everything about your little pack, or Jace here is going to charge you with aiding and abetting an interspecies murder."

Frankie's jaw dropped. "You can't do that. I didn't do anything."

Chet grinned. "Watch me."

In the background, Jace was shaking his head, jaw clenched. "She's right. You can't do that. There's no evidence to implicate her."

Chet glanced toward him. "Then make evidence."

The beat of silence that followed pressed into Frankie's ears.

Her heart raced, filling her with panic until with a resounding growl until Jace said, "No."

Chet's gaze narrowed. "Excuse me?"

"I said, no," Jace repeated. "I'll lose my job if that's what it comes to, but not even a piss poor excuse for a region lead like you could make me do that."

Chet laughed. "And how do you think you're going to stop me, McCannon?"

Frankie watched in horror as something dark in Jace's eyes flickered again. Something remarkably wolf-like, but it was there and gone so quickly she couldn't make sense of it.

A second later, the door to the interview room swung open once more and Damon Brock stepped in. "That's enough, Chet. Time to go."

Chet rounded on the division lead. "Shut your mouth, Brock, or I'll have your job, too."

The return look in the division lead's eyes was iced fury. "I don't care who the fuck you are. You're done here."

Frankie blinked. It didn't take a genius to gather there was more background to this moment than she was seeing. An unspoken corporate history.

"Fuck you both." Chet didn't appear to care that he both was out of line and outnumbered. "I'll have *both* your jobs for this."

Neither hunter seemed fazed by the threat.

Jace's eyes narrowed then, and he gave Chet a look as if he was seeing something new and even more disgusting that he hadn't seen before. "What's this case mean to you? Who at Headquarters has their hand so far up your ass they've made you their puppet?"

Chet snarled and stepped toward Jace. "Watch your mouth, McCannon."

Damon shook his head. "Not now," he warned Jace. For a moment, his blue eyes darted toward her.

Whatever silent communication passed between them, clearly this was internal business. Not for her ears.

Damon turned toward Chet then. "Threaten one of my team again and I'll end you." From the stern delivery and the chill which shot down her spine, it wasn't a passing threat. It was a promise. "Now get out," Damon growled.

With a look of petulant fury, Chet snatched the folder off the table, pausing only momentarily, before his eyes fell to her. "You would've looked like less of a bitch in the muzzle," he sneered.

Frankie stiffened. Fury coursed through her as Chet turned to leave. She'd heard more hateful words a thousand times before. Even more hurtful, perhaps. But somehow, she couldn't bring herself to let it go. Not this time.

"The only beast who needs a muzzle here is you," she said after him.

Chet stilled and the muscles in his shoulders writhed. Slowly, he glanced toward her.

Frankie knew it wasn't wise to bait him, but she'd had enough men in her life, human or otherwise, who thought they could talk down to her, treat her as less than, only for them to walk away unscathed. Never again. She was done playing nice.

Leaning forward, she met Chet's gaze from across the table as her eyes flashed to her wolf. She wasn't just defiant. She was pure lupine, proud of who and what she was, and she let him see it then as her voice dropped to a ruthless, animal growl. "Take your species hate and shove it up your ass, Chet."

For a moment, Chet didn't so much as breathe.

Instead, the color drained from his face, making him deathly pale for a beat as he held her gaze. She couldn't just see his fear. She could smell it. Taste it. The man's nostrils flared, his face twisting to one of embarrassed rage, causing Frankie to grin, though she quickly realized her mistake. Men like Chet lashed out when they were afraid.

The region lead dove across the table so suddenly, Frankie didn't anticipate it.

Without warning, he knocked her from her chair, sending her sprawling to the floor. Upon impact, Frankie growled, struggling to right herself, but before she could gain her footing, Chet grabbed her by her hair, using the leverage to hurl her toward the wall like she weighed nothing. She hit the cinderblock—hard—the wind flying from her lungs as she struggled to breathe. But he was on her again in an instant. His large hand gripping her by the throat. The whole thing happened so fast she hadn't been able to think.

Damn the E.U's freaking injections. Had this been a normal human, she'd have seen it coming, and fought him off with ease.

Apparently, Chet packed more power than it appeared.

Gasping for air, her eyes shifted to her wolf. He wouldn't last two seconds if she were in wolf form. But Chet moved too quickly. Drawing his gun, he pressed the barrel to her chin, before he hauled her into his arms, and positioned himself behind her.

The coward had turned her into his shield. Damn it.

Slowly, Frankie released her shift as she tried to remain calm. Steady.

He'd never have bested her if he hadn't caught her off guard. But even then, she couldn't have killed him. For her pack's sake.

The blowback from the Execution Underground would be a massacre.

The other hunters had their own weapons drawn now. That familiar Mateba from Jace and what appeared to be a Desert Eagle in the vampire hunter's hand.

Aimed at the human threatening her. A wolf shifter.

She hadn't seen that one coming.

Jace stepped forward, gun at the ready. "Let her go, Chet."

"Take another step and I blow her head off," Chet threatened. "Headquarters won't even blink." Chet's hot breath smothered her ear, and she cringed.

But the hunters obeyed, remaining still. Guns at the ready.

For her sake.

"Go ahead. Fire first." Chet smiled. "Whose it gonna be? Brock?" he taunted. "McCannon?" His malicious grin broadened. "Who do you think HQ is going to believe? Either of you pull the trigger and I own you, *and* your job. And you both know it."

Jace's lip curled.

"Now, we're going to try this my way." Chet shoved the barrel of his semi-auto a little higher, forcing her onto her toes. She wasn't short by any means, but he had several inches on her. "What were you doing in that alleyway?"

Frankie gaped. *This* was his plan? He thought he could *coerce* a confession out of her?

She'd sooner die than claim she'd committed those crimes. Doing so would cause irreparable damage to her pack, her species. Chet had greatly underestimated how willing she was to put her life in danger. To die for them.

So long as it protects them.

"I already told you," she spit. "I was doing my duty." She spoke each word through gritted teeth. "That's all."

The gun pushed higher. "Try again."

"I won't admit to something I didn't do." She didn't know why, but she looked toward Jace then, and the mixture of fury and fear in his eyes told her what her wolf instincts already knew.

Chet *would* kill her. He wouldn't hesitate.

She meant nothing to him.

Her heart raced.

And even if Jace or Damon dared to risk their jobs, their lives for her, she wasn't certain there would be any justice. No punishment or repercussions. As if she *and* her kind meant nothing. A chill shot down Frankie's spine.

For the first time in her life, she was just a woman then. Not a wolf or a packmaster more than capable of defending herself. Not even a looked-down-upon endangered species.

Just a defenseless creature in the hands of a powerful man.

The thought chilled her. Would her pack even know what happened to her? Mourn her? Or would they think she'd abandoned them, because she was their first female packmaster, and they thought she couldn't take the heat?

True fear took over, though she didn't dare show it.

Would anyone even miss her?

She felt more than saw Chet's finger move toward the trigger.

Her powers were useless in the face of human steel, of a bullet to the head.

"Wait," she suddenly heard herself say. The fear she held inside felt strange, foreign, but she held strong, refusing to show it. Among her pack, those who were eager to see her fail would have cut her down for it. "Please," she said, her voice remaining steady, powerful as she allowed herself this brief request for mercy, away from even harsher eyes that would judge her, scrutinize her every move. "I'll tell you everything I know, just...don't hurt me."

The look of pained remorse in Jace's gaze gutted her.

Like he regretted ever bringing her here.

Like he saw straight through her, to the true version of

her she kept hidden under the surface. The real her, complete with doubts, struggles, fears, and yet...

He didn't judge her for it or think of her as weak.

Something about that scared her more than Chet's threats ever could.

Chet's gun at her throat lowered ever so slightly, and from the almost imperceptible nod Jace gave, he encouraged her to keep talking. She wasn't certain why she was looking to him for guidance, for help and safety, but for some reason she was.

"The killer isn't a wolf," she said as she confessed the first valuable piece of information she could muster. Her pack would have to forgive her.

They'd have to.

She watched as Jace's nostrils flared.

Like she'd just confirmed something vitally important to him, and also...

Something he'd already known.

But how?

There was no hint of surprise in his eyes. His face appeared to be carved in stone, and his gun remained steady, his aim never faltering from where he'd trained it upon Chet.

Whose bullet would be faster?

Frankie couldn't even bring herself to look toward the other hunter at his side.

She locked her gaze on Jace, looking straight into his eyes as if she were speaking to him and him alone. If she was going to die, she could at least do this. Help bring a different sort of sadistic monster to justice. "There's something different about the killer's scent. It's...lupine and distinctly male, but not...not normal. Not like a regular wolf.

I've never smelled anything like it." Silently, she pleaded with him to listen.

"And?" Chet prompted from behind her. The gun inched higher.

Frankie shuddered. "And he likes to hunt at nightclubs nearby." She opened her mouth to speak, but her tongue felt too thick, and she had to force herself to speak around it. "I've...tracked his scent there," she choked out. She closed her eyes momentarily, a poor attempt to hide her vulnerability beneath strength. "I swear that's all I know."

She'd never felt so violated. So stripped bare and powerless.

But she'd never give this asshole the satisfaction of showing it.

From over her shoulder, Chet beamed. "There," he said. "Was that so hard?"

"You've made your point now, Chet. Time to let her go," Jace warned.

Frankie felt the tension in her chest ease, but then she heard the amusement in Chet's tone as he said, "And if I don't?"

Those cruel words were the last sound she heard before the first shot rang out. The sound ricocheted off the cinderblock walls. And Frankie couldn't help herself.

She screamed.

6

Jace fired the Mateba inches from Chet's head. It was a risk, but the moment it became clear that Chet didn't intend to let Francesca go, Jace had been willing to take it. Whatever it took to get her free from Chet's arms, to wipe that look of fear from her eyes, and that smug grin off Chet's face. Even if it cost him his job. He couldn't watch another second of it.

Not without losing his dignity.

The shot rang out, echoing in his ears in the small space.

But Jace didn't hesitate.

At the sound of gunfire, Chet ducked for cover, exactly as Jace had anticipated. Suddenly free, Princess stumbled forward, placing enough distance between her and Chet for safety. And leaving Jace room to act. He didn't think.

He was on Chet within seconds, tackling the other man to the ground. Chet's nine-millimeter flew from his hand as they hit the floor with an audible oof. The weapon skidded across the painted concrete with a clatter as Jace slammed the bastard down beneath him.

With any normal suspect, it would have been easy. Roll

them. Pin them. Cuff them. He'd done it a thousand times before. But every member of the Execution Underground was highly trained, including the corporate suits who worked office jobs, and even a little shit like his region lead wouldn't allow himself to be pinned so easily.

Chet threw the first punch, narrowly missing as Jace deflected, before delivering a hard blow of his own. Straight to the other man's teeth. The crunch of bone raked against knuckles, and pain shot through his fist. But Jace didn't stop. Didn't hesitate.

Not until he made the other man bleed.

Jace drew back his fist again, prepared to land another blow.

But suddenly Chet pulled the blade at his hip, a standard issue from HQ, slashing out. The tip of the dagger caught Jace's wrist, nicking him, though he blocked the blow. But doing so caused his balance to falter, and Chet seized the momentary advantage. Bucking, the bastard sent them both rolling in a tangle of limbs until he came out on top. Quick to reclaim his footing, Chet started to rise, blade in hand, but with a sharp pivot, Jace swept his legs, sending the other man down to the floor again. The region lead yelped like the worthless coward he was.

No way was Jace letting this bastard walk out of here unscathed.

Jumping to his feet, Jace stood over the other hunter, ready to tear into him. But Damon appeared by his side, his Desert Eagle trained on Chet and at the ready.

"Don't fucking move," the vampire hunter growled.

Chet dropped the knife and lifted his hands.

For a long beat, all Jace could hear was the sound of his own heavy breathing.

With a quick flick of his gun, Damon gestured for Chet to rise. "Get up."

Slowly, Chet rose, hands in the air. His gaze flicked toward Francesca again. "All this over some she-wolf cunt?"

The beast inside Jace roared, breaking free. He wasn't certain whether it was Chet's smug grin or his disgusting words. Or maybe it was the way the other man looked at her. Like if they let him out of this room, out of their sight for even one minute, he would find this innocent woman who'd done nothing but refuse to lessen herself and make her pay.

The abuse of power wouldn't stop here.

Hate burned through Jace until he could barely see straight. Until red clouded his vision.

Inside, the freed beast snarled, rearing its monstrous head. A feral protective instinct writhing and awakening its fury until it grew claws.

Mine. It snarled.

Before he knew what he was doing, Jace charged, gripping Chet by the throat and slamming the other hunter against the adjacent wall with such lethal force Jace felt the blow in his own knees. For once he didn't hold back.

"Threaten her again and I'll fucking end you," he snarled, his voice half-animal. The beast inside him stirred again.

Chet's eyes went wide, and for a moment, he stilled.

He didn't so much as blink.

Suddenly, Jace's blood ran cold.

It only took a moment to realize his mistake.

He'd been so hellbent on protecting the silently wary she-wolf in the corner, he hadn't been able to think, to judge his choices clearly. His strength was off the charts, even for a hunter, and he'd shown his full hand. He didn't need to flash his eyes to his wolf to fully reveal himself. The other hunters would know instantly.

They'd been trained for it.

Abruptly, Jace chanced a glance toward Damon. The vampire hunter was staring at him like he'd never fucking seen him before, though they'd known each other over a decade. But to Damon's credit, his gun remained steady, trained upon Chet.

"Holy shit," Princess breathed, like she couldn't believe what she was seeing.

Her shock raked through him. Unwelcome and grating.

Like something inside him couldn't withstand her discomfort.

But it was Chet's sly, shit-eating grin that did Jace in.

"Oh, this is rich," Chet laughed finally with all the amusement of a hungry hyena who'd found his prey was already wounded. "Wait until Headquarters gets a load of this." He cackled. "You're fucking dead, McCannon."

Jace didn't have the words to respond.

Instead, he did the only thing he could think to do then.

He growled, canines bared, eyes flashing to his wolf.

Chet blanched.

"What the fuck is happening right now?" Francesca looked as if she could hardly breathe. She stood on the opposite side of the room, watching in a mixture of disbelief and confusion. Like her mind couldn't wrap itself around the fact that a hunter, a human, had just growled like some sort of wolf-man.

Most would have said it was impossible. A hunter who was part wolf.

And yet...

For a moment, none of them moved, until somewhere else in the building, someone finally pulled the alarm. The sound of gunfire had alerted them. The emergency light on the wall overhead flashed red, the siren screeching out the worst kind of sound. It promised a whole mobilized unit of trained hunters. The emergency response team. The only question was who'd they'd deem the bigger monster.

Chet or him.

For the first time in his life, Jace froze.

Slowly, he released Chet, though doing so went against every instinct in him. Tentatively, the asshole slid lower on the wall, slumping in a struggle to catch his breath as Jace stepped away from him. He didn't know why he'd let Chet go that easily, but somehow he knew he had to. Knew he needed to take Princess and get the hell outta here. Head to the Chevelle, and then...

And then what?

He'd single-handedly ensured he could never come back here again. Changed the course of his life in an instant. And the terrifying part?

He'd fucking do it again.

So long as it saved her.

The beast inside him growled.

Mine.

Jace felt the blood drain from his face. For a moment, he bucked against it, attempting to fight, but its urge was immovable.

Fuck.

"Jace," Damon said, drawing his attention enough to break him from his stupor. His division lead's voice was uncharacteristically soft as the hunter's blue eyes held his. The singular look Damon gave him then provided the only answer Jace needed to know.

Chet was right. He *was* a dead man, if HQ got ahold of him.

But not by Damon's hand.

Slowly, Jace met his division leader's eyes as Damon breathed out his one and only warning. "Jace," Damon said again. "Run."

~

AT THE VAMPIRE hunter's command, Jace's hand was suddenly in hers, pulling her alongside him and leading her out of there. Fast.

Frankie had suspected there was something different about him from the moment she'd first gone head-to-head with him in the alley, but she hadn't *known*. Known that feral look in his eyes. Known that alpha male instinct to protect.

Suddenly, every heated interaction between them made sense.

Didn't it?

The conclusions her brain was jumping to were out of the question, her mind still reeling from the altercation so much that nothing made sense.

A hunter who wasn't human?

It wasn't possible.

"What the hell happened in there?" she demanded again once they were out of the interrogation room, leaving the other two men in their wake.

Jace silenced her with little more than a passing glance as they rushed through the observation area. The sound of the facility's alarm screeched overhead. They hurried into the hall before he finally released her hand. Losing his touch shouldn't have chilled her, but somehow, it did.

The building was a white-washed maze of cinderblock pathways lit with the too bright glow of florescent lights, which seared her wolf retinas as he led them. But from the sure-footed way he navigated, she held no doubt he knew all the nooks and crannies of this place.

Where to hide. Where to duck and cover so they could escape sight unseen.

A hunter like him *would* know.

He couldn't be anything but human, could he?

They snaked their way through the facility, undetected. Only stopping once to duck into an alcove as what appeared to be a fully armed S.W.A.T team of hunters rushed by. A few turns and locked doors which Jace keyed through, and the chill of Rochester's freezing winds hit her face. In an instant, she was reminded that she was still wearing little more than his buttoned-up trench coat. But she couldn't bring herself to care.

Not when she was this close to freedom.

To returning to her pack. Her family.

They made their way across the nearly empty parking lot, back to the Chevelle he'd brought her here in. When she reached the vehicle, she hesitated, not certain whether to part ways now or risk getting into the car with him.

But before she could make up her mind, he spotted the crack she'd left in his rear window and cursed. Despite his clear frustration, he didn't stop to assess the damage. Instead, he simply wrenched open the driver's side door, before he looked toward her. "Get in."

She didn't need to be told twice. She'd place further distance between herself and here by riding alongside him rather than making her way on foot. Not to mention she'd need to get past the gates. This time, she slid into the passenger's seat, slamming the door behind her and trying not to smile at the pine-scented air freshener hanging from the rearview.

A wolf's favorite scent.

Though it smelled like a fake version of the real thing.

But was he a wolf or was he something . . . different?

Jace shoved his key in and the engine turned over seconds later. He didn't bother to tell her where he was driving, and she didn't ask. All that mattered was placing distance between them and that godawful place. Escaping from Damon and the guards and Chet. At this point, she wasn't certain which of them posed a danger to her and which didn't.

The moment Jace had fired his gun, every bit of gray in the already shady situation had blended, until who was her enemy and who was her alley had become unclear.

Hell, she still wasn't certain.

When they finally pulled to a stop, they were parked outside a run-down apartment building that looked as if it hadn't seen a renovation in years.

"Stay here," he grumbled, before tearing out of the vehicle.

"Like hell." She climbed from the cab after him.

He strode toward the apartment building like a man on a mission, which by her guess, she supposed he was. Though what exactly either of them were doing here she couldn't be certain.

"What are you?" she called after him.

Boy, if that wasn't the question of the year.

She suspected he was a wolf shifter. Maybe some kind of half-breed. But neither of those possibilities made sense given his occupation. Or his lack of scent. Not to mention, she couldn't wrap her head around how he would have been able to keep it hidden from his colleagues all these years. But he was something lupine. A distance species cousin at least.

That much was clear.

It made whatever this...this...tension between them was a hell of a lot easier.

Explained what had happened back there.

The way he'd torn into Chet hadn't been like a hunter. Hell, it hadn't even been like an alpha wolf. It'd been like a mate.

Her shoulders stiffened, filling her with unease. *No.* She shook her head. *Not a chance.*

She couldn't allow herself to go down that line of thinking. Not when she was promised to another for the betterment of her pack. Her mind was reeling. That's all. Jumping to conclusions in order to explain how the foundations of her world had been shaken. Anything to find an explanation of how a man who was supposed to be her enemy had sacrificed everything for her.

Like she was someone.

Like she mattered.

Even though he barely knew her.

If he heard her question, he didn't bother to answer. Nor did he miss a beat in his step. Still not entirely certain what she was doing, she trailed after him.

He marched right up to the apartment entryway before he paused and entered the door code. As soon as the green button lit up, he pushed inside and they both paraded up the stairs.

They climbed two flights and finally reached a shabby wooden door sporting a pitted brass number six hanging a little too far to the right. He pulled a key—on a chain like a dog tag—from inside his shirt and jammed it into the lock. The tumblers clicked, and Frankie followed him into the run-down apartment.

Bleak. That was the one word to describe the small

space. A flattened, faded, brown couch sat in the middle of the room, facing an arms closet and T.V. From the dust on the screen, it was rarely, if ever, used. A small gas stove, a refrigerator, and of course, every man's best cooking pal, a microwave, sat against the far wall—no division between the living room and the makeshift kitchen. An open door stood across from her, leading into what appeared to be his bedroom. The faint scent of long dissipated cigarette smoke hung in the air.

"Nice place you've got here," she said as he herded her farther inside.

He shot a glare toward her, ignoring her sarcasm before he closed the door behind them.

Standing there, almost naked save for his coat, she watched him wander into the bedroom, peel off his shirt and throw it onto the bed. "It's a burner apartment. HQ won't track us here."

In other words, a safe space he'd kept for exactly a time like this.

What was going on at Execution Underground Headquarters that he'd had that kind of foresight?

She glanced around, fighting the urge to ask what the hell they were doing here. She could still feel where the silver handcuffs had burned her skin. Why hadn't she left already? She didn't owe this jerk a damn thing.

No matter if he'd saved her. Defended her.

She glanced up again, and her breath stopped short as the hunter turned and met her gaze. A warm flush crept through her, and a flood of heat pooled in her core. His appeal in the alleyway was nothing compared to the rugged man who stood before her now. In the light, his dark auburn hair glistened and the vibrancy in his emerald eyes took on a life of its own.

With his shirt gone, he sported a pair of low, straight-legged jeans that conveniently hugged his muscular body in all the right places. She slouched in on herself, trying to hide her interest. Now that she knew what he was, she could admit there was attraction there, even if she couldn't explain it, and the thought of his hair brushing against her cheek while he laid her down crossed her mind. She tensed at the thought. She shouldn't even *be* here.

Let alone be thinking about him like this.

She lowered her stare to the floor. "If it's all the same to you, I'm getting the hell outta here." A moment later, when she dared look at him again, all the air rushed from her lungs. His eyes ran over her, like he could smell exactly what sort of thoughts were going through her head—hell, he likely could—and she could have sworn his irises flashed a hint of gold, the familiar color of a wolf's

She shook her head.

"Nobody's stopping you," he said, his voice rough. "You're free to leave." He looked at her for another long moment before he walked into his room. He returned with a fresh shirt on, a white ribbed undershirt that hugged the muscles of his chest closely.

Which didn't make what she had to do any easier.

He stalked toward her, his gait smooth and graceful like an animal's. At the sudden onslaught, she stumbled and nearly bumped into the door. Her whole body froze. She clenched her thighs together as a wave of desire rolled through her, leaving her hot and ready.

Why did he have to prowl toward her like that?

"Here," he said, offering her the handle of a gun she didn't realize he'd been carrying. "If Chet or anyone else tries to fuck with you, use it."

Reluctantly, she took the weapon. The weight of the

standard nine-millimeter felt strange against her palm. She knew how to use a gun, how to shoot. She was even a decent shot, but among her kind, weapons came second to what she could do in her wolf-form. Though he clearly thought she'd need it.

Accepting the sign of peace for what it was, she tucked it into the trench coat pocket. "Thank you," she whispered.

At that, he turned away from her again, heading toward the arms closet.

"Thank you for saving me, I mean…" she added, perhaps a little too breathlessly. "Even though it cost you your job. And for the gun," she said quickly. "Thank you."

He paused then, shaking his head, though he didn't look at her. "I didn't do it for you."

She blinked. His response caught her off-guard. "For who then?"

"For myself," he said. "And anyone who's ever been powerless."

A lump formed in Frankie's throat. She wasn't certain what to say. Her hand fell to the door handle, but before she even knew what she was doing, she turned toward him. "So, what's your plan, exactly?"

He finally turned to her, one dark brow lifted. "What's it to you?"

She shrugged. "Humor me."

He blew out a long breath and rubbed at the back of his neck. "Gather as many weapons as I can and get the hell outta Dodge."

"And then?"

"And then I run. Or else I'm a dead man."

"What about the killer? What about your job? Clearing your name? Vindication?" She gaped at him. "You can't tell me that none of that matters."

He smirked a little. "Why do you care, Princess?"

"Like I said, humor me."

He sighed again. "It ceased to be my problem the moment I fired at Chet. Even if I wanted, I can't do anything about it now."

"So that's it?" She couldn't hide her disappointment. "You're going to let the killer run loose? Don't tell me all that cryptic communication with the vampire hunter means there's not a deeper problem going on with the E.U. I'm smart enough to read the subtext."

"And what do you expect me to do about it, sweetheart? I'm persona non-grata now. You got a better plan?"

"As a matter of fact, I do." She lifted her chin defiantly. "But this time, you're going to have to come with me."

7

"What are we doing here?" Jace's gruff voice carried over the winter wind.

It was a few hours until dawn and they stood outside on the darkened sidewalk, the din of the city cutting through the morning quiet. Nearby the sound of an early garbage pickup whirred its electric gears, and the far-off screech of a distant firetruck followed. The air was rent with sewer and the dampness of melted snow. Not surprising. This side of Monroe Street, everything wreaked with the stench of the city.

Fumbling with the lock for a moment, Frankie jiggled the key until finally the door came unstuck. Stepping inside, she checked down the block for anyone watching them, though they'd already parked the Chevelle and traveled on foot for several blocks. Assured the coast was clear, she ushered Jace in, not bothering to flick on the single working light overhead. The orange glow of the streetlamps outside would stream in through the windows.

That would have be enough. For now.

Once the door was closed and locked again, she gestured

to the abandoned dance studio. "You needed a place to hide out. This is it."

Dust and silence greeted them. One full wall lined with floor-length mirrors. The adjacent wall sported a colorful array of street tags and graffiti she'd never found the time to paint over. Frankie exhaled and watched her breath swirl through the chilled air. It was nearly as cold as it was outside, and Rochester had already dropped to well below freezing, but she hadn't paid to turn on the heat.

Jace stepped further into the open room, his large frame instantly dwarfing the height of the aging, abandoned barre. Behind him, the concrete and brick jungle that was downtown loomed, barely visible overtop the curling paper which covered the business windows. Through the crack in the newspaper, she could see snow flurries had started to fall, looking like a sky speckled with ash through the orange glow. On the city streets, the snow would become gray slush within a handful of minutes, if it even stuck at all.

A tense moment passed, neither of them saying anything, before finally Frankie cleared her throat. "What? You can't tell me this is any worse than your dingy excuse of an apartment? And there's no way they can trace this place to you." She cast the key on top of an abandoned box in the corner.

Amidst the pressing silence it made an audible *thunk* against the cardboard.

She always forgot how quiet it was whenever she came to hide out here.

Even alongside the sounds of the city, this place was a kind of sanctuary.

"Lying low wasn't the plan," Jace grumbled in answer.

Frankie huffed. "And this from the man whose only plan was 'get the hell outta Dodge.'" She headed into the studio's only bathroom, turning on the light overhead. The cramped space sported little more than a lightbulb with a pull string, a cracked sink, and a working toilet, but she always kept a small travel bag stored under the exposed sink pipes.

"That's still the plan," he called after her.

In other words, she was simply stalling him, but for some reason, he was indulging her.

Closing the door, she stripped off the damp trench coat in exchange for the jeans and an old t-shirt sweater from the travel bag, before she emerged. "And did your plan include an untraceable, 'for sale' property off the E.U's radar?"

Silence followed, and Jace frowned.

She cast him a smug grin. "That's what I thought."

She stepped closer, offering the trench coat back to him.

Shaking his head, he reached inside the pocket of his leather coat. "Keep it." He removed a flask before he unscrewed a cap and took a drink.

She lifted a brow, but he simply cast her a smug grin and extended the flask to her.

She shook her head, before turning her back to him.

In the mirrors, his eyes followed her, like it didn't occur to him to look elsewhere, or like he didn't want to. A delicious pressure built low in her belly, stirring something there. Temptation, or something close to it.

"So this is your brilliant plan? Hide out? In the city?" he asked. "For how long?"

"No. You're mistaken." She shook her head, giving him an incredulous look. "All I've done is given you lead time to *formulate* your brilliant plan, and get the hell outta dodge isn't that." She grabbed a refillable water bottle she kept by the barre, for occasions such as this, and filled it with tap water from the sink. She took a quick drink. "Consider it payment for standing up to that asshole you called a region lead for me."

Jace huffed, something close to a laugh, but not quite. He tipped back the flask again. "No payment needed. I'd been biding my time, wishing I could take out that bastard for years." Slowly, he eased toward her then, a test, like he wanted to come nearer but saw her hesitate.

At her reluctance, instead he brushed past her, allowing himself to wander. His steel-toed boots echoed against the old wood floor as he traced a large hand across a curled graffiti letter. "I should've put a bullet in him when I had the chance." His tone was gruff, strained.

"But you didn't because you're a good man."

He glanced toward her then. In the dark, lupine gold flashed.

She smiled. "Or something close to it, at least."

She held her water bottle out to him, offering to share, but he refused. A quiet, heavy tension settled between them again, neither of them certain what to say.

She nodded to the open space. "Sorry it doesn't have heat. It's going to get cold tonight."

Jace lifted a brow. The way he looked at her made it feel like she had a secret she hadn't yet shared with him. "Why do this?" he asked. "Why help me?"

She set her water down on the floor, softly. "Because everyone deserves a fighting chance." She drew closer to him, placing her hands on the barre surface to rest her weight there. "You put your own life on the line to help me, even if you say that wasn't why." She met his gaze. "That means something."

The tension between them stretched for a beat.

"So what is this place?" Jace asked, glancing toward the window.

"My dance studio. Or it would have been anyway. If I had opened it." Frankie lifted a shoulder and shrugged. "Technically it belongs to the pack for tax purposes, but it was purchased from my personal funds. It's my name on the deed." She nodded to one single picture she'd hung on the far wall. A younger version of herself in costume at some dance competition or another. She couldn't even remember which. It'd been aspirational placing it there.

A dream of something she'd never have.

Of a life that was shaped for herself alone.

Not the life of a pack wolf.

Jace eyed the old photo. "Dance?" He lifted a brow. "Really?"

The costume she wore in the picture was red and glittering. A little revealing from the devious grin that sparked when he looked at it. An old favorite of hers. She'd been proud of how she looked in it.

"Salsa dance," she answered.

He grumbled a low grunt of acknowledgement under his breath, running a rough hand through his hair. "Suppose you have the legs for it." His gaze cut to her and he cast her that smirk of a grin.

Heat flooded her cheeks, and she glanced away again. "I'll take that as a compliment."

He looked back to the photo. "A salsa dancing wolf shifter." He shook his head, and she watched something spark in his eyes then. "Show me."

She laughed, unable to stop herself. "You sure that's not an excuse to get me in your arms again?"

Something dark flickered in his gaze. Like temptation. Only...more sinful.

"Do you want it to be?"

The question hung in the air between them.

For a moment, Frankie struggled to breathe. "I... I haven't danced in years." She held his gaze. Unwittingly, her tongue darted out to wet her lips, and his stare fell there.

"Give me your hands," she said, before she even knew what she was doing.

The growl of approval which came from him rumbled through her.

Slowly, Jace prowled toward her, each step languid and lethal, like a predator stalking its prey. He didn't stop until he stood in front of her. Gently, he placed his palms in hers.

What am I doing?

The moment their hands touched, an electric shock pulsed through Frankie. Every nerve, every desire inside her stood on edge. Awakened and wanting. No matter how forbidden.

Without prompting, he pulled her into his arms, pressing her flush against him, until she could feel the hardened length of him against her, how the low ache between her legs called out to him, exactly as it'd been in the alley. His warmth flooded over her skin. The heat of him enveloped her, instantly making her chilled skin warm, and it took every ounce of self-control she had not to close the distance between them then, to kiss him right there.

Kiss me or I'll die. The thought rolled through her again.

What *was* this? She shouldn't want whatever this tension was between them.

She hated the way her body responded to him so readily, and yet...

Frankie swallowed down the lump of nerves in her throat. What if she didn't stop it this time? What if she...indulged it?

The thought instantly shook her. She shouldn't even be considering this. She was promised to another man, another wolf. But her engagement was a decision not of her own choosing, an arrangement on behalf of the pack with someone she barely knew, and with that harsh reality catching up to her so soon...

When would she have another chance like this?

To be with a man of her own choosing?

Simply because she wanted to be.

The thought alone shook her.

"The man normally leads in salsa," she suddenly heard herself saying, "but for now, let me lead you." She glanced up at Jace again. His broad shoulders towered over her, making her feel strangely small and...protected, in a way she hadn't known she'd longed for. She told herself the reason she couldn't stop watching him was because it was hard to look away when he was so close. But deep down, she knew that was a lie.

Fuck, she wanted him. She couldn't keep fooling herself anymore. Keep denying it.

Kiss me or I'll die.

Damn it. She'd wanted him from the start.

And what did that even mean?

She tried not to chase that thought too deeply, as an intense longing burned in her chest and Jace's touch pierced her again. His gaze raked over her, igniting a trail of heat as it went.

It didn't seem to matter that they didn't know each other. That they were practically strangers. Not really. She'd already seen the true heart of him, in the way he'd put himself on the line for her. Would it be the same if he were another man, another hunter?

Or was it something about *him*?

"Step back," she instructed, tentatively. "Now forward."

He did as she commanded, the unbridled heat in his

eyes turning into a devastating smolder. Like he'd have her on her back and moaning within minutes, if only she allowed it. The thought sent a fresh wave of heat to her core and she knew the moment he sensed it, smelled the affect he had on her from the way his nostrils flared.

She wasn't the only one affected by their closeness, and they both knew it.

She could feel every inch of him, every bit of leashed power behind the taut muscles of his arms, his back, his chest—and growing length of his cock pressed against her stomach, the way his fingers tightened on her hips in a delicious, bruising grip, promising a primal, pleasurable kind of punishment, if she let him.

His hand dipped lower.

"Now back, and extend your left foot," she heard herself say.

Her voice was breathy, little more than a whisper, her need barely contained.

She wasn't certain how long they continued like this, each movement, each step singeing her like she was a candle and he was the flame, until the throb between her legs nearly came to a head, built in a slow steady ache, and she wasn't certain she could take it anymore.

Not without coming apart.

"We're supposed to step away now." She stopped moving, uncertain what else to say.

Jace's eyes were dark, lustful. "And if we don't?"

The forbidden promise behind that question burned through her.

He cradled her in his arms, like he refused to let go, though she couldn't bring herself to pull away. Maybe because she didn't want to.

He was a natural lead, his movements surprisingly

polished and smooth. Nothing like the gruff man she knew him to be every time he opened his mouth. He was tender with her now.

Different.

She bit her lower lip. Allowing herself to go further with this would do neither of them any good. Still, for a brief second, she considered telling him the truth, willing herself to let her words flow freely, but she quickly snapped her jaw shut. There was no point. Knowing her luck, it would only make things worse.

His hand slid from her hip onto her lower back, pulling her from her thoughts.

Shit. She couldn't do this.

There was no doubt in her mind now—her body wanted him, needed him like she needed air, water, food, and some part of her heart did, too.

But she couldn't. Not now. Not ever.

Sensing the change in her, Jace's breath slowed, and for several long moments they lingered there, a hairsbreadth away from moving closer, or stepping apart. His emerald gaze locked on hers, but she forced her gaze away. Navigating this situation just wasn't possible. They were enemies. Nothing more.

That's all they ever would be.

She turned away from him then and folded her arms over her chest, as she tried to hold herself together. If she didn't stop now, she wouldn't be able to control herself; she would want him too much to resist. Having him so close but being unable to have him was pure torture. She wasn't sure how much longer she could take it.

Frankie cleared her throat. "You can stay here a few days. There's a studio apartment upstairs. Hide out until you get your bearings. Hopefully by then this insanity with your organization will have blown over."

As if her words had brought some sense to them both, the tension between them dissipated. The spell broken.

"It won't." Jace shook his head, before raking a hand through the stubbled shadow on his chin. "You heard Chet. I'm a dead man. Headquarters won't take lightly the fact that I've been hiding what I am for years."

"Which is?" She lifted a brow.

He scoffed, suddenly gruff again. "Hell if I know."

She waited, silently hoping he would elaborate, but he didn't.

Jace leaned against the wall, raking a hand over his face. "Shit...I said I don't know, okay? Some sort of half-breed? I don't even know what your kind would call it."

"But you're a wolf shifter? You're certain?"

"If you mean, can I shift into a wolf like you can? I don't know. Never bothered to try."

She blinked at him. He had to be nearly thirty-five, but he'd never...

"You're kidding."

Jace shot her a hardened glance. "Do I look like I'm kidding?"

"You've spent your whole life knowing what you are and never shifted?" Somehow, she couldn't bring herself to believe it.

"If by knowing what I am, you mean having my father walk out on me and leaving me with this curse, then yeah, I am."

"I'm sorry," she said softly, her whisper carrying through the empty studio. "I'm sorry he left you like that."

Jace chuckled then. An unamused laugh. "I don't need your pity, Princess."

"No, but you do have my empathy. My understanding." She took another sip from her water in search of some reprieve for how she'd burned for him. "Take it as you will."

Silence fell between them again, pressing and heavy.

Hitching a thumb over her shoulder, she indicated the stairs up to the studio apartment beyond. "Look, if it's all the same to you, I'm going to crash here too. I already put in a call to my pack, and it's likely a good idea if I lie low. At least for a little while."

Jace shrugged. "It's your place."

"Right." She nodded.

The air between them seemed to hesitate, cut through them.

For a moment, she thought that might be the end, that they'd make their excuses and then finally part ways, until suddenly she heard herself say, "Hey...are you...hungry? There's this little greasy spoon diner around the corner that's perfect for when you have a hangover."

Jace chuckled. An actual laugh. "Hangovers require you to *stop* drinking." He gave the flask a little shake.

Five minutes later they were seated across from one another in a cracked vinyl booth, the cherry red color faded from one too many bright days. The smell of maple syrup mixed with bacon, hashbrowns and grease filled the air, and Frankie's stomach growled.

She could feel her wolf practically salivate.

She and Jace stared across the booth at one another, both of them clearly uneasy, but the quiet persisted, considering they were the only two people in the restaurant at this hour. Save for the sound of the coffee dripping into the hot plate percolator and the waitress they could hear in the back talking to a single line cook. Frankie adjusted herself in her seat. The mist of fry grease that clung to everything in the place made her shoes stick to the checkerboard tiling which lined the floor.

Jace was the first one to crack. "So you come here often?" he asked.

Frankie smirked. "That's the best pickup line you got?"

Jace leaned back in the booth, spreading both arms over the seat with a shrug. "I've used worse."

She smiled. "I've come here at least once every winter since I was a little girl."

The waitress showed up a moment later, interrupting them. They both ordered and handed over the sticky plastic menus, though the aging brunette didn't bother to scratch out their choices on her notepad. She hollered their order back to the kitchen before leaving them alone again. They waited for their food in a tense, companionable sort of silence.

Finally, Jace said, "What are we doing here?"

Before Frankie could answer, the waitress returned, their dishes stacked in a line down the length of her arm. She set down Frankie's buttered toast and sunny-side eggs, and Jace's enormous plate of country fried steak with biscuits and gravy, before leaving them to it.

Jace didn't say anything else before he quickly tucked in.

For a few minutes, Frankie watched him eat with fascinated amusement. "You definitely have the appetite of an alpha wolf," she mused once he was more than halfway in.

Suddenly, he paused mid-forkful before he abandoned the utensil on his plate. He frowned. "Maybe I'm not so hungry." He slowly pushed his plate away.

Frankie scooped up a bit of her eggs. "How long have you known you were a wolf?"

Jace let out a long sigh, shoving his hands in his coat

pockets beneath the booth. "Is this the part where we play twenty questions or something?"

Frankie lifted her fork. "I'm just trying to understand."

Jace drew his coffee mug into his large paw of a hand. "What's to understand, sweetheart? My old man walked out when I was a teen. Bastard saddled me with whatever this," he glanced over his shoulder, ensuring they were alone, before his eyes flashed to his wolf briefly, "is. I stuck around long enough to graduate high school, then joined the E.U. That's it."

Frankie found that hard to believe. "And you've never embraced it? Never wondered about who or what you are?"

"Oh, I've wondered plenty." Jace grabbed his fork again, using it to push around a large clump of sausage gravy. "But that doesn't mean I have to embrace it." He met her gaze.

"Doesn't it?" she asked. "It's who you are."

Jace's expression turned grim. Pulling out his wallet, he dropped several twenties on the table, more than enough to cover the bill and then some. "I don't have time for this."

He slid from the booth, coming to stand.

His back was fully turned toward her by the time she said, "On the night of the full moon, do you feel its pull? Like something living is crawling underneath your skin, threatening to burst out?"

Jace froze.

"I bet you get the same feeling when you're angry. You constantly fight to control your emotions and hide your identity from the other hunters."

His spine cracked when he moved, hands clenched.

"And when you're hunting and you smell a female wolf shifter, it turns you on more than a human woman ever could, doesn't it, and you hate yourself all the more for it."

Jace remained silent, his body language speaking

volumes. The muscles in his back flexed, and she could feel the rage which radiated from him.

"And right now, I'm making you angry," she said, pushing him to his limits. "Because every mention of your true nature pisses you off. You'd rather loathe yourself your entire life than embrace what you really are."

Silence answered her, as powerful and forceful as if he'd spoken.

He needs to know this, she reassured herself.

"How can you hunt your own kind?" A pang of sadness hit her in the chest. A part of her felt sorry for him, because she was challenging all his preconceived notions about himself.

It was part of why she'd put a stop to the heat between them.

How could she be with him when the part of himself he hated was also a part of her?

"I'm not one of you."

"You are."

He spun to face her, his face flushed and his hands clenched as his eyes flashed to his wolf. "I am nothing like him." Walking to her side, he leaned down staring her square in the face, and Frankie saw the resolve in his gaze. "I'm nothing like you."

He was so close to her that she could feel the heat pulsating from his body. Clenching her thighs together, she tried to ignore her undeniable interest in him. The intoxicating smell of his hair, and that keen absence of scent on his skin. She inhaled a sharp breath, balling up her courage. "You can't hide from the truth forever."

He broke eye contact and stalked from the diner, grabbing his coffee as he went.

"We're not all monsters," she called after him. "I had a family once, and I never would have betrayed them."

"Bully for you," he called back.

When she returned to the studio, she was surprised to find him there once again, already safely hidden inside. Clearly he had no problem jimmying a lock. She made a mental note to invest in an upgrade as soon as this mess was over.

Without exchanging so much as a word with one another, they headed up the stairs to the apartment studio. The decorations there were sparse, nearly as barren as his own place, though with a touch of feminine flare thanks to an artsy streak from back in her college days. Her old left-over furniture remained there. He glanced about the space, and for the first time since he'd been there, his presence felt like an invasion.

She'd never brought anyone else here. Not even the members of her pack.

Why had she chosen to do so with him?

"There's only one bed," she said, getting the matters of necessity out of the way.

"I'll sleep on the couch," he volunteered.

She nodded, making her way toward the open bedroom door before she paused. She wasn't certain what it was that made her turn around then, but suddenly, she said, "I'm sorry I pushed you. I...know this can't be easy for you."

Jace cut her a hardened glare, and something withered between them. Crushed by the harsh lines and rough surfaces of him. There was more to him underneath, she could feel, had seen it in the way he'd risked himself for her, in the tenderness with which he held her when they'd danced.

But she didn't see it then.

He didn't take a seat, instead he stood there, looking at her like her face held the answers to every question he had about her world. Finally, something in his gaze softened. "Don't worry about me, Princess. I'm a big boy. I can handle myself."

She turned back to the bedroom, but felt herself hesitate. "I...know the feeling."

He lifted a brow, and she turned back toward him.

"That voice that tells you that you have to be self-reliant, invulnerable," she said. "But you don't always have to be." She placed a hand on the door frame, casting a glance back at him as she nodded. "Goodnight, I guess."

She moved another foot into the bedroom.

"Hey, Princess," he said, causing her to pause once more. "Answer me something, will you?"

She nodded but didn't look toward him.

"In the alley..." His voice was rough, charred with whatever burned between them. "Did you mean it?"

Frankie couldn't help herself. She couldn't bring herself to breathe.

They both knew what he was asking. What else *could* he mean?

Had she really wanted to kiss him?

Earlier she would have said she didn't know the answer, but now...

"Yes," she finally breathed a moment later. "Yes, I meant it."

Her wolf felt more than saw him stir behind her. His grumble of acknowledgement sent a shiver into her knees. But she couldn't bring herself to look at him. Not now.

"Fair enough," he ground out, then paused again. "Night, Princess."

"Goodnight, Jace." She stepped into her room, sealing

the door closed behind her as quickly as she could then, because if she didn't, she wasn't certain she'd be able to put a stop to what they both wanted.

FRANKIE LAID awake long into the early hours of the morning, unable to sleep. Her mind too busy reeling, too full of questions about the what and why of all she was doing. Eventually, a stir of movement down on the street and someone's stray car alarm broke her, and she gave up on rest in favor of rising from her bed.

She tiptoed into the studio apartment's main area, careful not to wake a sleeping Jace as she snuck past him. She was down on the street and closing the door behind her within a minute.

"This isn't wise." A voice from the darkness said from behind her.

Frankie turned, unsurprised, at the sight of the man the shadows helped hide. Her wolf had sensed him there, blended among them. "Alejandro." She nodded in acknowledgement.

Her second-in-command eased forth from the darkness, his russet skin helping him blend into the street's darkened corners. His lineage descended from Mexican immigrants, red wolves who'd crossed over the border by way of Texas to New York City, and then eventually upstate. But she'd known him since they'd been children, since long before Rochester had been *her* pack.

Never one to beat around the bush, Alejandro joined her side then. "You know I'm not one to question your judgment, packmaster, but as your friend..." She felt him hesitate, though whether out of respect for her position or the repercussions of her anger, she wasn't certain. "...whatever deal you think you're making with that hunter in there, Frankie, this wasn't the plan."

Frankie folded her arms over her chest, an attempt to keep herself warm. "You're not the first alpha male to have told me that tonight." She stepped further out onto the street, staring up at the apartment. To the unknowing eye, it appeared empty. Abandoned. In some ways, she supposed it was, and would continue to be. "You were watching us? At the diner?" she asked.

Alejandro stiffened at the implied intrusion. "It's my job to protect you, in whatever way I can." It was the safe answer, the practiced one. Meant to show deference to her position.

But it didn't accomplish what he'd intended.

"And would you have said the same to my father? If I were a man?" She glanced toward him, and Alejandro lowered his eyes in submission. "I respect your opinion, Alejandro, but I have this situation well in hand. Leave this to me." She blew out a slow breath, watching the heat of it swirl in the early morning light. "And there's more at play here than meets the eye."

Alejandro lifted a brow.

"He's a shifter," she answered. "A half-breed, or something like it."

Alejandro's eyes grew wide, like he couldn't believe it, though he didn't dare defy her or say it was impossible. Though it still certainly felt that way. Even to her.

"Shit," he swore. Though that familiar concern in his expression returned quickly. "And you think you can use this to our advantage? To get out of the deal with the white wolves?"

Frankie's lip curled at him. A flash of canine teeth. "Are you suggesting—"

"—That you're doing this for your own advantage? No. Never," Alejandro finished quickly. He shook his head. "I know you'd sacrifice everything for this pack."

She punched at his arm playfully, but didn't grin. "Now you're ass kissing."

Alejandro smiled a little. "Don't look so offended, packmaster. All of us wish you didn't have to go through this."

"Not all of you," she corrected. "Some are far too eager for it."

She stepped away from him, placing one slender hand flat against the studio's glass. The warmth of her hand left a foggy imprint. "No, I'm not trying to get out of the arrangement with Rock." She shook her head. "I'm not that foolish."

"What then?"

Frankie lifted a shoulder and shrugged. "He saved me. I owe him. I got hauled into division headquarters and he got me out."

Alejandro's expression turned grim. "You mean that man…"

"Is a wolf hunter? Yes." She removed her hand from the glass. "Jace McCannon."

Alejandro swore. She'd known he'd recognize the name. Her second was good at his position, highly trained and aware of every threat against them. Plus Jace's reputation preceded him.

Alejandro shook his head. "Whatever it is you're planning, Frankie. I don't like this."

"I don't remember asking your opinion," she said, perhaps a little too defensively. He rarely, if ever, used her name anymore. She softened her tone then. "He saved my life."

Though he held his human form, Alejandro's brown eyes seemed to glitter in the fading dark. "You don't know that man."

"And neither do you," she said. "But he *did* save me. I owe him."

Alejandro swore again. "I'm begging you, Frankie. As your friend. Leave this now. Before it ruins everything we've planned."

"You mean everything *I've* planned," she corrected him. "It's my sacrifice to make, and make no mistake, Alejandro, you may be my friend, but first and foremost, I am your packmaster and you are my second. You will defer to my judgment on this and on all things. Do I make myself clear?"

Alejandro dropped his gaze. "Yes, packmaster."

"Good." She turned to head into the studio again.

"Can I...at least know your plan, packmaster?" He tacked her title on at the end with a small grin. Like he respected her, but also wouldn't let her forget he was her friend.

She smiled at him. "I already told you. I owe him." She turned the studio doorknob. "I plan to help him, that's all." Alejandro didn't appear to be pleased by the answer, so she said, "I'd do the same for you, or any wolf who laid their life on the line for me."

"Your life wouldn't have needed saving if it weren't for that man."

"That wolf," she corrected again. "Hunter or not, he's no human man. No matter how much he wishes to be." She reached out and gave Alejandro's hand a quick squeeze. "Trust me. I know how to handle myself, especially with the support of an old friend."

Alejandro nodded. "I'll leave you to it then."

Frankie opened the door to the studio.

"But packmaster," Alejandro said again.

Frankie glanced over her shoulder from where she stood in the doorway.

"Should you need us." Alejandro's lupine eyes glared through the darkness as he became one with it. "We'll be waiting in the wings."

8

Jace woke to the creak of a door closing as Francesca slipped back in, then didn't stir again until well into the following night. He was used to this. Sleeping in bursts. Claiming his rest when it suited him and foregoing it as needed. It'd never fazed him like it did the other hunters. He'd always taken a strange pride in that. Chalked it up to dedication. Perseverance. Though maybe the true reason was worse.

A sign he really *wasn't* one of them.

On that grim thought, he rose from the couch where he'd slept, raking a hand over the stubble on his face that was quickly turning into a beard. He'd need to duck back to the burner apartment, shave, and grab a bag. Or on second thought, maybe he'd leave it. When a man was on the lam, maybe it wasn't half-bad to grow a beard. He'd always kept it close, out of concern that growing it would make him look like even *more* of a fucking wolf man.

Goddamn it. He pushed the thought away.

"Finally, you're awake."

Before he could rub the sleep from his eyes, Francesca

pushed a steaming mug of coffee into his hand. "Careful. It's fresh. I know you're not used to that."

He grumbled his thanks, lifting the drink to his lips before sputtering it back into the mug. "Fuck, that's hot."

"I warned you."

He could hear her amused grin.

He examined the porcelain mug in his hand. The familiar logo on the side read: Waffle House. He'd eaten there one too many times before, and he probably would soon, considering he'd need to be back on the road again. To where, he hardly knew.

He blew on the coffee, before daring another sip. "Better."

A far cry from the sludge at division headquarters.

"So what's the plan?"

He looked toward her. "That really is your favorite question, isn't it?"

In the glow of the streetlights that streamed through the window, a hint of red flashed in her dark hair. "What can I say? I'm a plotter by nature." She gestured to the surrounding darkness. "And I did give you the day to sleep on it."

Jace shook his head. "I didn't ask you to give me anything."

"No, you didn't." She watched him expectantly.

They were talking about more than where he slept, or so it felt like it.

With a grunt, he placed the Waffle House mug on the table. "I need to head back to the burner apartment, gather a bag."

"And then?"

"And then what I do no longer concerns you." He allowed the gruffness to return to his tone. The rough edges. They couldn't keep playing this game. Whatever it was.

"You're really going to start with this again?" She shook her head. "Rochester is our jurisdiction and if you think I'm going to wait around for Chet to take this further and blame those murders on us, you've lost all sense."

Jace stood. "Do what you like. It doesn't need to concern me."

"So that's it?" She set her own mug down on the counter, a little too forcefully. "You just drop this steaming pile of shit in my lap and expect to leave?"

"No one said anything about leaving."

"I thought that was the plan? To get the hell outta Dodge?"

He'd never dare tell her it, but that hadn't ever been the plan. At least, not since she'd speared him with that look of disappointment. Like she expected more from him.

Expected him to be some sort of hero.

"Plans change." He scratched at his stubble.

She grumbled, and thankfully, she didn't press him further. Though somehow, she *did* end up riding in the Chevelle with him all the way back to the apartment. Hell if he knew why.

He was eager to place some distance between them. For levity's sake. But she kept coming at him like a Conrail freight train he didn't have the strength to stop.

Once they were safely inside the burner apartment, Jace had fully cemented his plans. In any case he'd need a hell of a lot more artillery than was currently on him. Breaking into E.U headquarters would require that.

Crossing the sparse apartment space, he retrieved a black duffel bag from the bedroom and headed to the arms closet.

Francesca stood there, lingering awkwardly near the doorway, watching him. "So, do you intend to fill me in on the new plan, or are we making this up as we go?"

"There's no *we* in this." Jace shook his head. "Not a chance, sweetheart." He tore open the weapons chest, removing another semi-auto and flipping off the safety lock. He didn't know what the hell she was thinking, but whatever scenario she'd concocted in that pretty little head about them making friends, teaming up, he wanted no part in it. He couldn't, wouldn't, cause her to get further involved in this mess. No way in hell.

He might as well place a target on her back.

He cast her a glance. "Look. I appreciate you letting me crash at your place, but like I said before, you're free to leave."

"So that's it then?" She dropped her hands to her sides with an audible flop. "You won't even hear me out?"

Jace paused. What part of no didn't she understand? "You think I didn't know about that little rendezvous with your packmate down on the street last night?"

Her eyes widened. Clearly she'd thought he was asleep then, but he'd been trained to wake at the slightest sound, the smallest movement. She hadn't been so stealthy.

"Any plan of yours is no doubt going to involve your pack. When shit hits the fan and word makes its way to HQ, you want them caught up in this?"

She started to respond, then hesitated.

Good. That seemed to knock some sense into her. At least, temporarily.

Her hands made their way to her hips, and his gaze shouldn't have followed the movement there, shouldn't have lingered, but he couldn't help himself. He could still feel the curve of her against his hands, the way she'd melted for him.

That was quickly becoming a problem with her.

Falling to temptation. Changing plans. That much was clear.

"So you save my life and then expect me to never see you again?"

He cocked a half-grin. "Don't go getting all emotional on me now, Princess."

He tried to tell himself that she didn't mean anything deeper by that, but his head was too busy reeling from the consequences of his actions. Formulating alternatives. Making plans. Tempting as she was, she was just another block in the road he had to deal with. Another complication in a life already full of clusterfuck after clusterfuck.

He couldn't allow it to be anything more than that.

His thoughts turned to the rage that'd coursed through him the previous night. When Chet had threatened her. Jace couldn't stand the thought of watching someone hurt innocents, but Lord knew he'd seen plenty of injured and hurt women out on the street far too many times before. Kids, too. He'd always felt a drive to protect them, sure. Not to be a hero, but to do his job. Protect those who couldn't protect themselves. The way no one had ever done for him. But nothing outside the realm of logic and reason. Nothing that would get his ass handed to him, or hold the potential for weakness.

Nothing like he'd felt in that interrogation room.

Logic and reason wasn't *that*.

The thought of her scent, the feel of her against him made his cock stiffen, casting all sense from his head.

As if she could see that raw, vulnerable spot inside his

mind, she chose that moment to poke at it. "What happened back there? Between you and the other hunters?"

Jace shook his head, opening the gun's chamber to check if it was fully loaded. Five out of six. He loaded up another bullet before he cocked back the hammer. In the empty apartment the sound echoed with a solid metal shift. "Nothing that concerns you."

Princess grumbled. "Like hell it doesn't."

He shook his head, though internally, he chuckled to himself.

Princess. The nickname was fitting. Hell, she was certainly making demands like one. No matter how he tried, he still couldn't bring himself to think of her by the name she'd given him. Not really. It was likely a fake anyway.

Francesca? It didn't suit her.

At the thought, that same instinct from the interrogation room echoed in his mind, igniting his primal side.

Mine.

Jace swallowed, hard.

He fought the urge to look toward her, and lost—miserably. "Didn't you say you were leaving?"

She shook her head. "Not until you tell me what you are. Or what the E.U.'s doing."

He scoffed. Hell if he knew the answer. "I'm a hunter. Or I was. Until you showed up."

He wasn't entirely sure why he held himself back. Why he didn't tell her the truth, but some part of him told him not to, told him to play his cards close, if he wanted to stand even a chance of letting her walk away.

When it came down to it, whatever the hell was happening here, he was still a trained hunter, and she was still a wolf. There would never be anything between them.

"And Headquarters?" She lifted one sculpted brow.

He cut her a silencing look.

"Answer me," she prompted.

He shook his head, busying himself with unloading one of his glocks. Why couldn't she let sleeping dogs lie? "I have my suspicions, but I'll handle it."

"Bullshit." She stepped toward him. "I saw the way you looked at Chet. Like the gears inside your head were turning. On something big. Not to mention, the way your fellow hunters reacted. If you expect me to believe nothing happened there, you're full of shit."

"You saw what you wanted to see, Princess." He stalked toward her, drawing close, a poor attempt to use his size to intimidate. "Hate goes both ways."

She growled. "I don't know what you mean by that."

"It means maybe you're trying to justify whatever you're feeling about how I saved you." He gestured between them. "Kiss me or I'll die, remember?"

"I don't know what you're talking about."

"Don't you?" He smirked. Placing his weapon in the cabinet where it belonged, he prowled toward her. He placed a rough hand on the door overtop her head. "You seemed mighty eager back in that alley. Last night. You think I didn't notice?"

He'd say whatever it took to get her to leave. To slam on the brakes and put a stop to this. They were like shooting stars both hurtling toward a black hole. The distance between them narrowed until they were certain to collide and combust.

She snarled. "Fuck you."

"Gladly." He raked his gaze over her. Hot and full of wanting.

"You're an ass."

He eased closer. "And you're a goddamn thorn in my

side. I think that makes us even."

"I could say the same." She eased against the door, as if she could escape him.

He chuckled. "Look I don't know what you want, Princess. You want to leave? Leave." He gestured toward the door frame. "I've already given up my life for you."

He watched her breath stop short.

For a moment, neither of them seemed to breathe.

"I didn't ask you to do that," she whispered.

"No, you didn't, but I did it anyway." Her gaze seared through him. "And I'd do again in a heartbeat. You wouldn't even have to ask."

"Jace..." she said softly.

He shook his head, stopping before she could pity him or God forbid thank him again. Like he wouldn't do it all over, if he had the chance. "What else did you expect, Princess?" He reached for her, but then stopped and let his hand fall again. "For me to stand there? To do nothing while I watched you suffer?" He sneered. "What kind of monster do you take me for?"

"A human one. Clearly." She stared up at him. "I don't know why I ever would have thought different."

"Because you wanted to. Anything to justify this." He reached for her, and the moment his fingers brushed a stray strand of hair from her cheek, she gasped.

It was like electricity shot through them, charging them both like a live wire.

Every time they touched.

"I don't think it's the fact that I'm a hunter that scares you." His voice dropped to a low purr. "I think it's that you don't want to walk out that door."

Her lip quivered, before she jerked away from him. "I'm leaving. For real this time."

"Go ahead." He stepped back, giving her ample space. "Don't let the door hit you in the ass on the way out."

For a moment, she hesitated.

He chuckled. "Cold feet?"

"I can't," she said, back still turned to him. "Not until I know why you saved me."

It was a piss poor excuse and they both knew it. "I already told you."

"No." She shook her head. "That answer's not good enough for me."

He wasn't good enough for her. Hell, he likely never would be.

It didn't take a genius to determine that.

"What do you want me to say, Princess? That if we weren't who we are, things would be different?" He growled, pushing her to her limit.

The flicker of shared recognition in her warm brown eyes as she turned hit him then, and from the fire in her eyes, suddenly, he knew he'd miscalculated, made a mistake pushing her away. Knew he couldn't let her walk out that door without being honest. He'd made enough messed up decisions the past few nights.

He wouldn't let *her* be the one he'd regret.

"What's that supposed to mean? I—"

"I want you," he said boldly, cutting her off. The words fell into the charged space between them. "There. Happy now? I said it." He growled. "Now you can go scurry back to that little pack of yours and have a good laugh about it."

Her jaw clenched. "Is that what you think of me? I wouldn't. I—"

"Don't hide behind your anger now, Princess." He shook his head. "There's no beat cop to interrupt this time. No more excuses."

He watched her expression as her denial, her frustration, slowly turned to resolve.

He'd admitted the truth. Now it was her turn.

"Fine. You're right. That *is* what I wanted to hear." She gave a dismissive shrug. "Maybe things would be different. I don't know how or why, but maybe they would be."

He nodded, faking a tip of a Stetson he hadn't worn for months now. "Appreciate that." He moved closer. "But you're wrong."

"What?"

"Things wouldn't be different." He gestured between them. "Whatever *this* is would still be there." He met her gaze. "But neither of us would be foolish enough to walk away from it."

This time, she looked at him. "You think it's that easy, huh? That I'm just going to fall into your arms, because you saved me?" She shook her head. "Think again."

"No, I don't think it's that easy, but you want this as much as I do, otherwise you wouldn't still be here." His gaze swept over her from head to toe, blazing a trail of heat over every inch of her. He may not have been a true wolf, but he had that sense under control, knew she wanted him. "What are you afraid of, Princess?"

She gave him an incredulous look. "I'm not afraid."

"You certain about that?" Slowly, he eased closer, carefully, tentatively.

With each step he drew near, he could see the war that raged in her. A battle between whether to step toward him or ease back.

"Are you?" he asked.

"Don't come any closer," she warned.

He quirked a brow. "Why not?"

The expression she gave him then was almost pained.

"Because I don't think I'll have it in me to go."

Something broke inside him then. Like his desire had been unchained. "You're playing with fire, Princess." He took another step closer. "But I think you want to burn."

He saw her resolve change. The moment she lost the fight.

She stepped toward him, meeting him toe-to-toe. Like she had in that alley. "Is that a challenge?"

Jace grinned. "It is if you make it one."

"What are you saying?" she asked.

"One night. What's it going to hurt?" Jace gestured to the apartment around them. "No one needs to know but us."

She lingered there, still caught in her indecision. He saw it play out on her face. Caught between what she wanted and what she thought was right.

"Don't tell me you're backing out now, sweetheart."

"No, I'm not." She finally nodded. "Okay." She nodded again. "Okay."

Jace shook his head. "I need to hear you say it, Princess."

She swallowed, hard. "Come here." She took another step toward him, both of them working to close the gap. He planted both hands overtop her head, dipping his head until she was pressed forehead to forehead with them.

"I *am* afraid," she admitted. "Afraid I want this too much."

He sucked in a hard breath as she leaned in, gripping two fistfuls of his shirt.

"Kiss me," she whispered to him.

Slowly, he moved in, but she shook her head, her throat rumbling with a low growl as she gripped him. "Like I'll die if you don't."

Jace grinned. "Don't worry, sweetheart. This time I'll make it count."

9

The moment Jace's lips met hers, Frankie knew he was right. *This* was what she'd been waiting for, why she'd stalled leaving. She'd tried so hard to convince herself otherwise, that helping him, sticking by his side, was repayment for what he'd done for her, and by proxy, her pack. But none of those reasons held a candle to the electricity that coursed through her.

To the way even a slight brush of his hand did her in.

Jace's lips pressed against her, hard and punishing. A bruising kiss coupled with the gentle sweep of his tongue. It wasn't a kiss meant for exploring. Instead, it was a stealing. Staking a claim on what he intended to be his.

As powerful and forceful as the hunter who wielded it.

She felt herself fall into his arms, softening and opening for him until she became little more than a simpering mess of want in his embrace.

What was she even doing with a wolf hunter like him?

She still didn't know the answer, but whatever it was, it failed to matter now. Not as his hands gripped her hair, or trailed her throat, or when the hardened length of his cock pressed at her entrance. Good God, he was everywhere. Filling her body and soul, though he hadn't yet entered her. But he would. She knew it was inevitable before the night's end.

Without warning, Jace broke the kiss between them, leaving her gasping again. He palmed her breasts, running his tongue over the flutter of her pulse at her throat before abruptly, he dropped to his knees. He had her jeans ripped open and around her ankles within seconds. "I've been wanting to do this for weeks."

"Weeks?" she panted, confused.

She'd only known him a handful of nights.

"Since I first smelled you."

Realization caused her to choke, and he grinned up at her, a wry smirk on his lips. They may have just met, but he'd known her scent, desired it—her—for much longer. Her pants and underwear were off a moment later, leaving her pussy exposed and bare. Her top and bra followed.

"Fuck when you're wet it's even better." He wasn't tentative or gentle as he cupped her in his hand, his thumb parting her and dipping inside her heat.

But gentle wasn't what she'd needed.

She wanted *him*. Gruff and coarse as he was.

"Is that all for me?" His voice was a rough growl as he smeared some of her wetness from inside her onto his fingers, lubricating her clit.

She whimpered, and bit her lower lip, but she managed to nod.

"Shit, Princess, all you needed to do was ask and I'd have taken you last night. Put us both out of our misery."

"I...I couldn't." She panted. "You're supposed to be my enemy."

Jace let out a dark laugh. "And who says enemies can't

fuck?" He stared up at her from where he was already making her tremble. "You're weeping for me." He dipped another finger inside her before drawing it to his lips, sucking her sweetness off it.

Frankie shuddered. It was like he *wanted* her sore, wanted to make her ache. As long as it was in want of him. It was a sweet, slow torture.

"Should I make you beg first?" he asked.

"Jace," she gasped. Her chest was so full of want she struggled to breathe through it.

He lifted a brow momentarily, staring up at her. "No one's ever taken charge of you like this, taken care of you. I can tell." He licked the taste of her from his lips. "And it scares you how much you like it." He cast her a knowing grin. "Don't worry, sweetheart. We'll start slowly."

Frankie cried out the moment Jace buried his face between her legs.

His hot tongue parted her folds, lapping and spearing her before zeroing in on her clit. He cupped the bare skin of her ass in one large hand before hooking her legs over his shoulders with a forceful pull. To her surprise, she let him, not only allowing him, but *wanting* him to take charge. He pinned her there against the door before he used his other hand to slip a finger inside her. Only giving her a moment to adjust, before he started probing, fucking her with a mix of his mouth and his fingers until she started moaning.

"Jace," she threw back her head with a gasp.

He paused, chuckling against her sensitive skin. The vibration of it shook through her. "Don't be quiet on my account, sweetheart. Wake the neighbors for all I care." He pulled back enough for her to see the gold of his wolf eyes, the supernatural gleam, and her slick heat all over his chin. "I've been dying to make you scream."

Before Frankie even knew what she was doing, she'd let herself go, yielding control. She cried out, burying her hands in his hair as she rocked her hips into him.

Closer. Closer.

Burning need built inside her, nearly reaching an apex. Far quicker than she was used to.

Her core grew warmer, and she felt herself slicken, preparing for an uncontrollable orgasm. Fuck, he was feasting on her like he was an animal, more rabid and wolfish than she'd ever seen. She threw back her head and howled. She came out of her skin all at once, bucking and writhing. Until she felt like she'd left herself. An out-of-body experience.

The red digits of a nearby clock flashed as she clutched hold of Jace's head, taking her pleasure. 3:00 a.m. She didn't know why she marked the time, nor did she care. She was going to have wild sex with a man she barely knew, but she wanted Jace inside her, his hands and lips and tongue and cock exploring her again.

Now.

"Jace," she panted, crashing down from her climax. "I want you inside me."

He chuckled. "You sure? She was just getting used to me." He petted her slit like she was his favorite pet.

Frankie's eyes flashed, and she growled, teasing. "I'm not your plaything."

Jace's eyes glittered with mischief. "Tell me you don't want to be, Princess, and I'll stop." He eased back from her, and another wave of longing rolled through her. He stripped off his shirt, revealing a large masculine torso. Ample muscle tapered down to a tight, firm ass beneath his jeans. His chest alone was better than any fantasy she'd ever imagined.

And she'd had him on his knees before her.

It was all too much.

The electric current that shot through her whenever they touched spiked higher, leaving her wet and even more ready than before. She was never ready again this quickly, but she was with him. Jace glanced down at her, their eyes locked, and she admired the beautiful, gold flecks in his. The sound of the door frame creaking as she leaned against it sent her heart racing.

No doubt they'd woke his neighbors. She wasn't beyond a little noise voyeurism.

His eyes filled with knowing. "Tell me what you want, and I'll give it to you."

"Jace, I..." She shook her head.

But he caught her chin between his thumb and his fore-finger, cupping it gently. "Don't play games with me, Princess." His gaze was rough, searing. "Tell me."

Frankie gaped at him, but before she knew what she was doing, she was confessing her darkest fantasy to him. To this man who was supposed to be her enemy. Even though she knew he could use it against her. "I...don't want to be in charge," she whispered. "I wanna lose myself."

He smirked at her like he already knew. Like her deepest desires were a locked away secret, and only he held the key. "I know, sweetheart," he purred. "I wanted to hear you say it." The grin he gave her then was pure deviance. He cupped her in his hand again, and his finger brushed featherlight over her sensitive clit, making her shiver. He growled against her ear. "I knew you needed a good fuck the moment you melted into my arms."

The gasp which tore from then wasn't intentional, but the next thing Frankie knew, he was lifting her, carrying her into the bedroom, before he laid her sprawled out on the bed. The mattress let out a low creak, promising a chorus of squeaky rails once they shook the headboard.

Unbuckling his jeans, she watched him strip down, until he stood over her. Her gaze traveled from his torso to the strain of his cock below. To his massive erection.

Good Lord Almighty.

Well-endowed didn't even begin to describe it. Frankie's mouth watered. She wanted to lick and suck at that pulsing vein at the base until he coated the inside of her throat.

Jace crossed to the bedside drawer, pulling it open, and for the second time since she'd met him he dangled a pair of cuffs between his fingers. These ones coated in leopard print fur.

She giggled.

"Do you trust me?" he asked.

It surprised her that she didn't hesitate. It didn't matter that he was her enemy.

She nodded. "Yes."

He lowered himself over her, his hands on either side of her head. He made quick work of cuffing her to the headboard, before he hovered over her again. He slid the length of his arousal over her entrance, instantly finding that sweet bead at the top of her core, and she whimpered. "Will you be a brat or a good girl for me?"

Her eyes flashed gold and defiant. "What do you think?"

He chuckled and ran his tongue over his canine teeth. "The safe word is enemy."

"Enemy?" She nearly laughed.

Something dark flashed in his eyes. "Because I'm going to fuck you like that's what we are here." The sudden change in his demeanor sent a thrill down her spine. He ducked his head, his hair to falling into the ethereal golden glow of his eyes.

His beast had taken hold.

"You couldn't help yourself, could you?" He shoved his hips against her. "You've been begging me for it."

"I—" Her voice was half moan, half whimper.

"And you knew I'd oblige." He balanced himself on one hand and slid the other to her lower back, pulling her closer. He lowered his head to her ear. "You're lucky I didn't take you in the middle of that alley."

Blazing heat radiated from her every pore, and she teetered on the edge of climax again, stimulated by his words and touch alone.

"I could make you come for hours." He positioned his fingers outside her entrance. "Just like this." He stroked between her legs, and her body seized.

She rode another release so intense her stomach muscles burned from the strain. She'd never come so quickly—and whether it was Jace, the control she'd given him, or both, she didn't care. All she wanted was him.

"Look at me." He turned her chin, forcing her to meet his eyes. "I can have you unchained or keep you tied up. Whatever I want." His lips grazed hers. "Do you know what that means?"

She inhaled sharply, incapable of forming words.

He let out a low growl. "I asked you a question."

"No," she panted.

He slid his face across her collarbone, his warm breath tickling her skin. "Ask me what it means." He ran his tongue over her skin.

She gulped. "Wha...what does it mean?"

He nipped her earlobe. Her mouth opened, but she couldn't even gasp.

He grabbed her hair in his fist and ran his canine teeth

over her neck. "It means you're gonna take everything I give you."

JACE'S HANDS TRAILED from her hair to her smooth thighs, and his cock throbbed as he admired her pink slit. His eyes wouldn't leave her body, and he rubbed two fingers over her. Fuck, she was gorgeous. Perfect in every goddamn way. She twitched beneath his touch, and he inhaled the smell of gardenias on her skin, mixed with the scent of her sex. His mouth watered. The sounds she'd made had torn him to shreds. Her touch. Her taste.

He could hardly stand it.

He snaked his hand up her stomach, then slipped it over the delicate bones of her rib cage until he squeezed her tit. He rolled her nipple between his fingers, playing with her like they had all the time in the world. She gasped, and pushed her hips forward, exactly how she'd rode him against the door. The sweetness of her cunt still coated his throat.

Damn. He couldn't get enough.

A devious grin spread across his face. She was hot, and so fucking wet. His cock stiffened with a painful urge. He would devour her. But he would draw out the moment. She would be screaming, begging before he finished with her. He intended to take his time, make both of them wait. A slow, agonizing torture.

Crawling on top of her, he teased her with painful slowness. She'd looked like sin in his coat, but that was nothing compared to when she was naked beneath him. When he positioned himself outside her entrance, her chest heaved, and he feasted his gaze on her breasts. A light blush blossomed across her skin, and he smirked.

"Fuck, you're gorgeous."

He lowered his head, brushed his tongue over those hard, pink nipples. She shuddered, and her hips rose, teasing him. Yeah, he wanted that, too, but not yet.

With a control he didn't think he possessed, he grazed his teeth across her glistening flesh, lightly pulling against her skin. She moaned again. He tortured her with slow circular motions, paying equal attention to both her breasts. He kneaded one as his mouth claimed the other. She trembled with each lick, and he damn near lost his mind when she whimpered.

The urge to take her hard and deep was overpowering. His dick pulsed with eagerness, and abruptly he shoved her up the bed until her shoulders hit the headboard, releasing the tension tugging at her wrists. He wrenched at the handcuffs, suddenly dying to roll her over, feel her ass against him. The wood of the bedposts creaked, and he squeezed the cuffs until the metal broke.

Holy shit.

He let go of the broken handcuffs, impressed by his own strength, but refusing to linger on it, before he grabbed hold of her thighs and dragged her down the bed. Moving with languid speed, he flipped her over and her body hit the mattress. He gripped the curves of her hips, then slid his hands up her sides.

He lifted her so her back was flush against his chest, gripping her throat with one hand. "Say you want it."

Nothing but a pleasured groan escaped her.

"Tell me you want it."

Her heartbeat was rapid but steady; his own matched the same pulsating rhythm.

"I want it," she whispered.

Nuzzling into her neck, he inhaled her scent. In the bedroom mirror, he could see the pink tips of her breasts shining where his lips had taken them. He pushed her onto the bed again, reaching beneath her to massage her clit. He pulled her ass closer to his hips and bent over her. "Louder."

Her spine arched, and her muscles tensed in anticipation. "I want it."

"Like you mean it," he growled. His fingers dug into her sides, and he slid his cock between her thighs. He ran the length of his shaft over her warm center. She writhed and ground her ass into him.

"Fuck me." She was breathless, panting.

"What was that?" He rubbed across her slit again and chuckled as she moaned.

"Please," she gasped. "Jace, fuck me."

"You better hold on to something, Princess."

She grabbed the sides of the mattress, and he thrust into her in one stroke, filling her to the max. She fit around him perfectly, hugging him in all the right places.

"Fuck me, you're tight."

A need more intense than he'd ever experienced raced through him. He had to take her. Hard. Fast.

Without warning, he pounded into her. With each loud smack, the heat rose, and they both teetered on the edge. Her muscles tightened around him, and the bed creaked underneath the blows. Her legs shook as she started to climax.

But he clamped his hands tight on her hips and stopped moving.

"Jace..."

He ran his hand over the curve of her behind, scanning the view of him sheathed inside her. His cock was held tight and bathed in her wetness. "You don't come until I tell you to."

"I can't stop. I—"

He let out a low growl. He wanted to flip her over, pull her against him and nip at her collarbone, but pleasuring her while watching her gorgeous behind, seeing the curve of her spine arch in ecstasy, was too sweet. "You *will* stop, and you'll be thanking me later and begging for more." He slammed into her, and even with his hands holding her hips, she staggered underneath his strength.

"More," she breathed.

Running one of his hands down her side, he groped her ass, and she slickened.

Fucking her was sweet bliss. Her legs and ass vibrated against his hips. With one large hand, he cradled her in place. His pace and force increased with each move.

"Jace," she panted. "I... I can't..."

"Tell me what you want."

"I..."

He exhaled a long hiss. "Tell me what you want, and I'll give it to you."

"Oh... I... make me..." She moaned and shoved her hips into him.

A dark chuckle escaped him. "You win, Princess. I'll settle for that."

He couldn't wait any longer.

He pulled out of her and flipped her over on the bed. Wrapping her legs around him, he slipped deep inside her. Heat flowed from her core. His cock throbbed, and he strained as he held himself back from the edge.

"Come for me," he growled.

Given permission, her body shook for him. Waves of ecstasy rolled over them. His seed rushed into her, and he bent down and kissed her hard. Her hands ran down his shoulders, and the sugary taste of her lips made him groan. He couldn't get enough. It would never be enough.

He wanted all of her, and now that he'd had her, he needed her like he needed air.

"Say my name, Jace." Her words came out as a breathy moan.

When he broke away, her golden eyes were filled with a craving for more than sex.

His heart jumped, and his stomach flipped. "Princess," he whispered. "What more do you need?" A large lump crawled into his throat.

Damn it. He was so fucking screwed. One night was all they'd agreed, but already he wanted more. But couldn't go down that road now. Couldn't allow himself to think about the consequences for them both.

Because if one night was all they had, he wasn't nearly finished with her yet...

10

Frankie stared at the ceiling of the apartment and sighed, sinking into the old mattress, which enveloped her like a huge cocoon. She glanced to her right, where Jace lay next to her, sleeping. He was an alpha, a wolf in every sense. But when he slept his chiseled features softened. She stared at his peaceful face, and her heart melted. The hard stare he normally wore, filled with suppressed rage, had disappeared.

She relaxed into the comfort of the bed and thought of the burning fire that had blazed behind his eyes when they'd been intertwined. He was good—damn good. Those large muscular arms, his silky auburn hair, and those toned abs he'd put to such good use...

She'd peaked faster and harder than she ever had. His touch had sent something wild and heady coursing through her veins, and she'd ridden on the natural high for so long she hadn't been able to think of anything but him.

He stirred, and her whole body tensed. Rolling over on his side, he flopped on the mattress, his deep sleep unbroken. She bit her lower lip. As much as she longed to stay by his side, she knew better. Her loyalty lay with her pack.

I can't leave them.

And this could be her last chance to escape.

She'd already proven she wasn't one for goodbyes.

Placing her feet on the ground, she slid off the bed. The hardwood floor squealed underneath her, and she froze.

Nothing. He didn't even twitch. She snatched his shirt off the floor and pulled it on. The smells embedded in the material wafted into her nose—cigarettes, whiskey, musky cologne and the woodsy scent of his hair. She clutched the shirt to her body. She didn't think he'd mind if she kept this small part of him. Something to go along with her memories.

Tiptoeing to the door, she grabbed the handle and it creaked open. A sliver of light from the hallway crept in. She paused and considered turning around. A large lump filled her throat. Everything between them had been so intimate, so personal. But now she was leaving, without him even knowing her real name. She swallowed past the pain and hurried out the door before she could change her mind. There was no point in ruminating on it.

One night.

That's all they'd agreed.

The latch clicked, and she rushed down the stairs. Her spine cracked into place, courtesy of Jace's inventive positions. She couldn't even count how many times they'd done the horizontal mambo or a variety of other moves that burned up the sheets. She grinned, but the wave of sadness caught back up with her, washing her smile away. She jogged from the building, the cold night air nipping at her hot skin.

She scanned the area. How would she get home? Streetlights tinted the concrete orange. Cars, trash cans and buildings. No people.

Hot-wire a car or shift?

She eyed his Chevelle, then remembered that it had an alarm. Not to mention he'd never forgive her if she wrecked it. Glancing over her surroundings one more time, she stripped off the shirt, knelt to the ground and concentrated on the adrenaline buzz.

The burn erupted inside her, and she winced at the feeling of her bones snapping, her appendages transitioning apart. The brief discomfort led to relief when her fur sprouted into place, blocking out the cold air. The usual heightened smells and sounds barreled over her senses. She let out a breath and collected herself, gathering the shirt in her jaw, then bolted down the road. The calluses on the pads of her paws scuffed against the pavement.

She ran for blocks, slipping among the city's shadows until her muscles strained. The thought of her home, her warm bed, soft sheets and silky nightgown comforted her. She wanted to fall onto her mattress and curl up into a ball, but she had something to do first. She rounded the final corner, then dashed down the alleyway. The backpack she'd brought with her two nights ago sat exactly where she'd left it, untouched. She had to move quickly in case the cops were nearby, checking out the crime scene.

One whiff and she knew she was in the clear, but that could change.

Moving behind the dumpster, she crouched down on her hind legs. Her wolf form filled her with adrenaline, and she thrived on the energy. She focused on the calm in the eye of the storm and allowed herself to shift into her human skin.

She fell against the wall of a bakery, exhausted.

Exhaling a long breath, she grabbed her clothes, stuffing Jace's shirt she'd carried in her muzzle in, and pulled on the jeans, tank top and jacket. She left her jewelry and lingerie in the backpack. She didn't give a shit about a bra.

Home. Bed.

That was all she wanted. There she could escape the sadness and anxiety balling up in her chest. Why had she slept with Jace?

A one-night stand?

That wasn't her style and yet...

She didn't regret it. One night of freedom.

Before reality and her obligations to her pack came crashing down again.

She threw the bag over her shoulder and sprinted down the road toward her apartment. Not the burner, but her home. It wasn't far. When she reached the entrance, she jammed the key into the lock and fumbled with the handle.

She scrambled up the stairs, then strode down the hallway to her door.

Finally.

Her muscles weakened, threatening to collapse. She pushed the door open and stopped. Her keys hit the floor.

"No. No. No. This isn't... No." Her eyes locked onto the phrase painted across her wall. Bile rose up in her throat, and her stomach flipped.

A LOUD BATTLE cry rose above the sounds of clashing swords, drowning out the noises of the surrounding forest. A large man decorated in the skins of a wolf towered over the beautiful woman standing before him. His weapon pushed against hers. Despite his size, she shoved against his blade with the strength to match his.

"Give up, you Valkyrie whore."

As she spun with her sword in hand, golden hair swirling around her shoulders, Freyja's sword collided with the man's shield. "The Brighasmann is mine and mine alone, Loki. I'll be more than happy to kill you for it."

A sneer crossed Loki's face, and a deep growl ripped from his throat. "If you so much as wound my flesh, I will destroy your precious warriors one by one."

Freyja let out a scream so loud and shrill the ground beneath them shook. "You won't be able to touch them. They're too powerful to destroy." She gritted her teeth and slashed her sword across his body. The edge of her blade bit into his arm.

He stumbled back, clutching his wound. Blood gushed from the tear. "I am the God of Mischief. I can't destroy them, but I will wreak havoc in their lives until they destroy one another." He grinned, then chuckled hysterically. "Look into my eyes and see for yourself."

Freyja met Loki's gaze. Reflected in his eyes, Jace lay in the middle of a pool of blood while the light faded from his pupils.

JACE JOLTED AWAKE. Cold sweat poured over his skin as he snapped upright, and he fought to calm his breathing. Fuck. What kind of dream was that? He flopped back down onto the bed, eyes closed. He wracked his brain to remember the names of the man and woman. Damn. The image of himself lying dead and bloody invaded his thoughts. It was so vivid. If he could just get back to sleep... Without nightmares.

He rolled onto his side and tried to let sleep reclaim him, but it was no use. He lay there, still groggy, until his alarm on his phone blared like a damn foghorn. He cracked one eye open and glared at the clock. 3:00 p.m. He smacked at the buttons until he hit the right one. Why the hell had he set the alarm to go off this early in the afternoon? A nocturnal creature in all senses of the word, he waged an ongoing war against the sun, vowing to ignore its existence.

He sat up and stretched, his muscles tight. What the hell had he done last night? He ran his fingers through his hair and glanced down at his morning wood.

He'd fucked a werewolf. Only *after* losing his job the night before. His vision spun.

Shit.

He slid off the bed and stumbled into the kitchen. Whiskey. He needed whiskey. Yeah, his head would clear after a swig.

Placing his hands on the countertop, he looked up at the top shelf. What the...? A small prickle of pain cut into his hand, and a droplet of blood pooled on his pinkie finger. Broken shards of glass and sticky, dried liquor covered the counter. Shit. The last bottle had broken in his hand. When she'd followed him into the kitchen, dropped to her knees and...

His cock throbbed. She'd taken the full length of him in and sucked him like it was her calling. Those full breasts and those sweet, pink nipples had jumped like mad as he slammed into her after. He could run his tongue over her all night long. But when she'd run her tongue over him? He hadn't known what to do with himself he'd gone so wild. Princess was like his personal brand of heroine. Addicting. He'd had her in every way he wanted. She'd...

Wait...

He wandered into the bedroom again. Nothing but his tangled sheets lay on his bed. He let out a groan.

"Well, I'll be damned." He ran a hand over his five o'clock shadow.

She'd hit it and quit it.

Exactly as planned. He swallowed the lump in his throat.

He grabbed his leather coat off the couch and pulled out the unopened pack of Marlboros. Opening the pack, he slipped one out and placed it between his lips before he looked at the bed again. Never once had a woman left *him* behind before.

Though that'd been their agreement.

One night. Nothing more.

The cigarette dangled from between his lips. Nicotine billowing into his lungs would calm him, instantly, but he took the cigarette and stuffed it back into the pack again as he mulled over the night's events. Her brown eyes had shimmered with flecks of liquid gold as she rode him, and her long, dark hair danced around them. A burn erupted in his chest.

He rubbed his hand over the area. Heartburn?

Yeah, he hadn't eaten much the night before.

After a short shower and a quick shave, he brushed his teeth and yanked on his clothes, then threw on his leather coat. His phone buzzed. A text from David asking where he was. By now David would have learned what happened. Grabbing his keys and the black duffel he'd packed with gear the night before, he hoofed it out the door and down to the street, where the sunlight hit his eyes, momentarily blinding him.

Squinting, he jogged to the Chevelle, grimacing at the cracks spanning the back window, evidence of Francesca's fight for freedom. With a disgusted grunt, he hopped into the driver's seat, revved the ignition and sped off. He cranked up the radio and drowned his thoughts with the sound of Kansas. Anything to block out memories of last night.

The last thing he needed to be thinking about was her.

Jace didn't remember any details of the drive other than the open road and the sound of the classic rock cassette playing in his ears until suddenly he was pulling the Chevelle to a stop in a patch of woods a stone's throw north of Ithaca. Placing a ball cap on his head, he made his way through the trees, the black duffel bag in hand, until on the other side of the landscape nestled on an old patch of farmland the view of Execution Underground Headquarters emerged. He crouched down, hidden among the forest brambles.

The former nuclear laboratory had been purchased and renovated on the inside post buy-out, but on the outside, it still looked like it was meant for research. Wrought iron fence surrounded the perimeter topped with barbed wire, the entrance manned by an armed guard. Insurance to be sure anyone or any*thing* being held there couldn't escape.

Nothing went out or in without clearance.

Jace knew that, but he was just fucking desperate enough to try it.

Francesca was right. He needed to know what exactly was motivating Chet and the other corporate suits in there. Sure, Chet had always been a prick. That much was certain, but until Jace knew what had pushed him across the line from asshole to evidence-planting dick, he couldn't know how to address it, how to vindicate himself. Or if it was even possible.

All that he was, all that he had, he'd poured into that organization.

He couldn't walk away and never look back again.

Hovering and observing until twilight fell, Jace slipped among the shadows. Carefully, he circled the perimeter, looking for a hole or a snag in the fence. Nothing.

He cursed. As much as he hated having his balls busted, this was the only job he knew. Francesca was right. He was a damn good hunter, and he wasn't about to lose his job. Nor would he let the killer walk free and Chet go unpunished. Not if he could help it, but alone he couldn't even get past the fence to get inside the damn building.

Defeated, he retreated to his car. Inside the Chevelle, he revved the engine and burned rubber, listening to the music once again. But this time, his heart wasn't in it.

Back in Rochester, after driving for several blocks, he parked the car outside a liquor store and stared out the windshield. He wasn't even fifty feet away from where he'd found Francesca two nights ago. She'd offered to help him, but he'd been too stubborn and refused.

"Damn it all to hell." He banged his fist on the steering wheel.

He got out of the car and immediately detected the trace of her scent. He strode down the nearest alley. His visit to Headquarters had scraped at his already raw nerves. He'd been punished over who and *what* he was—and damn if he hadn't done the same thing to Princess. He couldn't blame her for running away the first chance she got.

He really was a worthless bastard.

He followed her scent for several blocks. He told himself he just needed to be sure she was safe. That was all. But his heart jumped in his chest at the thought of seeing her again. Hung up on a wolf shifter? God, help him.

Following her scent, he stared up at what he guessed was her apartment building and repeated his mantra of curses.

He was a complete idiot. He'd stooped to a new level of stupidity with this one, and he was past the point of no return.

Digging around in his coat, he found the lock pick he always carried and let himself into the building. He waltzed in like he owned the place, right past a bewildered-looking family. They eyed him up and down, and the mother squeezed her baby a little closer as they hurried past him.

The door slammed behind them as he walked toward the stairs. "Nothin' to worry about folks," he muttered under his breath. "Just your friendly, neighborhood wolf hunter."

He sniffed the air. The smell of her perfume lingered, mixed with something he couldn't quite identify, but the familiar trace tormented him. He followed the scent of gardenias up two flights and to the second apartment on the left.

Was he really going to do this? Drag her into this?

He knocked hard. "Francesca?"

He listened for a long moment, but no one answered. He let out a loud sigh and pounded on the wood again. "Hey, Princess, you in there?"

He rocked back and forth on his heels, not sure whether he was praying she wouldn't answer or whether she would open the door and make it easy on him. With all his senses on edge and his adrenaline pumping, he knew she was home. But there was another scent mixed with hers. The rank smell of...

Damn it.

Jace smashed open the door and burst into the room with his Mateba pulled and ready to fire. The door hit the wall in an echoing bang. He charged through the entryway and tightened his finger on the trigger. He would blow the fucker's head off.

A small sniffle came from the middle of the room and Jace's eyes locked onto the woman he already thought of as his. She was sitting on the floor with her legs tucked underneath her, clutching a broken picture frame. The shattered glass cut into her hands, and drops of her blood speckled the hardwood.

Holy hell.

He holstered his gun and stood at her side. "Are you okay?"

She gave a small nod. Clutching the broken frame tighter, she glanced to the wall and back to the mess around her.

The apartment was trashed. Pieces of broken glass, torn fluff and splintered wood from the furniture were scattered everywhere. Jace walked to the wall and saw what she'd been looking at. Dried blood. The words that monster had written there read: *Take it like a bitch.*

Taped underneath was a professional, full-length photograph of Francesca with two people whose faces had been scribbled over with a permanent marker, blacking them out. Pasted over her photographed body were pictures of torn flesh from the original crime scene photos, a way of making sure she knew how she would look after the killer got hold of her.

After her death.

Jace ripped down the picture and examined it more closely. He knew each victim whose bodies had been pasted over hers.

He stared at Princess sitting on the floor, a look that was half-violation, half-rage contorting her face. Though she didn't fit the usual profile, he was sure she knew that monster intended to make her his next victim. Jace had made a huge mistake in so many different ways. Sleeping with her. Involving her. He needed to fix this. He would not let that psycho destroy any more lives. Especially hers.

"Was the room like this when you showed up?" he said.

Her hands trembled as she nodded.

Jace's anger peaked, like a bomb ready to explode. "No one hurts my girl."

Mine. The beast inside him snarled.

Jace froze. Whoa. Where the hell had *that* thought come from? Not to mention what he'd said. He shook his head. No, she wasn't *his*. "He's not going to hurt you, Princess. Not over my dead body. I'll rise from the grave to drag his ass down to hell. You got me?"

"I don't need anyone to protect me," she said without looking at him.

Her eyes widened, and all the color washed from her face. But then her mouth drew taut with underlying anger. His arms itched to wrap around her. He wanted to torture the SOB who'd done this.

"My parents..." She opened her mouth to say more, but nothing came out.

His attention captured, he asked, "What about your parents?"

"The photograph." Raising her bloodied right hand, she pointed to the picture he was holding, barely able to speak around her rage.

His palms clenched into fists, and he swallowed down a feral growl. "Where are they? Did that damn psychopath go after them, too?"

"No, my....my parents died in a car accident five years ago." She stopped trembling, and some of her color returned to her cheeks. Her eyes glazed over, masking her emotions as she collected herself.

"I'm sorry."

"Don't be. They wouldn't want to be the object of anyone's pity..." She stood and walked toward him, still clutching the frame. Her gaze returned to the picture. "He ruined my only recent portrait of us, all three of us, together as a family." She stared at the photo with such calm resolve, her sadness dissipating and shifting into another emotion he couldn't quite identify.

The silence hung thick in the air, suffocating him.

"I don't know what to say. I'm not used to dealing with..." *Living victims.* "Do you...is there somebody I can call for you?"

She shook her head. "No. I'm fine."

Jace raised a single brow. "You're sure? You don't have anyone?" He regretted the words as soon as they escaped his mouth, and he wracked his brain, trying to think of something better to say. Preferably something that didn't make him sound like an insensitive moron.

"I don't want to put anyone in danger," she said. "All I want right now is to find this low-life piece of shit and tear him limb from limb." Her volume escalated until she sounded powerful and firm.

He cringed as her hands tightened on the broken glass, not a single trace of pain on her face. He reached out and cupped her hands in his.

An electric jolt shot up his arm and down his spine.

She jumped and pulled back.

"Whoa there. If you want to rip him apart, then you better stop cutting up your hands. You're going to need them." He rubbed his thumbs in gentle circles on her skin until her hold loosened.

Taking the frame from her, he placed it on the ground. Shards of glass protruded from her smooth skin.

"Sit on the bed."

Without another word, she walked to her swanky four-poster, slow and lifeless, like she was in a daze, before resting her hands on her lap.

He scratched his head, not really sure of his next move.

What would I do if she were another hunter? What would I do for an ally? First aid?

"Do you have any peroxide?" he asked.

"There's some under the bathroom sink." She gestured to a door on the other side of the one-room apartment.

He rushed into the bathroom and stepped around the mess. The brown peroxide bottle had rolled behind the toilet amid all the vandalism.

Snatching the bottle and some spare toilet paper, he hurried back out. If Princess was anything like him, her wolf genes would kick in and she would start healing in no time. The glass needed to be pulled out pronto before the wounds started healing around it.

He knelt in front of her, and she stuck out her hands.

"Ready?" He looked her in the eye.

She gave him a single nod, and he plucked the first piece of glass from her palm. She winced.

"You okay?"

She inhaled sharply. "Just get it over with."

Trying not to be too rough, he picked the shards from her skin one by one and tossed the bloodied pieces onto her bedside table. When her hands were glass free, he screwed the cap off the peroxide. "This may sting a bit."

She gave him a rueful grin. "I know."

Jace poured the liquid over her flesh. The chemical sizzled and popped as soon as it hit the wounds. She hissed in pain, but her gaze didn't falter. She took it like a pro.

"You do this often?" he asked.

A little smile curved her lips. "More than you'd think."

"No offense, Princess, but you don't really seem like the fighting type." He paused as he patted the toilet paper across her skin, cleaning off the blood and excess peroxide. "You've got the attitude, and don't get me wrong, you handle your-self well in a brawl, but...." He hesitated. "Something tells me you don't like to do that."

"It doesn't matter what I want. It's my duty to my pack." She cocked her head to the side and eyed him up and down. "You're not going to pull the whole 'I'm a big bad wolf' and 'I don't need any help hunting this monster' crap, are you? This is my fight too now."

Jace shrugged. "Don't get me wrong, I'd rather not draw you into this. But considering you want revenge and you could use someone by your side protecting you, I think us working together is the best solution."

She shook her head. "I already told you. I don't need anyone to protect me."

"I know you don't, but I want to." He swallowed the nervous lump in his throat. "Humor me?" he asked, echoing her words from the other night.

Her eyes lit up, a beautiful burn behind them like when they'd...made love? Was that what they'd done? His stomach dropped down into his feet, and he looked away. Son of a bitch.

"Although, who am I to make your choices for you?" he grumbled.

For a moment, she didn't say anything until...

"*Un amante.*" Her voice barely registered above a whisper.

Jace froze. He didn't speak Italian, but he sure as hell knew what that meant. *A lover.* His mouth went dry, and his stomach churned as if someone had grabbed his insides and twisted his intestines into knots. Slowly, he released her hand.

Rushing to the other side of the room, he searched through his trench-coat pockets for his cigarettes. "You mind if I light up in here?" He pulled one out and stuck it in his mouth before she could answer. "I've been trying to quit." Not that it was going too well at the moment.

He glanced back toward her, the way she was watching him whispered a thousand things he wasn't certain he wanted to hear. Fumbling, he grabbed his lighter, flicking it several times before the flame caught and sweet smoke rushed into it his lungs.

He shouldn't be doing this.

Shit. Shit. Shit. He glanced in her direction and his stomach flipped again. *One night. That was all it was supposed to be, and yet...*

He burnt halfway through the cigarette before he could stop himself, sucking the gray fog into his lungs. The smoke gave him just enough calm to keep his cool. A bucket of ice dumped over his head would have been better.

He took another drag. "Pack your bags. We need to get out of here."

Her head snapped toward him, her eyes wide-open and attentive. "We're going hunting *now*? Don't you think that's a little stu—"

"Don't get your panties in a knot. We need to get our shit together first. But we can't talk here. We need to be prepared before we go at him, and because he's a sexual sadist and gets off on all this, it's likely he'll come back here to..." He shrugged.

She walked over to her wooden wardrobe and sifted through the clothes. "To what?"

Jace sighed. "Flog the bishop."

Her long hair whipped through the air as spun to face him, gaping like a waterless fish. "You can't be serious?"

"Who knows what this bastard is capable of? You've heard of crimes of passion? There isn't much that's more passionate than sex, and everything this guy does is so he can yank his own chain. Much as I'd like to camp out here and stake him out, we'd be just as likely to trap ourselves. We do this, we do it right."

"To vindicate your name?"

"And get the heat off your pack." He shrugged, flicking his ashes. "In my world we call that a win-win scenario."

She nodded in agreement, before she turned and bent down to grab something from the bottom drawer, treating Jace to a prime-time view of her tight, round ass squeezed into a pair of low-cut jeans. His cock jerked.

Damn.

He'd thought one night would be enough to satisfy the ache. What a fool he'd been...

He ripped his gaze away and shook his head. He shouldn't be ogling her in the middle of a crime scene after she'd been traumatized by a serial killer. He scanned the room. The sound of Chet's voice mocking him pounded in his head. One more thing to mess with him.

"That's disgusting," she said, interrupting his self-loathing, clearly still caught on the killer's motivations.

Jace shifted his weight and rearranged himself. The last thing he needed was for Princess to think he was some creep who got his jollies off scared women. "You bet. Now grab your things and let's get outta here."

When she finished stuffing everything into a purple backpack, she threw the bag over her shoulder.

He nodded to the door. "Let's go."

She headed out, but paused near the entryway, stopping by a photo the sicko had knocked askew on the wall during his rampage. She took it down, and he looked at it over her shoulder. The big grin she wore in the photograph highlighted the beauty of her features—he'd never seen her smile like that. The man next to her wore a puffy white shirt, like the ones on the covers of the old romance novels his mom used to read. But whoever he was, he was holding Francesca in his arms.

He indicated the photo. "Who's he?"

She stared at the image, and a small smile crept onto her face. "That's Alejandro."

"He your cousin or something?"

A blush blossomed across her cheeks. "No, he's a member of my pack...and my partner."

Jace lifted a brow.

"Not like that," she added hurriedly. "But Jace, I think you should know. I *am* engaged. It's a political arrangement, on behalf of my pack."

Jace's jaw clenched. "And when exactly did you plan to tell me that?"

A RUSH OF heat prickled underneath her skin. Frankie ran her thumb over the edge of the snapshot. Alejandro was everything she *should* have wanted in a man, but they were no more than friends. She'd once had a fleeting crush on him when they were teens, but nothing had ever come of that. She'd long ago accepted her fate, agreeing to mate with the packmaster of a larger pack, an attempt to fuse their independent territories into one and not get swallowed up by the massive leadership play that was the Grey Wolves out west. But that'd been before.

Before Jace.

She'd convinced herself she would eventually come to love her new arranged mate, to want him—but now she wasn't so sure of that. Jace had saved her from that fatalistic thinking, and she'd never felt freer.

She was grateful for that.

Without another word, Jace brushed past her and stormed into the hallway. She straightened the photo and trailed after him. His face looked strained, his mouth drawn into a thin line. She could tell he wanted a fight—and soon. It'd been unfair to tell him like that, but it also would have been unfair not to. Especially now that they were going to be working together.

Her brow furrowed as she watched him stomp down the stairs. She figured he wouldn't be pleased, but she hadn't expected him to seem...hurt like that. She hurried after him, following him to the Chevelle while ignoring the searing pain in her hands as she gripped her bag strap.

The drive back to Jace's apartment was long, tense and awkward as hell. Jace stared at the road with extreme tunnel vision, his fingers white on the steering wheel. His tension was suffocating in the small, enclosed space.

Frankie didn't know what caused his sudden shift in mood. They'd agreed to one night, only that, and it wasn't as if she had any kind of emotional relationship or meaningful engagement with her fiancé. It was a political move. A power play with a man she had only met a handful of times, meant to help preserve the legacy of her people, but from the angered look on his face, she wasn't about to ask.

They'd promised each other no more than the one night.

When they finally pulled up in front of the apartment complex, she leaped from the car, eager to escape the tense atmosphere. Jace followed more slowly, stalking from the vehicle to the door. Short of steam coming out his nose, everything about him reminded her of an angry bull, ready to charge. Where was her red cape when she needed one?

He punched in the combination and headed up the stairs. She jogged after him, admiring how swiftly he moved despite his massive frame. She remembered the sculpted muscles hidden under his trench coat shifting beneath her hands as she lay underneath him.

She swallowed the huge lump in her throat. She needed to stop this. Even though Jace was gorgeous, masculine eye candy, even though his ferocity and passion matched her own, and even though he'd rocked her world in bed, he hunted his own kind.

She wasn't sure she could be with someone like that. Not for more than an evening.

She did the same thing, in a way, but she only hunted rogue wolves, killing them to preserve the safety of her pack. But Jace... She couldn't help wondering how he'd react if he knew her true identity. Would he have risked himself for her? Put himself in harm's way if he knew she wasn't just any wolf, but a packmaster? The leader of the entire Rochester pack.

She couldn't be certain.

They reached the door with the crooked number six, and Jace stopped mid-stride. The door was cracked, but no light came from inside. Definitely not how he would have left it.

Frankie stiffened.

He unclipped his gun and prepped his aim. Carefully, he nudged the door open farther and glanced inside. He slipped in, and she followed close at his heels. A loud creak echoed from the bedroom, someone stepping on a floor-board. As Jace crept forward, she inched toward the makeshift kitchen. There was no way in hell she was fighting anyone unarmed, not while she was in human form. Any old knife was better than nothing.

The sound of a large boot hitting the hardwood sent a chill down her spine as the invader stepped out of the bedroom. She hit the light switch, unsure of whether Jace's night vision was as keen as hers.

A man as large and intimidating as Jace stood in the bedroom's door frame. He had a wild look in his eye and a gun at his side, and Frankie's heart paused at the sight of him.

"Who is *she?*" The trespasser's gruff, rumbling voice shook her to her core as he pointed in her direction.

What?

Frankie's eyes shot to Jace. "You know this guy?"

Jace lowered his gun and clipped the piece back in place, but he ignored her and answered the man's question instead. "She's none of your business. What the fuck are you doing here, David?"

"What do you think I'm doing? I'm looking for your sorry ass. Damon's been blowin' up your phone nonstop with no answer."

Frankie eyed the man from head to large leather boots. With buzz-cut black hair, a coat that could hide a load of heavy artillery and a silver Star of David around his neck, there was only one thing this man could be: a hunter. He had to be another hunter. Her head spun. Two hunters in her territory, while she was already chasing after a rogue killer was enough. But a whole damn division. She hadn't really allowed herself to ponder that. She shouldn't have been surprised, but she wasn't quite sure how much more she could handle.

"I ditched my phone on the way to HQ."

Frankie lifted a brow. "When were you going to tell me you went to Headquarters?"

Jace shot her a look, like she was one to talk about keeping secrets, and she supposed she deserved that, before his friend quickly moved on.

"Well losing that phone was probably a good idea. You're in some deep shit, but..." The hunter named David gestured to the blood on his clothing. "There's been a double killing. The local P.D is losing their heads over it."

Jace groaned. "You gotta be shitting me."

David shook his head. "No B.S. involved. The bodies were dumped less than a mile from the division warehouse. Chet's gone wild looking for you. I came by here to warn you."

"I don't need any warning about Chet. He and Headquarters can kiss my ass. Losing my job isn't enough? He needs to twist the knife too?"

"Apparently so." David lowered his eyes to the floor and cleared his throat. "Your name was carved into their forearms, J."

11

FRANKIE STEPPED BACK and placed her hand on the kitchen counter, gripping the edge for support. The anger rolling off Jace triggered all her primal instincts. Goose bumps rose on her arms, and even though he was directing his rage elsewhere, her body urged her to shift into defense mode. His hands shook at his sides, and his jaw clenched.

"Was it Chet or the killer?"

David cleared his throat. "I don't know, but now Chet's covering his ass by saying there's a possibility you may be involved. He and Headquarters put out the word that any hunter who encounters you is supposed to bring you in. You and I both know what that means."

Jace practically growled. His rage made her jittery. She wanted to help him, but she suspected that her help was the last thing he wanted.

David sighed. "Look, man, I'm sorry but—"

The door burst open, and the bang as it hit the wall echoed through the small apartment. She jumped. Screws and wooden splinters from the shattered wood scattered across the floor. The man who stepped through sent chills down her spine. She backed away before she could stop herself. Cold eyes seared into Jace's, and she was glad she wasn't on the receiving end of that stare. Her stomach churned.

Two other men stepped in behind the latest intruder, one with golden blond hair, the second with his face shadowed by a Mets cap—the muscle to back up Mr. Ice Eyes. Frankie eyed Ice up and down. Not that he needed any backup muscle with his massive biceps and natural scare tactics.

"Would you look at that? Easy to find and a supernatural piece of shit. You're a disgrace to your division." Ice shook his head. "We came up from Brooklyn to send a message."

Jace let out a harsh snarl, unable to control his anger. His eyes burned with a golden fire and he flashed his canines.

"Holy motherfucker," Blondie said in a slow, southern drawl. "It's true."

The Mets fan's jaw dropped. "Damn it, McCannon. You're a fucking shifter?" he said, and she heard traces of a Jersey accent in his voice.

David stepped forward. "Look, man, it's not what you think."

"Shut up, Aronowitz, and move out of my way or you're going down with him as a traitor." The muscles in Ice's throat strained and his fists clenched as he stared Jace down. "I didn't want to believe it, but you haven't left me any choice, you woman-beating whoreson. You just signed your own death warrant, you werewolf piece of shit. Those dead girls can all trace back to you, and now Chet says you've got the same mutation as the killer you've been hunting."

Frankie yelled before she could stop herself. "Stop!"

Ice turned toward her. The power pulsating off him was

staggering. Her breath caught. She fought not to step back and show her weakness. There was no backing down now. She shoved her fear aside and concentrated on absorbing the anger that hung thick in the crowded apartment air. It would make it easier for her to shift.

She willed herself to stand straight and stare him in the face. She told herself she could take him. "You can't kill him. He didn't murder those women."

"Who the hell is *she?*" Jersey shouted.

Frankie shot him a glare. "You shouldn't be asking *who*, you should be asking *what*." She bared her canines and the wolf-gold flashed through her eyes, her pupils narrowing to thin slits.

"Just perfect. A piece-of-shit half-breed and his loyal bitch." Ice's jaw clenched so tight she thought his teeth might shatter.

She let out a low, feral growl. "He may be a half-breed, but I'm full-blooded, and you'll be screaming when I rip out your jugular."

Jace straightened to his full height and pointed a single finger at Ice. "Go on. Give me an excuse to tear you limb from limb and send you crying back to Chet." His voice was disturbingly calm, but rage flew off him like darts, with Ice as the bull's-eye.

Ice turned to Jersey. "Take the dog outside while I deal with this."

Frankie swallowed her anxiety in one large gulp. She knew the drill. "Bring it. We'll see who the real bitch is."

"Take care of her, Brent."

"Don't make me do this, Eli," Jace said to Ice. "We're on the same side."

Ice—Eli—ripped a gun from inside his coat. Hooking his finger around the trigger, he aimed straight for Jace's head. "You lied about your identity from the very start. You were never on our side."

Before Eli could fire his first shot, Jace grabbed hold of his wrist. He twisted the other, then swept him to the ground. The gun fell to the floor as the two men battled. Eli kicked Jace in the stomach, knocking him off balance. He stumbled back as Eli crawled toward the gun.

Jace drew his knife and threw the weapon across the room with the accuracy of a well-aimed bullet. The blade pierced Eli's flesh between his collarbone and his shoulder. A wet stain blossomed across his black shirt, and several drops of blood hit the floor as he clutched the wound. Frankie's adrenaline kicked into overdrive.

"I don't beat women," Jace said through clenched teeth. "And no one calls my mother a whore." He threw himself forward at the other hunter.

As Frankie stared, she felt a large, iron-tight hand grab her elbow. She tore her eyes from Jace to find she was staring into Jersey's pissed-off face. A surge of adrenaline pumped through her, and she flung her head back, using the momentum to head-butt him full-force. Pain shot through her skull, but the bruise would disappear within the hour or, if she shifted, even sooner.

Jersey stumbled back and bumped into the wall. His cap fell off his head and onto the floor. She crushed it under her tennis shoe. "This is Yankee country, asshole."

"You bitch!"

"Mind your manners."

Deep inside her chest, her inner animal shifted as it fed off the adrenaline. She had to do something fast, or Jersey would charge her. She might have him in the brains department, but even with her wolf strength, he was still twice her size and packed a whole lot of muscle. They would be an equal match. She clenched her jaw. She could beat him.

She kicked off her shoes and crouched to the floor. A look of recognition crossed Jersey's face, and he shot forward, determined to stop her from shifting, but he was too late. Speed-shifting was her specialty. Her clothes ripped to pieces as she went from woman to wolf.

A deep snarl ripped from her throat. They stared at each other, unmoving. He stopped midstride, and Frankie seized the moment. Diving for him, she sank her canines deep into the flesh above his ankle. The nasty iron taste of human blood filled her mouth, but she held on. She jerked her head from side to side in an attempt to snap the bone.

Jersey howled in pain before he kicked her off. His boot collided with the side of her stomach, and she yelped as all the air rushed out of her lungs. He unhooked a silver chain from his belt loop and swung it around.

"You're going to like this new necklace. I picked it out just for you."

Frankie's paws slid against the hardwood. She scrambled away and tried to bolt for the hallway, but Jersey threw himself on top of her. Flipping onto her side, she writhed as he wrapped the silver chain around her neck. As the metal touched her skin, igniting a scalding heat, she slashed out with her paw and slashed her nails across his face. Blood trickled in their wake.

He reared back and clutched at his face, yelling profanities. The silver chain slipped from her neck. She was free. She darted away from the screaming hunter, only to collide with another. Blondie skidded into her as he was thrown across the floor by David, who had clearly appointed himself Jace's ally.

He looked down at her and grinned. "Sorry," he said, as

he grabbed Blondie and slammed his fist into the man's nose.

Frankie didn't waste another second. She could hold her own in a fight, but against several well-trained hunters with silver weapons? That was ridiculous, and she wasn't stupid. She bounded into the hallway, ready to escape the whole thing, but a crushing hand grabbed her tail and yanked her back.

Jersey used the spare moment to slip in front of her. He positioned himself in front of the stairs, blocking her only exit. It was either back into the apartment with all the other hunters or time to teach this piece of shit a little lesson about girl power. She decided on the latter. She ran toward him and slid to a halt in front of his knees, a massive wave of adrenaline making her stronger than ever.

Before he could move, she shifted into human form and punched him hard in the kneecap. He doubled over in pain, clutching hold of his leg. She tried to crawl past him, but he grabbed her shoulder, his multiple silver rings searing her skin. She screamed and pulled away.

Her skin tore where the enhanced metal had burned her, and pain radiated through her.

THE SIGHT OF blood pouring from the Brooklyn division lead's shoulder sent a buzz surging through Jace's veins, and he smiled. He didn't give a flying shit that he'd stabbed the leader of an entire Execution Underground division or that he was getting a little too much satisfaction from the pain of his newest enemy. Beating Eli into a pile of quivering flesh would be a sweet, addicting high. Fuck him for believing Chet's bullshit.

For seeking him out like there was a damn bounty on his head.

With a low grunt, the bastard dislodged the blade from his shoulder and dropped it onto the floor. "You're going to pay for that, you worthless mutt."

Eli lunged toward Jace, hitting him right in the belly and knocking him clean off his feet. His breath flew out of him as he hit the ground. Jace felt his jaw pop out of place as Eli's fist collided with his face, his uninjured arm swinging like a massive club as blood from his shoulder soaked Jace's clothes.

Jace maneuvered his legs onto Eli's chest and thrust forward, flipping his fellow hunter to the ground. He straddled Eli's stomach and pounded his fist into the dickhead's nose, treating him to the same blows the bastard had just dished out. Anger pumped through him.

Eli bucked in a fruitless attempt to throw Jace off. His blood pooled on the floor, filling in the cracks between the boards. The more Eli fought, the more blood gushed from his stab wound and Jace could feel him weakening with each hit.

Eli was the best fighter in his division, or so he'd thought. Jace had never unleashed his full strength in front of the other hunters for fear of revealing his identity—his unfair advantage, or disadvantage—until now. Until Chet. Now he wasn't holding back. The combination of his bloodline, natural strength and the serum all the members of the E.U. received made him a force to be reckoned with.

The bastard squirmed beneath Jace's grip until he'd positioned himself just right, then brought his knee up hard in a low blow to the crotch, a move Eli would never normally make, a sign of how close he knew he was to passing out. Jace groaned but kept on pounding Eli's face.

Black and purple bruises were already forming across the hunter's cheeks and around one eye.

"That was a cheap shot, you fucking cocksucker." Jace slammed his knuckles into Eli's jaw and felt the crack of bone beneath his hand. He grabbed Eli by the front of his shirt to hold him down. "You hit like a bitch," he growled.

"Like your bitch?" Eli said through a mouthful of blood.

In one quick twist, Jace snatched his blade from the floor and held the sharp metal against the skin of Eli's throat, then leaned into his face, each word sending his warm breath over his enemy's skin. "If you *ever* call her a bitch again, your smile will run from ear to ear." He lifted the blade and traced it across Eli's mouth up to his cheekbone. "You and Chet both."

Eli didn't even flinch. Instead, he spat a glob of bloody spit into Jace's face. Jace threw down a punch at Eli's temple so hard he swore he felt the bone soften beneath the hit. He delivered the final blow, knocking the asshole out cold. But that wasn't enough. He wanted to kill the bastard. God, how he wanted to end this.

His fist collided with the mauled flesh of Eli's face again, and he couldn't stop swinging.

A large hand clutched hold of Jace's arm and wrenched him back. "Jace, man. Stop! We've gotta get out of here."

Jace's arm kept swinging with the force of a pendulum. But David hooked him under the arms and hauled him off Eli's limp body.

"Get a grip and let's go. If I'm going to be a fugitive because of you, I'm at least gonna be smart about it." He shoved Jace between the shoulder blades. "Move it. We're wasting time."

Hands shaking from the adrenaline rush, Jace placed one foot in front of the other. He stepped past Rich, who lay like a dead man—though on closer inspection he was still breathing—on the floor, presumably courtesy of David.

A high-pitched and angry scream echoed from the hallway, and Jace snapped to attention. *Francesca.* He bolted into the hall. Brent was standing at the edge of the stairs with four bloody claw marks slashed clear across his face as he blocked Francesca's access to the only exit.

She must have shifted, because she was stark naked, her hair in total disarray. Blood trickled from her collarbone, where her skin was raw. Brent had used enhanced silver on her.

Jace snarled.

Francesca growled, an animal sound from her human throat. "Move out of my way, asshole." Throwing herself against Brent, she knocked him down.

Despite how small she was in comparison to him, she held his throat between her thighs and beat his face with her fists. He gasped for air as she cut off his breathing. She snarled and drew her hand back. The air bent and quivered with energy as her hand shifted into a wolf's paw while all the rest of her remained human.

At the sight of her claws, Brent managed to throw her off. She flew back into the wall. Her head hit the plaster with a loud thump, and Jace shot forward, but David beat him to the punch with those long-ass legs of his.

David pulled his .40 from his jacket and aimed it straight for Brent's head. "Get out of here."

Brent didn't move. He stared David directly in the eye.

"I said, get the fuck out." David fired a shot right past Brent's ear. Brent stumbled to his feet and down the stairs as he clutched at the side of his head to cover his throbbing eardrum. David gave a satisfied smile and slipped his gun back inside his jacket.

Francesca groaned, and Jace turned to see her getting to her feet. "Thanks for coming to my rescue, guys. My head? Oh, it's fine. No concussion at all." She stared at the floor and rubbed her palm across her forehead.

Jace scowled. "You didn't give me time to ask."

"If I had, would you?"

"What kind of question is that?" Jace snapped.

"Well if he isn't going to ask, then I will. Are you all right?" David placed a hand on her shoulder.

She shied away from his touch. "Yeah, I'm fine. Who the hell are you?"

"I'm David."

She nodded. "Francesca."

David stuck out his hand. "Nice to mee—"

"Look," Jace interrupted, "usually I'm all for warm and fuzzy introductions, but can we please get the hell out of here before those two assholes wake up, or Brent decides to be a hero and comes waltzing back in here?"

David zipped up his leather motorcycle jacket, no doubt preparing to hop on his Harley. "We can't go back to my place, so I'm going to split. I can't take the chance of hanging around you, J. I've gotta save my own ass and I've already screwed myself over by fighting on your side. If you need anything, call." He clapped Jace on the back before he jogged down the stairs.

Jace and Francesca stood alone in the silent hall. He cleared his throat and padded back toward his apartment. "I need more weapons."

The door stood open and would clearly never close again, and the crooked six had toppled to the floor in the midst of the chaos. He kicked the rusted numeral across the hardwood and stepped over his fellow hunters. He thought about giving Eli another good blow to the face with the heel of his boot, but he could save that revenge for another time.

He pulled out the chain around his neck and chose the key to his weapons closet. He unloaded the rest of his artillery—every standard handheld on the market, short of an Uzi. He'd had one on order, but the delivery had fallen through at the last minute.

Francesca walked into the bedroom behind him, already wearing a set of clothes from the backpack she'd brought. She leaned up against the wall and sighed. "What now?"

He packed the rest of the weapons into a large black duffel bag and locked up the closet. "If there's been a double killing, I need to check it out." He thought of the face of the man in the photo—Alejandro or whatever the hell his name was. Then the faceless fiancé she'd mentioned. "You can do what you want. I won't keep you any longer. I've got bigger prey to kill." He tried to tell himself that if anything happened to her he wouldn't give a shit, but his gut said otherwise.

Damn it, she wasn't his responsibility.

She shook her head. "If you're going to try and kick me out at this point, you're nuts. How can I go to my pack knowing what I do now, being a target, and tell them I haven't done anything about it?"

"Why take it on by yourself? Leave the work to someone else."

She placed her hands on her hips. "It's *my* responsibility, and I'm going with you. Besides, you need backup."

He didn't need backup and he'd never had any before, but he wasn't going to bother pointing that out. He walked out of the bedroom, and she followed behind him.

"Where are we going?" She stepped over Eli's bloody body as if he were a nasty stain on the carpet.

Jace waited until they were out of the apartment and on the stairs. The last thing he needed was for a seemingly unconscious Eli or Rich to hear where they were going. "We'll have to get a motel room. Somewhere they wouldn't expect me to go."

"That sounds like the worst pickup line ever."

He smirked. "If I wanted to pick you up, I wouldn't even have to use a line."

"Are you calling me easy?" She titled her head to the side in annoyance.

"Most women I sleep with are easy. But you, no"

She crossed her arms over her chest. "I wouldn't blame you if you thought that. I did sleep with you the first night I met you."

"Second night, but who's counting? Do you need an excuse to justify what we did? We're consenting adults, so why not have a little fun?" He glanced over his shoulder and saw the skin of her cheeks flush.

12

———

FRANKIE TRIED TO concentrate on anything other than the throbbing feeling in the back of her skull as they climbed into Jace's Chevelle in silence. Pain throbbed throughout her body. She needed to shift. Her human wounds would heal faster if she were in wolf form.

They continued driving even once they'd passed the majority of the cheap motels he'd said they would be looking for and reached the nicer part of the city. Frankie leaned back against the headrest, and her eyes flickered closed. A large hand gripped her shoulder and squeezed hard enough to jerk her awake.

"Don't you dare fall asleep. You hit your head. I don't want you going into a damn coma."

Frankie focused past the blur of exhaustion. She had to try several times to make sure what she was seeing was real. Jace had pulled the car into the parking lot of the Imperial Hotel. The brightness of the lights beamed down on her, and she drank in the opulence like a ravenous animal. Beds. This place would have soft, warm beds.

Jace stopped the car and stepped out. She hopped out,

too, and took her backpack off the floorboard. With this much beauty surrounding her, she looked like a peasant in her scruffy clothes, not to mention her wounds and bruises. Jace opened the hatch and grabbed his duffel before he threw his keys to a nearby valet.

He pointed two fingers from his eyes to the young employee. "I don't care if the back window is already cracked—scratch this baby and you're dead."

The valet nodded, as if he often received death threats from random guests. Maybe there were a lot of uptight car owners in this part of the city.

"Don't worry, sir. I'll take good care of it," the valet said.

Jace gave the guy a pointed look, but he must have been satisfied, since he shoved a majorly generous tip into the valet's hand turned and walked toward the entrance.

She hurried after him.

With the marble flooring and the crisp clean atmosphere, the hotel was absolutely stunning. Jace strode right up to the front desk clerk and dropped his duffel bag on the ground, then pulled a thick wad of bills from inside his coat pocket. Frankie choked back a laugh at the contrast between his rough and tough appearance and the post-modern décor. The clerk's eyes widened as she eyed Jace up and down. Her attention jumped between Jace and the bills, then she took more time with his face and his clothes. Frankie wasn't sure whether the visual examination was prompted by Jace's rugged appearance or his divinely hand-some face.

He slapped the wad of bills on the countertop. "We need a room. Give me the nicest one you've got."

The clerk blinked several times, interrupted by her examination of Jace. "Excuse me?"

He sighed, then leaned forward on the counter and

overly articulated each word. "Give me the best room you have."

The woman just stood there.

Frankie stepped up to the counter and nudged him aside. "I think what he's trying to say is, could you please tell us the best room you have available?" She flashed the girl a sweet smile, careful not to show off her sharp, protruding canines.

The clerk shook her head a little to wake herself up before she turned to her computer. The click of her fingernails against the keyboard combated the canned piano music playing in the background.

Finally, the woman cleared her throat. "Besides the penthouse, the top room we have available is the Town—"

"We'll take it."

"All right, the Townsend suite—"

"No, the penthouse."

The clerk's mouth fell open a little, and Frankie whirled around. "What?"

Jace ignored her and shoved the money across the counter. "You heard me. The penthouse. If you get me the key in less than two minutes, I'll give you an even bigger tip than that." He slapped five hundred-dollar bills on the counter, then glanced up at the clock. "Starting... now."

The woman grabbed the phone and punched in a string of numbers while mumbling under her breath. Jace flung an ID over the counter—probably a fake one—and continued his countdown.

Frankie's jaw dropped. "What the hell was that all about?"

"We don't have any time to waste. Not with other divisions already coming at us like that." He gave her a pointed look.

Shock flew through her, and she battled her jaw to keep it from dropping. "That's not what I'm talking about. I'm referring to the fact that you just booked the penthouse at the Imperial. I mean... Jace, for lack of a better term, you live in a crash pad of an apartment."

"I told you, that's the burner. I just sleep there sometimes."

"And is your regular apartment any better?"

He snorted. "Fuck no."

When she continued to stare at him, he lifted a brow. "And?"

"And how are you going to afford this?"

He picked up his duffel bag from the floor and tapped the bills on the counter. "You think I stole this, don't you?" he asked, too soft for the clerk to hear.

She lost the battle with her jaw and gaped at him. "What? I didn't say that."

"You didn't need to say it. But for your information, Headquarters pays all their employees, all around the globe, *very* well. I don't want for anything. How do you think I bought the Chevelle?" His eyes narrowed as he waited for a response.

"But..."

He sighed. "I live in a shit-hole apartment because I choose to. I'd rather deal with shitty and realistic than fancy and fake any day."

The clerk cleared her throat to get their attention and held out the key.

Jace took it and looked at the clock. "You were nearly late. Don't let it happen again." Then he winked at her and shoved a ridiculous amount of bills into her hand.

He turned on his heel, shot Frankie a grin and strolled toward the elevator. She hurried after him. Catching the closing elevator doors, he held them until she joined him inside. She hated elevators. The air closed around her and slowed her breathing.

"If you don't like fancy, then why are we here?" She closed her eyes and leaned onto the inside railing. The elevator hummed as it shot up to the top floor.

Jace reached inside his coat and pulled out a flask. He unscrewed the cap and chugged a swig. "If you'd put a bounty on my head or were looking to kill me, would you start here?"

Frankie thought of the other hunters searching every slummy motel in Rochester for a sign of him. "Point taken."

When the elevator finally reached the penthouse level, the bell dinged as the doors opened into a small lobby. The floor was covered with fluffy white carpet, and she had a feeling that lying on it would be as comfortable as lying in her four-poster bed. A white double door faced to the elevator, only the slight tan of the lobby walls adding any color.

Jace walked to the door, his dirt-covered boots leaving dark footprints all over the white carpet. She cringed at the sight. After unlocking the door, he stepped inside as if he'd been there a hundred times.

She followed him, and let out a low whistle at the sight of the penthouse. "This is absolutely gorgeous."

He dropped his bag of weapons on the floor of the master bedroom. "It's a little too gorgeous to be comfortable, in my opinion. Though I guess if you like gaudy, it's all right."

"Why does anything nice make you so uncomfortable?"

He grumbled like he didn't want to answer that.

She grinned, ready to throw his words back verbatim. "You said you'd 'rather deal with shitty and realistic than fancy and fake any day.' I want to know why."

Jace raised a single eyebrow.

She put her hands up. "Your words, not mine. I'm just trying to understand them."

He unzipped the duffel and slipped one of his many handhelds underneath the pillows. "Shitty and realistic is what I'm used to, and I'm comfortable with that."

"You're a creature of habit."

"No, I just don't like change." He tucked another handheld in the nightstand drawer.

"Same thing." She looked at him. "Change can be good."

"Change can screw you six ways `til Sunday."

She dropped the subject and walked over to the bed. Sitting on the edge, she felt like she was invading someone else's room, someone else's space. She peeled her tennis shoes off her feet and wiggled her toes, then arched her spine. Her neck and back could really use a good straightening.

Jace strolled into the master bathroom and flicked on the light. He shrugged out of his coat and laid it across the counter, then leveled his face inches away from the mirror. He examined his eye, running his fingers over the bruises, which had already begun to heal. She watched as he stood up straight again and pulled his shirt over his head, then threw it on top of the coat.

Thick muscles defined his torso, and his back flexed every time he moved. Her stomach filled with evil, torturous butterflies. Every part of her body that he'd touched burned. A trail of heat washed through her, and she forced herself to look away.

She stared at the fluffy white carpet. A low grunt came from the bathroom, and she couldn't help but look up again. Jace was attempting to pour whiskey down his back and over the scratches lining his shoulder blades from his fight with Eli, Mr. Ice-Blue Eyes. She walked slowly into the bathroom. As soon as Jace saw her reflection in the mirror, he stopped making a mess with the whiskey.

"Here." She took the flask from his hand. "Let me help."

"I can do it," he said, though he dropped his hands to his sides and didn't reach for the flask again.

"No, you can't. You're getting it all over the tile." She unfolded one of the bathroom towels and stepped closer to him. "Can you kneel? I'm not tall enough." Even though she was tall for a woman, standing next to him, she realized she barely reached his shoulders.

He got down on his knees, and she bunched the towel in her hand.

"This will sting." Before he could protest, she poured the whiskey onto his wounds. He hissed as she patted the excess liquid off his skin.

She looked at his reflection in the mirror. A large purplish-yellow ring hung under one eye. His cheeks looked swollen from where he'd been punched in the face, and the cut on his lip was scabbed over with dried blood. But he was still ruggedly handsome and, in many ways, even beautiful. Part of her hated him for that.

"You should put ice on that. I'll get some for you."

He shook his head. "Don't bother. You don't need to take care of me."

"Why not? You took care of me earlier." She refolded the towel and set it on the counter.

"That was different."

"How?" she asked as she exited the bathroom.

He followed her into the bedroom but didn't answer.

"Sit on the bed." She pointed to the king-size mattress before hurrying into the kitchen to retrieve some ice. She wrapped it in a towel and walked back out to the bedroom.

Jace's shoulders slumped as he sat down. He placed his hands on his knees and hung his head. Frankie sighed. Just looking at his defeated posture drained all her energy.

She went to his side and knelt in front of him. "Close your eye."

He did as he was told, and she pressed the makeshift compress onto his shiner. He groaned, and his grip on his knees tightened.

"From the way you're acting, I'd swear you'd never been punched before." She smiled.

"Believe me, I've had my fair share of beatings throughout my lifetime."

She shrugged. "Such is the life of a supernatural."

He opened his one good eye and glared. "I'm not one of you."

"You are—at least partially. You might have been able to fool those goons we took down back there for a long time, but you can't fool me. I know an alpha wolf when I see one."

"I'm no wolf, and I'm no alpha."

She rolled her eyes and nodded to the compress. "Hold this in place while I get some more ice for the rest of your face."

He held the compress as she went back to the kitchen. When she returned, she held an unwrapped cold cube against his lip. Despite the cold ice in her hand, her body filled with heat as she thought of his warm mouth running across her thigh. Her finger slipped, and the pad of her thumb rubbed against the smooth skin of his lip.

She glanced away and pulled her hand back. Her cheeks flushed red. "Sorry. I—"

He grabbed her wrist until she slowly raised her gaze to him. "Don't stop."

Even after he released her, she fought to keep her

breathing even. Lowering her gaze, she tried to think of something to break the silent tension. Anything.

He's a hunter. He's a hunter.

She steadied her trembling hand as she tried to soothe his wound again.

"So who were those guys?" she asked, glad to have come up with a logical change in subject. "I know they were hunters, but why hunt one of their own?"

Then again, he hunted his own kind, too, even though he wouldn't admit it.

"You heard David. They're from the Brooklyn division. Chet might as well have put a hit out on my head, telling everyone I'm not human. There are certain guys in the organization who will take that personal. See it as a betrayal. Brooklyn probably came up here looking for me to get brownie points with Headquarters and Chet."

"They're like the freaking supernatural police."

Jace shook his head, putting down the compress. "More like dirty cops. Not every hunter is a good guy."

She drew a deep breath. "Like Mr. Ice."

"Who?"

"The one you stabbed and beat the crap out of. Eli."

"True." He nodded. "Well, 'Mr. Ice' is the head of the Brooklyn division. He thinks he's tough shit because he slays vamps. You've gotta be more than a good shot to take down a bloodsucker, so he thinks he's got all the right moves. He's not dirty. He's just a miserable person, and clearly a kiss ass to Chet."

Frankie pitched the half-melted ice cube into the trash can near the dresser. "Why's Chet have it out for you so bad, anyway? Other than the smack down in the interrogation room, I mean."

Jace shrugged. "The killings have been going on sporadically for a few weeks now, and since I haven't bagged the guy yet, Chet got it in his thick skull that I'm not doing my job. Now that he knows I'm a half-breed and with the whole name-carving shit, he's clearly aiming to paint it like I'm involved. Gives him all the more reason to get rid of me. Hell if I know why yet."

"Not sure why you'd want to be involved with guys like that, especially considering what you are."

"They're not all bad. There's gotta be someone to protect humans when they don't stand a chance on their own, but since the Cronos buyout, things have been tense. Feels like we've been split down the middle. It's the guys like me who've been around the block a few times versus the new. Not sure where it originated from, but it's come to a head with this. This conflict with Chet was a small spark in an already lit powder keg. I should've seen it coming."

"But you did, didn't you? Hence the burner apartment."

He shrugged a shoulder. "You could put it that way."

She nodded at that. "What sort of grudge does he have against you?"

Jace grinned ruefully. "From day one, I've refused to put up with his bull. That's why he's got it in for me."

She sat down near his feet. "And now that he knows what you are, he pretty much hates you."

"You got it, babe."

"So all we need to do is find the real killer and you can clear your name, right?"

He shook his head. "No can do. I'm branded for life with this wolf stuff. I always knew that asshole would come back and haunt me."

"Asshole?" Frankie stared at him with wide eyes.

"My old man."

"He's dead? I'm sorry to hear that—I guess."

"Hell no. I have no clue where he is, and I haven't since I was sixteen. And if he's dead, I'm sure as hell not sorry. Good riddance." He grabbed a gun and some bullets from his duffel bag.

"Oh." A constricting feeling plagued Frankie's chest as she stared into his face. She could see the pain behind his eyes.

He loaded the shells. "He just up and left one day. Hung us out to dry."

She remembered what it had been like when her parents died, how alone she'd felt even though she'd been an adult. Facing that kind of pain when still a kid seemed more than unfair. She imagined that knowing his father had chosen to leave made that pain even worse. "You must have been devastated."

"My mom was. I was sad for her sake, but mostly I was glad he was out of our lives." He locked the gun's barrel into place before he laid the fully loaded weapon at his side.

"You didn't get along?"

Jace laughed. "Sure, we got along—when he wasn't beating me up or smacking my mom around."

Frankie's stomach flipped. "That's horrible. I don't know what to say, Jace. Have you ever talked about it with anyone?"

He reached into his bag and dug around. "I don't need a shrink."

"I didn't say you did. I meant anyone. A friend. That's the sort of thing that you need to get off your chest."

He shot her a glare. "There's nothing on my chest."

She put her hands up in surrender, unwilling to push the subject. "If you say so." She leaned her weight back on her arms and winced. A sharp pain tore through her collarbone.

"Shit. Brent got you with his silver chain, didn't he?"

Her hand trailed up to the top of her shirt. She pulled down the material to show her maimed collarbone. Since the fight, the blood had clotted into flaky bits, but the few places that were still raw burned at the touch of her blouse.

"Let me get something for you."

She held up her hand to stop him. "No, it's okay. You're worse off than me. Just take care of your eye."

"Do you really think I'm going to sit here and baby myself when you have second-degree burns? Who cares if they heal fast? I may seem like an ass sometimes, but I'm not *that* much of a jerk." He stood and stalked into the bathroom.

Frankie smiled a little. "I don't think you seem like an ass. Or a jerk."

He glanced over his shoulder and eyed her for a long moment. "Thanks." He grabbed his flask off the counter and strolled back into the room, bypassing the bed. He sat down on the floor in front of her, their knees almost touching.

Before she could protest, he wrapped his arms around her and scooped her into his lap. All of her senses snapped to attention and her mind went rigid—but her body had other plans. It melted into him, all her muscles relaxed.

A small smile crept over his face, and she suddenly wanted to hide in any available space. Anywhere, as long as his smoldering stare couldn't run over her body and leave her wishing he would undress her with more than his eyes. She glanced down at her hands.

He hooked his index finger under her chin and tilted her head up. "Hey, what's wrong?"

She swallowed hard. For such a simple question, it felt oddly intimate rolling off his tongue. "Nothing." She forced herself to be realistic. This was going nowhere. He hated her kind. She could tell by the way he thought of himself.

"I know from dealing with my mother that 'nothing' always means 'something.' When my dad would come home drunk and rough her up, every time I'd ask her how she was, she'd always say nothing was wrong."

Crossing her arms over her chest, she folded into herself. "I guess I don't want to talk about it."

"That's a better answer, though I wish you would."

"I wish *you'd* talk, too—and don't say that's different. It's not."

A moment of silence passed between them, a suffocating lull.

Frankie sighed. "I'm thinking about what my actions will result in when I return to my pack."

"I'm sure they'll be glad that you're back. By now they're bound to have realized you're missing, and can they really punish you for hunting a killer?"

She shook her head. "It's not that simple."

He stared at her, waiting for elaboration.

She let out another long sigh. "I'm in a position of power, an especially high position for a female."

He looked at her expectantly. "What's wrong with that?"

"There's nothing wrong with it. I'm ready to accept my obligations and fulfill my duties, but it's...hard for me to live my life when I'm confined by such strict rules."

"I try not to play by other's rules," he said.

She rolled her eyes. "And we've seen what sort of trouble it gets you in. If I step out of line, my position could be challenged, and because I'm a powerful female, there are loads of males who wouldn't hesitate to kill or defeat me in order to usurp me. I live with the constant knowledge that someday my pinkie toe may barely cross over some line and I'll end up with a knife in my back."

"Sounds like a shitty position to be in."

She thought of all her duties. "In some ways, yes. In others, no. It depends. I know I should do what I want and not allow anyone to dictate to me, but it's hard, in my position. I have others to think about, people I'm responsible for. I wish I could be like you."

"Why the hell would you want to be like me?" His brow furrowed like he couldn't begin to understand that.

"You don't let anyone intimidate you. I don't scare easily, but I'm not immune to fear like you are."

He let out a short huff. "I wasn't always this way."

"Maybe, but you are now."

Jace's jaw clenched as if he were fighting not to grind his teeth. "I swear to myself every day that I'll never give in. I refuse to be like my bastard of a father. But each morning I look in the mirror and I see him staring back at me, and there are so many things that take me back to that place. I let him haunt me, and I can't help it. I still choke at the smell of cigars." He twisted so she could see his forearm. A series of perfectly circular scars marred the inside of his arm. Bile burned at the back of Frankie's throat at the thought of someone hurting a child in that way. "Don't be like me. You can't allow them to get the best of you. Don't let yourself be abused."

She didn't know what made her do it, but she gently gripped his face in both hands, holding his gaze as she spoke to him. To underscore the seriousness of her words. "Jace, you can't blame yourself for what happened to you, and you can't be angry over frightening memories. All the pain you felt was real. It would've been too much for anyone to handle, and you were just a kid. That sort of pain leaves scars that go way deeper than the surface. And you don't need to spend so much of your energy fighting not to be like him. You may have a lot of anger, but it's easy to see that you're a good person." She ran her hand over his cheek, then released him.

He cleared his throat, glancing away from her, before he stared blankly at the wall, like he was reliving memories she couldn't see. It took a moment before he responded. "And what does that say about me? I have to fight every day not to be some crazy, abusive drunk? Not to treat people like shit and kill the innocent? And half the time I'm barely succeeding. Lord knows I drown myself in liquor, even if my damn supernatural metabolism burns up the alcohol so quickly that I'm rarely drunk. What does that say about my character?"

"That you're a good man. Because, despite any past trauma, you keep trying to do the right thing. Everyone has demons."

He held up the flask. "This is going to hurt a little." He tipped the container over and allowed the whiskey to pour across her burns. The wounds screamed with pain as the alcohol sanitized them. His hand fell back to his side. "I've never told anyone that before."

She smiled through the pain. "I'm glad you told *me*."

"Do you want me to put a bandage on this?" he said.

"No, if I can shift, it will heal quickly. I'll wait until you're asleep. I know you don't like—"

"No, don't bother. I may hunt criminal shifters, but... well, I wouldn't hunt *you*."

Her heart jumped, and she mentally scolded herself as she asked, "What makes me different from any other shifter?"

"You're useful. I need inside information. If the killer

really is a rogue, I'll need to cooperate with your pack, at least temporarily."

Something inside her deflated a little. "Oh."

She glanced down at her hands and gritted her teeth. She was an idiot. What sort of answer had she expected?

"I'm going to shift. I'll be right back." She rushed into the bathroom and shut the door behind her, a little harder than she intended.

Pushing her spine against the wood, she slid down to the ceramic tiling. What was wrong with her? Their one night was long over. And *why* was she interested in him?

She was a wolf shifter—his sworn enemy. The only thing he would remember about their time together was the fact that he'd fucked a wolf. He'd saved her, had her in his control, and that was all that mattered. She was nothing but a piece of leverage that allowed him to say, "Take this, fur-faces. I banged one of your bitches."

Destined mate, her ass.

Burying her face in her hands, she thought about making a run for it. If she bolted now and caught Jace off guard, she could make it to the stairs. Her body shook from the adrenaline buzzing through her veins. No. She couldn't run. She needed his help to find the rogue.

She let out a long sigh. Why had she told him about the precariousness of her position? She'd never told anyone that, not even Alejandro. She'd likely messed with her chances on that score, too. She'd never wanted to marry into another pack, but her little rendezvous with Jace hadn't solved anything. And as a result, here she was, sitting in the bathroom of an overly done-up penthouse pining for a wolf hunter who couldn't care less.

Useful.

The word echoed in her ears. That was all she was to

him. Useful. That was what she got for having sex on an animalistic whim, then letting her dumb-ass brain try to rationalize her actions with delusions of romance and destined mates. Use*less* was more accurate. He undoubtedly only wanted her in order to get to the Rochester packmaster.

She scoffed. Little did he know...

She pulled her cell phone out of the pocket of her jeans. She stared at the screen. Alejandro's name flashed next to a missed call message. She pressed a few buttons and the blank slate for a text message popped up. She started typing.

Alejandro, I'm okay. Will explain everything later. Sorry I missed your

She stopped typing in the middle of her sentence, staring at the words until she finally hit the delete button. The sound of phone's screen cracking snapped her mind back in place, and she realized she'd thrown it at the bathroom wall.

"Damn it."

She crawled toward the broken pieces. It was fixable, but she would need a whole lot of glue and possibly duct tape, and....who was she kidding? She needed a new phone. But that wasn't the real issue. What mattered was whether she was really going to run from this. Especially from her deal with Rock. She stripped off her clothes and laid them next to the bathtub. The feeling of the cold tile against her naked flesh sent shivers up her spine. Crouching on her knees, she clenched her teeth. She wanted to scream, but the only real release was to shift.

13

J ACE SAT ON the edge of the bed with his head buried in his hands. What the hell had he gotten himself into? She was a wolf shifter *and* a powerful one. Not to mention, she was engaged. How much lower could he stoop? He ran his fingers through his hair and tightened them around his skull. No matter how hard he squeezed, he couldn't hold himself together.

A small crash resonated from the bathroom, like the sound of cracking glass. Damn. He walked to the door and leaned his ear against the wood. No sound. He knocked and waited for a response. Nothing.

Worried, he knocked harder. "Francesca?"

Muffled by the closed door, nails scratched over the wood in an eerie response.

"All right, I'm coming in." Jace opened the door and immediately stumbled back.

Francesca's clothes lay scattered across the floor, her lacy panties hooked on the rear paw of a large ebony-colored wolf. The eyes staring at him were all too familiar, like molten liquid gold. The wolf cocked its head to the side, and its ears perked up.

No, *Francesca* cocked *her* head to the side. He fought the urge to swear under his breath. She was a wolf shifter. The wolf *was* Francesca.

"Am I still supposed to call you Francesca when you're… you know?" He rubbed his fingers over his temples and stared at the ceiling. "I can't believe I'm talking to an animal."

The wolf grumbled in response.

He let out a long sigh and pushed his fingers through his hair again. "So am I supposed to call you Francesca? Bark once for no, twice for yes."

The wolf barked twice.

"All right, then, Francesca it is."

She huffed and trotted over to the side of the bed. She leapt onto the mattress with grace, stretched luxuriantly and then curled into a ball. Jace glanced toward the door. If she was planning to sleep, he supposed he could go check out one of the other bedrooms.

Francesca followed his gaze. She rested her head on her paws and whimpered.

"It's okay. I'll use one of the other beds."

She made a noise between a growl and a whimper.

He realized that she didn't want him to go. "I can take the floor in here, then," he offered.

She whined again.

"Come on. I bet you'd be more comfortable without me anyway." He took a pillow from the bed and dropped it onto the floor. It hit the carpet with an audible poof, and he realized it was probably softer than anything he'd ever slept on in his whole life.

He sat down next to it and leaned back against the wall.

Reaching across the floor, he took the flask, then unscrewed the cap and lifted it to his lips, ready to chug down however much whiskey was left. When nothing came out, he threw it on the carpet next to him. Damn. He would need to restock if he was going to make it through bringing a rogue werewolf to justice with Francesca there to distract him every step of the way.

He glanced up from the stark white carpeting. Golden wolf eyes stared back at him, monitoring his every move.

"Do you distrust me so much that you need to watch me, or am I that pretty to look at?"

The wolf pawed at its muzzle and buried its head in the comforter. The thought that Francesca was in that wolf—that she *was* that wolf—made the gesture all the more human. He had a feeling she would have been blushing if she could have.

"So, if we're going to stay organized and keep one step ahead of this sicko, we'll need a plan." He glanced at his watch. "The sun should be coming up soon, so we'll get some shut-eye first, and then, when evening rolls around, we'll head out to where the double killings were." He looked her way to make sure she was listening. She watched him with attentive eyes. "We'll have to touch base with David, to find out where it all went down. The bodies will be long gone, but once we examine what's left of the crime scene, we can take it from there. Hopefully we can still catch a trace of his scent. As long as we can find the bastard, we can take him out. Locating him will be the big problem."

He eyed her again. "Bark once for okay, twice for 'I have a better plan.' I'm sure you have something to say, as usual."

The wolf snarled and barked once.

"Agreement. That's what I like to hear. I'll set the alarm to be sure we don't sleep too late." He pushed himself off the ground, walked over to the bedside clock and punched several buttons before he figured out how to program the alarm.

The sheets rustled as Francesca shifted onto her side.

"How are those wounds looking?" He sat beside her on the bed. He hesitated before he pushed aside the fur on the wolf's collarbone. The burns were visibly healing before his eyes.

"Looks good. You should be better by tonight."

The wolf laid her head on her paws and closed her eyes. Her fur was a rich, ebony black, as dark as night itself, undertoned with bits of red, the same gorgeous color as her hair—both beautiful and a deadly camouflage to hide her from her enemies. And man, those eyes—wild, untamed and majestic. They held an entrancing quality, one he had never encountered in a normal human being, the eyes of a free animal.

That asshole packmaster of hers was too much of a coward to send out his troops, so she was out there on her own. What type of leader sent a lone female as his muscle to track a rampaging rogue?

Jace pulled his gaze away and flicked off the bedroom light. He could see perfectly in the dark, and the weight of her gaze as she watched him hung heavy on his shoulders. He moved back to the pillow. He took a deep breath, and the words slipped out before he could control himself. "For the record, you're a beautiful wolf."

Without looking back at her, he lay down on the floor and rested his head on his pillow. He thanked God she couldn't respond.

～

THE SCREECHING SOUND of the alarm rang in his ears, and something wet licked at his hand. *Wolf.* His eyes shot open, and he scrambled to his feet. Adrenaline propelled him until he realized the wolf was Francesca. Right, he'd slept in a room with a wolf shifter all night—probably not his brightest idea. If she'd wanted to, she could have ripped his throat out.

Though he supposed they'd already slept together in more ways than one.

"What do you think you're doing, waking me up like that?" Jace demanded as he stood and strode over to the alarm, hitting the off button with more force than was necessary.

Francesca's tail bristled, and a shiver ran down her spine. Jace's eyes widened as her fur melted back into her skin. Her muzzle shortened. Her tail folded in on itself, and her ears shrank and rounded out. A moment later he was staring at Francesca, propped on all fours and completely naked.

She threw her long hair over her shoulder and sat up. "I could've barked in your ear or bitten you. If I were you, I wouldn't complain about a little tongue action."

He frowned. "Bite me again and you'll find a silver knife against your throat."

She rolled her eyes. "How gentlemanly of you." She stood.

Jace drank in the beautiful curves of her nude figure. Slender, muscular legs, round, smooth hips, a toned stomach, and breasts that could make a man wild with lust.

He ripped his gaze away from her and turned around. He felt his cock grow hard, and he tried to ignore the strain against his jeans. "I never claimed to be a gentleman."

"Good, because you didn't have me fooled for a second." He could practically hear the amused grin in her voice. He heard her pad lightly toward the other side of the room, where her backpack lay against the wall.

"You can turn around now," she said after several moments. "I don't care if you see me naked again."

He turned to find her wearing a white tank top and a pair of worn jeans. His gaze slid over her curved frame and his dick jerked. Damn, even when she was clothed—or barely so—he wanted to run his tongue over every inch of her skin. He forced himself to ignore the deep urge tugging at his groin.

As if she read his mind, she glanced down at her clothing. She met his stare again and frowned. "These are my work clothes. I don't dress like this *every* day."

"I didn't say anything." He tried not to dwell on the way her jeans squeezed her perfectly round ass or how her tank top framed the most perfect pair of breasts he'd ever laid eyes on.

She shrugged. "You implied it with your eyes."

Jace pretended he didn't hear her comment and took his leather coat off the dresser. "Grab your things while I call David. I don't know if we'll be coming back here or not." He shrugged on the coat and used the hotel phone to dial David's number.

After a few rings, the call went to David's voice mail. Jace hung up and redialed, and kept redialing until David finally answered.

"Hello?"

"What's with you not picking up your phone?"

"After helping you, I'm on the lam, J. I'm trying to be cautious."

"Yeah, and I'm trying not to waste time."

"Then hurry up and spit it out," David said.

"We need to know where the double killings were."

"We?" David asked. "You know, I really don't like the idea of you—"

"Mind your own business. Either help me or hang up the phone."

"I can't tell you where it's at. It's hard to find. I'll have to show you."

"Meet me at the place in an hour. You know where I mean. Make sure you ditch your phone in case they can track it."

Jace hung up the phone without another word—David would be there.

After Jace thoroughly chewed out the valet for slamming on the brakes too hard when he pulled the Chevelle up to the hotel doorway, but then tipped him far too generously because even he knew he was an uptight prick about his car, they drove toward the edge of the city. He ordered Francesca to check the rearview mirror every couple of minutes to ensure they weren't being followed. He'd checked his ride religiously for tracking devices, and while nothing electronic had been attached, there was no arguing with the fact that a Chevelle stood out.

"I don't see anything," Francesca said. He could tell from her quiet demeanor that her nerves were as on-edge as his. The last thing they needed was to be tracked down by his fellow hunters again.

When they reached Honeoye Falls, Jace took the back way to the Lucky Bastard. The bar was usually dead this early on a Tuesday night, and tonight was no different. With the tiny lot nearly empty, he parked the car and surveyed their surroundings. David's restored 1947 Harley FLH, one of his many motorcycles, was parked at the side of the lot. Two nondescript cars, which Jace recognized as the bartenders', were parked across the blacktop.

Francesca stared at the sticker on the bar's front door, which read: *Welcome to Honeoye Falls.* And scribbled beneath it in thick marker: *Three bars, one graveyard and four hookers.*

She let out a small laugh and walked inside.

Jace shook his head. Four hookers who tried to hit him up for free on a regular basis, the three bars where his dad had drank himself into the ground, and the one graveyard where his mother was buried. Yeah, welcome to Honeoye Falls all right.

With one last look over his shoulder, Jace strolled inside.

The dark cherry wood of the bar shimmered in the dim lighting. Francesca stood next to an old jukebox that only played well-known Garth Brooks and Johnny Cash songs, flipping through the selections with a blank look on her face. David sat at the bar sipping a craft beer as he watched Francesca with a wary eye.

Jace sat down at the bar next to David and watched as the bartender cleaned a tall beer mug a few feet away.

"Hey, John. You want the usual?"

It took Jace a moment to respond to the bartender's question. He spent a lot of time here, even now that he'd moved deeper into the city, but only the owner, Jimmy, knew his real name.

"Yeah, slip me a couple bottles of Bushmills, will you? I need to restock." He actually didn't, but he knew they needed that kind of business in this place.

"Coming right up."

He watched the bartender walk away before he turned to David. "So where were these bodies at? I need to map where the attacks took place and check out the scene. There has to be some sort of pattern to what this psycho is doing, and if there isn't, there's a reason it's random."

"I can't concern myself with this for too long, J." David

sipped his beer, then set his glass on the bar top, staring blankly at the liquor shelf. "I've got a baby downtown who's been possessed by that demon that's been giving me shit, and she doesn't have much more time. If I don't rip that thing out of her soon, she'll be dead, and the demon will move on to its next host." David turned toward him. "Have you ever seen a possessed baby? It's horrifying. I can't have baby blood on my hands."

"I promise I won't keep you too long, David. Just show us the spot and then you can go save some babies."

"They're not *all* babies. Just the *one*."

Francesca walked up to the bar. "As much as I'd love to stay here and listen to Johnny Cash all day, if you guys are done making small talk, I think we have more important business to attend to."

David set down his glass. "It's not that simple."

"What do you mean, 'It's not that simple'?" Francesca crossed her arms over her chest.

"The bodies were found in Manhattan Square Park on top of that big metal piece of shit. You know, that little structure thing."

"Okay, yeah, I know what you're talking about, but I thought you said it was somewhere hard to find," Jace said.

"I didn't want to say much over the phone. You know how good Headquarters is with anything electronic. They could've hacked into the line. I've got a new disposable cell now. I can't give you the number, but I can call you and then throw out the phone, if needed." He stared at his drink for a moment. "The site is easy to find, but there *is* something I want you to see there, and I'll need to show it to you."

The bartender returned and pushed three bottles of Bushmills toward Jace, who slapped some large bills on the counter in return. He turned back to David. "Fine, I needed to restock my liquor, anyway. Finish your drink and then meet us there."

COLD, DREARY AND downright sketchy, Manhattan Square Park was the last place Frankie wanted to spend her night. Not that she currently had many other options. She walked next to Jace along the park's dim pathways. Even though her naturally high body heat warmed her, she wrapped her arms around her chest and pulled her jacket closer. How many times had her parents told her to stay away from here at night when she was a teen? The thought of being mugged gave her the heebie-jeebies, even though she could easily hold her own in a fight.

She scanned the surrounding darkness, thankful for her heightened night vision. Nothing, as far as she could see. They continued on for several more minutes. Just as her shoulders started to relax, Jace reached for his gun. She heard it, too. Footsteps. He pulled his weapon as David stepped into the dim glow of the moonlight. They'd taken different routes from the bar.

"I don't think it'd be a good idea to blow my head off." David grinned. "You wouldn't get your clues, and the city of Rochester might start to have a demon infestation problem. Follow me."

Without a word, Frankie and Jace trailed behind him until they reached the metal structure. David climbed the aluminum steps two at a time, and they stayed on his heels. When they reached the top, he crouched down and pointed at the ground.

"This is where they were found. Right out here in the open. But as a precaution, I scanned the place. Watch this."

David reached inside his leather and removed a copy of the Old Testament. He flipped to a page written entirely in Hebrew. He dug inside his pocket, then scattered rock salt across the platform as he continued to read. As his voice rose, obviously leading to the climax of his chant, he pulled a lighter from inside his coat. He stood and raised it high above his head before he knelt down again, pressing the flame to the cold metal. A trail of fire ignited, and a large symbol appeared—a perfect circle with two wavy lines perpendicular to each other running through the middle.

"What the hell is that?" Frankie asked.

For a brief second an image flashed through her mind: a blond woman with a long sword battling an enormous man wearing wolf skins. *What the hell?* She pushed the thought aside, but the image was so vivid and clear.

Where was her imagination going?

David stared at the burning flames. "I'm not sure. A circle is one of the universal conduits, like water. It can give you full access to the beyond, usually a one-way ticket to hell." He looked at Jace with a grim expression behind his eyes. "I don't think you're dealing with a regular wolf shifter. I think you've got a shape-shifting demon on your hands, and one I've never encountered."

"I have to say, I've been called a lot of things, but shape-shifting demon is a first," a deep voice drawled from behind them.

Jace and David had their guns drawn and aimed into the darkness within seconds.

A chill shot down Frankie's spine. The silhouette of a man hidden within the shadows loomed over them. She dropped into a defensive stance, bared her canines and growled. The small hairs on the back of her neck and arms stood on end. She recognized the scent instantly.

From the flash of rage in his eyes, Jace was aware of it, too. He growled, his gun held steady. "I don't give a shit who or what you are. You're done."

"I had a feeling you'd say something like that."

The man stepped into the light, and Frankie stared.

It was...strange to put a face to what had been done to those young women. Horrific in its own way, because he was...just a person, supernatural or not. No different from her, or David, or Jace. Tall, with broad shoulders, auburn hair, sea-blue eyes and muscled. With human eyes and hands and feet. The heavy scent of his skin hit her full force.

Her eyes widened as she sucked in a harsh breath.

He may have looked like them, but they couldn't be more different.

He was a *monster*, through and through.

A smirk crept across the man's face. "Seems like you and your bitch have a keen sense of smell." He stepped forward. "My name's Robert, though your papers have been calling me the new-age Jack the Ripper—surprisingly accurate. Tell me, what do you think of my work?"

"I think you're one sick fuck." Jace pointed the Mateba at Robert's head. "One sick fuck who needs to be buried six feet under."

Jace fired.

Robert dodged faster than Frankie would have believed possible, and instead of his head, the bullet hit his shoulder. He yelped and stumbled back, knocking into the metal railing. Blood poured down his shirt. He clutched his hand to the wound.

A satisfied grin crossed Jace's face and he surged forward as Robert fell to his knees, still clutching the bleeding bullet hole. Jace raised his gun, and pressed the barrel against Robert's forehead. "You better say a prayer and hope that

Satan doesn't make you his bitch every day for the rest of eternity."

"I think you're in for a surprise." Robert pulled a hunting knife from his belt and stabbed Jace in the thigh.

Blood spurted from Jace's leg as he doubled over in pain. The crimson liquid splashed over Robert, turning his twisted features even more demented. Panic filled her.

"Jace!" Frankie moved to lunge toward him, but Jace held up a hand, urging her away.

"Stay back." Pain and warning flared in his eyes, communicating the rest. He was protecting her again.

We don't know what he's capable of.

Frankie stilled, watching in horror as Robert stood, smiled in self-satisfaction and plucked the bullet from his shoulder. The blood trickled to a stop.

Frankie couldn't bring herself to breathe.

He held the bullet out in his hand. "You think you can kill me that easily? And you're a hunter?" He dropped the bullet in front of Jace.

It hit the metal with a loud clang.

Frankie's heart raced. How the hell could he do that?

David cocked his semi-auto then, drawing Robert's attention. "We might not be able to kill you—yet—but we sure as hell can cause you a lot of unnecessary pain." David fired.

The sound of the shot rang in Frankie's ears.

This time, Frankie didn't think.

She ripped her gaze away from the action, trusting David could handle it. For now. Jace was kneeling, spewing curses she had never even heard before. His blood formed a small pool of crimson around him, the heat from the liquid billowing with steam in the freezing cold. With David drawing Robert's attention, she was at Jace's side in an instant. She pressed her hands against the wound and applied as much pressure as she could, but his blood continued to flow with frightening speed.

"Shit." She stripped off her coat and rolled it into a long strip. Using all her strength, she forced Jace to straighten his leg. She looped the material underneath his thigh and tied it off above the wound. She hoped that bastard hadn't hit an artery.

She grabbed Jace's face and forced him to look her in the eye. "Don't take the tourniquet off." She turned to leave, to help David in the fight, but Jace grabbed hold of her wrist.

"Don't you dare get hurt. Give him hell." He released her.

David was fighting hand-to-hand with the bastard—or hand-to-gun. He had jammed the butt of the revolver into Robert's jaw.

Blood spewed from Robert's mouth and stained his teeth red.

Frankie ran straight for him and thanked God she had enough focus to transition. She dove for Robert and shifted mid-jump. Her canines collided with his stomach, piercing deep into his flesh. He toppled over from the force of her attack.

Take that, asshole.

Except within seconds, he had hold of her by the scruff. Lifting her as if she weighed no more than a newborn pup, he threw her away from him. She hit the platform hard and skidded across the smooth metal.

Fuck!

Her back legs slid over the edge of the structure. Her stomach dropped and her fur bristled as she clawed at the platform and tried to hold herself in place. She yelped. Just as she was sure she was about to fall to her death, a pair of large hands clutched her paws. Jace hauled her back onto the platform.

"What did I say about not getting hurt?"

She whimpered to say "I'm sorry" and panted to catch her breath.

A loud groan echoed through the night, a jolt of adrenaline kicking her senses into overdrive. The sound of David's strained voice mumbling in Hebrew registered in Frankie's sensitive ears. A low growl escaped her at the sight of Robert lifting David into the air by his throat. David grasped Robert's hand and clawed at his fingers, to no avail, his face turning from pale to pink. His mumbling grew fainter as his air supply was cut off.

No. She couldn't stand here and watch Robert kill Jace's friend.

She leapt at him. The sharp points of her canines latched onto his throat, and the sick taste of him filled her muzzle. David fell from his clutches as the three of them toppled over the railing, plunging off the metal structure. Frankie closed her eyes on instinct. She heard a loud shrieking yelp and faintly wondered if she'd hit the ground yet. She couldn't feel her body, the impact.

All she knew was pain.

The next she was aware, someone shook her shoulder, and a fresh wave of nausea coursed through her as her consciousness faded to black.

JACE DIDN'T GIVE a shit that his leg was injured or that he was bleeding like a stuck pig. He skyrocketed down the platform steps, leaving a blood trail as he dragged his leg behind. He sprinted to Francesca's side, adrenaline fueling him. At the force of the impact, she'd shifted into human form, and her naked body lay on top of the frozen grass and half-melted snow.

"Francesca? Francesca? Fuck, Princess! Don't you pass out on me. Don't you do it, damn it!" He probed her neck for a pulse and massaged the bones. Pulse steady, and her neck was perfectly intact. But her right arm and shoulder were a whole different story.

And that bastard had gotten away on top of that.

Shit. He couldn't move her and risk injuring her further, and he couldn't call the cops. An unconscious naked woman and two men covered in blood, with bullet casings scattered everywhere, wouldn't make for an easy explanation.

No doubt they were on their way already, after all that ruckus.

He glanced at David, who lay on the ground several feet away. His leg was bent unnaturally, but he had managed not to pass out. Instead he stared up into the night sky with wide, shocked eyes.

"David, are you okay?" His words sounded slurred, and he swayed a little, but...he wasn't drunk.

Jace glanced down at his leg. The blood was still coming hard and fast.

He blinked.

Too much. He'd lost too much.

The world spun, and Jace steadied himself with his free hand. In one quick rush, the blood drained from his face and a frosty cold nipped beneath his skin.

"Shit," he mumbled, only vaguely aware of what came next.

David glanced in his direction. "Jace? Jace? Oh, fuck."

~

When Jace finally came to, he was sprawled across an old beat-up sofa, the cushions beneath him crying from his muscled weight. He cracked one eye open to find a pair of shiny thin glasses reflecting the light straight into his retina.

"What the hell? Get that fucking light out of my eye."

The glare dimmed, and Jace peered up at a pair of large hazel eyes and a mop of wavy brown hair. Who the...?

"Shane?"

"Good, you recognized me. Hopefully that means we won't have to test for any brain damage due to blood loss."

"What?"

"Shane, I think I can take it from here." A large hand brushed the kid aside, and David slid into focus. "Hey, man. You okay? You looked whiter than a ghost the last time your eyes were open."

Jace groaned in response. His whole body felt drained and devoid of any energy.

"You lost a ton of blood, J." David paused. "By the way, you may need to repurpose the interior of the Chevelle. Just sayin'."

The image of the sadistic killer's face flashed in Jace's mind, and he suddenly recalled why he felt like complete and utter shit.

"Where's Francesca?" Jace pushed himself up on his elbows.

"I'm right here." Her gorgeous voice sounded in his ears like a sweet melody. "My arm was broken, and I was a little bruised up, but I'm fine now. I heal fast, you know."

Jace wanted to snarl, but he didn't have the energy in him. "That is *not* fine," he grumbled. "I'm going to torture that son of a bitch when I get hold of him."

David pushed lightly against his shoulder, trying to ease him back down. "It's cool, J. Take a breather. We're lucky we got out of there with so little damage—other than my leg, that is."

Jace's eyes widened as he remembered. "How bad is it?"

Shane cleared his throat. "He broke it pretty badly. Then he was forced to walk on it to get you and Francesca into the Chevelle before I got there. Even with extensive physical therapy, he might still have a permanent limp, and he'll definitely be out of commission for a while."

Jace met David's gaze. David's eyes burned with rage, and Jace knew that if David had the ability, he would kill Robert with his bare hands. If there was one thing David couldn't handle, it was people screwing with his job, and being physically impaired was practically number one on the list of things that would completely mess up David's hunting skills.

"David, man, I'm sorry. I shouldn't have—"

David shook his head and cut off Jace. "Don't even go there, J. I'm a big boy. I can handle myself, and I chose to get involved in this, so leave it."

Jace nodded and grumbled as he shoved himself into an upright position. Francesca was sitting in a brown suede La-Z-Boy with a blanket wrapped tight around her body. A sharp pang hit Jace hard in the chest; he'd never been so envious of a blanket. He wanted to hold her, touch her, make sure she was okay. His body stiffened, and a slow ache throbbed in his chest as he pictured her wrapped up in his arms, his hands stroking her smooth skin.

But she wasn't his to comfort.

She belonged to another man. Another goddamn wolf shifter.

He shifted his weight, and a pain in his thigh snapped him back to reality. He was ass-deep in a hunt for a sadistic killer, and the last thing he needed was to be hung up on a beautiful woman, much less one who wasn't available.

Still, the thought of her naked and passed out on the grass where she'd fallen chilled him.

He never wanted to see her injured like that again.

The beast inside him stirred, weakened, and yet...

Mine. It growled. Again.

This was getting tedious. Jace pushed the thought aside. There was no point in it.

She'd made a choice for her future and it didn't include him. She'd only promised him one night after all.

He examined his leg, assessing the wound. It was bandaged up nicely, and he felt the pull of stitches underneath—professional level work. Shane must have been the one to dress the gash, and Jace shook his head and wondered if a medical degree was another item he could add to the long list of the hunter's intellectual assets.

"Thanks for fixing me up, Shane."

"You're welcome." The other hunter nodded, shoving his hands into the pockets of his slacks. "Consider it payment for never calling me kid again." Shane cast him a sly grin.

Jace shook his head with a chuckle. "Not a chance." His gaze turned toward David then. "David, you shouldn't have brought him into this." He nodded toward Shane. "What the hell do you think Chet's going to do to him when he finds out that we were at his place?" He glanced at Shane. "This *is* your place, right?"

"Actually, this is my grandmother's apartment. She's out playing bingo tonight. We already took all the necessary precautions to keep Chet and any other members of the Execution Underground from finding us." Shane's smirk widened. "And I gave you a new phone for contact purposes. No trackers on it, obviously. It's in the console of Chevelle."

Jace had to admit. He was impressed, and his expression must have shown it.

"I'm a big boy, Jace," Shane said, rolling up the cuffs of his button-downs sleeves. "Still going to call me kid?" He lifted a brow in challenge.

Jace frowned for show, though his heart wasn't truly in it. "Don't look so full of yourself." The side of his mouth tilted with a barely hidden grin.

David cleared his throat as he managed to stand with the help of a large wooden crutch. "Jace, we can't beat around the bush here. There is something seriously scary about that fucker."

"Were you able to figure out what type of demon he is?"

Jace couldn't believe he was entertaining this line of thinking. He'd been so convinced the killer was a wolf shifter, or something similar, but since they'd seen him pull a bullet from his chest like he was indestructible, there were too many other options to consider.

David shook his head. "That's just it. When he was strangling me, I recited Psalm 91 three times. Add in a shofar and that's the big fat Jewish mother of all exorcism rituals. He didn't even flinch. He's not a demon, J. And whatever the hell he is, I don't like it."

Francesca snuggled deeper into the blanket, as if to shield herself from the gruesome details. "If he's not a demon, then where did that symbol come from?"

David shrugged. "I honestly have no clue. Maybe he's got one of those hell-crawlers working for him. They'd do anything for a little bloodshed."

"I don't think it's a demon. I've seen that symbol before, and I've never crossed paths with a demon in my life. As far as I know anyway," Francesca said.

David's eyes widened. "You know that symbol? He's a werewolf?"

Jace snorted. "I thought so, but now... A werewolf hopped up on steroids, maybe."

"No, he's not a shifter. And no, it's not one of *our* symbols." She eyed Jace, forcibly including him with her people. "I can't remember where I've seen it. I just know I have."

"Well, that doesn't give us much to work with."

"Look, I'm sorry I can't remember. I'll keep thinking about it. But don't act like that's our only hope. We've got information to work with." She held up a hand, ticking things off with her fingers. "First off, we know that he *is* able to shift, most likely into wolf form, since that's what his scent smells like, but we can't rule out any other possibilities."

Jace and the other men nodded.

"Secondly, we know he has abilities that a regular werewolf doesn't. Did you see how easily he lifted David and me together? He's got extra strength. Not to mention the healing thing. That guy pulled a bullet out of his own chest, for God's sake. I'm guessing a demon could have similar strength, but since he's immune to David's exorcism, that rules out the possibility that he's a demon. Third, there's the symbol. We have to figure out what it means."

All three men stared at her in silence.

She sighed. "So, we need to take a different approach. There is no way we can fight this guy with just two men and one wolf."

"Make that three," Shane said, his expression turning deadly serious, fast.

"Still," Francesca said. "We're going to need an advantage, something he isn't expecting."

Jace leaned back on the couch. "And what exactly would that be?"

"You'll need to shift, Jace."

He blinked several times, unsure if he'd fully processed what she said.

"You're the only one I know who even comes close to matching his strength," Francesca continued. "And you doing so would catch him off guard. Be something he isn't expecting."

"But Jace *can't* shift, can he? He's only half wolf," David said.

Jace cringed. Hearing the words said out loud in a room with two other hunters stung like a bitch. Anything was better than being one of the monsters. Hell, the black plague would have been preferable.

Francesca sat forward. "It's not that he can't shift, he just *hasn't* shifted."

Jace gritted his teeth and swallowed his rage at the whole discussion. "What are you talking about?"

"With some training, you could learn how to shift."

Jace shoved himself off the couch and hobbled from the room, courtesy of his damaged leg. "No, I won't do it," he called back over his shoulder. Anger ripped at his insides.

David caught him by the arm. "J, at least listen to what she has to say."

"Don't you start this with me. You know—"

"J, we're talking about people's lives here! Would you stop thinking about yourself for one damn minute and listen to the woman?" David growled.

Jace stepped back into the living room. In all the years he'd known David, the man had never so much as raised his voice to anything other than some sick demon wearing a human's body like a swanky new suit coat. Let alone snarled at him.

"Thank you." David turned to Francesca. "Continue."

Francesca nodded. "As I was saying, all you would need is some training."

"And you could train him?" David asked.

She let out a long sigh. "Yes, but we'd need somewhere safe to hide out while he learned, a place to lie low. My pack can provide that. Shifting for the first time isn't easy, and the presence of other wolves lessens the difficulty. Supernatural strength in numbers. There are a lot of things he'd need to learn, but the best place to do that is among other shifters, other wolves like you," she chanced a look toward Jace. "Best case scenario, you learn with the alpha of the pack."

"A packmaster?" David supplied.

Francesca nodded at that.

Jace scoffed. "There is no way in hell your asshole packmaster would allow a hunter into his pack."

She shoved the blanket away. "It's not the packmaster's approval you'd need to worry about—it's the pack's. Wolves are territorial, clannish. Quick to make enemies of those who aren't their own. It's a survival strategy for our species. Nothing personal. But if you're willing, I can guarantee they'll accept you, at least temporarily."

"How do you know you could get me past the packmaster? All he sent to look for that son of a bitch was you. No offense, Princess, but you're only one person. If he cared so much about catching this killer, why didn't he send more people?"

Her jaw set into a hard line. "Look, even though more people weren't sent, it doesn't mean anything. Trust me."

"And what about the Execution Underground?" Jace asked. "You don't want that kind of blowback for your pack."

"We'll deal with that," Damon said, suddenly emerging from the darkness of the apartment's shadows. "Formulate a plan to clear your name."

"Shit," Jace swore. He hadn't even realized the vampire hunter had been standing there.

"God, I hate it when he does that," David grumbled.

Damon scoffed, ice-blue eyes glaring.

"We're in this as much as you are now, J. Remember that." David cut Jace a hard stare, instantly sobering his pride. "The whole division. Ash and Trent included."

Their division leader nodded his approval.

Jace tipped his head toward each of them, an acknowledgement of his appreciation. From David, he'd expected as much, but the others? It was more than he could have asked.

His colleagues, no, his *friends* were putting their asses, their own jobs and lives on the line for him. He needed to make it worth it. At the very least, he could do that.

"Okay." He nodded slowly. "Okay. If you're all up for going against Headquarters, we'll handle that, figure out what's motivating Chet, but there's two parts to this plan and how do we know her packmaster will cooperate?"

He directed his attention to Francesca then. "How do you know so much about what he thinks? Answer me that."

Her hands clenched into fists, and she stood, power radiating from her until he could feel the full force of her strength. Her eyes transitioned to their wolf-like gold. "Because I *am* the packmaster."

14

FRANKIE'S HEART WAS pounding so hard she could feel the pulse in her neck. Silence hung in the air as the room filled with palpable tension.

"My name isn't Francesca. Francesca is my mother's name." She cleared her throat and fought down the bile rising in her stomach. "My real name is Frankie. Frankie Amato. *I'm* the Rochester packmaster."

After several long moments the men's utter shock and confusion passed. Frankie watched in dawning horror as Jace's face tightened with hurt.

For deceiving him. For lying to him.

Her stomach dropped. She hadn't realized what a betrayal of trust it'd been until that moment. She'd only considered her own survival, her own protection.

Jace turned to his fellow hunters. "Give us a minute, will ya?"

The other men exchanged knowing looks, clearly understanding the sudden need for privacy. "I'll be in the kitchen," Shane nodded, retreating to the other side of the apartment and out of earshot, before David and Damon stepped out.

As the door closed behind them, Jace turned toward Frankie. The already constricted feeling in her chest tightened in a sharp pain. She'd expected nothing less than pure, unadulterated rage from him. Swearing. Curses. Hurtful words. Anything but this.

The pained expression across his face was so much worse.

She'd disappointed him, hurt him. Not with who or what she was, but because she hadn't trusted him with the truth, and maybe worse, she'd underestimated him.

How could she have been so wrong?

"Did it amuse you that I didn't know your real name? Actually, no. Don't answer that." Jace held up a hand, before dropping it again, his voice surprisingly calm. "Forget it. You don't owe me anything."

She stepped toward him, attempting to bridge the chasm she'd created. "Jace, I'm sorry I didn't tell you. I didn't mean to hurt you. It was a survival strategy, that's all. Your kind has killed mine for less, and at first, I was...scared, of who you were, of what you'd do. Not to mention, I needed to keep my identity off the E.U's radar, for my pack's sake," she admitted. "Once you let me go and we started working together, I...I didn't know how to come clean. But why does my role as packmaster have to change anything? Why does it matter?"

He huffed, a humorless, pained laugh. For a moment, he buried his face in his hands. "Why does it *matter?*" He raked both hands over his face. "It matters because I trusted you. That means something, remember?" He met her gaze. "But you didn't trust me," he breathed.

Frankie's breath caught. "You... You never asked me to," she whispered.

"Did I have to?" he asked, gesturing around them as if to indicate the situation.

She'd known he'd risked himself for her, of course, but until she watched the pained look in his eyes then, she hadn't fully understood.

That he'd done it all for her.

That he'd do it again in a heartbeat.

Even though he'd told her that, hadn't he?

Yet still, she'd doubted him. Treated him like a monster.

Exactly how she'd expected him to treat her.

Shame filled her, harsh and fierce. She opened her mouth again to speak, but suddenly, Jace was on his feet. "I need a minute."

"Jace—" She reached for him, but before she could stop him, he'd left her alone in the room. Nothing but her own guilt-ridden thoughts and the memory of his pain there to linger. Pain she'd caused him. How could she have been so stupid?

Before Frankie had even sorted through her emotions, a tear ran down her face. It fell onto her hand, catching her by surprise, causing her to reach up and touch her own cheek.

What exactly was she crying for?

They'd made no promises, and yet...

She'd known there was something more between them. There *had* to be. Even though it was happening so fast.

But she hadn't trusted in it. Not truly.

And how could she? How could she let this feeling between them grow without suffocating it? Let it take root in her heart, her life when she was already promised to another? When Jace still hated himself for what he was?

She wasn't certain she knew the answer, or if she ever would, but before she could even wipe away the single stray tear, someone was nudging a hot beverage into her hand. Warm and comforting.

She glanced up from where she'd sunk down onto the floor.

One of the other hunters stood over her. What was his name again? Shane?

She accepted the steaming mug, uncertain what else to do. "Sorry, if you want me to clear out, I will. I don't want to intrude."

The only reason she was here at all is because Jace had wanted her to be, had agreed to be a team, but she wasn't certain that was the case anymore.

"Oh, no, stay. Grandma stays out late. She loves her bingo."

She glanced down at the mug he'd pressed into her hands. The chocolate liquid was steaming, speckled with tiny marshmallows. Cocoa.

"Gran says a hot drink makes everything better, and also chocolate is a woman's best friend." He shrugged. "I figure cocoa is a win-win."

Frankie tried to smile at that, but that only prompted a fresh round of guilt.

There was something about him. This hunter. She couldn't decide whether it was his gold-rimmed glasses, his hollowed-out cheekbones or the fact that underneath all the displays of intellect he was fiercely attractive—in a harsh, dark academic sort of way. But if he took off his glasses and put his hair in a ponytail, there was almost something... tender underneath.

Or maybe it was that he'd brought her cocoa.

She'd always had a soft spot for chocolate, despite the fact that too much wasn't great for her wolf's tummy, but one cup wouldn't hurt.

"I don't think I ever introduced myself. Dr. Shane Gray." He nodded and gave her a smile, one that reminded her a little too much of a young Harrison Ford.

She smiled a little, though it likely looked a bit forced.

With a grin like that, she'd bet his classes filled fast.

"Frankie. Nice to meet you, Doc." She blew on the steaming mug before she finally took a sip. The smooth chocolate liquid coated her throat, and she had to admit, it *did* make her feel a little better. Like her problems were a bit more manageable. "Thanks for the cocoa, and for fixing me up. Guess your years of med school and caring for people worked in my favor."

"Actually, I'm not a physician."

She lifted her eyebrows. "Then how did you—"

"I read...a lot," he said.

She blinked at him. Why wasn't she surprised by that? "So you're a professor?" She lifted a brow to guess. "And a hunter, too?"

He bit his lower lip before he answered, as if he wasn't sure he wanted to share. "I don't really work out in the field as often as Jace and David do. My doctorate is in the study of the paranormal and the history of religion, specifically the occult." He glanced at his feet. "But yes, I'm a hunter."

From that spark in his eyes, one she wouldn't want to cross too.

Brains plus brawn made for a dangerous breed, and that didn't even account for the fact that he was easy-on-the-eyes. Not her type, personally, but still alluring.

And caring.

Like Jace, even if he was rough around the edges.

She let out another long sigh.

"I guess witches are your specialty then?"

He nodded.

A moment of silence passed.

"He'll change his mind, you know."

"What do you mean?" She tilted her head to the side.

She wasn't certain how much of her and Jace's conversation he'd heard exactly.

"Jace is stubborn, but he's not a bad person. What happened to those women will motivate him, and if it doesn't, David will get Jace to agree. He'll shift."

"And he'll hate me." She sighed, deflated. "I didn't want to lie to him, but in the beginning, I thought he might take advantage of that knowledge, if the opportunity presented itself. Once we started working together, I guess I thought..." She inhaled a sharp breath. It was the first time she was fully admitting it, even to herself. "I guess I don't know what I thought...maybe that the truth would cause things to end between us?" She looked down into the cocoa again. "Guess I was right."

"Jace won't be deterred so easily."

She lifted a brow.

"If he cares for you, he won't allow this to stand in his way." Shane extended a hand toward her, offering to help her stand again. "But trust is a two-way street."

She accepted the gesture and he helped pull her to her feet, but it felt like more than a helping hand. It felt like an offer of friendship, despite everything.

"The question is, Frankie..." Shane asked, "are you willing to meet him half-way?"

Jace barreled down the stairs despite the pain in his leg and out into the street. David and Damon were standing outside, talking in low voices. When he burst out the front door, they both glanced in his direction. Damon didn't say anything, before he cast a parting nod toward David and Jace a look of pity, then disappeared into the ether, swallowed up by the shadows of the city, but David stood his ground. Jace perched on the edge of the stoop, reached inside his coat for a Marlboro and lit up.

"I thought you were tryin' to quit?" David asked.

Jace nodded. "Would you try to quit through all this?" He gestured around them as if to indicate all the shit they were dealing with lately. "Quitting ain't going so great."

The sweet smoke filled his lungs, but nothing could calm him now. He thought back to the other night when he'd found Francesca...Frankie...whatever...in that alleyway, the way she'd reacted to the sight of his gun. As hard as he tried, he couldn't even count how many things had gone wrong since then. Where was his head at?

Nestled into the part of his heart she'd laid bare, that was where.

He swore under his breath as he remembered how her body felt pressed against him. The taste of her lips. It'd taken everything in him to pull away from her then. But he'd thought she trusted him. Boy, what a fool he'd been. In more ways than one.

A deep growl rumbled in his chest, and he sucked hard on his cigarette in a vain attempt to drown out the memories. If he was going to get her out of his head, he would need something a lot stronger than a nicotine, but even he wasn't enough of a fool for that.

"You need a minute to yourself? Or can I pick your brain?" David said from behind him.

Jace nodded to the empty space on the stoop next to him. "Be my guest."

With some careful maneuvering, David lowered himself

down to Jace's side and nodded at the cigarette. "That's gonna kill you some day, you know."

The orange glow of the streetlights was illuminating, and the concrete beneath them was cold enough to make a man shiver. Jace was used to the cold. He could handle that. What he wasn't used to was having this much conflict thrown at him. Being this hung up on a woman.

He'd never had that problem before.

Every woman before her had been faceless, nameless. A sea of meaningless connections meant to satiate their mutual needs and little more. He'd hated it.

Jace dragged in another long smoke-filled breath. "Now you sound like her. Besides, it doesn't affect me as much as it would a human. You know that."

"What's going on with you and her, J? You're usually more focused than this."

Jace shrugged and blew out more smoke. "I don't know."

Sighing, David rested his elbows on his knees. "She's beautiful, and she's gotten under your skin."

Jace ignored him and flicked away his ashes. That much was obvious. They sat in silence for several minutes before Jace cleared his throat. "She's a wolf shifter."

"I know. So?"

"She's Rochester's packmaster, David. I hunt her kind for a living, you know that better than anyone, and she's one of the head honchos. How the hell am I supposed to do my job when I'm sleeping with the enemy?"

"It's not as cut and dried as that and you know it."

Jace chuckled. He held the cigarette out toward David, but the other hunter passed, and Jace stomped it out shortly after that. They sat in companionable silence. Nothing but the sounds of an occasional passing car, and a couple arguing from an upstairs apartment to disturb them.

"Since when have you cared about playing by the rules, J?" David asked, breaking the silence. "At the rate you're going, unless you bring this asshole's head to Headquarters on a silver platter, you're out, and even then, you better pray on bended knee that Damon can get the higher ups to have one forgiving bone in their bodies. You lied about your bloodline so you could be a hunter. Why start sweating the details now?"

"What are you saying, David?"

His friend cast him a hard stare. "I'm saying, you've risked everything for that woman, J. Don't lose her over this. Fight for her, or I promise someday, you'll regret it."

Jace ran a rough hand through his hair. "You talking about me or about you and Ally?"

David grumbled at the mention of his ex-fiancé. She'd been the one who got away, and Jace knew it still haunted the man. "Both? Does it matter? Its good advice. Listen or don't."

"When did you get so lenient about the guidelines, Mr. 'Be at the Meeting on Time and Don't Disrespect Damon'?" Jace mocked.

David crossed his arms, a grim look tightening his features. "Since Headquarters forced me to choose between my job and my friends."

Jace stubbed out his cigarette and clapped David on the shoulder. "Thanks for having my back."

David relaxed a little and leaned back against the door. "You owe me big-time. Like 'sacrifice your firstborn child' big-time."

Jace chuckled and offered David the flask from inside his coat.

David refused, but tapped his forefinger against the

metal. "Take a large shot of that before we keep talking. You aren't buzzed enough to discuss this yet."

Jace didn't need to be told twice. He swallowed three large gulps, nearly draining the flask dry. The warm liquid sloshed down his throat.

"You know that you seriously need to consider taking her offer, right? About learning how to shift?" David said.

Jace shook his head. "I can't, David. You know I can't."

David frowned. "No. I know you don't want to. There's no *can't* about it, J."

Jace shot him a glare and tightened his grip on the flask, wishing there was still whiskey in it. "You should know better than anyone that I can't, David. I refuse to be anything like that dirtbag piece of shit who was my father."

"I hate to say it, Jace, but forget your daddy issues for a minute and screw your head on straight. Shifting doesn't mean you're anything like your lowlife father. You're not a coward. You need to face any personal issues you may have and do this. The longer you wait, the more women that monster will slaughter. And the only way you'll be like your father is if you sit around and do nothing to save them." David slowly rose from the stoop and reached for the door.

Fuck. He was right.

Jace sighed. "You sure have a way with words."

David paused. "Being a closet book nerd all those years in high school came with a few perks, kept me golden in Allyson's eyes. She always loved it when I'd read the books she liked."

A smirk crept across Jace's face. "You were such a pansy back then."

"Bite me."

"Gladly."

He and David fell silent for a beat.

"I was in love with her, J. Hell, I still am. People do crazy things when they're in love. You're no different. So quit sulking and go be the man your girl needs you to be, whatever that may be." David stood like he planned to return inside, but instead, he lingered in the doorway, burning holes into Jace's back with his heavy gaze.

Jace stared at the concrete in front of him. The image of the victim's bodies, shredded and abused, was seared into his memory. Their faces would never leave. They'd had years of life ahead of them, families and loved ones to miss them. And so would any others who that bastard targeted. Yet here he sat, wasting precious time as he sulked about his pathetic issues and tried to preserve his own sanity. And for what? So he could spend the rest of his days alone, living like a drunken bum?

He hadn't let her walk away from whatever this...*feeling* was between them before.

Why let her walk away now?

Jace ground his cigarette butt further with his foot. "That was a shitty move, David, playing on a guy's emotions like that. But I'll do it." Then he mumbled a few creative profanities to show what he thought about that decision.

David laughed and stepped inside the building.

"We're leaving soon, for Headquarters. Get a plan together, before I change my mind," Jace yelled after him. Then he let out a long sigh. The killer knew who he was, had known right where to find them. Why had Robert bothered with him? Dared to show himself? Why would he want Jace's attention?

The bastard's cold blue eyes lingered in Jace's mind.

There was something familiar about them, but he couldn't place his finger on it.

A gust of cold wind slapped against Jace's back and sent

a shiver down his spine. He forced himself to remember the contorted look of rage on his father's face as he transitioned, stopping somewhere between man and wolf, the ripping sound his claws made as they tore into his mother's clothes. His eyes had been as cold as Robert's.

At only ten years old, Jace had wanted to carve out the man's heart with a dull-bladed knife. The bastard deserved a slow and painful death, and Jace hoped he'd had one. And now he was about to become a monster, just like his old man. He was all in now.

With both shifting and Frankie.

And if there was a God, Jace really needed his help.

THE DOOR TO the apartment creaked open, and Frankie shot to her feet from the chair she'd been perched in, scrubbing the worry away from her face and straightening her clothes as Jace stepped into the room. His gaze darted between her and Shane while David disappeared into the kitchen.

Not accusing. Just acknowledging the other man.

Shane cleared his throat. "I'll go downstairs and check in with Damon. David can go with me. I might've missed something when I was examining him earlier," he said coolly, cleaning his glasses with the edge of his shirt as he went.

David grumbled from the kitchen. "But I was just out—"

Shane hushed him, quickly ushering the other hunter outside despite David's muttered protests.

A moment later, the door closed and locked, and Jace leaned his weight against it.

He pointed over his shoulder with his thumb. "Shane is wicked smart, but kind of a nerd," he said. "A badass nerd."

She nodded. "Yeah, I noticed."

A long moment passed. Frankie stared at her feet, while Jace shoved his hands into the pockets of his jeans. She watched him from under her lashes. She tried not to imagine where the zipper of those jeans, where those pockets led. She blushed.

I shouldn't be thinking about him like that, especially now.

He was the first to break the silence. "I'll do it," he said.

She glanced toward him, hoping he meant what she thought he did. "Do what?"

"You know what I'm talking about. Do I need to spell it out? I'll learn how to shift."

Her shoulders relaxed. "You're serious?"

"No, I'm telling you this just for shits and giggles." He nodded. "Yeah, I'm serious. I can't let any more women die."

She wanted to run to his side, throw her arms around him and tell him he wouldn't regret it, but she didn't think that would go well, so she settled for plain and simple. "Good for you."

He pointed at her. "Listen. I'm not doing it for you, I'm doing it for those girls."

She sighed. "Can you stop hating me for just one minute?"

He turned away.

When he didn't respond, she stood and marched toward him. "I never wanted to lie, Jace. I'm not a liar."

He faced her again and his jaw clenched into a sharp angle. "No? Because it sure seems to me like you lied."

"I made a mistake, Jace. You held a gun to my head when we first met, and you expect me to think you wouldn't have killed me, hell, at least threatened me, if you'd known?" She dropped her hands to her sides. How could he not understand her reasoning?

He growled as if she'd insulted his manhood. "I don't kill women."

"Yeah, well I'm not a normal woman. I'm a wolf shifter, and you hunt women like me. Remember?"

He stepped forward, towering over her. If she'd been a weaker woman, she might have been intimidated, but the tenderness with which he touched her face stilled her. "I've never hurt a woman." He stepped away from her and moved to the other side of the room. He pulled aside the ugly flowered curtains and stared into the dark street. "And I'd never hurt you."

Frustration gripped her. How could she make him understand? "I know that now. How was I supposed to know that then?"

He closed the curtain. "You didn't seem to think I'd hurt you when you were lying in my bed."

Her breath caught. She bit her lower lip and swallowed down her hurt. She wouldn't let him see her hurt. "I am *not* a whore."

"I never said you were."

"You implied it."

He shook his head as he walked back toward her. "I'd *never* say that."

She covered her face with her hand and sighed. They couldn't keep doing this, pushing one another away, treating each other like enemies when in truth they were something more.

They had been since the moment they'd decided to sleep together. Hell, maybe even before. If she'd learned anything from this, it was that for once, she needed to be real with him. Admit the truth. Trust her instincts. As difficult as that may be.

She'd known that from the moment she'd seen the hurt

in his eyes, his pain at her admission she was packmaster. One of them had to take the first step.

Why not her?

Be brave, Frankie. Internally, she encouraged herself.

Why was it so hard to be real with him?

Perhaps it was because she was so used to hiding the real her with every man who'd came before, and even with her packmates. But Jace had seen through her from the start, hadn't he? Recognized the vulnerability that lay beneath her hardened exterior.

What would it hurt to show him that one time more?

She sighed. "Look, I know it was just one night for you, but for me." She struggled to breathe. "For me it was more."

Jace stared at her for a beat, and for a moment Frankie thought she might have been wrong in thinking he felt the same, but then a fast flash of relief crossed his face, before suddenly, he was on her. Her back hit the wall so hard all the air rushed out of her lungs, but she didn't care. Not now that she was in his arms. She gasped as he hoisted her ass up once again, pulling her legs around his hips. He ground his cock into her until she bucked against him. A wave of heat radiated through her core. Massaging his fingers against her spine, he cradled her. Pleasure coursed through her, hot and wanting, and she leaned into him.

Pent-up frustration radiated from him, yet his touch relaxed her. He tucked his head between her neck and shoulder. Inhaling her scent, he let out a low growl, before he slowly he ran the length of his tongue over her earlobe. "Fuck, it was more to me too."

Frankie couldn't form words.

"I've been dying to tell you, Princess, but I didn't know how." His teeth grazed the tender flesh, and she moaned. He dragged his lips down the skin of her ear, her neck, her shoulder, until he nibbled on her collarbone. His tongue swirled over her skin in sensual movements.

After several moments he pulled away. Before she could comprehend what he was doing, her panties were around her ankles and his thick cock was rubbing across her entrance.

"Do you want me?" He ground himself against her.

Every logical cell in her body screamed no. But her body said otherwise as she rocked her hips against him eagerly. "Yes," she panted.

Apparently, that was all the response he needed. He sheathed himself inside her, stretching her wide. She took every inch of him. He filled her completely, until she ached with the burn of it.

She breathed against his ear, tickling her breath over him, and his cock jerked. A feeling of hot need filled her, and she pushed her hips harder against his.

"Did you miss this?" He slid out and rubbed his length over her thin pink slit. "I did."

"I missed *you*." She shivered beneath his touch. "I missed all of you."

A smirk spread across his face, and he drove himself inside her again. She cried out as he pounded into her, each thrust sending electricity shooting through her.

As he rode her hard, he palmed her breast outside her shirt, then slipped his hand inside and under her bra. He circled each of her nipples, using his thumb and forefinger until they were hard and aching for his touch. Then he trailed his fingers over her skin, down the line of her abdomen, until he quickly found her clit. He rolled his fingers over her in sensual circles. The seat of her sex pulsated, and her body shook.

She slickened as he slid in and out of her with

increasing ease. Adrenaline raced through her veins as he claimed her. The sounds of his pleasure sent chills down her spine, and she inched closer and closer to climax.

She let out a deep-throated moan.

How had she not known what she meant to him?

She felt it in every touch, in every stroke, in every way he was tender with her, despite his strength.

"Do you like it when I take you deep like that?" He thrust into her again. "Make you mine?"

His body was heaven—her own little slice of divine bliss. She nearly laughed at her own thoughts as she watched him push inside of her. "Little" had nothing to do with it. Her body ached for him.

When she said nothing, he reached up and lightly tugged a strand of her hair. "You didn't answer me."

The small jolt sent waves of desire through her. She wanted him so badly, so...

"You still didn't answer my question," he whispered next to her ear. "Do you want to be mine?"

"Yes." She gasped and nodded. "You know I do."

He tugged on her hair again. "Yes, what?"

Her whole body tensed as she neared her peak.

"Yes...." She smiled and her eyes flashed to her wolf in challenge. "Sir."

Jace snarled his approval. "God, you're such a brat." He gripped her hair. "But I love it." Another feral snarl ripped from Jace's throat, and his irises flashed wolf-gold, almost like he had something else to say, but chose not to. He bared his canines and growled. "You're going to come for me, and then you're going to tell me just how deep you like it."

Frankie's heart pounded as he rubbed harder and harder against her clit with his fingers, never losing momentum as he thrust deep inside her. "Now, *Frankie*," he purred her name.

Hot ecstasy rolled through her as she reached her release at last. She shook against him as pleasure engulfed her body, consuming her until she couldn't take it anymore. Everything she was threatened to crumble to pieces beneath his skilled hands.

She gasped. "Jace, I want to be yours, but...I... I can't..." She tried to tell him she'd never felt this much pleasure before. That her body was so overwhelmed that she...

"I know you need time," he said. "Time enough for me to convince you. Build trust." He kept shoving into her, pounding into her flesh as he fingered her. Her whole body tensed as she felt herself climbing toward a second climax.

"Jace." She whimpered. It was too much and somehow not enough. A delicious kind of punishment. She felt like she was coming out of her own skin. Already she was shattering again, and she wanted him to come with her.

A low growl ripped from his throat. "Tell me you don't want me now and I'll stop. Let you run back to that goddamn fiancé."

She opened her mouth. A small moan escaped her lips.

"Tell me, Frankie."

She was acutely aware every time he used her name when addressing her. Words...words...why couldn't she find any right now?

He pushed against her with his chest, and she melted into his touch.

She *did* want him. No matter what he thought of her, she still wanted him.

"I don't want him." Closing her eyes, she tried to gather her thoughts. "I want you, Jace." She didn't want him to leave. Ever. Didn't want to hurt him again. Everything between them was happening so fast and yet, she felt it bone deep. It was real, a part of her. Finally, she breathed. "One night was never going to be enough."

"Fuck, it wasn't for me either, Princess."

His grip on her tightened, and she could feel his erection push against the soft skin of her pussy. He leaned his face into hers, and she fought hard not to gasp as his lips lingered dangerously close to her ear. His warm breath danced over her skin.

"Just stay with me," he whispered.

Tears pooled in her eyes again, but this time she didn't let them fall as she buried her face in his neck. "I wish it were that easy," she whispered back.

"Then let be," he said. "If only for tonight."

15

"You have *got* to be shitting me."

Jace let a long string of profanities rip under his breath, muttering into the darkness where he, Damon, and the other members of the Rochester division were now crouched outside Headquarters in the woods. Since Jace had last been here, security had increased tenfold. No doubt they'd likely found his lost phone and anticipated him coming.

Shit.

"Don't tell me you were enough of a dipshit not to expect them to up security?" Trent hissed. Despite the harsh question, the Jersey transplant cast him a wry smile from beneath his ball cap, his wide-toothed, grin visible through the darkness with ease.

Jace growled softly, his eyes flashing to his wolf.

He was *not* in the mood for Trent's goofing. Not tonight.

Not in the face of what they would soon be doing.

Breaking into Headquarters would put them *all* at risk. He'd warned his friends as much, but they hadn't listened, had refused to hear any of his reasons—or in Trent's words

—his self-sacrificing bullshit. They'd all been far too ready to put their lives on the line for him, and who was he to contradict that decision?

He'd already placed them in a tough enough place with this whole mess.

Beside him, Ash exhaled, low and easy, just short of a whistle. He shook his head slowly, the movement as loose and languid as his Cajun drawl. "Damn it, I'll never get used to that," he said, glancing to Jace's glowing gaze.

Trent snorted. "Ya think?"

Jace allowed his irises to change to their human form again. He was getting more used to making the change at will as of late. He wasn't sure whether or not he hoped that meant good things were to come when he tried to shift. He still wasn't exactly keen on the idea, but he'd go through with it. For his friends' sakes. For the sake of the victims. To ensure they didn't lose another innocent life to this senseless violence.

"Bite me," he grumbled at Trent.

"Gladly," Trent grinned, though his heart wasn't in it.

"Used to it or not, cut the shit," Damon growled from between them, his tone as cold as the frozen winter ground beneath their feet. "Both of you can it before one of the guards hears you."

"We're not within hearing distance," Jace said confidently.

The other men's eyes turned toward him in the darkness, the sound of his voice guiding them, though he could see all three of them clearly. He knew they couldn't say the same.

"They're talking about some stupid video game or something." Jace shrugged, gesturing toward the men who stood guard. Even from here, he could hear every word the guards said. Like he was standing beside them, or at the very least nearby.

Damon frowned. "You've gotta be joking."

"Hey man, video games are their own art form," Trent said, defensively.

"Says the man with a collection of comic books longer than my—" Jace's jab was cut short as Trent, unsurprisingly, cut him off with the push of a finger to his lips.

Jace growled.

"Leave my comics out of this." Trent's face went from joking to lethal in an instant. "You don't think you could have used that little hearing ability of yours during that shifter raid last month?" Trent had nearly broken an arm during that, and from the harsh look in his eyes, he was no longer amused. The hunter may have specialized in shifters as strange and diverse as he was wild, but that didn't mean he approached his position with anything less than deadly seriousness.

"No," Jace said, flatly. "You all would have lost your shit then, remember?" He glanced between the three of them pointedly. They may be by his side now, but he hadn't known whether they would have stood with him then, considering what he was. All the more reason he couldn't have stayed mad at Frankie. He understood, really. "Not to mention that would have taken away my chance to piss Damon off." He grinned as Trent smiled again.

The division lead had taken issue with the way he and Trent had rushed into the situation then, but what else was new?

This time, it was Damon's turn to growl.

Trent shot their division lead a questioning look. "You *sure* you're not a wolf shifter like Jace or something?" Trent lifted a dark brow.

From the spark of iced fury in Damon's eye, Trent had no doubt asked the same thing more than once before.

Damon's growl turned closer to a snarl. Nearly feral.

"What?" Trent made a face like he couldn't believe Damon found him irritating—Jace and Damon both. "Vampire hunter or not you can't blame me for asking when you keep snarling like that. Not to mention all this new shit with Jace."

"Shane and I are tired of listening to you four already," David's voice came over their earpieces.

Thanks to his now bum-leg, at Damon's orders, David had begrudgingly stayed behind in the van to help Shane man the CompHunt maps and the van's computers and satellite controller, while meanwhile Frankie had returned to her pack to give them a lead on what was happening, and to prepare should shit go down, which left Jace alone with their vampire hunter division lead, alongside a disgruntled Ash and a far too enthusiastic, Trent.

"Roger that," Shane added, clearly having wrestled the mic away from the exorcist again. Jace could practically hear the razor-sharp focus in the kid's voice, as he imagined Shane's gaze locked onto the computer screen, where he'd no doubt tapped into Headquarters security cams by now. Apparently, it wasn't enough that he already had a doctorate, but he had to go and be a literal genius when it came to computers and tech shit. It was disgusting, really.

"There's about to be a shift change in two minutes. Be ready," Shane warned over the comms.

Trent rubbed his hands together like Shane had announced he was getting him a new Star Wars t-shirt for his birthday. "Showtime."

"Ash, you're the look out," Jace said, not hesitating to take the lead.

It was *his* life they were dealing with after all. His name they needed to clear.

Damon cast Jace an annoyed glance, but didn't protest. The vampire hunter knew when to pick his battles, and as a leader, he played his cards closely. Damon wasn't in it for the glory or the power.

"You think you can handle it?" Jace asked Ash then.

Ash nodded, slow and steady. "I might not be able to tell you whether who I'm seeing is dead or living, but either way, I'll keep the eye out for you." He tapped the center of his forehead as if to indicate his sixth sense, the one that gave him his abilities as a ghost hunter.

Jace knew for a fact the Ragin' Cajun, as Ash's old division had nicknamed him, was more than a little... haunted by his own abilities. No pun intended. The native Louisianan was hardly ever without a drink in hand to keep the voices of the dead at bay, and coming from Jace, who knew by his own estimate that he drank like a fish, that was saying something.

"Just get us in there while Trent gets them stirred up a bit," Jace said.

Trent's grin was filled with unnecessary glee. "Distraction is my specialty."

"The amount of joy you take in that is concerning," Damon dead-panned.

"Says the man who keeps growling like a frigging cougar shifter," Trent quipped.

Damon's lip curled like he planned to address that, but Jace cut him short.

"Quiet," he hissed. "They're listening now."

The guards' conversation had fallen silent.

Damon nodded to Jace, giving him the go ahead.

Jace didn't hesitate to take it. "Your move, Jersey."

"Watch and maybe you'll learn something." Trent cast them all one last grin, before he slipped through the darkness—Jace sensed the man's movement through the trees—until he was positioned far enough away, so as not to expose their hiding place. Then without warning, Trent strolled out of the dark from the woods, suddenly covered in dirt to the point his face was unrecognizable, and to their collective shock, buck ass naked, as if he owned the place.

The guards' gazes locked onto the intruder's nude form in an instant.

"Evening, gentleman." Trent flashed that stupid, over-confident grin.

"That crazy motherfucker," Jace swore under his breath.

Damon muttered something that vaguely sounded like "shit" before he placed his head in his hand and groaned.

"*Laissez bon temps rouller*," Ash raised a flask beside them and chuckled at the sight of Trent's bare ass facing toward them in the distance and took a swig.

The guards' guns were pulled on Trent in all of two seconds, but if Trent was even slightly concerned for his own safety, he didn't act fazed by it. The hunter's eyes darted between the guards and the nine-millimeters in their hands, like he hadn't expected them to pull them that quickly, and he was estimating if he could outrun a bullet.

Not to mention, he was still naked.

Trent let out a slow breath. "Shit."

Abruptly, he darted back into the woods, hightailing it into the darkness again as if the hounds of hell were on his heels, though that area was more David's specialty.

"Please tell me he wore a bulletproof vest," the exorcist said over the in-ear mic.

"He wasn't wearing *anything*," Jace said.

"It's Trent," Damon answered grimly, his tone brusque

and tinged with fury, like he couldn't believe he'd somehow chosen *this* rag-tag group of men to form some kind of cohesive team. "He likely forgot it on purpose." The vampire hunter grumbled.

Jace clapped the division lead on the back. "They grow 'em different in Jersey."

Ash took another swig. "Swear he has a death wish," he crooned. "But it's impressive."

"Trent isn't who I worry about on that front," Damon shot back.

Ash's expression turned sour, but the ghost hunter didn't dare say anything or try to defend himself before the sound of the facilities sirens set in. A few minutes later and half the guards from Headquarters were out in the woods, searching for a very naked, and potentially armed Trent, combing the very woods they hid in.

"Now's your moment," Shane said over the headset.

Jace held his hand on the Mateba, prepared to have his gun at the ready if needed, as he, Damon and Ash ventured in.

Thanks to Trent's distraction, the guard tower was now unmanned. What would have been a glaring oversight on HQ's part, if it hadn't been for Shane hacking into the security cameras and placing a false feed on loop in order to let them in. Whoever was watching the gate from inside wouldn't even see them. No doubt the facility had gone on immediate lockdown, but what they didn't anticipate was someone having an active badge to key him in. David, God bless him, had maintained the peace of mind to nab one of the IDs off one of the Brooklyn division, before he'd hightailed it out of Jace's burner apartment.

He'd known he called the exorcist his closest friend for a reason.

At one of the side entrances, Jace pulled out the badge from his pocket. He placed it against the scanner with a grin toward Damon and a gruff mumble of "So much for rules." With this, HQ wouldn't be able to trace any of this back to them.

Unless they managed to get caught.

Jace tried not to think about that possibility as they ducked inside the building. The sound of Shane's voice ringing in unison in each of their ears.

"You have maybe ten minutes tops before they figure out I've hacked in."

"In other words, get a move on it," David grumbled from beside them.

"You don't need to tell me twice." Jace glanced toward Ash and Damon.

Ash nodded and separated off from them, heading toward the security room to serve as a lookout on the few screens Shane didn't have access to. Even a tech genius professor like their witch hunter couldn't be everywhere at once.

Alone with Damon, Jace continued his trek into the facility. The only sign of intelligent life from Ash over the earpiece. A few grunts as he took out whatever poor security guard happened to be in the control room over their shared feed.

For all the voices of the dead in his head that haunted him, the way Ash Devereaux could move undetected through a room was downright ghostly. Jace had heard a rumor once, long before he'd met his friend, that the Ragin' Cajun could do more than simply communicate with the dead, though he'd never had the chance to put that to the test. There was talk Ash had left the New Orleans E.U division because his fellow hunters had been too spooked by his abilities.

It was rumored he could move between planes. Not the skills of a simple mortal medium, but something more akin to a god of dead, though Ash was fully human as far as Jace knew, and Jace had never witnessed it for himself.

But he hadn't ever forgotten the rumor.

Not with the way Ash's eyes sometimes looked as if he always had one foot inside the grave.

"I'm in," Ash said over the headset. "Only took a blow to the head."

"Keep your eyes on the screens," Damon said.

"I've got you, *ami*," Ash drawled. "Incoming. On your right."

Jace and Damon ducked into an alcove, side-by-side, as they heard a set of footsteps hurry past.

"Clear," Ash said.

They continued on, making their way slowly, careful enough to not draw attention, but also heeding Shane's warnings that their time was limited. With Ash and Shane's guidance, there was no one in their way to inhibit them.

When they reached the first of the office suites, they ducked in. All they needed was one internal computer to gain access to Headquarters' main database, enough time for Shane to make a full download of their system, and for Trent to create enough of a distraction to keep the guards busy until they could to get the hell outta there. Then they'd be good as gold.

Easy enough, though it shouldn't have been.

Jace couldn't shake the feeling something, or maybe someone, was watching them.

It all felt too easy. Though who was he to look a gift horse in the mouth?

The thought sent gooseflesh prickling across his skin, despite that adrenaline coursed through him, making his pulse race. They needed to take care of this, and fast.

"Three minutes," Shane warned.

That was barely enough time. Shit.

But Jace couldn't allow himself to panic. Not now.

What the hell did he have to lose anyway?

Anything he'd already had, he'd lost. Save for the friends he'd made along the way.

Once he and Damon were safely sealed inside the office, Ash and Shane continued to keep guard muttering updates into their ears, whilst David let out the occasional grumble telling them to hurry the hell up. Jace wasn't saying it was David's Jewish upbringing that made him a worrier, but he also wasn't *not* saying it.

David himself had made the joke plenty of times before.

Jace sat down in desk chair, entering several passwords, that should have worked only to find them failing. "They've wiped all my codes." He wasn't certain why that should have surprised him. Of course, they had.

"Move out of my way," Damon grumbled, nudging him aside. Seconds later, the vampire hunter was logged in, using something other than his personal code.

He was inside the database within seconds as if...

Jace swore. "Holy fuck, you've done this before, haven't you?"

Damon shot Jace a look that was somewhere between *we'll discuss this later*, and *don't ever mention that again*, before he plucked the thumb drive from Jace's hand and loaded it into the computer. Once the drive was inserted, over their earpieces Jace could hear Shane's fingers flying across the keyboard as he raced to download the information.

"Shit," Ash swore. "Incoming."

"Who?" Damon growled, while Jace swore in unison. "Not now damn it."

"Trent's headed inside. The guards are hot on his tail."

"You've got to be shitting me," Jace said again.

"That wasn't part of the plan," Damon snarled.

"Plan or not, he's headed in, which means I need to get the hell out of the control room," Ash said, then a sudden rustle sounded on his end.

"Fuck, his mic went out," David said.

Damon swore. "Son of bitch."

"He'll get out of it," Jace assured him. "He always does."

"The guards are back in," David warned.

Which meant within less than two minutes, the entire facility would be searching for them. "Fuck!" Jace roared.

"Two minutes," Shane mumbled.

"We don't have two minutes. Do it in one!" Damon ordered.

As if in warning, the building's internal sirens suddenly rained down from overhead, an electronic female A.I voice bellowing out a repeated, "Breech. Breech. Breech" in time with the siren's whistles.

"Fuck!" Damon echoed.

Jace ripped the thumb drive from the computer just as Shane shouted, "Got it!"

Neither of them bothered to shut any of the open tabs before diving toward the door, but it was wrenched open from the outside at the same instant. A very naked, heavily armed Trent, stumbling in.

"Shit," Jace bellowed.

"What in the flying fuck, Trent?" Damon swore, as the other hunter slammed and locked the door behind him. A pounding immediately started on the other side of the door.

Jace's gaze fell to the heavy artillery in the other hunter's hands and then to his nude form. Trent hadn't been armed when he'd first created a distraction. "Where the hell did you store those?" he snapped.

Trent cast him a half-amused grin. "Don't ask."

Jace wrinkled his nose in disgust.

But another sudden thump brought him to his senses. The door was seconds from caving in.

"How do you get out of here?" That brilliant question came, of course, from Trent.

"Air vent," Damon said, already rolling the desk chair over.

"Me first." Trent stumbled forward.

"Hell no," Damon snarled, the chilled blue of his eyes downright frightening, despite that he then growled, "I am *not* having your naked ass in my face."

Had it been any other moment, Jace would have snorted at how Damon could say that with an entirely straight face, but the pounding at the door had only grown louder, causing the wood of the frame to bend in.

Jace pushed past the other two men. "Damon: second. You last. It's me they want." He shot a glance toward Trent, who had the gall to make a pouty face.

"Why?"

"Because Damon and I agree," Jace grumbled as he hoisted himself up and into the rafters. "Not to mention your sorry naked ass was supposed to lead them *away* from here."

"I had to get them off my tail somehow."

"And you ran to the very room we were in?" Damon barked, wild with frustration.

But Jace was already army-crawling his way into the tightened space. Fuck, he was not built for stealth. Damon and then Trent followed a moment later. He heard Trent replacing the vent just as the office door caved in.

Jace waited a moment, holding his breath as he waited for the sound of bullets, for the holes to pepper the metal sheet beneath him, before slowly, silently, they eventually heard someone close the door. They made their way through the enclosed space, not bothering to question it. But it wasn't until all three of them had dropped down onto the floor in an adjacent office space down the hall that Jace allowed himself to breathe.

"Couldn't they have at least pulled some badass Die Hard shit?" Trent faked a frown, before he smiled impishly.

"Fuck you, and your movie loving bullshit," Damon snarled.

Jace could scarcely believe that for once, *he* was the voice of reason. "Can it," he said, mimicking Damon. His eyes flashed to his wolf, and to his surprise, the sight seemed to spark some sense in his friends, because the other hunters fell silent then.

Together, the three of them made their way out into the hall again, nearly making it to the edge of the facility without incident, before Ash rounded a corner and collided with them.

Jace had never seen the ghost hunter move so fast.

"Chet," he panted. "Following."

"Shit." Jace shoved his friends toward the facility door ahead of him. "I'll handle it. Leave that asshole to me." No way was he letting them take the fall for this. Thankfully, the side-entrance had already closed behind them by the time Chet rounded the corner, his eyes darting straight to where Jace lay in wait in the hall of the old lab facility.

Anything to buy his friends time.

He was already up to his eyeballs in all this Headquarters shit.

What was one offense more?

Chet's dark eyes practically glimmered with unfettered hatred. In his own sick way, the bastard enjoyed this. "I thought I warned you that you're dead, McCannon." The region lead lifted his nine-millimeter, aiming it toward Jace, as Jace drew simultaneously drew the Mateba.

To think, he'd spent years out west but he'd had to haul his ass all the way back to the east coast to finally have a full on western shoot-out. Only Quinn Harper, his division lead back in Montana, would have found the humor in it.

Jace stepped forward, aim locked on Chet and unafraid. No way was this bastard getting to him again. "You see, Chet, the thing about threats is...you have to actually follow through with it." Jace fired at Chet without warning, causing the hunter to duck once more, but Jace surged forward, drawing again only once he was standing point-blank, barrel to the man's forehead.

"Give me your gun," he commanded.

Chet snarled, but a moment later, he handed the weapon to him.

Jace kept the Mateba steady, staring Chet down as he refused to move. His eyes flashed to his wolf. He wasn't about to kill a fellow hunter at point-blank range, but Chet didn't know that. Hell, if he knew why, but he couldn't do it.

Not when he'd once considered them on the same team.

Jace wasn't a monster. Not like his old man.

He never would be.

"Come at me or mine again and next time, I'll kill you for it."

"Is that a threat?" Chet sneered.

"No." Jace shook his head. "That's a promise."

Slowly, he backed toward the side-door. Chet's gun still in his hand. He lifted the nine-millimeter and gave it a little wave as he slipped out the door. "Thanks for this."

Before the door even shut behind him, Jace beat feet, running into the woods so fast his peripheral vision was a blur. He didn't stop moving until he was safely in the van. The sounds of the guards and the other hunters pouring from the facility in search of him followed.

"Drive!" he shouted, once David had slammed the van door behind him.

"*Please* tell us you offed Chet?" Trent made a set of praying hands like he was pleading.

Jace shook his head.

"What the fuck, Jace?" Trent whined.

At least someone had given him some goddamn pants.

Damon shot a silencing look toward them from the driver's seat as they all sped off. None of them spoke again until they were all sealed safely within Shane's office at the university, a location too public for HQ to follow. No way could they chance going back to division headquarters at this pace.

They were all perched in various stages of wait as Shane tapped away on his keyboard, until finally Jace said, "Well?" He was leaned against a bookshelf and from his position, it was hard to read what exactly the witch hunter's expression meant.

"It's not good news," Shane answered.

"When has it been good news lately?" Jace lifted a brow.

But something in Shane's expression turned dark. "I think you need to see this for yourselves." He twisted his computer screen toward them.

Jace scanned over the contents on the screen. Slowly, he tracked what Shane had been doing, piecing the puzzle together. Buried deep within Headquarters database behind several encryptions was another level of access code, something Jace or Damon, considering their seniority, *should* have had access to if it'd been official, and yet...

The internal memo read a recent date, identifying their division by name.

"Shit," Jace swore for what had to be the umpteenth time that evening.

"It gets worse. The split we've all been sensing in the organization is real. Several of the higher ups from Cronos have sold-out, bought into what appears to be some supernatural-targeting hate group. Essentially home-grown supernatural hating terrorists. Chet's one of them. Anyone not on their side or who hasn't been brainwashed into wanting to join their in-group is basically the enemy. Which makes someone who is both supernatural *and* a hunter, like you Jace, public enemy number one."

Shane shot a glance toward Jace. "They've been all talk up until now, but their first point on their latest memo detailed a coordinated attack to take out all the shifters on the east coast. Namely, Frankie's pack among a few others. In their minds, if they can reclaim the east coast as a shifter free territory, they can start taking out other supernaturals with a series of targeted hits."

"Those hateful fuckers," David swore.

"It goes further. Anyone within the Execution Underground that opposes them has been marked potentially dangerous—a person of interest to either convert, or eventually eliminate. And our division..." Shane looked toward Damon then, "...has been deemed a rogue brotherhood among the opposition."

"Christ," Ash swore.

"It will take me some time to figure out how deep this

fully runs, but if what I suspect is correct, this isn't just an issue here in New York. It's a problem with the whole organization. An organization-wide infiltration."

The muscles in Damon's throat writhed. "I had a feeling it might come to this."

Jace stiffened. "What are you talking about?"

"This has been brewing ever since the Cronos buy-out. It goes far deeper than one person." Damon cut him a harsh look. "You didn't think it suspicious when a corporation was suddenly allowed to purchase a government sponsored entity like the Execution Underground? If you think there's not dark money involved in his, think again."

Jace had thought it was suspicious, but some small part of him had hoped it was his own cynicism getting to him. "And you didn't think to tell us this?"

"We all have our secrets, Jace. You included." Damon's stare was so sharp it could cut. "And I needed to be certain. Announcing Headquarters was taken over by a hate group is a lofty accusation to make."

"And now?" Shane prompted.

"And now, I'm certain." Damon's expression turned grim. "Faced with all this," he said, "there's a choice to make." He glanced between them. "Stand with Headquarters or stand against them. We work to take them down from the inside. Together."

Jace blinked. He couldn't believe he was hearing this, let alone from Damon. "Are you suggesting we help tear apart the same organization we helped found?"

"Yes," Damon answered without hesitating. "Yes, that's exactly what I'm saying, Jace." He stepped closer. "We built it and it's our responsibility to end it now that it's rotting from the inside." Damon stuck his hand out between them. "Are you in or out?"

"I'm in." Trent threw his hand over top Damon's like they were Boy Scouts around a campfire. "Let chaos reign, baby!"

"Fuck, I'm in too." David put his hand on Trent's.

"Me three." Ash stepped forward.

"Shane?" Damon turned.

The professor shook his head. "I didn't bust my ass earning tenure to be afraid of some hate group. The course of history bends toward progress."

"In simple language?" Ash drawled at him.

Shane shrugged. "I'm in."

"Jace?" Damon lifted a brow.

Jace steeled himself, drawing in a long breath. He wasn't sure what made him hesitate, until finally, he sighed. "I was in the moment they held what I am against me, instead of favoring all that I've done." He stepped forward. "Fuck it. I'm in."

"Yes!" Trent hissed. "Avengers assemble." He wiggled his fingers like he was a kid.

Damon glared. "Don't ever fucking say that again."

It took several hours more of discussion and negotiating before Damon and the rest of the division finally came to an agreement about how this would work. When Jace finally exited Shane's office with David by his side, he couldn't help the optimism coursing through him. Maybe they *would* actually pull this off. Clear his name, and then take down Headquarters for better or worse. Weirdly, he was okay with it.

The past several days, he'd seen the darkest parts of what the Execution Underground had become. It wasn't something he wanted to be a part of, nor was it the dream he'd planned, but the plan he and his friends had formulated in its place was.

Hell, it just might make a fucking difference.

That's all he'd wanted back in those early days. Back when he and Damon and Quinn and others like them had been out for vengeance for their families' sakes.

All he'd ever really wanted was to make sure nothing like that ever happened again.

To protect others from his own brand of pain he'd experienced. At the abandonment of his supernatural old man. Ensure no shifter ever hurt a helpless human woman like his mother again. Or a defenseless child like he'd been.

"What's going through your head right now, J?" David asked, suddenly interrupting his thoughts. They were headed to the other side of the university, where Jace had parked the Chevelle leading up to all this. Jace grinned. He had half-a-mind to tell David to park himself on a bench and he'd drive the car to him, considering he was still dragging that leg of his and would be for a while, but he didn't think being coddled was something his friend would appreciate.

"Just thinking it'll be like the old days again," he said.

"It will be," David agreed. "But there's a storm coming, J. We need to be prepared for it."

Jace knew that. Had felt it in the past few days more than most, but as he and David headed toward the Chevelle, to K9s, the club where Frankie had said she'd wait for him, he couldn't bring himself to stamp down his own optimism.

16

Frankie had insisted on accompanying Jace and the other hunters to Headquarters, but deep down, she'd known she couldn't risk it. Not when she'd been skirting her second in command for days, leaving the pack's management in his, albeit capable, hands while she'd handled this quickly escalating...situation. But that didn't mean she didn't owe him and her inner circle an explanation, and her time, especially considering what she was about to spring on them.

Frankie exited her Mazarati, silently tossing her keys to the valet as she donned her packmaster face. She'd never show any hint of vulnerability here. Striding to club's front entrance, her black stilettos clicked against the damp pavement. The five-inch Jimmy Choos were far more comfortable than they looked same as the strapless black minidress she wore, but when she was here, she needed to impress.

As packmaster, she had to be capable of the power plays every male before her had been, but she also had to do it in heels.

The line outside the club leading down to the basement

entrance snaked around the building. A sign of the establishment's trending popularity among the supernatural community. Among her own, it'd been a controversial decision to open K9's exclusive doors to outsiders, to non-shifters, but the immediate influx of money it'd brought to the pack's then dwindling funds had spoken for itself. She'd never once regretted the decision. Until tonight.

She really needed fewer eyes watching.

She cut around the waiting patrons to the chorus of a few disgruntled mutters, and descended below, to where pack security anticipated her.

"Packmaster," Aidan purred, dropping his eyes to the ground before her.

She placed a tender hand on his cheek, then slid the back of her knuckles across the other side, marking him with her scent. "Aidan." She smiled.

The bodyguard unclipped the velvet rope for her, before he opened the door. As she entered, Frankie paused near his ear, whispering to him. "There'll be some hunters from the Execution Underground here in plain clothes, unarmed, later tonight. Have Tiberius bring them in through the back. Straight to me."

Aidan's eyes widened at the mention of hunters, but he didn't protest. "Yes, packmaster." He nodded dutifully.

She placed an affectionate hand on his cheek again, patting him gently, before she slipped inside.

The red neon lights which lit K9's interior cast an ethereal, otherworldly glow, instantly transporting its patrons to another world. One where sin, and sex and money interplayed with greed, where the monsters that ruled Rochester's nightlife took literal form amongst the shadows, circling, dealing and wheeling their unique brand of vice.

And where *she* was their queen.

The club's patrons parted for her, instantly recognizing, not who, but *what* she was. The vicious ruler of this dark, glittering kingdom. A supernatural mafia queen.

She snaked her way to the bar where Allyson, her Fae head bartender, was busting her ass to get out a round of flaming, neon drinks.

Frankie leaned over the bar and whispered into the other woman's ear, the pulse of the club's thumping music drowning her speech. "Hate to interrupt, but..."

The Fae bartender immediately paused what she'd been doing, turning a pointed ear toward her.

"Two hunters will be here tonight. Maybe more."

Allyson stiffened, though Frankie wasn't certain why. The Fae weren't often targets for the Execution Underground, their glamour allowing them to blend in easily among humanity. Save for their beauty.

"They're welcome here," she continued. "Make sure the staff knows."

Allyson nodded, silently returning to her task while whispering to another member of the wait staff. The whole of K9s servers would be aware of the situation in a matter of minutes. The knowledge of the pack's leadership would soon follow.

That would be a tougher conversation, but one she was prepared for.

Satisfied, she made her way toward the stairs. She moved about the club with uninterrupted ease. To any patron, she was just another beautiful woman, but to the monsters in the dark who waited...

They knew better than to disturb their queen.

Not until she was ready for them.

Climbing the stairs, which led to her office, she escaped the stifling noise. As she approached, she passed her secretary, Jeanine's, open door. At the sight of her, Jeanine's eyes widened and she scrambled from behind her desk, scurrying into the hall.

"Packmaster," she breathed.

Frankie reached her office and scowled at the crack in the door which indicated it'd been left open. She pushed through it as she said over her shoulder, "Jeanine, what have I told you about leaving my door..." Frankie's words trailed off, her directive cut short at the sight of the wolf who sat across from her executive chair.

Amarok "Rock" Saila. Newfound packmaster of the Toronto white wolves.

And for all intents and purposes...

Her fiancé.

"Packmaster," Jeanine squeaked from behind her. "I tried to tell him to wait in the meeting room, but—"

"Not now, Jeanine," Frankie said curtly.

She cast the other she-wolf a cursory glance, a look that clearly said she'd address the oversight later. Once Jeanine was dismissed, Frankie promptly closed the door.

The moment the latch clicked into place the available space in the room shrunk considerably, until breathing became a chore, but Frankie didn't dare show it.

"I hear you've been quite the absent ruler as of late." Rock swirled the whiskey in his tumbler glass, dark eyes watching her, considering. The first several buttons of his shirt were open, to where she could see the white wolf paw tattoo, which marked his pack affiliation, against handsome russet skin. His heritage was Inuit, or so he'd told her at one of their last meetings. Many of the white wolves were.

"Absence makes the heart grow fonder." She shrugged dismissively. "And I don't think you came here to criticize how I run my pack."

"Criticism was never my intent." Rock smiled at her. A flash of white canine teeth. "Consider it observation. Nothing more."

Frankie crossed the room and stood behind her desk. "You could have warned me you were coming."

"I had Henrik send word to Alejandro two nights ago."

Two nights ago...

Frankie nearly winced. When she'd conveniently ignored her second's calls and smashed her phone to bits. It felt as if a lifetime had passed since then.

She placed a hand on the cool leather of her executive chair. "What brings you here, Rock?"

Rock had the balls to look amused by that question, though she didn't think offense was his intent. "When my fiancé's in trouble, what kind of man would I be if I didn't come to your aid?"

She lifted a brow. They both knew he was nothing to her... yet.

"I hear you have a killer on your hands." He swirled his whiskey, inhaled the scent. "Not to mention the human hunters are circling."

"I'm handling it." Frankie's red nails tightened against the chair's leather, digging in. "What I do is none of your concern."

"You're right. It isn't." Rock met her gaze, unafraid. Why would he be? They were equally matched in both influence and power. "Until our packs combine, and then..." He raised his glass to her, before setting it on her desk. "Then it will be my concern, packmaster."

"If you have something of actual interest to discuss, Rock, best get to it," she said, stiffly. Frankie didn't dislike the white wolf. She wouldn't have agreed to their arrangement otherwise, but that didn't mean she wanted him here. Especially now, of all times.

"I'll get to the point, then." Rock sat back, crossing one long leg over the other. "I'd like to move forward with our mating-ceremony. Post-haste."

For a moment, Frankie stiffened, before she quickly recovered herself. She covered it by sitting down in her chair. Their mating ceremony wasn't supposed to be for another year, but now he wanted to move it forward? To a new date? "Why the sudden rush?" she asked.

"Considering the threat you and yours are facing should this killer's..." Rock paused momentarily, as if he were trying to find a diplomatic description, "more unsavory actions fall back on you, you don't find it wise to have a plan in place? What will stop the Execution Underground from coming for you?"

"I already told you." Frankie leaned back in her seat, feigning ease. "I'm handling it."

"And you could handle it with considerable more ease, with more wolves at your disposal," Rock countered. He wasn't wrong, and from the confidence in his face, he knew it. "I'm trying to help you, Frankie. That's all this means." He reclaimed his whiskey glass. "Consider it an early mating gift." He lifted the glass to his lips and took a considerable sip.

Frankie watched him for a moment. Rock was handsome, powerful, and, in his own way, considerate. He'd make a fine mate for somebody. Somebody who was more enthusiastic about the idea than her. Someone whose heart didn't belong to another.

Frankie shook the thought from her mind. She was being silly. She didn't want to be mated to Rock any sooner, but she saw the logic in it.

It wasn't the right decision for her, but it *was* the right decision for her pack, and though the idea grated on her, she couldn't ignore the fact that he was coming to her aid, offering her help in the only way he knew how. There were poorer ways to start a partnership. She couldn't very well be angry with him for it, and yet...

She swallowed down her pride.

Her growing feelings for Jace weren't Rock's problem.

If he was even aware of it, which she'd make sure he wouldn't be.

"Wait for me in my private booth," she said then. "Jeanine will take you there and we'll discuss this further."

Rock nodded amiably, rose, and headed toward the door.

"And Amarok," she said. "When we *do* join packs, do not think for even a minute that I'll kowtow to you and your leadership." She cast him a hard stare. "Your pack will be mine too."

Rock smiled like he was pleased. "I never anticipated anything less, my queen."

Amarok exited the room then, as Alejandro entered in behind him.

Once more, the door closed with a quiet snick of the lock.

"Why didn't you tell me he was coming?" Frankie hissed.

"I tried to warn you," Alejandro said, a little too defensively for her tastes.

"Your text asked if I was okay. Not 'by the way, packmaster, the fiancé from your arranged marriage is heading this way.'"

"Clearly, you didn't see my later texts."

"My phone broke." She didn't deign to tell him that she'd been the one to break it.

"Have Jeanine order you a new one." Alejandro waved a hand. "One with more obnoxious notifications to ensure you answer," he added with a sly grin.

"I don't answer, because I trust you to handle the pack in my absence." Frankie looked toward him then, challenging. "I've never been gone when you truly needed me."

Alejandro nodded his agreement. "I know."

"I'll need you there for this meeting." She nodded to the door, to indicate where Rock had exited, only moments ago. "For moral support."

"And this situation with the hunter?"

Frankie stared down at her desk, at the pile of paper's that had accumulated there. "I'm handling it."

"You reek of him," Alejandro commented.

"That better be observation, not judgment, Alejandro," she snapped.

Alejandro shook his head. "Never."

Frankie breathed out a long sigh. "He needs help shifting, and I've offered to give it to him."

Alejandro's eyes widened. "And his division? How do we deal with them?"

She'd anticipated this question, but still, the lack of trust in her decision grated. "There's a rift within their organization. His division is with him. I'll fill you in on the rest of the details later this evening."

"You mean to tell me that this...hunter, and his team are on our side?"

"Yes," she nodded. "For now." She shuffled the papers together into one organized pile. "The killer targeted my apartment."

Alejandro's expression tightened. Eyes flashing to his wolf in protective rage. "And you didn't think to *tell* me?" he hissed.

"It's been less than forty-eight hours, Alejandro." She pegged him with a sharp stare. "What *exactly* could you have done about it?"

The harsh question seemed to leash him and his frustration with her, at least for the moment.

"The killer isn't a wolf," she continued. "Not a regular one anyway. We already knew that, but now he's made himself known, shown us his face. He knows I've been working with Jace."

"Jace." Alejandro rolled the wolf hunter's name around on his tongue. "You speak of this hunter as if you know him."

"I *do* know him. Intimately." Frankie didn't dare glance away. She wasn't ashamed. Why should she? Her body was her own, to do with as she pleased. Even if her hand in marriage wasn't. "As you've already pointed out tonight."

Alejandro glanced away to hide his embarrassment, his shame.

"We've had this discussion already, Alejandro. You'll defer to my judgment on this." Frankie glared. "Don't make me keep asking."

"Of course, packmaster." Alejandro nodded, dropping his gaze again. "But at least, tell me he treats you well. This...Jace." He said Jace's name almost as if it was a strain for him.

She smiled a little. Though he was her second-in-command first and foremost, Alejandro was ever her friend, her trustworthy confidante.

"He treats me better than any other man I've ever been with," she said, softly. "He's rough around the edges, but underneath it." Her friend met her eyes then. "He's tender, Alejandro, truly. A wolf befitting of our species if there ever was one." Her features softened. "He just doesn't know it yet."

Alejandro nodded his approval. "Just be careful, considering..."

He didn't need to finish his sentence for Frankie to understand his meaning.

Considering the white wolf packmaster waited for her below stairs.

"You know I will be." She plucked a pen from her desk and opened her laptop, pointedly. A clear dismissal. "I always am."

Alejandro left her office then, leaving her in peace as he no doubt disseminated updates to the rest of the pack's leadership on her behalf, minus the intimate details of what was happening between her and Jace, of course. She still wasn't certain what she planned to do on that front, especially now that Jace had laid all his cards on the table, admitted he wanted more than a single night with her, a chance at a relationship.

She wanted that too, if she was honest with herself, but she was stuck between her own needs and her commitment, her leadership.

She couldn't walk away from her deal with Rock so easily. Their intent to combine packs was a strategic move, meant to prevent them from being swallowed up by the massive operation that was the Grey Wolves. Her parents, her ancestors, who'd run this city, their territory which expanded from the downtown of Rochester all the way to the Adirondack foothills, would turn over in their graves at the mere thought of bowing down to other leadership.

They'd built this city. Made it their home.

That wasn't something she could erase away. Her pack had a history here, a purpose.

There had to be a solution. She…just hadn't found it yet.

Either way, exiting her agreement with Amarok wouldn't be easy. She didn't intend to make an enemy of the Toronto white wolf pack, which meant she was stuck. Trapped, really. And she couldn't ask Jace to continue to be her lover, something akin to a male mistress. That wouldn't be fair to him. Or herself. And now that she was here, returned to the sanctuary of her office and among the safety of her pack, she wasn't certain she could continue this.

Keep putting her deal with Amarok at risk, all because she wanted Jace.

She'd been selfish, foolish over the past several days. Alejandro hadn't needed to say it. She'd already known that the reality of what and who she was would come back to haunt her.

She hadn't anticipated it'd be her, rather than Jace to slam on the breaks between them.

She slumped into her executive chair, feeling her spirit deflate, but nevertheless, she got to work, as all powerful women did, as every packmaster had before, tending and caring for everything that'd gathered on her desk while she'd been away.

Amarok could wait.

She tackled anything remotely urgent first, Jeanine filling her in on the details from while she'd been away. Then she set about tasking the secretary with finding a cleaning crew that could discretely restore her apartment, answered a few necessary emails, ordered a new phone, and then finally, made her way downstairs.

It wasn't an awful night, but the work was tiring, tedious, and considering Amarok's unexpected arrival and the topic she planned to discuss with him, she couldn't see how the evening could get any worse. Until she arrived at her private booth, Amarok lounged back against the plush cushions, a fresh drink in his hand, and Jace sitting across from him in wait.

For a moment, all she could do was blink. She wasn't certain, which of the men to address first, but from the subtle, murderous glint in his eye, she decided on Jace.

"The wait staff was supposed to bring you straight to my office," she said.

He cast a cursory glance toward her. "That'd require them to know I'm here."

She lifted a brow. "How did you get in?"

"The usual way." He leaned back in his seat, propping his arms over the back of the booth. He said it as if he'd been here a dozen times before.

She'd have to have a talk with Aidan about that.

"And David?" she asked.

Jace chuckled. "Pretty sure he's chasing down that bartender of yours. The blonde. Allyson." Jace nodded toward the bar.

"Allyson?" she repeated. How did Jace know...

In an instant, Frankie put two-and-two together.

K9's head bartender, Allyson O'Hare, a Fae woman who Frankie also considered her friend, had disclosed in her initial interview for the position over a year ago that she'd been previously engaged to an Execution Underground hunter, once upon a time. Frankie hadn't thought much of it then, other than concern for what it could mean for the pack's safety should the two get back together. But Allyson had assured her it'd been a long time ago, a high school sweetheart gone wrong situation, and that there was no chance of the two reconciling.

"You mean David is..." Frankie's voice trailed off as Jace

nodded. "Well, that's a development I wasn't expecting." Rochester's underground was a small city, she supposed.

"And neither was this," Amarok said, his presence suddenly coming between them.

Frankie glanced between the two men, more aware than ever that she'd need to use... subtlety if she expected to navigate whatever this situation with the three of them was.

"Rock," she said sternly, "allow me to introduce you to—"

"We've met," Jace said, cutting her off.

The wolf hunter was full of more surprises than she knew. Another way she'd underestimated him.

She glanced between them then. "Please tell me you're not—"

"Enemies?" Rock finished for her with a lift of a brow. He set his drink down on the table. "No. I don't share drinks with any man I have the intention of cutting down."

Frankie had no doubt he would then. Cut his enemies down, that is. With his pack, his friends, Rock was amiable, considerate, but among his enemies he had a reputation that could only be described as fierce, ruthless. Any newfound packmaster had to be.

"But we're not exactly friends either," Jace offered, interrupting her thoughts. "Are we?" he said to Rock.

Amarok only smiled at that.

Now that she knew there was a history between them, Frankie supposed it made sense. She'd known Jace had been previously assigned out west, and until recently, when Rock taken over the last independent white wolf pack in Toronto, he'd been a valued mercenary for the Yellowknife Pack, a larger clan of white wolf shifters close to the Grey Wolves territory.

"Small world," she said tersely.

She was eager to get the two men separated in any way possible, before this situation quickly went from bad to worse. Sticky. Tricky. No matter what adjective she used, she didn't foresee this interaction ending well.

"Rock here was just telling me about your plans to move up your impending nuptials," Jace said, immediately dropping a proverbial bomb on those plans.

"Mating ceremony," Rock corrected.

"It's all one and the same though, isn't it?" Jace cut back.

"I suppose." Rock took a sip of his drink, holding Jace's gaze. "Either way, she'll be my wife."

Frankie watched Jace's jaw tense enough she feared he might crack one of his own teeth, but he didn't dare say anything, didn't try to argue that she was his.

Frankie wasn't certain why that...irked her.

She shouldn't be disappointed in him that he didn't fight for her, claim her as his. She had no right to be, but somehow, she couldn't escape the feeling, though she didn't dare show it.

"It's something we were planning to discuss," she said, quickly in a poor attempt to appease him, and also to get Rock in line. "We haven't come to any agreements yet."

"In any case," Jace said, "my congratulations to you both." The look he cast toward her then was cutting, his frustration barely leashed.

She hadn't known he had it in him to be so...cold.

It was impressive, really.

And only reminded her that she was really just beginning to know him.

Despite the bone deep longing that coursed through her every time she looked at him.

"It's good to see you made your way east again," Amarok

said to Jace, placing his drink on the table in a clear dismissal. "My old pack grew tired of evading you."

Jace huffed, though he wasn't amused, clearly. "No wolf has to evade me if you play by the rules. My job's to protect humanity. That's all."

Frankie once would have debated him on that point, but now that she knew him, she knew it was true. For him at least. "Are you two done posturing here?" she asked. "I'm growing bored quickly." It's something she never would have said had she and Jace been alone, had she been allowed to be her true self, but they weren't alone, and she had an image to maintain.

She'd never be her true self when she was here.

Only a more glittering vicious version of it.

"No posturing involved." Rock smiled a genuine grin. "I'm actually quite fond of your friend, Jace."

"The feeling isn't mutual," Jace dead-panned.

"Jace," she said, a little colder than she intended. "Can you give us a minute?"

The glance he cast toward her then reminded her far too much of the man she'd met in that darkened alley. "It's good to see you again, Amarok. I wish you both the best, truly." Jace's harsh eyes fell to her on that last word, and a shiver ran through her.

Amarok raised his glass toward him.

Then before she could get another word in, Jace was gone, having disappeared into the din of the club. He lived up to his reputation fully. Had earned her people's fear. She needed to remember that.

"So how long have you been sleeping with him?" Amarok asked.

Frankie sputtered. "Excuse me?"

Rock waved a hand, as if to indicate he didn't care.

"What you do before we are mated makes little difference to me." He picked up his glass again. "But once we are mated," his dark eyes pierced through her, "I won't be so amused by it."

Frankie wasn't intimidated by him in the least. "And until then, I expect you to keep your opinions about me, my personal life, and how I run my pack to yourself."

Amarok smiled again. "I meant it when I said I like him, truly, but a hunter is not for a packmaster like you, Frankie, and you know it."

"Apparently, I didn't say it clearly." Frankie stood tall, looming over him. "Whatever your opinion is of me, of Jace. I expect you to keep to you yourself." Her eyes flashed to her wolf. "Starting immediately."

"Duly noted." Rock nodded with a lift of his glass. "You'll make a formidable leader to my people, Frankie. I don't regret the choice." She knew he said it for her benefit, to keep things civil between them, but somehow, it didn't appease her.

"Of course you wouldn't." She knew her worth, her value, and she let it show in every way. In how she held herself, how she spoke to him, how she looked. She was a powerful wolf in her own right, and she wouldn't soon allow him to forget it.

She slid into the booth across from him. "Now, I believe we had a date to discuss."

17

J ACE STORMED OUT of K9's and into the street, his heart pounding like a construction worker's jack-hammer, each blow heavy and fast.

Not just a fiancé, but a wolf he fucking *knew*.

Another packmaster. A respected warrior among his kind, and from all Jace had gathered on Rock over the years, a decent man. Someone who would be more to her than an arranged marriage, someone who would treat her well. Jace wanted that for her, wanted her happiness—how couldn't he?—but somehow it'd been...easier when Rock hadn't had a name, a face. When Jace still had a hope she wouldn't forget him, that she'd be with someone she could never love.

Someone who wasn't him.

Love.

The word slammed around in his head and he swore. What the hell was wrong with him? He paced, cursing under his breath. Sure, they'd slept together, promised each other it'd meant something more than the single night they'd agree upon, but bottom line? She was still *engaged*. Not only had he messed up before he'd known, but then he'd fucked her again once he had known. Had thought he could convince her to end the engagement.

What kind of man did that make him?

Clearly, one who didn't deserve her. She hadn't even been able to acknowledge what she was to him. How many times was the universe going to stick it to him?

"You gotta be fucking kidding me!" Jace yelled.

A woman passing by on the other side of the street clutched her purse tighter and sped up her pace.

Jace growled. "I don't need this." He pulled a cigarette from his pocket and lit up. The smoke filled his lungs, but didn't calm him. How could he calm down when faced with this guilt inside him? She was perfectly willing to sleep with him, but she couldn't even admit who he was to her, not to mention she was promised to someone else.

Adrenaline pumped through him, and he flexed his free hand into a fist at his side. He'd made a total idiot of himself, thinking for even two seconds that he could win her. Dumbest idea he'd ever had. What a fool he'd been to think she had real emotions for him. He wasn't one of them, and he never had been.

Never would be.

He sighed and blew out a puff of smoke. "Of course, I'm not one of them either." His gaze darted to the human woman scurrying away in the distance. All sense of the belonging he'd felt among his friends, his brothers in arms, drained from him.

"You're not what?" a male voice said from behind him.

He turned to find David leaning up against the brick building.

Jace ran his fingers through his hair. "Nothing."

"Well, something's up with you."

Jace raised a brow. "You're one to talk. You look like shit."

"Thanks for the compliment, Sugarplum."

Jace shrugged. "Any time. So what happened in there? You went running off like a bat outta hell." The moment David had spotted K9's bartender, he'd beat feet without so much as an explanation.

David shook his head. "You saw. Allyson was here. What about you?"

Jace took another drag on his cigarette. "You go first."

Jace watched as David stuffed his hands in his pockets and stared up into the dark sky. You could never see the stars in Rochester. Every night, the lights from the city obscured them. That was one thing Jace missed about Honeoye Falls. About his time out west, too.

"David, how come you never told me the ex you're still hung up on is a werewolf?"

David shook his head. "Because she's not. She a bartender here now. I guess she wanted to work with other supernaturals."

"What do you mean 'other supernaturals'?" Jace lifted a pointed brow.

David sighed. "She's Fae. Half pixie, specifically."

Jace cleared his throat. "Excuse me?"

"You heard me."

"Pixies? You're in love with a damn pixie?" He lit another cigarette and took a hard drag. "What is the world coming to?"

"Most of them still live on the Isle of Apples. You know, Avalon. It's hidden off the coast of Scotland. So when her mother passed away a few years back—her mom was full-blooded—Allyson didn't have any other faeries around. Your girl hired her here, sort of let her join their pack, even if she's not a wolf shifter."

Jace raised his eyebrows. He couldn't believe what he was hearing. "That's wild."

David rolled his eyes. "Tell me about it."

A moment of silence passed before Jace cleared his throat. "She's not my girl, David."

David scoffed. "Oh, shove it, Jace. Just because she's a wolf shifter, that doesn't mean—"

"She's engaged. Arranged mating."

David's eyes widened. "What?"

Jace nodded. "You know that wolf I was waiting with? Amarok? She's set to be mated to him. It's like their equivalent of marriage. Bastard flat out said she was going to be his wife."

David fiddled with the collar of his shirt, like he couldn't find enough room for his neck. "I'm sorry, J. That's rough."

"Nothing to be sorry for. But I don't know how I'm gonna work with her now." Jace watched his smoke climb toward the sky.

David scanned him up and down as if he'd grown ten extra heads. "What do you mean, you can't work with her?"

Jace paused. He glanced at David but didn't respond. He didn't want to get into this discussion.

"No. No." David shook his head. "You still have the hots for her after all that?"

Silence stretched between them.

"That's rough, J. But you can handle it. You didn't know she had a fiancé or a mate or whatever."

"At first," Jace corrected.

David winced.

Jace flicked his ashes. "It was easier when he didn't have a face or a name."

David nodded. "I get that, but past mistakes don't mean you can't change course now. So deal with her on a business level only. Hands off. Doesn't matter if you're attracted to her. You can think she's the greatest woman to walk this earth, just keep it in your pants and you'll be fine."

Jace rolled his eyes. "You always did have a way with words."

"Tell me something," David said. "What does this woman mean to you?"

Everything.

Though Jace didn't allow himself to say it. The beast inside him stirred.

"More than I want her to."

Damn if that wasn't the truth.

David nodded. "Then fuck off with your sense of guilt about her having a fiancé. Is she in love with him?"

Jace shook his head. "No. No, she's doing it for her pack."

"Then don't let her cast you aside so easily, J. Like I told you before. Fight for her. Be the man she needs you to be. If you are, she'll change her mind about this Rock guy, and if she doesn't, then well...it wasn't meant to be."

The beast inside Jace snarled at that possibility, but he didn't indulge it. He was getting better at keeping it in check, but hearing Rock say Frankie would be his wife had nearly unleashed it. Full fury.

"Meant to be, huh?" Jace cast a glance toward David. "What are you now, a psychic?"

David chuckled. "No, just been listening too much to my *bubbe.*"

Jace was about to respond when the door to K9's burst open and Frankie strode smoothly out into the street. Her eyes locked on him, making her look every bit the powerful packmaster she'd been inside the club. Great, just as he was starting to calm.

She made her way toward him, heels clicking. "Jace, we need to talk."

"You don't need to explain anything to me, Frankie. Believe me. I get it."

"I meant about the raid on HQ," she said, "that's what you came here for after all, to share what you found, how it relates to Robert."

Jace shrugged her off. "Later."

Her sharp stare cut through him, seeing too much. "Jace, Rock and I—"

Jace lifted a hand. "Give it a rest. I saw everything I needed to see in there." Jace cast her a dismissive glance. "You're all his."

"Jace," David hissed.

Fight for her. His friend's advice rang in his ear.

Frankie opened her mouth again, but Jace raised a hand. "I'm done with this drama. Unless you have something to tell me that will lead to catching Robert, I don't want to hear it."

Even in the dark, he could see her stiffen. "Well *I'm* not done with it," she challenged.

Over her shoulder, David lifted a brow as if to say: *See? Told you.*

Maybe David was right.

He couldn't fold the first moment the going got tough. When had he ever let that stop him before? He may not have had much experience competing when it came to women—hell, he'd never had to—but all the same, he knew how to play the game. How to best an opponent in a power play. How was this any different?

The only change was this time it was more than his life at stake.

He'd almost allowed himself to retreat at the first sign of

trouble, because his heart was on the line, but he'd already known it wouldn't be easy the moment he'd admitted he was all in with her.

Why not take the risk?

"If we're going to start training tomorrow, we're going to discuss this," Frankie said, undeterred. "Now."

Jace frowned, but this time, his resolve remained intact.

If she wanted a fight, he'd give it to her.

Even if she didn't realize it was *her* he was fighting for.

Looking completely unperturbed, David smiled a little, like he recognized what was going through Jace's head and said, "Well, have fun, you two." He clapped Jace on the shoulder. "Call me when you need a drink, J, or when you learn how to shift, whichever comes first." Then he limped down the road to the garage where he'd parked his car, since he wasn't going to be riding his motorcycle for a while with the condition his leg was in.

Jace stubbed out his last cigarette, turning toward Frankie as if he didn't have a care in the world. If she wanted to play, he'd play, but he wouldn't make it easy on her. Not by a long shot.

When a silent beat passed between them, Jace shoved his hands in the pockets of his leather. "You wanted to talk. Talk."

"What kind of game were you playing at in there?" She gestured toward the club.

Jace lifted a brow. "I don't know what you're talking about, Princess."

"Really?" She placed her hands on her hips, glaring. "Congratulating me and Rock, like I mean nothing to you?"

Jace ducked his head for a moment, glancing at the ground while he stifled a smile. David knew his way around women. Jace would hand him that. He saw what David meant clearly now. She didn't want to marry Rock. She was just scared. Scared of what the consequences of leaving her agreement with the other packmaster would be, and it was his job to convince her. Fight for her until she couldn't walk away. Because he sure as hell wouldn't.

"Is that what you want? Is that what you would have wanted me to do? Fight for you?"

She glanced away, but didn't answer.

Fuck, if she wasn't as stubborn and fierce as he was.

"Is that what you want from me, Frankie?" he asked again, though her pursed lips tightened, like she refused to answer. "Because I will, if that's what you need from me. I'll go back in there and tear him limb from limb, if that's what would make you happy." When she still didn't respond, he whispered. "I'd do anything to make you happy."

"Stop staying that!" Something inside her seemed to snap at that offer. Lose control.

"Why?" he challenged, easing closer.

"Jace." She growled in warning.

He smirked. "Because that's what you want?"

"Stop."

"Because you're scared I'll make good on it?"

"Yes!" she shouted, her hands suddenly clenched and angry. She glanced around them, seeming to realize anyone could hear them, before she dropped her voice low. "I'm scared I'm going to run out of reasons to tell you no," she whispered, deflating slightly.

The look of conflicted agony on her face nearly killed him.

But he couldn't ease up on her. Not if he ever wanted there to be more possibility between them. Jace chuckled, gripping her by the chin and forcing her to look at him like he did whenever he was inside her. He cast her a wry grin. "That's the goal, sweetheart."

Her chin quivered. "To wear me down?"

"No. Never. If you really didn't want this, I'd leave no questions asked, but we both know that's not your goal or mine."

"Then what *is* the goal?" she said, a little incredulously, her chin lifting in defiance.

Fuck, he loved watching that hot temper of hers flare. It ignited something primal in him. Made him want to claim her. Fuck her tame. He'd always been a good brat tamer. But only for him and never to take away that fire.

She'd be a good girl by the time he was through pleasuring her.

"The goal is to let you know what you'll be missing should you decide to walk away," he answered. He shook his head, leaning in to whisper. "Because I don't want to walk away from you, Frankie." He brushed his lips against the tender flesh of her ear, and she shivered. "And I don't think you want that either."

She sucked in a harsh breath. "That isn't fair."

"You know what they say, packmaster." He smiled a little, and stepped back, resolved that for tonight, he'd leave her wanting, aching for him. Let her desire flare. "All's fair in love and war, and the line between love and hate is dangerously thin."

Her wolf eyes flashed in challenge.

"Do you want to risk it?" He grinned, his gaze raking over her, blazing a trail of heat in its wake. He didn't need to caress between her legs to know she was wet for him. He could smell it on her, practically taste her sweet heat on his tongue.

"Tell me, *packmaster*," he growled her title like she

belonged to him, or he belonged to her. He wasn't certain. "Can you walk that line without stumbling across? Because I don't think you have that kind of resolve in you. Not now that I've been inside you."

She bristled, angry with him, but still wanting. "We'll see about that." She crossed her arms over her chest. A poor attempt to hide her erect nipples beneath.

But it was too late, he'd already noticed them. Wished he could suck each one into his mouth until she was crying out again.

Lord, it would be a long, lonely night for them both, but he'd make the payoff worth it.

"You're right. We'll see." He cast her a wry grin, before he turned, and whispered. "Goodnight, Frankie," he said, leaving her standing there alone on the sidewalk.

Frustrated and full of wanting.

"You're awfully confident for a man who barely knows me," she called after him as he made his exit.

Jace turned and cast one last smirk toward her. "Oh, it's not confidence, Princess. It's reality that you want me. I know you do," he called back. "And given enough time, I'll prove it to you."

FRANKIE COULDN'T POSSIBLY HAVE KNOWN what that sinful promise could mean, until she arrived in her office the next morning in a now empty K9s, only to find a delicate satin-lined box on her desk. Jace hadn't returned to the Imperial where she was still holed up as her apartment was cleaned. She hadn't expected him too, of course, and she'd known better than to ask him where he was headed when they'd parted ways last night.

But now, the black satin box waited for her. It's branding and label crisp and pristine, a sign of its luxury quality.

She deposited her purse on the edge of her desk and opened it first thing, her heart racing at the possibility of what she'd find inside.

The interior of the box was lined with pink silk, revealing the lacy matching bra and panty set beneath. The lingerie was a stunning ruby red. The same color as her old salsa costuming, and exactly her size. As she lifted the undergarments from the box, a small note on thick, matted cardstock fell out. She grabbed it from the desk and read the inscription.

Since you like playing dress up. Maybe you'll wear this for me?
There was no signature, but she didn't need there to be.

The jewel shade said it all. There was only one person who'd seen that old photo of her recently. She glanced down at the lingerie again, trying not to smile or act giddy. The color was such an exact match it was uncanny. How had he—?

"Is it from Amarok?" The sudden sound of a woman's voice drew her attention.

Startled, Frankie's gaze shot toward the door, where Jeanine was smiling and wiggling her shoulders suggestively. Of course, she'd likely been the one to place the box there, though Jace had clearly managed to be discreet about who its sender had been.

Frankie blushed, feeling her entire face turning beet red, an impressive feat considering her olive complexion. Shoving the lingerie back into the box more forcefully than necessary, she snapped, "Not now, Jeanine."

Her secretary only smiled knowingly, and grinned before exiting.

Later that afternoon, when it came time for her and

Jace's training, Frankie cast the now closed lingerie box onto the empty bartop. At this time of day, K9s was entirely empty. Eerily vacant and quiet. Save for the two of them.

"Lingerie, really?" She lifted a sculpted brow.

Jace shrugged with a nonchalance that was both delicious and infuriating. "You didn't strike me as a flowers kind of woman. Not after last night." His gaze raked over her, taking in the low-cut pantsuit she wore. It showed off her cleavage perfectly. "Seeing you play queen was..." He considered her for a long moment. "Interesting. Made me figure fancy is kind of your thing."

"That's an interesting observation." She shrugged casually, before pinning with him a stare full of challenge. "Considering you said it wasn't yours." He'd made that clear when they'd booked the room at the Imperial. It'd struck her then how different they were, but she hadn't had the courage to point it out or explain it.

Jace smiled at her, a devilish grin. "Just because fancy isn't my thing, Princess, doesn't mean I can't spoil you for my own pleasure."

She sucked in a sharp breath, though she hoped he hadn't heard.

"If you give me the chance, that is." His gaze raked over, lingering on that exposed bit of cleavage.

She was suddenly aware of exactly how much this suit showed, but she wouldn't apologize for it. She wouldn't bow down to those who thought that because she was powerful meant she couldn't flaunt her sexuality, claim her prowess. Use it like a weapon when it suited her, even.

"Are you wearing it?" Jace's voice was an aroused, grumbling purr.

Enough to make her quiver during the times when he was inside her.

Heat pooled between her legs. "That's none of your business." She smiled coyly.

"You are." He grinned, his expression absolutely wicked. "I can tell from that blush on your face."

She shrugged. Attempting to play it off. "I like expensive things, including lingerie. What can I say?"

Jace nodded. "I'll keep that in mind." His gaze darted to the booth she'd seen him and Amarok in. "I could wear a nice Armani suit too, if that'd suit you better." His personal style was blue-collar to say the least. Leather jackets and jeans.

She shook her head. "No. No, it wouldn't." She liked that about him, that he was genuine. Real. That's what she cherished about him most, that she didn't have to pretend, to play the packmaster, or the vicious mafia queen. She could just be Frankie.

With all her attributes and faults.

He saw the whole of her, the unpolished stone underneath the guise of a diamond, and still he wanted her. Was attempting to fight to her.

As much as she feared what that would mean.

How things would end between them.

Jace gestured to the lingerie box as if to indicate the intimate contents which were no longer underneath the sleek lid. "I figure once you change your mind, maybe we can ruin those on that desk of yours." His gaze speared her. "I like to tear things."

The thought of him ripping that lingerie off her, no doubt only to turn around and spoil her with more, was more than a little appealing. She shook her head. What in the world was she going to do with him? They couldn't keep going on like this.

"I won't change my mind, Jace. I want to, but I can't."

She spoke clearly, confidently, trying to make him understand.

But still, he didn't believe her. She could see it in his eyes.

She wasn't even certain she'd truly convinced herself. Let alone him.

"So you've told me," he said. "For your pack's sake."

She nodded, hoping that maybe, someday, he'd understand.

"And what about your sake, Frankie?" He stepped closer.

She was entirely too aware of his position in the room, how even one look from him could fill her with wanting, stop her breath short.

"It's not about me," she breathed.

"Isn't it?" One dark brow lifted. "I think it's less about what it would mean for your pack and more about what's at stake for you—personally, that is."

"Which is?"

"Having to admit you're afraid again. Having to admit that you've known since that first night what I am to you."

He didn't have to say it for her to know the word he'd left unspoken.

A mate.

And a destined one at that.

They'd been skirting around it since the very beginning, though she hadn't even been certain she believed in that sort of thing before him. Hell, she still wasn't.

But what else could that immediate connection between them mean? The way he'd given up everything for her? Even if it'd been the right thing to do.

She pushed that thought aside, not quite ready to deal with the repercussions of it yet. "Don't sound so cocky," she said, refusing to admit to anything.

"Cocky or convinced?" Jace grinned. "You tell me."

Frankie let out a bemused huff. She liked this side of him, really. The banter and chase of it. But what she really wanted from him was the tenderness underneath. The man who could do more than meet her quip for quip, the man who could care for her. Kiss her worries away.

Or at the very least, make love to her until she forgot her own obligations once again.

Until she lost herself a little.

He'd been her perfect escape.

And he would be again, if she could only let him.

"You're stalling," she said, quickly changing the subject. Though it was more for her own sake. "The pace of the attacks may have lessened, but there's still no time to waste."

Ever since Robert had made himself known to them in Manhattan Square Park, things had been surprisingly silent on the killer's end. Not that Frankie wasn't more than grateful for that. Still, she couldn't shake the feeling that this was simply the quiet before the storm, and that didn't even take Jace and his division's confrontation with Execution Underground Headquarters into consideration.

Time was ticking, though what the fallout would be, she still wasn't sure.

She couldn't speculate what their world would look like once the organization could no longer hide their obvious division, when Jace and the rest of the Rochester division would no doubt separate themselves. Form a new organization.

She supposed only time would tell.

Jace rolled his shoulders, squaring himself up in a way that highlighted the strength of his form. Frankie had more than a passing feeling the show was more for her benefit than his.

"Okay, you win. For now. Let's get this over with."

Frankie rolled her eyes. "It's not that easy. You're not going to learn it in a few hours."

"It seems simple enough for all of you. You do it within a matter of seconds."

She sighed and shook her head. "We're full-blooded. It'll be harder for you. And even we had to learn how to control it, when we were pups—kids," she clarified at the lift of his brow.

Jace's face fell into a frown. "How long does it usually take to learn?"

She let out a long sigh. She hadn't been looking forward to disclosing this part. "Weeks. But we can't afford that. We both know you only have a few days at most."

"Shit," Jace swore, his bravado wavering. "I may be good, but I'm not *that* good."

At least he had something in the way of modesty.

She placed her hands on her hips, and the look which crossed her face was pure attitude. The face of a fair, but dissatisfied packmaster. "Unless you want more women to die, you'll shift and you'll do it soon. Exactly like I show you. We're going to be working all our available waking hours until you get this mastered."

It was his turn to roll his eyes then. "If you say so, teach."

"Don't be a smart-ass," she snapped, though it was belied by a teasing grin. "Are you ready?"

He shrugged. "For you?" A smirk twisted his lips. "I'm always ready, Frankie."

18

————————

It'd been several days and still Jace hadn't shifted.

Working with him so closely on this and not indulging the heat between them had become a chore. A tedious. Awful. Tantalizing. Chore. Jace stood across from her inside the empty club, rocking his shirtless arms back and forth as he tried to get his head clear. The predatory grace with which he moved reminded her of a caged animal.

Frankie's eyes widened, the memory of his arms flexing as he drove himself into her invading her mind. Heat shot to her core. And she'd had to stand here, watching him flex and train and move like this for the past several days.

Not once had he come to the Imperial, kept her bed warm, despite all the teasing and flirting going on when they were together.

She couldn't decide whether she was disappointed about that, or whether it was a saving grace. Rock was still here, his presence among her pack a lingering reminder of her duties, of the oath she'd sworn, and the wariness of her packmates to trust the hunters, despite that they trusted her.

They'd obeyed her orders to accept Jace and the others implicitly.

Anything else was a distraction.

A wanted, welcome, ridiculously enticing distraction.

She tore her gaze away from Jace. She shouldn't be thinking like this. About the way his packed stomach tightened when he thrust into her... The thought lingered. She bit her lower lip, attempting to snap herself back to reality. "You know what to do, so why aren't you doing it?" she finally managed to say, once he seemed to have cleared his head from the last failed attempt.

At least he was being a good sport about it.

They'd both known this wouldn't be easy, but there was something holding him back, something beyond learning the basics. A deeper emotion she couldn't quite put her finger on, even though she could see it.

"You want me to get down on my hands and knees?"

She waved him forward. "Don't ask me. Go ahead. We've been through this."

"I can't believe I'm doing this," he muttered, the first thing he'd said that had even come close to a complaint within their past few sessions. Jace knelt on the platform, the sight reminding her way too much of how he looked when his mouth was on her, then lowered his weight onto his hands. "All right," he said. "This is all you're getting out of me. You've got about three more seconds of this before I stand up again."

She shook her head and sighed. "You can get up now."

He stood and faced her. Her eyes drank in the lines of his body and the hard muscles disappearing under his jeans. She clenched her jaw and tried to focus.

"Okay. Remember what we talked about? Basically, there are three methods of shifting. The first is to stand as tall as possible, usually with the spine arched back, and allow the energy to flow through you from the bottom up." She straightened her back and imitated the pose. "It's not very common."

She shrugged. "The second is to crouch down, like you did. You can drop into a deep knee-bend and arch your spine, or you can get all the way down on the ground. Crouching is more typical because it allows you to focus all your energy in one condensed space, and since you're in a similar position to your wolf form, it's easier to transition. Then there are shifters who can switch in either stance, but that takes more practice than we have time for. So since none of those are working for you, just...do whatever feels intuitive while you focus on the energy inside."

Jace nodded. "Instincts. Got it."

"Okay. Now do whatever feels comfortable."

Jace bent his knees and arched forward like a large animal waiting to pounce.

"Channel your energy wherever its strongest. Focus on pushing all your energy there."

He raised a single brow. "What energy?"

"What do you mean, 'what energy'?" She sighed, exasperated with him.

She'd been more than a little on-edge lately. A combination of her lonely nights, working with Jace, Amarok's unintentionally oppressive presence, and the knowledge that there was still a killer on the loose in her territory. Something had to give. And soon.

"You keep saying focus on the energy and I don't feel any energy."

She sighed and walked to his side. "Straighten up again."

He rolled his shoulders back to stand at his full height, towering over her. The closeness of his body to hers sent a fresh wave of heat straight through her. "It's the energy inside you. The kind you feel when the moon is full. That sort of stirring. Right here in your chest." She placed her palm over his solar plexus, and their eyes locked.

Something heated flared in his gaze, feral and untamed. But she couldn't address it.

Not without revealing how much his absence from her bed had affected her.

Apparently when the lingerie hadn't worked, he'd taken a different approach and ghosted her.

Like he was bidding his time, taunting her until she came to him.

And from the fire in his eyes now, he had no doubt she would. Eventually.

Her will wasn't made of titanium, though she wanted it to be.

She tore her gaze away. She had to fight to get the words out. "It's right here. It pulls at your whole being, like something connected to your soul." She glanced at the floor. "Do you feel it?"

Jace placed his hand over hers, his voice an aroused growl. "Only when you touch me."

Frankie couldn't help herself. She met his eyes again, and her breath caught.

They stood in total stillness.

He stroked his thumb over the top of her hand. "I'm sorry I can't give you what you want," he said, barely above a whisper. "Not without ruining everything you need."

She swallowed, trying to find the ability to speak. "I'm sorry, too."

He kept staring, and Frankie wasn't sure how to handle it.

Unintentionally, she inched closer.

Jace cleared his throat and stepped back.

Her hand fell from his chest to hang limp at her side. Yeah, she was an idiot. Thinking she could have him both ways. He wanted her. He'd made that much clear, but the distance he'd placed between them over the past few days said he wouldn't play second-fiddle to Amarok. He'd only have her again if she was ready to go all in, and in the meantime, their constant flirtations were driving her wild—exactly like he intended.

It was all or nothing with Jace.

And he was playing to win.

She stepped away from him. *Learn to take a hint, Frankie,* she chastised herself.

Jace cleared his throat again. "I can feel it when the moon is full. But I can't feel it now. So how am I supposed to gather it?"

"You're going to have to learn how to feel it." Her palm tingled from where she'd touched his skin. Her arms didn't feel right hanging at her sides, so she crossed them over her chest. She wanted to wrap them around him. Instead, she tightened them around her body, trying to hold herself together. "You've probably suppressed it so long that you can't feel it anymore. Can you think back to the last time it was there?"

"When I hunt."

"What do you mean?" she said.

He stared at the wall as if he didn't want to look her in the face. "When I'm out hunting... well, you know." He glanced at her to gauge her reaction.

"Wolves? Our people?"

Jace frowned. "Only the criminal ones. Ones who hurt humanity," he amended quickly, making it clear that despite all her darker dealings as a packmaster, he didn't consider *her* to be one. "When I'm hunting, I can feel something stir inside me. Almost like an animal living under my skin. A beast."

"Is there any way we can simulate the feeling you get when you hunt?"

He squared his jaw and rubbed his temples in slow circles, a slight smirk crossing his lips. "Not unless you bring Rock in here and let me tear into him."

"Aren't you funny?" she said coldly. "What's your problem with him, Jace?"

"I have a problem with any man, wolf or otherwise, who has what I want."

A moment of silence passed between them as he scanned the length of her body and her skin seemed to catch fire. He could caress her with one look.

"Come here," he said.

Without thinking about what she was doing, Frankie shuffled forward a few inches. He pulled her against his body, lacing his fingers through her hair, until a blush heated her cheeks.

"If you stand close to me, I might be able to shift."

"Why does this strike me as an obvious ploy?"

"I don't need a clever ploy to make you want to be in my arms, Frankie." His grip on her tightened, and she could feel the hard length of his cock push against the soft skin of her stomach. He leaned his face into hers, and she fought hard not to gasp as his lips lingered dangerously close to her ear.

His warm breath danced over her skin. "Just stay with me," he whispered again.

And for a moment, she almost indulged him.

Before suddenly, she heard someone's throat clear.

Frankie tore herself away from Jace so fast, she realized her swiftness likely only made her look guiltier.

At the edge of the bar, Henrik, Amarok's second in command, a white wolf who'd found his way to Toronto by way of Denmark, watched them. He had made it more than clear over the past several days that he was no fan of hers, of her association with Jace in particular.

Despite that, until now they'd been nothing but discreet.

Not that there was anything to worry about in that regard.

Considering there was nothing intimate happening between them as of late.

At least since Amarok's arrival.

And she refused to apologize for the time before. Monogamy before their mating ceremony hadn't been part of their agreement. An agreement that she was all too eager to remind Henrik was purely political.

Amarok meant nothing to her.

And likewise, she meant nothing to him.

Other than what their union could mean for the benefit of both their packs.

Henrik gave another rough clear of his throat. "A word, packmaster," he said, using the honorary title in deference to the fact that he was in her territory—and a less than subtle reminder of who she'd become to the white wolves, given time, should she fulfill her duty.

Should she... *Am I really considering breaking the deal?*

No. She couldn't. Her pack needed this. She and Amarok planned to rule side-by-side.

Frankie glanced toward Jace quickly, all too aware of every harsh line and tense muscle. He'd seen the way she'd torn away from him and from the disappointment in his eyes, she couldn't continue to keep rejecting him and expect him to go on fighting for her like this.

Eventually, he was bound to take no for an answer.

In an instant, it struck her how keenly she should want that.

For both their sake's. But she couldn't make herself want it.

"I'm sorry," she muttered lamely at Jace. "If you'll excuse me."

"You don't have to apologize to me for doing what's best for you, Frankie. Or anyone else for that matter." Jace's gaze shot toward Henrik or not. "Packmaster or not, your choices are your own," he said, clearly speaking about more than Henrik's sudden interruption. "When I told you I'd wait, I meant it, so whenever you're ready I'll be right here." His features softened and the longing in his eyes tore through her. "Just try to make a decision before it kills me."

IT WAS HOURS LATER. Well past nightfall, and still Frankie couldn't get Jace's haunted look out of her eyes. What was she even doing? Playing these kinds of games with him? The roar of the club surged around her. The music rising to an ear-splitting apex. It was the Friday night crowd, heading into the promise of weekend, and the club was always the wildest on Fridays and Saturdays. She drummed her fingers in time with the music.

This wasn't like her, warring with herself in a constant battle of indecision. She'd always been the kind of woman who'd claimed all she could want, made no apologies. Just like when she'd been in that interrogation room with Chet, she wouldn't lessen herself or make herself small. Not for anyone else's convenience.

She was strong and stubborn and proud.

Exactly as her parents had raised her to be.

But lately, she felt less and less like she fit that description.

She sat at the edge of the bar, trying not to let her eyes wander over the sea of patrons. Jace and David were here. After Henrik's pointless interruption—a tedious question about some of the finer logistics of moving up her and Rock's mating date, and what that meant for the training schedule of the warriors and bodyguards for both packs— she'd given Jace the night off from attempting to shift.

They'd been pushing and working non-stop for days, and continuing to push until the point they were both burnt out would only get them nowhere.

She struggled not to lift her gaze to where the wolf hunter and demon exorcist drank.

"Can I get you something, boss?" Allyson shouted to her from overtop the music. Her voice muffled, but audible.

"You know better than to call me, boss," Frankie said back, a smile curling her lips. More than other members of the staff, Allyson was her friend, in part because being Fae meant she placed no added obligations on Frankie, held no expectations simply because she was packmaster. To Allyson, she was just another woman.

Albeit a powerful, supernatural one, and her boss.

But another woman all the same.

"What's up with you tonight?" Allyson called to her over the music again. A thumping ballad Frankie couldn't begin to identify. "You don't normally hang out down here."

Allyson was right about that. She was usually too busy taking meetings in her office, to linger among the patrons for long, but she had been keeping her schedule light to work on Jace's shifting. Besides, she didn't have it in her to deal with the underground politics of Rochester.

Not on top of everything else.

"It's nothing. Don't worry about it."

"Nothing takes a certain kind of medicine to fix." Allyson shook one of the bar's tumblers at her. "Just my specialty."

Frankie shook her head. "No, thanks."

Allyson nodded, but poured a vodka shot into a glass and threw back one of her own.

Frankie lifted a brow.

Allyson inclined her head toward Jace and David's booth. "It's stressful him being here."

"I can ask him to leave," Frankie offered. "If it bothers you."

If Allyson wanted David gone, Frankie would make it happen in a heartbeat.

No matter if it'd annoy Jace.

She didn't know what had happened between the demon hunter and her Fae bartender, and she wasn't about to pry. Allyson would tell her when and if she was ready. But from the way Allyson cast the occasional longing look at David when she didn't think anyone was noticing, Frankie had a feeling that there was still some romantic feelings left there.

"You don't have to do that for me," Allyson said, shaking her head. "He's just... a reminder of what could have been, that's all."

Frankie nodded. "I understand the feeling."

That's exactly what Jace would become to her if she continued like this.

A reminder of what could have been.

Something about that thought sent her reeling. Made her pity herself over the loss of him, even though he was still sitting on the other side of the club. She smoothed her hands over her dress, her features softening for a moment as she briefly searched the crowd for him. She'd worn this particularly revealing little getup in hope of getting a rise out of him, making him jealous of the heated looks she'd no doubt get, but Jace's resolve was iron-clad.

He wanted her all in or not at all.

There would be no half-measures with him.

No matter how much these past few days without him had filled her with longing.

Her gaze fell to him, laughing and talking with David, enjoying himself without her. Another woman nearby watched Jace, clearly interested, though she hadn't yet approached his and David's table. And what if she did? Frankie had no claim on him.

The hole that had seemed to form inside her chest every time she looked at him ached.

Allyson moved to take care of a waiting patron, but Frankie caught her attention. "On second thought," she said. "I'll take that drink after all."

"My special heartache medicine coming right up." Allyson grinned. The glint in her eyes was pure Fae mischief. Her ethereal beauty was barely hidden by her glamour.

A moment later, she returned, carrying a martini glass full of pink liquid. She slid the drink on a small napkin toward Frankie, who quickly took a sip. The drink was strong, yet sinfully delicious. The kind she'd no doubt regret come morning. Allyson's bartending skills really were one of a kind, almost magical.

"It's so good it's dangerous," Frankie said.

Allyson winked. "Only if you let it be," she said, before she returned to her work.

Frankie wasn't certain drinking was the answer to her

problems, but she grew a little more relaxed with each sip. A little less worried.

She quickly finished her glass, then ordered herself another, vaguely aware that it probably wasn't wise, but it was her club, her pack's business. Who was there to stop her from having a little fun?

She was already well into her second by the time she thought that maybe she should have a little chat with her bartender about if she used Fae magic to liven up the club's drinks. But at the moment, Frankie was having too much fun to care.

She made her way out onto the dance floor, losing herself in the music's pulse and the sea of writhing bodies. Frankie danced like she hadn't in years, pulling out every move in her past repertoire until she could feel the music in each sway of her hips, each gyrating beat.

Her vision blurred and she stumbled slightly, giggling as she collided with some cougar shifter out on the dance floor...Or was he a panther? She couldn't be certain.

She laughed uproariously, slurring her words as she attempted to apologize to him. But she hadn't thought about or seen Jace in hours. She hadn't even looked for him.

Until a large hand gripped one of her hips.

"Okay, Princess," Jace grumbled, low against her ear. "That's enough."

"Hey, man. We were just—"

Jace's eyes were liquid fury. "Beat it," he growled.

The cougar-panther went pale, before quickly scurrying off to another part of the dance floor. Frankie turned toward Jace then, swaying a bit.

"Why are you..." She poked at his chest. "Spoiling. My. Fun?" It was like poking at bricks, he was so stacked.

She giggled.

His face all seriousness—which wasn't that a drag?—Jace plucked the half-drained martini glass from her hand and sniffed it. He wrinkled his nose. "What's in this?"

Frankie waved a dismissive hand, swaying with the music. "Hell if I know."

"Allyson and I are going to have a little talk." Jace wrapped an arm around Frankie's waist, drawing her to him. He led her through the club as she strutted along with him, working to keep up her balance.

"Where is Allys-son?" she slurred. "I need another drink."

"Her shift ended, thankfully." Jace slid the martini glass he'd confiscated from her across the bartop. "And, no. You don't."

Frankie stuck out her lower lip and pouted, but she couldn't tell whether or not he'd noticed. The room and the patrons were going by in a spinning, colorful blur. The firm pressure of Jace's arm around her waist, his hand on her hip, her only anchor.

He led her to the stairs. She stumbled several times once they were firmly out of sight of the patrons, before suddenly she was in his arms, being carried like she was some damsel-in-distress.

"Now I really *am* a princess," she giggled, then hiccuped.

Jace's lips curled in mild amusement, his touch and his care for her tender. The next thing Frankie knew, she was deposited on top of the desk in her office. Her high-heels kicked off her feet. She groaned in ecstasy at the feeling of her toes finally escaping those godawful gorgeous shoes.

Jace swore, biting his lip.

She wiggled them with another little moan. "Why won't the world stop turning?" she whined to no one in particular.

Jace didn't bother to answer her. Instead, he turned to close the door.

Frankie didn't know why, but she suddenly felt hot all over her. Like she was ready to burst out of her skin, or her clothes, at least. She slipped down the little minidress she wore, the one she'd changed into earlier. It'd been a poor attempt at catching his attention, but apparently, it hadn't worked. She kicked off the dress, thankful she was wearing nothing underneath, save for the very sheer lingerie he'd bought her, just as Jace turned back toward her.

"Christ," he swore as the door latched. "You don't make anything easy, do you, Frankie?" Her eyes darted to the strain of his fly, that impressive bulge against his jeans.

She fanned herself with her hand, leaning back onto her desk. "I don't know what you mean." She sighed. Now that she wasn't dancing, she was magically tired, dizzy.

A second later, the door burst open and Rock suddenly stepped in, his eyes instantly falling to her nearly naked form. Jace growled slightly, though nudity wasn't as secretive among shifters.

"Oh, it's Rocky," Frankie crooned, trying for affectionate, and ending with tipsy. "Still want to marry me?" She batted her eyes suggestively, then laughed.

At the nickname, Rock's jaw tensed, his gaze falling to Jace. If her naked form did anything for the white wolf, he didn't show it. "I don't know what you think is going on here, but—"

"I'm taking her home." Jace interrupted. "That's all."

His gaze was so intense it made Frankie's head spin.

"She's *my* responsibility." Rock growled.

The fire in Jace's eyes grew murderous, his eyes flashing to his wolf, though his voice remained eerily calm. "And if it wasn't for me you would have let her drown herself on the dance floor." Those last words were spoken through nearly clenched teeth.

Rock stiffened slightly. Lip curling. "I didn't anticipate this kind of behavior from a fellow packmaster."

Jace scoffed dismissively. "Fuck off with that bullshit, Rock. I've seen you drunk as a skunk more than once. Cut the misogyny."

Rock bristled but didn't protest. He glanced between them, warily, before he turned his gaze back toward Jace. "I expect you to see her home, safely. That's an order."

"I don't take orders from you or anyone, Rock." Jace shook his head. "But she'll be safe with *me*." Even in her drunken state, Frankie recognized the emphasis on that last word.

Rock didn't say anything, simply nodded, before he turned and stalked out the door.

Frankie was still swaying, and attempting to fan herself, when suddenly Jace was directing her to shrug into his leather jacket, after only managing to pull her dress up over her waist.

He zipped up her jacket, ignoring her bare breasts before him with another mutter of "You couldn't make this easy" to which she only stuck out her lip and pouted.

"Why won't you touch me?" she whined.

"Later," he grumbled with small smirk, his words a dark promise.

He carried her back down the stairs again, and then out to his car, but she sat down the moment her feet touched the curb. "I think I'm just going to stay here a bit," she muttered, before he promptly scooped her up again.

He loaded her into the vehicle with an almost clinical patience and care.

His touch only purposeful, never explorative.

Much to her disappointment. She supposed she *was* drunk. Though she didn't want to be.

It wasn't until he'd closed them safely in the room at the Imperial, that he pointed toward the bed and said, "Sleep."

Frankie stuck out her lip again.

"That's an order, Princess."

She grumbled at him, but it didn't take a genius to figure out she needed to sleep this off. She collapsed into the bed, sleep claiming her in a way it hadn't in the past several days, because with him beside her, she knew what'd he'd promised Amarok was true.

She was safe.

Safe in a wolf hunter's arms.

A LARGE HAND *clamped down on Thomas's shoulder. The voice of the shadowed man echoed as he said, "You will not be limited by mortal bounds." His voice filled the small clearing where they stood, the forest painted in blue hues as if the brush were made of the sky.*

Thomas's eyes widened. A light sparked in his irises, and a smirk spread across his face. "You mean I'll be immortal?"

The shadowed man stepped in front of him. "Don't overestimate your abilities. No one is immortal but the gods. You will age, but at a slow pace, and no minor wound will harm you, but make no mistake, your time will come. Like your father, someday you must pass down your power. You will choose when that time is. A respectful son shall wait until the time is right, just as you must wait now."

"Like a respectful son..." Thomas looked up into the face of the shadowed man, who towered over him in his enormity. "What do I do now?" he asked.

"Go. Return to your rightful place at your father's side. He will tell you when his time is up. Until then, learn what wisdom you can from him. Great power lies ahead of you."

The shadowed man lifted his hand, and with the wave of his wrist, the blue forest melted.

When the blue world had faded from his view, Thomas scanned his surroundings. He stood in the middle of a fenced-in backyard behind a small redbrick home. Inside, framed in a window, a middle-aged man stood at a kitchen sink, his hands buried in suds.

"Wait and learn his wisdom?" Thomas shook his head before he strode toward the house. He wrenched open the patio door and stepped inside, his boots tracking dirt onto the once-white linoleum. "Hey, Dad. I'm home."

Thomas's father glanced up from the dishes and smiled. "You're later than I expected, Tom." He set the plate he'd finished washing onto a towel along with the other cleaned dishes—three stacks of plates, several bowls, a single glass and some well-used silverware. He turned to the casserole dish in his hand and scrubbed at the leftover macaroni. "What were you up to? Your mom put some dinner for you in the fridge. The macaroni is in the yellow Tupperware container, and there's some steak on a plate in there. It's covered with tinfoil."

Thomas walked to the fridge, keeping his eyes trained on his father. "I was just... uh... running late at work, Dad. We had an extra shipment come in." He pulled the refrigerator door open and removed the covered steak. After unwrapping the aluminum foil, he shoved the plate into the microwave and hit start.

He scanned the room. His gaze paused on the block holding the steak knives. "Can you hand me a knife, Dad?"

"Sure." His father reached over the counter, selecting one of the steak knives from the wooden block. Still facing the sink, he held the knife out behind him, and Thomas took it from his hand.

He clutched it in his palm as he stared at his father. The blade gleamed in the light. "Hey, Dad, I have something interesting to tell you...." He stepped forward.

"Yeah?" His father looked up from the dishes and saw, reflected in the window, his son standing over him. His eyes widened. "Tom, what are you—"

Tom met his gaze as he stabbed the knife into his father's spine. "I just wanted to tell you, I'm sorry."

JACE'S EYES SHOT open as he woke from where he'd fallen asleep next to Frankie. He blinked several times, his heart pounding in his throat. Holy shit. Dreaming of his father killing his grandfather—a man Jace had never even met? Damn, he had too active an imagination.

He didn't need to be thinking about this shit.

His nightmares were freaky enough without delving into family drama, the dreams having grown more intense and vivid lately. The thing was...what if that shit was true? Damn. No wonder he was as fucked up as he was.

He rolled over onto his back and glanced at Frankie. She lay sleeping beside him, hair sprawled over the pillowcase, fast asleep. He wanted to touch her, but would never even consider doing so until he knew she was fully sober. As much as he was angry with her, resented her for making him feel so much when she yielded so little, he couldn't find the strength to detach himself completely, though he wished he could. She'd insisted she wanted to be with him, but couldn't, but as the days wore on, he was struggling to believe her. And yet...

He could have moved into another room in the suite to sleep elsewhere. But as he'd drank his demons away with more than a little Bushmills, he'd found himself settled beside her on the bed, neither disturbing her sleep nor touching. Sleep had claimed her quickly, and he'd been content to watch her rest, to hear her breathe. Yeah. Maybe it was in his genes. A level of debauchery and greed that went bone deep.

He was hungry for her always.

He'd considered more than once that maybe it was selfish to fight for her like this, to not allow her to walk away with ease. He knew the trouble it'd cause her, her pack, but it wasn't so easy.

Not since he'd realized she was his mate.

He didn't know when the realization had hit him exactly, or even if the word fit, considering he still hadn't shifted. But the moment it'd settled in his mind, it felt like he'd known. Like he'd always known.

From the moment he'd first laid eyes on her, they'd been meant to be. Like David had said.

If they could only find a way to work through all this.

The wheels of Jace's mind where still turning.

He let out a long sigh and shook his head. If the nightmares in the early morning hours were any sign of what lie ahead, he was going to need a lot more whiskey.

19

Frankie woke some hours later, her head aching, but no longer hazy.

"Jace?" she whispered into the darkness.

She searched the shadows, recognizing quickly that she was in the hotel room. The penthouse at the Imperial. Her wolf eyes combed the dark for him, finding him at the edge of the bed. He was sitting there, hunched forward onto his knees, a glass of whiskey in his hand glittering like citrine each time it caught light from the nighttime glow of the city.

He glanced over his shoulder, but didn't turn toward her. "How's your head, Princess?"

"Better. Only self-induced pain now." She blinked, clearing the sleep from her eyes and sitting up. She was naked except for the red see-thru lingerie he'd bought her, the material soft and sheer, and she suddenly remembered how she'd gotten stripped down in the first place.

She groaned.

"Remembering what happened?"

"Yeah." She attempted to run the fingers through the mess that was her hair and failed.

"Next time, take it easy on the fairy wine," Jace muttered, though there was no judgment in it. He took a sip of his whiskey.

"You're one to talk." She nodded at his drink, teasing. "You're practically an alcoholic."

He snorted, a short laugh. "A functional one."

She smiled. "Duly noted."

She stripped the sheets from her body, and rose, coming to stand before him. In the dark, she knew he could see her nudity clearly through the sheer silk. His eyes widened at the sight of her, and she cupped his cheek.

"Thank you," she whispered. "For taking care of me."

He leaned into her touch, eyes fluttering like a tamed predator who couldn't help purring. A contented grumble poured from his chest. "No thanks needed." He cursed and looked out toward the night skyline. "I don't deserve you," he mumbled.

Frankie's breath caught.

"What did you say?" She knew what he'd said, but she couldn't comprehend it.

Suddenly, all her struggles, every emotion that'd been passing between them made sense. As if those words had brought her a sudden newfound clarity.

They were mates. Fated lovers.

A part of her had known it from the start.

And what would losing a mate do to him? To her?

She'd known it would hurt to let him go, but she'd told herself she'd get through it—survive—but what about him? What would her letting him go cost him? He'd already given up so much for her. Already come so far in accepting who, and more importantly, *what* he was, but how would that change if she abandoned him?

Something in the way he looked at her now told her that

despite all the power this hunter who sat before her held...if he lost her, he'd never recover...

He'd go on, yes, but all that kindness she'd seen in him would be lost in an instant.

She couldn't allow that to happen.

His eyes narrowed, before he took another sip. "I said I don't deserve you."

Her throat tightened.

"Taking you captive was the biggest mistake I've ever made, but I wouldn't change it even if I could," he went on. "I never wanted to have feelings for you." He met her eyes with a look that was half joy, half agony. "But I do."

Before Frankie knew what she was doing, she was kneeling before him, having dropped to her knees. She cradled his face in her hands. A fire ignited in her veins, and she pressed closer, positioning herself between his spread legs. "How can you not see that it's always been the other way around? It's me who doesn't deserve you. Not after all I've put you through."

For a moment, the depth of emotion in his eyes froze her despite how her heart raced, until suddenly he was pulling her into his arms. He kissed her so deeply, her world spun, their lips locking in an instant. Like they were born for each other, meant for each other, and this time, Frankie felt it.

Wholly. Fully. Completely.

It was there in every part of him.

His fingers tangled in her hair as his warm tongue moved against hers, the bittersweet taste of whiskey and the taste of his tongue filling her mouth in an intoxicating blend. His hands trailed from her hair down her spine, his palms settling on her lower back, and he slowly pulled her closer. Testing. Asking.

He would love her, if she let him.

She gasped against his lips, nodding her agreement. Palming her ass, he pulled her into his lap, spreading her legs so she was wrapped around him, and pushing his fingers into her quickly. A wave of heat spread between her legs, and she trailed kisses across his cheek as he made sure she was ready, his deft fingers probing. She sucked on his earlobe, her teeth gently grazing the skin. A low growl escaped his throat, and a fresh wave of heat flooded between her thighs as Jace rubbed his palm against her clit.

He kissed her collarbone. "I have to be inside you," he said. "Please, Frankie. I'm begging."

Lifting her with him as he stood, Jace pressed her against the nearest wall.

"I've wanted to take you every second since we were last together." He kissed her hard and sucked on her bottom lip.

She moaned and wrapped her arms around his neck. "Yes, *please*," she panted.

He pulled away. A slow smile spread across his face while he fingered the edge of her nightgown. "I'm going to rip this."

"Do you have to?" She smirked.

"Yes," he growled. "Don't be a brat." He nipped at her, slapping her bottom.

She squeaked at the sharp, pleasurable sting. "You'll buy me a new one," she teased.

She barely had time to grin back at him before he kept his promise and her panties fell to the tile in two quick shreds. The bra came next, falling from her body with flimsy ease beneath his powerful hands. As he held her in place, he claimed her breast with his mouth. He ran his tongue over her, and she melted into him.

Her nipples hardened, and she pushed her chest against him. He flicked his tongue over her nipples, then slowed to swirl over them. Her breath caught. Hoisting her into position, he held her steady as she unbuckled his belt. She stripped his jeans out of the way, and his pants hit the floor as he positioned himself outside her entrance, agonizingly close to claiming her.

"All I want is to pleasure you," he groaned. "I'll make you mine right now, if that's what you want, but only if you want me."

There was something vulnerable in his voice, almost a plea, though his eyes were hungry for her, and rather than take her now while she was wet and ready and already wrapped around him, he still stopped to ask. Was it any wonder she'd fallen so hard for this man?

"Frankie?"

She wanted to tell him she was already his, tell him he had been at the center of her thoughts since his body lay flush against hers in the alley, but all she could do was nod.

He sheathed himself inside her in one stroke, and she cried out. He rocked—slow thrusts that left her begging for more. He was a gift from the heavens. Running her hands over his shoulders, she quivered, barely holding herself together.

Warmth pulsed through her body. He slowed down, then worked his way from slow movements into a steady pace that caressed her deeply, thoroughly. She buried her hands in his hair.

"I want to make love to you," he whispered, pausing. He looked around them, frowning. "Can I take you to bed?"

She kissed him hard, and apparently that was the only response he needed. He lifted her against his chest and carried her the few feet, exploring her tongue with his own.

When he reached the edge of her bed, he lowered her until she stood in front of him. His eyes roamed over the curves of her body, and though she knew she should have been cold, her skin burned hot from his gaze.

He ran his hands over her shoulders in slow, circular motions. He was gentle and strong as he massaged her there, working the rough night away. She sighed as he reached her breasts, kneading them. He knelt and kissed his way down her body to her navel, until his cheek rested just above her mons. He caressed the insides of her thighs before he ran his tongue over her pink slit. He kissed her there, exploring and exposing her every weakness, lavishing her with attention over and over again. When her legs could no longer support her, he followed her onto the bed, smiling as if he'd been the one to receive all the pleasure.

She reached for him, urging him to join their bodies together.

He hesitated for a moment, then settled atop her and buried his face against her neck.

"Jace," she panted as he thrust into her.

He drew back, and their eyes locked.

Frankie watched as his irises slowly transitioned to liquid gold—the gold of a wolf's eyes. Her heart jumped, and an invisible pull tugged at every inch of her being.

Her destined mate.

"I love you, Jace." The words slipped out before she could stop herself, and perhaps, even more importantly, "I choose you," she whispered. "I'll always choose you."

A blazing fire lit his eyes. He pounded into her at a fevered pace, the quiet emotion of his response pouring into her core. In a blast of sweet warmth, he found his release, sending her over the edge until she soon found her own. She moaned as she rode him through her climax.

Without a word, Jace covered her mouth with his lips and kissed her hard, sealing her heart, her fate fully.

FRANKIE KNEW what she needed to do.

The following morning, she'd called Amarok first thing and requested he and his pack's leadership meet her at the club come evening. Her inner circle from her own pack would be there, too, to support her, to back her up. This wouldn't be an easy conversation, nor had she came to the decision lightly, but now she knew the truth.

Jace was her mate. Destined.

She couldn't walk away from him. Even if she'd wanted to, which she didn't. Not even for her pack.

She had to believe, to trust in the mating bond she'd sensed between them from the start.

She'd been too scared to allow herself to recognize it before. Too in denial about her own feelings, but she wasn't afraid now and she would own whatever consequences befell her from both Amarok and her pack. She had to believe her father, or any male packmaster before her would have done the same, placed the pack above all but their bonded mate.

That kind of connection held power. More than she'd given it credit for.

More than she'd given *Jace* credit for.

The sun was just starting to set, the cold city air still settling into the frosty bite of evening as she made her way into the club. K9s wouldn't open for a few more hours, but already she could hear the buzz of the wait staff preparing, the low beats as the D.J tested his sounds, the murmurs of voices.

As she entered through the back, on the other side of the club, the front entrance slammed. The sound of heavy boots echoing the click of her heels, before she heard a familiar voice bellow, "What the hell did you do?"

Frankie quickened her pace. Emerging from the storage area, she strode into the main section of the bar, only to find David prowling toward Jace, his gait more fevered than she would have thought possible considering his limp. "Where's your woman?"

Jace looked toward him. "David, slow down. What are you—"

"I'm right here," Frankie said, drawing the two hunters' attention.

David rounded on Frankie, pure fury flashing in his eyes.

She took one step back as he advanced toward her.

"You were supposed to protect her. Watch over her like she was one of your own."

Frankie's brow furrowed in confusion, but she didn't retreat.

Jace grabbed David's shoulder, catching him mid-stride. "Whoa, David. Back off. Where's who?"

David snarled, a noise that seemed far too animal to belong to him. "Allyson's missing, and you brought her into this." He jabbed a finger at Frankie.

Frankie's eyes widened. "What happened?" she demanded.

"That's what I want to know." David stepped toward her. "Why was there a message to you on the wall of her demolished apartment—written in blood?"

Frankie felt all the blood drain from her face in an instant. They'd all expected Robert to strike again, but she'd expected him to come for her, her pack. She hadn't anticipated...

Her mind combed over the events of the night before. The fragmented pieces where Jace had said Allyson's shift had ended early, though the Fae bartender had been scheduled until close.

Had Frankie had her wits about her, she would have noticed. Would have questioned where Allyson had gone. But this wasn't her fault. It was Robert's. His actions were his own.

Yet Allyson's protection was Frankie's responsibility, which meant she'd hunt Robert as if she'd taken one of her own.

"We *will* find her, David," Frankie said, speaking quickly and clearly, the words of a packmaster used to remaining calm among the fray of chaos. "Faerie or not, she's been one of us for a long time. We'll find her."

Frankie wouldn't allow another innocent woman to die on her watch, especially not Allyson. She cast a glance toward Jace and saw the same resolve in his features.

Together, they'd do whatever it'd take.

But from the murderous look in David's eyes, the demon hunter was far from satisfied. "I swear, if I find out you caused this, I'll force you to shift and then skin you for your—"

"David!" Jace grabbed his friend by the front of his jacket, shaking some sense into him. "Frankie's been with me the whole time. She didn't do this."

David panted hard, each breath so heavy it strained the leather of his jacket.

"We'll get her back, David," Jace promised.

"What's going on here?" Alejandro emerged from the club's office, the pack's other leadership in tow, already here for the meeting and clearly drawn by the sound of the commotion.

"Allyson's been taken," Frankie answered.

Alejandro's eyes went wide. "Shit."

"Gather our best warriors. Start searching for her—immediately," Frankie commanded the group of men and women. They were some of her best fighters, those among her pack strong enough to help her lead.

Her warriors nodded dutifully, immediately moving to set about their task.

"We'll go after her, David—and we'll find out where she's been taken," Frankie said. She met David's gaze.

"I can't wait around while you sniff her out," David snarled. "That's not good enough. I have to do something *now*. I won't sit around while he has her."

Jace gripped his friend by the shoulders, hard enough to still him. "David, if you go after her now, you'll get her killed," Jace growled. "If you go in there injured like you are, you're *both* going to be killed, and how will that solve anything?"

David's whole body trembled like the fury inside him was barely contained.

If Frankie had held any doubt that David still loved her friend, she didn't now.

And from the look in David's dark brown eyes, the thought of Allyson in Robert's hands killed him, and the fact that he couldn't save her, couldn't help her thanks to his leg would haunt him for the rest of his days.

"Listen to your friend," Rock's voice cut through the din, as he and his warriors joined the fray. "He speaks reason."

Jace gave a cut nod, an acknowledgement of his thanks before his eyes were on David again. "I swear to you on my life, I'll get her back. But you know we can't go out unprepared."

Frankie opened her mouth to express her agreement, but her words were cut short by the sound of the several of the club's doors bursting in, followed by a round of fearful shouts from the wait staff as someone called out, "It's a raid!"

Frankie had all of two seconds to prepare herself, before Chet and a whole legion of Execution Underground hunters swarmed in, guns trained on them.

The initial chaos of the wait staff calmed in an instant, a sudden stillness falling over the room where she, her warriors, and Rock's stood.

Wolves always became the most still before the kill.

Chet stepped forth, gun trained on her, but this time was different.

She may not have been prepared for him, but this was her territory, her turf, and this time she wasn't alone.

And she'd make him feel it.

"You didn't think I'd let you off the hook that easily, did you? Let you sully our organization?" Chet's gaze fell toward Jace, then her. "And not come for the bitch that helped you get away with it?"

Jace, Alejandro, and Amarok snarled in unison, the darkness of the room suddenly lit with dozens of glowing eyes from the wolves, and she was proud to see Jace among them, standing at her side, the side of her pack as if he were one of them. Frankie held up a hand, commanding the warriors to still.

"You made a mistake coming here," she said, stepping toward Chet, her voice strong, unwavering and without fear. "You treat us like villains and thieves, but this," she gestured to the surrounding club, to the beasts within its walls, "This is a den of wolves," she told him. "And you'll regret that mistake the moment I let them tear your throat out."

She held Chet's gaze for a long beat, before she glanced over her shoulder toward the wolves that were hers to command, her voice every bit the vicious queen she'd been groomed to be, as she growled, "Sick 'em."

20

Jace would have marveled at the way every wolf in the room descended at Frankie's command, had he not been among them. One among many. Chaos erupted, the club filling with the sound of gunfire, conflict, and pained human screams—the first of what would be many fights with the insurgents that'd taken over his organization. But not here in Rochester. He wouldn't allow them to take hold here. Especially not targeting Frankie. Not on their turf.

Not if he had anything to say about it.

Jace rushed Chet, not holding anything back this time.

Chet fired a shot, aiming for him, but missed narrowly, thanks to Frankie, who'd now shifted into wolf form. She tore into his arm. Chet shouted, crying out at the pain and dropped to his knees, but neither of them were even remotely close done with him yet.

Distracted by Frankie, Jace stripped the other hunter of his gun, using Chet's own wrist against him to break it free. He drew the weapon back, and pistol-whipped the bastard across the face, causing him to release the newfound grip he had on Frankie. Spittle went flying, and Frankie shifted back into human form beside him, naked, and wolf eyes blazing.

Some of Chet's blood dripped from her lip and she licked it away, her gaze downright vicious. Every bit the dark wolf mafia queen.

"Again," she commanded.

Jace wasn't sure why he listened, but the beast inside him demanded it, yielded to her in every way he refused to when they were alone together, and it was just the two of them—when it was his turn to command her.

Jace caught Chet by the chin again, blocking one of Chet's blows before he struck the other hunter. Howls and shouts from the battle around them rent the air, but Jace paid little attention to it, his full focus on Chet and Frankie.

"Harder," Frankie snarled, every bit the feral she-wolf he knew her to be.

Jace obliged and Chet toppled to the floor, but Jace was on top of him, wrenching him to his feet and shoving the barrel of Chet's gun against his throat, exactly as he'd done to Frankie. Chet bucked against him, furiously, clearly confused about how he'd been bested when he'd evaded them so many times before.

But what he didn't see was that this time, he and Frankie were a united front. A team.

And they wouldn't make the mistake of letting him go again.

"It's one thing when you come for me," Jace snarled. "It's another when you come for her." He shoved the gun a little higher and Chet cursed. "Say your goodbyes quickly, because this time, I won't hesitate to kill you. Unless you want to do it yourself, pack master."

Something dark glittered in the she-wolf's eyes. Something unlike her and yet not.

He could see her now fully.

The powerful woman she could be. When he didn't have her beneath him, begging.

"Finish him," she hissed. "For me."

Her dark eyes glittered.

Jace didn't need to be told twice. He'd given Chet ample chance to leave them be, to tuck tail and run. But men like Chet never knew when to leave well enough alone. To admit that a woman held power over them, that she could be a feared thing. So his hatred would die with him.

Jace shoved Chet to his knees, his gun positioned at the back of Chet's head.

"Say goodbye, you woman-hating fucker." Jace started to pull the trigger.

"Jace, wait." Another voice of command. One he was more accustomed to, but rarely heeded. Jace turned to find Damon, emerging amidst the melee.

Where the fuck did he come from?

The vampire hunter's blue eyes spoke volumes. "We need him alive."

For their rogue brotherhood. For information.

Jace's jaw stiffened, but he nodded his approval, as Damon took control of the situation, slapping a pair of cuffs on Chet and hauling the bastard to his feet.

The sounds of the surrounding fight had dimmed considerably. Frankie and Amarok's packs having clearly won. The few among Chet's crew that remained had been sent running.

"I would have killed him for you," Jace said, his gaze falling to Frankie, to where she stood naked and full of power before him.

"I know you would have." Frankie's dark eyes glittered. "You can later." She grinned.

"Packmaster!" Alejandro shouted from across the club.

Jace and Frankie raced toward the sound, to where an injured but still alright Alejandro, knelt beside a dead white wolf. The first casualty among the war they could no longer deny was brewing.

Frankie joined Alejandro's side and Jace didn't stop her, as she took lead of the situation, double-checking the white wolf's pulse before she called out for Amarok.

Soon, they were surrounded by wolves, the fighting now ceased as the white-wolf leader stepped forth. Amarok hung his head. Jace waited for the mournful howling that was no doubt to follow. He'd seen other packs, other wolves mourn their dead before. Sometimes at his own hands, though never undeserved. But before Jace could bow his own head out of respect, a sharp grip wrenched at his shoulder.

"You did this!" Henrik hissed. "You and your bitch brought this upon us."

Frankie snarled, but Jace quickly stayed her hand with a sharp look. She was fierce, but he would never allow her to fight his battles.

"I had nothing to do with this. I fought them the same as you did," Jace said, coolly.

"Henrik," Rock growled in warning.

"No," Henrik said, turning a defiant gaze toward his friend. "I won't allow you to continue to be cuckolded like this, packmaster." Without warning, Henrik charged at Jace full speed, hitting him under his arms in an attempt to tackle him. But Jace used Henrik's own weight against him and sent him stumbling across the club's floor.

Vaguely, in the back of his mind, he heard Frankie snarl. Like she would come to help defend him. But Amarok stopped her.

"Leave him. If you care for him, let him fight his own battles."

When Jace regained his balance, Henrik turned and threw his first punch. Jace dodged, but another punch came toward his face immediately. The white wolf was well trained, but in human form he was sloppy. Not as well equipped as he was when he was a wolf.

Unlike Jace.

Jace blocked Henrik's arm and tried to sweep him to the ground, but Henrik wasn't having it. He bent under Jace's weight and dragged Jace down with him. They rolled on the floor, until Henrik pinned Jace to the ground. He punched again, this time aiming for Jace's jaw. Jace twisted his head in time for Henrik to slam his fist into the platform. The warrior let out a loud yelp.

Grabbing hold of Henrik's injured wrist, Jace grasped his fingers and twisted them in the opposite direction. The bastard crumpled in on himself, completely under Jace's control. Jace slipped out from underneath him and pinned the werewolf to the ground, switching their positions.

Henrik bucked against him, trying to throw him off. "Aren't you man enough to fight?" he said as he strained against Jace. "Or can you only block my moves?"

Jace ground his weight against his opponent, needing to keep Henrik pinned down, and let out a low feral growl. "Don't push me, asshole."

"Or what? You'll finally hit me?"

"Henrik," Amarok growled again in warning, urging his warrior back.

Jace slammed his palm into the bastard's throat, then held tight, slowly crushing his windpipe. He could feel Henrik's veins pulse beneath this hand as the man gasped for air. "Don't make me do this. Listen to your packmaster."

Henrik's face reddened as he fought for air, but he gritted his teeth and shook his head.

"Have it your way, then." Jace's hold tightened.

"Don't! Please!" a woman yelled from the crowd.

Jace looked up, but the voice wasn't Frankie's. A petite blonde was running toward the edge of the stage, another white wolf, and that moment of distraction was all it took. Jace glanced back down at Henrik, only to rear back. Fur had sprouted across Henrik's skin, and his face had lengthened into the snout of a wolf.

Jace scrambled off Henrik just in time for the wolf to flash his fangs.

Shit.

The white wolf rose onto its feet and crouched, ready to spring. Jace backed to the edge of the platform.

"Jace, concentrate." Frankie's voice rang in his ears, and a surge of adrenaline shot through him.

The white wolf snarled as it bounded toward him. Jace focused on the anger rising inside him. Henrik hit him square in the chest and knocked him to the ground. They rolled around on the platform in a snarling heap. Henrik scratched his paws across Jace's face. A sting of pain shot through Jace's cheek, and a warm trickle cued him in. Henrik had been the first to draw blood. He wouldn't continue to hold himself back now.

As far as Jace was concerned, it was practically an invitation. He punched the wolf in the jaw. Yelping, the werewolf reared back. A snarl ripped from its throat. Jace howled in pain as the animal sank its canines into the flesh of his shoulder. Blood poured down Jace's chest.

The white wolf released his shoulder and prepared to strike again, like a venomous snake. Jace shoved against

Henrik's neck and focused all his energy into shifting as he stared into the wolf's golden eyes.

He felt the beast stir inside him, and a grin spread across his face.

Jace grabbed the wolf by the scruff of his neck and threw him off. Henrik skidded across the stage; his back legs fell off the platform, and he desperately clawed his way back up. But Jace was already on his feet. He crouched into a low stance and focused on the feeling inside him. He felt the beast stir again, and he latched onto the feeling in a desperate attempt to draw it out.

Henrik ran toward him, fangs bared and covered in blood.

All the muscles in Jace's body strained. He clenched his fists. He could feel it. It was working. He let out a ragged yell. A surge of power pulsed through him as Henrik dove for him.

The energy surged through Jace's veins. Then everything faded to black.

FRANKIE STUMBLED BACK as a pulse of blue light and energy hit her full force. Screams and yelps echoed through her ears. She nearly hit the floor, but managed to keep her balance. She couldn't tear her eyes from the platform. Her breath caught, and before she knew what she was doing, she was shoving her way through the crowd and running toward the stage.

Jace. She had to get to Jace.

David was at her heels. As the energy dissipated, several members of the pack howled and shifted into wolf form. But Frankie could only focus on Jace.

She threw herself down at his side and wrapped her arms around him, but he didn't move. He was kneeling in the middle of the platform, as still as a statue. She distantly heard herself screaming his name.

What the hell just happened? He was supposed to shift. That grin told her he'd figured it out. What was happening?

Lines of blue light gleamed on his body, as if he were covered in a glowing pattern of tattoos. His eyes had transitioned from their normal green to the gold of a wolf's eyes. He stared toward the sky, unblinking.

She shook him as hard as she could. "Jace! Jace!"

A second later, Rock was grabbing her arm, Alejandro beside him, attempting to haul her away to safety, but she couldn't leave him. She couldn't.

She turned on them, eyes feral and teeth bared. "Stay away from my mate!" she snarled.

Amarok and Alejandro's eyes grew wide at the connection she'd just declared.

In response, another pulse of energy flooded the room, emanating directly from Jace. It hit Frankie hard. Her head fell back, and pain boiled beneath her skin. The familiar feeling of her bones rearranging overtook her, and she felt herself involuntarily begin to shift. Within seconds she lay on the ground, transformed completely.

Hunkering to the floor, she whimpered. Her gaze darted around the room to the other pack members. The only human left was David, who couldn't shift. Howls and the sound of keening rang out as they all waited for the next aftershock of magic, of energy. She covered her head with her paws to block the sound from her ears.

What the hell was happening?

She'd never seen anything like this before.

Another wave of energy shot from Jace's body. He jerked

forward and rose onto his knees. Even in wolf form, Frankie stopped breathing.

A replica of the symbol they'd seen in Manhattan Square Park glowed between Jace's shoulder blades. Frankie howled as recognition washed over her.

She knew that mark. She hadn't been able to place it before, but now, God help her, she remembered.

Jace wasn't a wolf shifter.

He was a *berserker*. A wolf shifting warrior rumored to have been crafted by the Nordic gods of old, a shapeshifter, not a wolf, who she'd just declared as her mate. Frankie shook from head-to-toe, as realization tore her. Jace was a warrior crafted by long dead gods.

And to her abject horror…

So was Robert.

JACE'S EYELIDS FLICKERED open onto a haze of shining blue. Slowly he pushed himself off the ground, drinking in his surroundings. It was as if the world had been engulfed in a cerulean haze. He stared and could faintly decipher the outlines around him.

A forest. He was in the middle of a damn forest.

The same as that nightmare. He racked his brain to remember how he'd gotten there but came up with nothing. What had happened? And why was everything like an amorphous blue shadow?

He listened for some sign of life, but heard nothing except silence.

Where the hell was he?

He stood and scanned the area. A flash of what looked like an animal's tail rounded a nearby tree. Inching forward, he moved toward the elm and stared into the blue forest. A large wolf was peering around a bush, its eyes beckoning him forward. Like everything else, it looked like nothing but a shadow, an outline of what a real wolf would have been.

Shit. This was all wrong. Either he was dead or dreaming, or he'd swallowed one hell of a dose of LSD.

The animal turned and ducked behind the bush again. An invisible string tugged at Jace's chest, and though his mind briefly protested, he soon found himself trailing behind the wolf.

Weaving in and out of the twilight trees, he followed it through the forest.

After what felt like an eternity, the wolf disappeared. Jace stepped forward into the edge of a clearing. He tried to call out, but he couldn't hear his own voice.

No need to use words here. Thoughts are far more valuable on this plane.

The voice sounded as if it were coming from inside Jace's head. He spun around. A man stood engulfed in the shadows. He stepped out from the trees and stared Jace in the eyes.

Jace moved his lips, but the words refused to come. *What are you?*

A smile curved the shadow man's lips. *A Berserker—a warrior—as are you.*

The words sounded oddly familiar, but Jace couldn't place where he'd heard them. *A Berserker?*

The shadow man stepped forward, and Jace stepped back. *You have no reason to fear me, though your instincts are right. I am more powerful than you.*

Jace dropped into a fighting stance. *What do you want with me?*

The shadow man continued to move forward. *My job is to direct you to the right path. I am your guide from the gods.*

If this had been real life, Jace's jaw would have dropped. Instead, he just stared at the shadow in front of him. *A guide from the gods? You've gotta be fucking with me. What sort of drugs did I take?*

The shadow man frowned, the first human expression Jace had seen him make. *I assure you that I am not "fucking" with you.*

Jace straightened to his full height again. *Then who and what are you?*

The Norse called me Heimdallr, guardian of Bifröst—the gateway to what you call heaven—and I'm exactly what you are.

What the hell was going on? Jace closed his eyes, hoping he would wake up. When he reopened them, he found himself still stuck in the blue haze. *I'm not following your thoughts here. What is this place?*

The man beckoned him closer. *Come. Follow me.* The shadow man turned and disappeared into the trees. The same pull Jace had felt with the wolf tugged at his chest again, and he walked forward involuntarily.

The shadow man moved through the forest with ease, as if he knew every tree, every branch. *I'm your guide, Jace—the spirit of the wolf.*

Jace regained control of himself and stopped walking. *Wait, so you* are *the wolf?*

The shadow man turned around and met Jace's gaze. The wolf's eyes stared back at him. *Yes. The wolf and I are one.* Then the man turned into the forest again and wandered deeper into its depths.

Jace never took his eyes off the shadow figure in front of him. *Why am I here? What is this place?*

We are past Midgard, or what you know as Earth. We are near Bifröst, the bridge between your world and the realm of the gods, the holy Asgard, where I make my home.

Jace wanted to curse, but still no words would come out of his mouth. *So I'm dead?*

The shadow man ran his hand down a nearby tree, almost caressing the redwood bark. *No, you still reside among the living, though few are capable of entering our world. You are an elite warrior, crafted by the gods.*

Goose bumps prickled over Jace's skin, but he ignored them. *If you think I'm crafted by gods, you obviously never met my father.*

The man stepped over the shadow of a fallen tree and continued. *Your father chose a dark path and used his gift for his own greed. He was not worthy.*

The questions flooding into Jace's mind were overwhelming. His thoughts raced. The trees and brush of the forest thinned as they continued forward. Another clearing lay ahead.

When they stepped through the curtain of the trees, Jace's eyes widened. Before him, stood seven stone statues, each one three times his height. Each depicted a Viking-like warrior dressed in animal skins. The warrior in the center stood tallest—a spear in his hand, and the pelt of a wolf covering his body and head.

The Berserkers, the shadow man said. *The originals from which you descend.*

Jace couldn't tear his eyes from the stones. These statues were ancient. *What is a Berserker?*

The shadow man moved closer to the stone replicas. *We are shapeshifters, crafted as tools for the gods.*

We? Jace pointed to himself. *No, you're wrong. I'm no berserker. I'm a hunter.*

The shadow man stared up at the face of the wolf-skin warrior statue. *You are a hunter by choice, a Berserker by fate. A remarkable creation.*

Jace couldn't wrap his head around any of this. *What do you mean? There's nothing remarkable about me. I'm a half-breed wolf shifter. I'm not good enough for either side.* He remembered what had led up to this. The brawl with his fellow hunters, the fight with Henrik.

Now both sides are against me.

Walking toward him, the shadow man examined him carefully. *You are no ordinary wolf. You are a shapeshifter, a Berserker warrior. You have the ability to shift like the wolves you control, but you are set apart. They are wolves at heart, but you are a man, a man with the power of a wolf.* He gestured to the statues, before he continued.

We can shape-shift, but we are not limited in our choices. When you come into your full power, you will be capable of channeling any animal you choose, but you will always be drawn to the wolf. He pointed to the statues again, each man covered in a different animal: the pelts of a wolf, a bear, and a wild dog; the mane of a horse, the skin of a serpent, the feathers of an eagle, and finally, the tusks of a boar.

Because Frankie is my mate? Jace shook his head. This was so messed up.

But she was the only part of this he wanted, the only part that made sense.

The creature swept his arm out toward the wolf-man, the head warrior, but didn't answer his question. *It's time you learned.*

Strolling between the statues, the man ran his shadow fingers over the stone surfaces. *In the time of the Vikings, the Berserkers were an elite group of Norse warriors, bestowed power by the gods, who devoted themselves to nature. It was their belief that by wearing the pelt of an animal, they could harness the power of the beast they imitated.*

As generations passed, their belief became a reality—a gift from the gods. They became shapeshifters, their descendants capable of shifting form. For you, that is the wolf.

Jace glanced at the statue of... his ancestor?

The shadow man continued. *Someday you will assume your rightful place in Valhalla, the heaven of the fallen warriors, but until then...* His voice trailed off.

But Jace didn't need him to finish. He knew.

He'd spend the rest of his life fighting for those who couldn't fight for themselves.

A tool meant to mete out divine justice. He always had been.

But against who? Robert? The terrorists who'd taken over the Execution Underground? Why did these long-dead gods care?

The foundations of everything he knew began to shake and crumble. He thought of Robert, of the women the bastard had murdered. He may not have understood it, the role of fate in all this, but had to find a way to beat him.

What do I have to do?

The shadow man's expression turned even more serious, almost sad. *In exchange for power, a sacrifice must be made.*

Jace glanced down at himself. A large hole formed where the shadow of his body had once been. His panic rose, but he had to beat Robert. *What kind of sacrifice?* he thought.

Blood of your blood must be shed. Then and only then will you know true power.

The man faded into the cerulean shadows, which melted together, blurring until his image disappeared into the twilight. But his voice echoed inside Jace's head.

This is your fate, Jace McCannon. Embrace who you are and you will conquer your enemies.

JACE WAS WRENCHED BACK into reality with a gasp. He toppled forward, struggling to right himself. A pair of large hands gripped his shoulders, holding him in place.

"Jace, are you okay? Jace?"

Jace's eyes darted around the room. There were wolves everywhere.

David leaned into Jace's line of vision and stared him straight in the face. "J, wake up. Jace, listen to me. Damn it." He mumbled Yiddish curses as he repeatedly shook Jace to rouse him.

Jace clamped his hands onto David's shoulders, still dazed. "Stop shaking me, David."

David stopped, but he kept his hold tight. "Jace, are you okay?" he repeated.

Jace tried to steady himself, using David for balance. Swaying, he leaned on his friend. "What happened?"

"I don't know, J. Henrik was running for you, and the air started vibrating around you. I thought you were going to shift, but then you fell to your knees. It was like a pulse of energy shot out of you, and it kept coming in shock waves. It stopped Henrik in his tracks and forced all the pack members to shift into wolf form, even Frankie.

Frankie?

"Where is she?"

Jace shot to his feet. The world spun, and David caught him. He slung Jace's arm around his shoulders and acted as his support. As Jace searched the crowd, David lowered him onto the platform again. Jace didn't see her anywhere.

"She's okay, J. I was right there next to her. She's taking care of her pack. She didn't want to leave your side, but she had to."

The air filled with groaning as the members of the pack transitioned into their human form. Shredded clothes covered the floor, destroyed during the transformation.

David grabbed Jace's face with both his hands and forced him to meet his eyes. "Jace, look at me. We need to get you out of here."

David's words melted together as the blood drained from Jace's face and he passed out again.

21

IT TOOK EVERY ounce of strength Jace had in order to crack open his eyes and stare at the ceiling above him. Someone had taken all the energy in his body and sucked it out. What the hell had happened to him? He fought to keep his eyes open while he searched his brain.

The blue haze. The wolf. The shadow man. The Berserkers.

Holy shit. He tried to get up but quickly fell back onto the couch where he'd been lying. Damn it. He pushed against the cushions with his elbows. He had to get up.

Where was he? His gaze darted around the room. David's apartment?

Someone touched his shoulder and urged him to stay down. Shane's face swam into view, looming over him. "Don't try getting up. You need to save your strength if you're going to channel...well, whatever the hell that Berserker shit was again."

Jace gaped. "How in the hell do you know about—"

"I did some research based on what Frankie and David told me about what happened to you and the symbol on your back," Shane interrupted. The two hunters stood over him. "We know what you are, and when you tried to shift, part of your power unleashed."

The room spun. Jace covered his face with his hands and tried to steady his breathing. Out of this world. The whole situation was out of this world.

David's voice carried from the other side of the room. "Hang on, J, and I'll help you sit up."

Jace frowned and started trying to get up again.

David limped to Jace's side and supported him. "Don't push it. You need to conserve your energy, so you can do that again—and right this time."

Jace growled at him. "The hell I do."

David gripped him by the shoulders and held him firmly in place. "Jace, you have to. It's our only chance to beat Robert. To save Allyson." He dug his fingers into Jace's shoulder blades, his frustration clear on his face. He over-enunciated each word. "I will *not* let you fuck this up. If you don't do *everything* in your power to find Allyson, I will personally take a hatchet to your head."

If it were anyone else saying those words, Jace would have pounded them to a bloody pulp. Well, if he could have moved without feeling like he was about to topple over, anyway. He examined David's face, and he knew that underneath the anger, his friend was dying to get back the woman he loved.

Damn it. He couldn't mess this up. "How will this help me beat Robert?"

Shane raised his hand as if he were answering a question one of his fellow professors had posed. "I did some research once David described what happened to you, and I found all this information about Norse mythology and Berserkers. Most people believe the Berserkers were an elite class of warriors, but the older beliefs are more relevant here. According to this..." Shane picked up a large book off the floor.

The aged gold lettering glimmered in the light, spelling something out in a language Jace didn't recognize. Shane flipped through the pages. "Here it is. According to the writer, a berserker must go on a journey of spirit before he can reach his full potential. Then a select few of those become berserker warriors. Is that what happened to you?"

Jace's jaw clenched. He nodded.

Shane began to pace the room, the large book cradled in his arms. "The only problem is, it doesn't describe how you become a berserker and gain the powers of the gods. You need to go back. You have to find out."

Jace straightened and brushed David away. "I already know what has to be done."

Shane stopped pacing and stared at him, and David leaned forward eagerly.

Jace cleared his throat. "There needs to be a blood sacrifice. He said, 'blood of my blood.' I need to kill a member of my own family."

A brief moment of silence passed while Shane and David glanced at each other.

Shane let out a long breath. "Shit." His eyes turned toward David. "You can't ask anyone to do that, David, not even for Allyson."

David scoffed. He pointed a large finger straight at Shane. "Oh, yes we can." Turning toward Jace, his eyes filled with determination; he was ready for a fight. "J, you need to track down that deadbeat father of yours and pay him back for all those years of abuse."

Jace stood slowly and walked across the room. Aside from Frankie, who knew only the bare bones, David was the only one who was aware of his history with his old man. Jace swallowed his anger. "I don't know where he is. I don't even know if he's alive. I haven't seen him since I was a kid."

Shane slammed the book down on the table. "I'll get right on that." He hurried from the room, presumably heading off to find his ever-present laptop.

Silence hung in the air. Jace leaned against the wall, too weak to hold himself up, while David buried his face in his hands.

"I can't lose her again, J. Not like this," David finally said. "I would fight for her myself, if I could. But injured like this...you're right. All I'd do is get both of us killed." He glanced up at Jace, a look of pure desperation on his face. "You can do this, can't you?"

"Kill my father?" Jace stared at the wall. The memories of his father beating him, his mother until she lay sobbing on the kitchen floor invaded his mind.

His father turned his head, directing his anger toward Jace, his eyes glowing gold.

"If I knew where he was, I would've done it already." Jace shook his head. This whole situation was so messed up. "Where's Frankie? Is she okay?"

"She was fine the last time I saw her. Dealing with the fallout among her pack."

Jace lifted a brow.

"She told them all you were her mate, J. Went to bat for you. Told Amarok she didn't need to marry him for their pack's to be in partnership, and defended you, who you are, what you do, what you mean to her." David's eyes softened. "You would have been fucking proud of her, J. I wish you could have seen it. She's something fierce, and there's no doubt she's in love with you."

Pain squeezed Jace's chest. Fuck, he wished he'd seen it, too. Wish he could have been there to stand beside her.

I love you, Jace.

Her words had played in his head on a constant loop ever since she'd said them. But now, in the wake of everything, doubt crept in.

Would it be enough?

He wouldn't be certain until he saw her for himself.

A deep feeling tugged at Jace's gut, and he knew he needed to be by her side. Go to her. A low growl escaped his throat. He wasn't sure what instinct told him that, but it did.

"I need to see her," he said.

David straightened. "Jace, you can't. You need to stay focused right now."

Without hesitating, Jace said, "Aside from the brotherhood, she's been my only partner in tracking this sicko, and in life," he said, "I need to see her. We need to go after him *now*." He needed to tell her the truth. He'd never said the words back, and he should have.

He'd let his actions alone speak for him.

He wouldn't make that mistake again. She deserved both.

He shoved himself away from the wall, using all the energy his body had left to get himself out of there. Groaning, he stood up straight and stumbled toward the door.

"J!" David followed behind him as fast as he could. "J, listen to me."

"Trust me on this, David." Jace growled over his shoulder. "I know what I'm doing."

He never felt more powerful than when he was beside her, or more powerless, but there was strength in that vulnerability. He saw that clearly now.

Jace left and headed straight for the old dance studio.

He knew without a doubt that's where he'd find her.

FRANKIE SAT IN THE middle of the studio with her legs crossed. She stared down at the picture in her hands, the younger version of her face beside her parents. The photo Robert had ruined.

Jace is a shapeshifter. A Berserker.

And so was Robert.

A shiver ran down her spine as she thought of the symbol glowing between Jace's shoulder blades. As hard as she tried, she couldn't reconcile the two images. The two feelings couldn't coexist in her mind. Jace was rough, his temper befitting of any alpha, and his strength... insane. But he wasn't a killer. Not like Robert.

The image of his gun trained on her the first night they met flashed in her mind. Even though he hunted her kind, he hadn't killed her. She supposed she'd known from the start that he was...different. Like her and yet not. In all the best and worst ways.

She cursed under her breath.

The man she loved, her mate, wasn't even of the same species. He was human, or close to one really, a shapeshifting warrior whose ancestors had been blessed by ancient gods. The same creature that they were hunting. She shook her head. Her mother always told her life wasn't fair, but she'd never said that fate could be downright cruel.

Frankie had learned that for herself—the hard way.

Running her thumb over the photograph, she tried to remember what her mother's hair felt like, the feel of her father's touch, but she couldn't. Only five years since they'd passed, and already her memories of them were fading. She didn't know which was worse: the pain of remembering their deaths or the realization that they may not have approved of the man she loved, because of what he was.

Hate goes both ways.

She hadn't understood what Jace meant then, but she understood it now. Now that she'd witnessed firsthand the fallout his true nature had caused among her pack, but they'd make it through this. They had too. There was no other choice.

She set down the picture. The look of confusion in Jace's eyes when he'd come out of his trance had been enough to convince her of his innocence. He hadn't known he and Robert were the same kind of creature, and she couldn't blame herself for not realizing the similarity in their scent, considering Jace's injection from the Execution Underground, what made him a hunter, had masked it. Still, she couldn't shake the feeling there was some other kind of link. Some kind of connection between them. What was she missing?

Once the situation had been well in hand and it was clear Jace and all the members of her pack were safe, Rock and his crew had made hasty exits, and she'd bolted as fast as she could to come here. Since then, her thoughts had been racing nonstop, and she'd been unable to collect them so she could make any sense of how she felt.

The man I love and the killer are the same creature.

She cursed herself. How had she missed the connection?

His name carved in the girls' forearms, her apartment being targeted just after she met him, the killer knowing his name, and now the symbol. That all pointed to something more than random coincidence. But what?

A loud knock interrupted her jumbled thoughts. With mechanical movements, she wandered to the studio's door and stared through a crack in the window's paper like a peephole. Her heart jumped in her chest.

Jace.

Shit. What was he doing here? He should be resting, preserving his energy. Obviously, she didn't want him to injure himself, but she'd needed space. Somewhere quiet to think and he'd been in good hands. She cursed herself. She never should have left his side.

He's your mate, and you told him you loved him last night. How could you expect he wouldn't follow you to the ends of the earth now?

Another knock, harder this time, and the door rattled in its frame. "Frankie, I know you're in there. We need to talk." His voice came loud and clear through the wood, his tone tinged with frustration.

You said, "I love you," but he never said it back. He never said it.

How could she be certain that's how he would feel? She wanted it to be, yet...

"Frankie, please open the door." His voice softened.

She inhaled deeply, slid off the chain lock and quickly pulled the door open.

Jace was standing in the street, leaning against her door frame. Dark circles rimmed his eyes, and he looked drained of all energy, but damn him, he was still gorgeous—still perfect in every way. "Come on in." She turned away and retreated into the studio.

Following her, Jace stepped inside and shut the door. "We need to talk," he said.

"I know." She cupped his cheek. "I'm just not sure if this is the right time to do that when everything feels so charged, Jace."

Especially when we count the crazy coincidences or the mounting pile of problems with our names on it.

"Did I do something? Are you angry?" He placed his hand on her shoulder.

She stroked her hand over his cheek, the firm line of his jaw, grateful to see him up and awake. "No. No, of course not. I'm just...just thinking about our next move is all." She caressed the stubble of his cheek and he leaned into her hand, the rumble in his chest an aroused purr.

"I practically became possessed in front of your entire pack, and David said you just ran off afterward. It made me think..."

"Don't think that way," she reassured him. "I just...needed time and space to think, that's all. Time to process."

"And your deal with Amarok?" he asked.

"It's over," she said, quietly. "Fated mates are so...regarded among our kind it's something even Rock had to respect. Our deal is off. He won't come between us."

"And your pack?"

She released a long breath. "They'll come to terms with it. Give them time."

Jace stepped closer, so close that she could feel the heat of him against her back. He snaked his hand around her waist and gently pulled her against him. "I *can* get along without you, if you need me to, but I don't want to."

If David had told him what she'd said, how she'd declared him as her mate, he was no doubt talking about the fallout, the consequences for her pack and her broken deal with Rock.

"We're past that now." She wrapped her arms around his neck, resting her head against him. "I'm handling it."

"I'm sorry," he whispered against her hair.

"Don't be. Don't act like that."

"Don't act like what?"

"Like you have anything to apologize for." She pulled back to meet his gaze. "You don't. It's me who should be sorry. I should have recognized what you are to me sooner."

"You never have to apologize to me for needing time, for needing space, Frankie. For your feelings." Jace smiled a little as he shook his head. "Not today, not tomorrow. Not ever." He tipped her chin up toward him, meeting her gaze. "But there's one thing I need to know."

She shook her head. "Of course. Anything."

Jace's emerald gaze pierced through her. "What held you back?"

Frankie lowered her hands from around his neck, stepping away and he let her. She wasn't sure she was ready to have this conversation. Not yet. Not in the wake of all of all that'd occurred. Of all they still had to face.

"The deal with Rock..."

Jace growled, low in warning, but there was no true threat to it, only frustration. "Don't lie to me, mate."

It was the first time he'd addressed her as that, at least directly, and the weight of that word, of all they meant to each other, and all they would be to one another in the future, shivered through her, making her warm not only in her core, but everywhere, including her heart. She turned her back toward him. "It seems trivial in the face of...well, everything," she gestured around them, "but..." She turned to face him again. "How can you love me, Jace, when you still don't know how to love yourself? How to accept who and what you truly are?"

Jace stilled then.

The space in the studio between them filled with nothing but the sounds of their breathing as she waited for an answer. She might as well have asked him to wrangle the moon for her.

"You're right," he finally said, the rough pain in his voice tearing through her. "And I can't promise you I'll change that. Not today, not tomorrow, or hell, even ten years in the future." The sharp eyes of his wolf speared her. "But I'm trying, Princess, truly, and being loved by you makes it easier. All I can give you is that."

"That's more than enough," she answered. "*You're* more than enough."

They came together in a collision of loving arms and lips before Frankie had even realized they'd stepped toward one another. They continued like this, coming together in a harsh joining of tongue and teeth, until suddenly Jace was dragging her to the floor with him, burying himself in her. She accepted him willingly, claiming her pleasure as she rode the top of his hips. Their lovemaking was messy and fevered, just as they were.

But whatever challenge faced them, she knew that together they'd get through it.

She came on a hurried shout, Jace pumping into her as he filled her full, the warmth of his seed coating her. She collapsed on top of him in a fevered heap of kisses against his chest, his neck, but he quickly brought her mouth to him, claiming her lips.

"I love you, Frankie," he whispered against her as he finally pulled back.

A wave of breathtaking joy rushed through her.

"I should have told you every time I've been with you before."

"I feel the same," she whispered, joyful tears pooling in her eyes, before she kissed him again.

Everything between them had happened so fast, but it didn't matter. It was real.

They were real. The truth of that hummed through her.

They lay there like that for some time, collapsed on the studio floor together, united as one, until finally, Jace whispered, "We still have a killer to catch."

"You'll beat him," she whispered back. "*We'll* beat him," she corrected. "Together."

They pulled apart, righting themselves and their clothes.

"Let's go get Allyson," Jace said.

Frankie nodded her agreement. "I'll just be a minute while I close up here."

Jace nodded, but made his way out the door to where he'd no doubt parked the Chevelle nearby. The sound of the door closing behind him shivered through her. They'd need to form a plan, work together, her, Jace, his division, and her pack as a group if they were going to defeat Robert, save Allyson, but she knew that together, they could do it.

Resolved, Frankie quickly jogged up the stairs to the studio apartment to retrieve the coat she'd left there. She was just about to head back downstairs toward Jace before she quickly realized she wasn't alone.

Before she knew what was happening, Robert came at her full force. He pinned her against the wall and held his knife against her throat. The blade cut into her skin, and a thin line of blood trickled down her collarbone.

Robert sneered. "Nice to see you again, packmaster." He spat the last word and looked down at her as if she was nothing more than a pathetic dog.

Frankie pressed herself as tight against the wall as possible and fought to slow her breathing. Calm. She needed to be calm. "What are you doing here?" She barely managed to choke out the words.

"Retrieving you. You see, I kidnapped one of your little pack members. But apparently, she wasn't important enough for you to come save her." He grinned. "Turns out that she isn't a wolf at all. First time I've ever tortured a faerie. But I have to say, so far I'm finding it quite amusing. Who knew iron was such a useful weapon?"

"You bastard," Frankie growled.

He leaned more weight on the blade and the cut deepened just enough to exponentially enhance her pain. "Enough with the insults, my dear. Dirty mouths aren't appealing on women, even canine whores." He dragged the tip of the knife down her collarbone, stopping inches away from her breasts.

She hissed from the sting. Blood gushed from the tear in her skin, and pain seared through her.

"I'd absolutely love to take my blade to that beautiful chest of yours." He trailed the flat part of the blade over her right breast. "But we'll save that for later."

She glared at him, though she couldn't fight the shivers running down her spine. "You're a sick freak."

With his blade safely away from her throat, she kneed him hard in the groin. He crumpled over exactly as she'd expected. She brought her elbow up and slammed it down into his spine. He toppled to the floor, but he managed to grab her ankle in the process.

He was strong, and when he pulled on her leg she slammed to the floor. She scrambled to her feet, but not before Robert regained his footing, too. He grabbed her shoulder, his knife at the ready. Spinning out of his grasp, she unleashed a roundhouse kick that hit him square in the face.

With a loud curse, he stumbled back, clutching his bloodied nose. Before he could retaliate, she punched him straight in the solar plexus. Gasping for air, he fell to his knees. Now was her chance. She bolted for the door, but before she'd run even five feet, Robert stabbed the blade of his knife through her blue jeans and into her calf.

She screamed in agony. Pain shot up her leg and radiated through her entire body, but she didn't stop. She stumbled toward her door, moving as fast as she could. Blood gushed from her wound, leaving a crimson trail. She reached for the knob of the open door, and she used it to steady herself.

Without warning Robert tackled her from behind. He caught her off balance and slammed her into the wall.

"Back off, you filthy piece of shit." She clawed at his face with her fingernails, scratching anything she could reach.

He clutched both hands around her throat. Lifting her off the ground, he choked her as he pinned her against the wall. "I said, No. More. Insults."

Frankie clawed at his hands, trying to escape. She kicked her feet in hopes of hitting him in the groin, but it was no use. Black spots clouded her vision as she felt herself start to slip into darkness. The last thing she saw was Robert's twisted grin.

"Sleep now, little packmaster. You can rest until the fun starts."

RACING THE HALF block back to the building, Jace ran toward the dance studio with renewed intent. He didn't know how, but he knew something was wrong. From the moment, he'd whispered he loved her, it'd been like something between him and Frankie had connected, taken full form then. Like he could sense her presence, her feelings, her fears. He sensed that fear now and more acute than ever. She needed him. Now.

When he reached the building, Jace tore inside, bounding up the stairs. He ran to the apartment stairwell and stopped in his tracks.

Crouching to the floor, he rubbed his finger across a small red speckle. He lifted his hand to his nose and sniffed. The smell of iron filled his nostrils, mixed with the scent of his mate that remained there.

Blood.

Jace's stomach flipped. "Shit." He ran up the apartment at full speed but quickly skidded to a halt.

Blood. Frankie's blood.

There was a large pool on the floor, with small droplets leading out of the apartment, down the stairs. Robert had her. He knew it without question. All his fault. If he hadn't left her...

A loud roar ripped from Jace's throat as anger flooded every inch of his body. He barely took the time to scan the writing that dripped in fresh blood across the walls, his mate's fresh blood, before he stormed out of the apartment. He was going to tear that fucker to pieces.

Come to the abandoned warehouse in Honeoye. Better hurry, my dear Jace, before I kill them both.

22

____

F RANKIE'S EYES SLOWLY flickered open. Her head pounded, pain thumping in her temple like a fast-paced salsa rhythm. Her whole body ached, and her collarbone throbbed with pain every time she breathed. Damn him for using a silver knife. Pushing herself off the ground, she blinked several times until her eyes adjusted to the dim lighting. She scanned her surroundings and gritted her teeth.

A cage. He'd placed her in a freaking cage.

She grabbed one of the bars and shook it with all the strength she could muster. The iron creaked as it threatened to give beneath her strength, but it would take hours to bend it enough so she could escape. Something told her she didn't have that kind of time.

"We're in a warehouse. Don't bother yelling or trying to get out. It's impossible."

Frankie turned around. Allyson lay sprawled across the bottom of the cage, her arms and limbs spread wide as if she were the female equivalent of da Vinci's famous Vitruvian Man. She didn't move.

"Allyson, are you okay?" Frankie crawled toward her. When she reached Allyson's side, she cursed.

Iron. The cage was made of iron—even the floor.

"Holy shit, Allyson. I'm going to move you, okay? I'm going to move you so your skin isn't touching the metal." Frankie placed a hand on Allyson's arm.

The small faerie cringed. "Be careful, Frankie. My...my skin is stuck to the iron. If you move me, it will peel off."

"Shit." Frankie hit one of the metal bars of the cage in frustration. "I'm going to have to move you somehow. If you stay like this, the iron's just going to keep eating away at your skin."

Frankie eyed the length of Allyson's body. She didn't know where to begin.

Legs. She would start with her legs. The only skin showing there was a slight flash of her ankle just above her shoe, the only part of her leg not protected by her jeans.

Shifting toward Allyson's feet, she stared down at her injured friend. "I'm going to move your legs so that your shoes are touching the iron, instead of your skin. Okay?"

Allyson whimpered, unable even to nod.

Frankie cupped her hands underneath Allyson's kneecaps. Should she pull her legs off the floor quickly, like a Band-Aid, to lessen the pain, or move slowly in hopes of salvaging some of the skin? Frankie closed her eyes and quickly lifted Allyson's legs.

A blood-curdling scream pierced the air. Frankie's eyes snapped open. Her stomach flipped. She held back vomit at the sight of chunks of Allyson's skin stuck to the iron. The smell of burning flesh permeated the air. Frankie gagged.

As gently as possible, she propped Allyson's legs up with her knees bent and placed her shoes in contact with the iron. Her torso remained flat against the bottom of the cage.

Damn. The difficult part was next. Her arms and her head.

Frankie carefully slipped her hands underneath Allyson's shoulders. Her blouse had managed to protect most of the skin there.

I'm doing this to help her, not to hurt her. She repeated the mantra in her head for reassurance.

"No. No. Frankie, please," Allyson cried.

A large lump lodged in Frankie's throat. "Allyson, I'm so sorry. I know this is going to hurt, but I have to get your skin off this iron. If your head stays where it is, the metal will eat completely through your skin until it reaches your skull. I can't let that happen."

Inhaling a steadying breath, then chanting "sorry" over and over, Frankie hoisted Allyson's body off the metal floor. The sound was disgusting, like peeling an old bumper sticker from a used car. Allyson's screams vibrated through Frankie's head as if someone had shoved a tuning fork inside her ear.

In one quick swoop, she had Allyson off the floor and sitting in her lap. The other woman weighed practically nothing, but her blood poured onto Frankie, staining her white tank top a deep crimson. Allyson screamed and writhed in Frankie's arms.

"Shh. Shh. Allyson, it's okay. It's okay." She gripped her friend tightly around the middle to hold her still. She couldn't let her touch the iron again. "We'll be out of here soon. I promise."

"You shouldn't make promises you can't keep." The voice came from the other side of the room.

Frankie looked up as Allyson's screams started to fade to groans and her bleeding slowed. Leaning against one of the warehouse walls, Robert stared at her with unrelenting, cold eyes.

Frankie scoffed. "A cage, huh?"

A smirk crept across his face. "You like it? I thought it was very fitting."

She shrugged—anything to piss him off. Anger made people sloppy, and sloppiness meant a better chance for them to escape. "I've been in worse."

He frowned. "Dismiss me if you want, but you're the one locked up like the bitch that you are. You're nothing more than live bait."

Frankie stroked Allyson's hair, trying to calm her panic. "You have me trapped now. What else do you need? Why don't you just kill us already?"

"My, my, don't we have a large ego?" He moved away from the wall and stalked toward the cage. "Don't flatter yourself, packmaster. You've never been my target. It's your hunter I want."

Her stomach dropped. "What do you want with Jace?"

He grinned, gleeful despite how cold and flat his eyes were. "To kill him, of course."

It took everything Frankie had to hold back her anger and remain still for Allyson's sake. "What about ransacking my apartment, kidnapping me? What does that have to do with Jace?"

He chuckled and kneeled next to the cage. If he moved any closer to the bars, she could speed-shift and slip her muzzle through the opening. She would have liked nothing more than to rip his face off with her teeth.

"You must be even less intelligent than you appear. Let me spell it out for you." He pointed to himself, then to her. "*I* kidnap *you*, which leads Jace straight to me. He won't be able to resist saving you."

"And Allyson? What about her? She's not involved in any of this."

Allyson stirred. When she spoke, her voice was hoarse from screaming. "To lure *you* here," she said in a near whisper. "Only it didn't work."

"The troll's smarter than she appears."

"I'm not a troll," Allyson said. "I'm Fae." She winced as she said it, but her voice remained strong.

Robert ignored her comment and stood again. "When you didn't come for her fast enough, I took a more...direct approach. There's no question. He'll be here."

Frankie swallowed down the bile burning the back of her throat. Her heart thumped in her chest, its pace quickly increasing until she was near panic. Frankie's head spun.

She growled. "Jace is going to tear you to shreds."

Robert laughed as if she'd told his favorite joke, the kind that never gets old. "Don't fool yourself, packmaster. Do you think Jace can match my strength? My speed? My abilities?"

Frankie didn't say a word. She clamped her mouth shut, but a smug grin spread across her lips.

A fire lit behind Robert's eyes as his anger melted his icy shield. He marched to the cage and kicked one of the bars. "Tell me what you know."

She stared him in the face, challenging him to give it his best shot.

When she didn't respond, he snatched a key from his back pocket and unlocked the door to the cage, his knife pointed straight at her. "Get out."

She didn't move.

Robert let out a deep-throated growl. "Get out. *Now*. Before I get my gun and plant a silver bullet in the middle of your forehead."

Frankie shook her head. "You can't kill me. You need me

as bait to get Jace here. He's my mate. He'll know if I'm dead."

He chuckled. "That's where you're wrong. You see, as soon as Jace finds the little note I left him, written in some of the delicious blood from that neck of yours, he'll come here ready for a fight. Your death will only cause him more pain. Why wouldn't I want that?" He brandished the knife. "The only reason I haven't killed you yet is so I can kill you and fuck you right in front of him." He smiled, and the lack of empathy there stilled her.

He wouldn't just hurt her. He'd enjoy it.

A chill ran down Frankie's spine. Every animal instinct in her body screamed for her to run, but she couldn't. She had to listen to him, if not for the sake of her own survival, then for Allyson's.

"Let my friend out of the cage, too. I'll get out if she comes with me."

Robert eyed her for a moment, sizing her up as a potential opponent. "One at a time. Her first." He nodded to Allyson.

Allyson groaned, her body lying limp in Frankie's lap. Frankie gripped her shoulders and gave them a light squeeze. "Allyson. Allyson, you have to get up. We have to get out of here."

Allyson let out another moan and rolled her head to the side. Her eyes flickered open, and she stared at Frankie. "I can't."

"You have to. The longer you're near this iron, the weaker you'll get." Frankie placed a hand on her friend's cheek. "You can do this."

"This is all very touching, but I suggest you hurry the fuck up." Robert's voice rose as his impatience grew.

"Allyson, get up. You can do it. Do it for David."

Allyson inhaled sharply. Her whole-body language changed, as if she'd found a new resolve. Frankie helped lift her onto her feet. Stumbling, back bent so she didn't hit her head, Allyson escaped the iron enclosure.

Robert grabbed her by the arm and drew her into his body. He held the knife to her throat, then nodded at Frankie. "Stay," he commanded, as if she were a dog. He kicked the cage door closed, and the lock snapped shut automatically.

"Hey!" Frankie screamed. She crawled on all fours toward the door, then moved to stand. If she could charge at the lock with all the fury she could muster, maybe she could break it open.

Robert held the knife tighter to Allyson's throat, but all his focus was on Frankie. "Don't get up."

She put her hands up in surrender and sank back down to the floor. "I thought you wanted me to come out?"

"I've changed my mind." Robert's eyes remained on Frankie even when he leaned his mouth down to Allyson's ear. "You first." He backed away, dragging Allyson with him.

"What are you going to do to her?" Frankie yelled. She slammed her fists against the bars. The pounding rattled the inside of her skull.

Robert maneuvered Allyson several feet away, where a pair of shackles hung from the end of a chain that had been haphazardly attached to the ceiling.

"Let her go!" Frankie shouted. She barely recognized the voice as her own from the panic in her tone.

"Lift your arms," Robert said, positioning Allyson under the contraption. She lifted her arms like the perfect victim, threatened enough by Robert's knife to listen, but not scared to the point of immobility.

He clamped the wide cuffs around her wrists, and she cringed at their touch.

More iron, Frankie realized.

Shaking the bars of the cage, she tried to think of anything she could do to help her friend. As far as she could tell, she was out of options. It took everything she had in her, but she caved in. She begged. "Don't hurt her. Please, don't hurt her. She's not a part of this. Let her go and kill me instead. Please."

Robert laughed as he examined the blade of his knife. "Who said I was going to kill her?" He glanced over his shoulder at Frankie, his eyes unpredictable and mad. "We're going to have some fun first. I've had lots of practice. I've had women, wolves...but faeries are a new favorite." He slapped Allyson. "Isn't that right, my little troll?"

Frankie watched, completely horrified, as Robert stabbed his blade into the soft flesh of Allyson's stomach.

THE TIRES OF Jace's Chevelle squealed as he sped up to the curb outside his apartment. He barely took the time to throw the car into Park before he bolted from the vehicle. He rushed up the stairs and burst into the apartment, panting and out of breath, but full of adrenaline.

David stood. "J? Man, what are you—"

"Robert has Frankie and Allyson. Old warehouse in Honeoye."

David swore.

"We need to go *now*." Jace grabbed David's jacket off a nearby coat rack and threw it at him. "Shane, get your coat on."

Shane's eyes widened. "What do you need from me? I can—"

Jace let out a low growl. "Get your coat on and get in the damn Chevelle. Pronto."

Two minutes later Jace was speeding full-throttle toward Honeoye.

Frankie.

She was his sole focus, the only thing he wanted to live for. He imagined her face in agony as Robert drew his knife across her skin. The image sent his blood boiling. That sick fuck would pay. He would die the slowest, most painful death Jace could think of.

My fault. All my fault.

The words echoed in his head. Frankie. Allyson. The countless bodies piling up in filthy alleyways. All his fault. He choked down a battle cry that would have shattered the windows.

Shane cleared his throat and leaned in between the two front seats, his face hovering between Jace and David. "We need a plan."

Jace growled. "I'll tell you the damn plan. We kill that motherfucker and then carve his eyes out with a dull blade." Jace's grip tightened on the steering wheel. "No one touches my mate."

My mate.

He thought of the first time they'd made love, the way he had slammed into her and she had taken every inch of him and reveled in it. Being inside her had felt like coming home, the way her lips had sweetly caressed his.

Damn right she was his mate.

Because even when she was ripping out his heart and stomping on it, unable to choose him, he was still fucking in love with her. A weight lifted off his chest. Yeah, he could admit it. She was mate. He loved her. He didn't give a flying shit if she was a wolf shifter, if she were packmaster, if she'd lied about her name and who knew what else. He loved her, and he would be damned if he was going to let anyone hurt her.

"If either of you wants this to be successful, we *need* a plan," Shane said, raising his voice louder. Colder and more calculating than usual.

"What's the point of making a plan?" David said. He twisted around to look at Shane. "We're going to be massacred. Robert has been a berserker longer. He knows his abilities and how to control them. He has the upper hand, and there's no way Jace can ever one up him, because with his father dead, he'll never be able to access his Berserker powers."

"Dead?" Jace asked, stunned. "What the hell are you—"

"Sorry to be the bearer of bad news," Shane said, coolly from the backseat, his voice filled with that eerily calm detachment than made him so good at his job, "I did some online research after you ran out like the hounds of hell were after you, and... I'm sorry, Jace, but David's right. He's dead."

Jace felt as if the world had been placed on pause. There was little room for anything in his mind except for the news David had delivered and Shane had confirmed—and his fear for Frankie, his love for his mate. His drive to save her and her friend. He continued speeding toward the warehouse, but his vigor and anger flickered for a moment before reigniting.

His father was dead? The old bastard was finally dead? He wasn't quite sure how to feel. Sadness—that was what he should have felt, if he'd had a normal childhood. Instead, all he could feel underneath his drive to kill Robert was a sense of relief.

Coupled with fear for the woman he loved.

The rest of David's words finally penetrated his brain then.

He shook his head to clear it. "Wait. Is that true? That no matter what I do, I'll never be able to use any of the Berserker powers?"

Shane sighed. "Unless you can go back to the other-world again and find a different solution, yeah, it's true. You're the last of your bloodline. There's no one else left for you to kill, even if you wanted to. And even with your current abilities, Robert still has the advantage, because he's been using his gifts so much longer, and you still can't shift at will."

The tension filling the car was staggering. Jace felt suffocated. Several minutes of silence passed before he finally let out a long sigh. This was it, then. He was almost certainly going to die. But that was okay. He would do anything, give anything—even his life—if he could just save Frankie. Finally, he spoke.

"Here's the plan. We do whatever it takes to get Frankie and Allyson out of there. Shane, your job is to get them to safety by whatever means necessary. I'll give you the keys to the Chevelle. David, it's your job to get them out, then go with them and Shane and make sure they're safe. Don't even consider coming back to help me. There are demons in this city you need to take care of. The brotherhood can't lose you, and once I'm out of the picture, Headquarters will see that they can't either. I'll take care of Robert. No matter what it takes."

David shook his head. "Are you sure, J? Can you do this?"

Jace nodded. "I have to. All I can do now is pray it's my lucky friggin' night and I don't go down with him."

~

ALLYSON'S SCREAMS ECHOED off the warehouse walls and rang in Frankie's ears. Adrenaline shot through her, and she fought to hold in her anger—she couldn't allow herself to shift unintentionally—but the rage filling her was on the point of exploding.

"Let her go, you sick bastard!" She shook the cage bars so hard the damn thing nearly tipped over.

Blood poured down the front of Allyson's torso, staining her shirt and jeans. All the color had drained from her face, and Frankie could tell she was fighting not to pass out.

Robert laughed as he glanced at Frankie. "Don't worry. I'm not killing her." He brandished the knife again and stabbed the tip into Allyson's arm.

She shrieked and writhed from the pain.

"See that right there." He pointed to the wound, raising his voice to be heard over Allyson's screams. "It's a shallow wound. Deep enough to cause pain, but nothing that will cause her any permanent damage."

He plunged the knife into Allyson's thigh, inches away from her femoral artery. "Actually, you should be thankful I haven't taken her life already. I find myself growing bored."

Seeing him torment Allyson conjured thoughts of all those other women. Had Robert tortured them the same way? Her body trembled with fury. She couldn't let herself think about it.

"You are a sick, pathetic excuse for a human being," Frankie spat.

Robert paused with the knife in the air and turned

toward her. Blood dripped from the blade onto his hand as he began to laugh. His laughter filled the warehouse—the cackling of a madman. "A pathetic excuse for a human?" He walked toward the cage. "That's where you're wrong, you filthy mutt. You see, I'm not human. Not in the slightest." He knelt in front of the cage and pointed his blade toward her face. He lowered his voice to a near whisper. "I'm more powerful than any man will ever be."

He stood and backed away from her, but his eyes never left hers. "And now, courtesy of your little outburst, I've become very angry," he said, almost clinically, "and believe me, you *really* won't like it when I'm angry. Because when my anger builds, I need to relieve it, so if you'll excuse me, the faerie and I have some much-needed business to attend to."

He turned away, and Frankie heard him unbuckle his belt before he unzipped his pants.

Allyson screamed and struggled against the chains holding her. "No, please. Frankie, help!"

Frankie pulled against the bars so hard the metal bent several inches and the cage actually toppled over. "Don't you fucking dare!"

Robert chuckled. He pushed his body flush against Allyson's, and she cringed at his touch. "Don't worry. I won't touch her." He ground the bulge in his pants against her small hips. Allyson whimpered, and he placed the knife against her throat. "At least, not while she's alive."

~

SHOTS ECHOED THROUGH the warehouse as Jace fired three rounds from his Mateba straight into Robert's back. The bastard staggered, falling forward and sending Allyson, who was shackled and hanging from a chain, swinging in the air.

Jace's gaze darted around the room. Frankie was struggling with the metal bars of a large cage that had tipped onto its side, her attention trained on him.

Tears poured down her face and blood covered her chest. "Jace!" she yelled.

Jace placed a single finger over his mouth to silence her and pointed to the rear exit door where David was slipping inside the building. As Jace watched, David limped toward the cage, making sure Robert didn't spot him.

Slowly Robert rose to his feet, still much too close to Allyson. The bullets pushed their way out of his back as the skin stitched itself back together, visible through his torn shirt. He turned to face Jace, the desire of a murderer burning in his eyes.

"Haven't you learned? Your silly little bullets can't kill me, Jace." Robert smirked.

Jace held his gun steady, pointed straight at Robert's head. "Maybe. But they can sure as hell cause you a lot of pain."

Robert stepped forward, arms wide in a welcoming gesture. "Why bother fighting, Jace? Give yourself up now and I'll let them both go. Untouched."

Jace shook his head. "You really think I'm that stupid? You won't yield that easy."

A wide grin spread across Robert's face. "That's debatable. But considering your bloodline, for my own sake, I hope your lineage alone makes your intelligence above par."

"What the hell are you talking about?" Jace focused on Robert, trying hard not to glance in Frankie's direction as David quietly picked the lock on the cage. If only Robert would move toward him, David could get to Allyson, too.

Robert stepped toward Allyson and ran his hand down the length of her thigh. She writhed in a fruitless attempt to avoid his touch. "You still haven't figured it out yet, have you?" he said, then turned to leer at Allyson.

While Robert wasn't looking, Jace inched forward. One step. Two.

Turning to face Jace again, Robert wiped the blood off his knife with the edge of his shirt. He eyed Jace up and down. "You never once questioned why? Why your name was carved into the arms of my masterpieces? Why that werewolf bitch was attacked just after you fucked her like the whore she is?"

Jace let out a low growl. "I don't try to understand the logic of psychopaths. If you wanted to kill me, you should have just done it that night at the park. Enough with the theatrical games."

Robert frowned. "Killing you then would have been too easy and entirely lacking in emotional satisfaction. I wanted you to know exactly why I chose you as my sacrifice. We have so much more in common than you realize."

"I am absolutely nothing like you." Jace's jaw clenched into a tight line, and he ground his teeth together. If he didn't fight back his rage, he would charge Robert right then, and that would be a mistake. He needed to wait for the opportune moment.

"We're both a rare breed. Beserkers destined to follow a warrior bloodline." Robert laughed mockingly. "To think that you were convinced you were werewolf. Self-right-eously killing for years to atone for your absent-daddy issues. No reason to cry in fear now, Jace. He's long dead."

Jace stepped forward. He couldn't let this creep get into his head, under his skin. But how...?

"How do you know about my father?"

Robert shook his head and clicked his tongue as if he were disappointed in a small child. "I thought you would have been smarter than this, Jace McCannon."

Anger pulsed through Jace's veins. "You heard me, asshole. How do you know about my father?"

A twisted look twinkled behind Robert's eyes. Jace had seen that look before. His breath caught.

Robert grinned in triumph. "Because Thomas McCannon was *my* father, too."

———

23

Jace stood frozen in a vacuum of his own thoughts as he processed the words Robert had just spoken. His stomach churned.

Robert was his brother?

No, there was no way. He didn't have any brothers. He had been his parents' only child.

Jace shook his head. "You're bluffing—another one of your sick mind games. Are you so desperate that you have to fuck with my head? Be a man and just fight me already."

Robert wagged his index finger at Jace. "Now, now, don't throw a hissy fit because you're no longer the only child, big brother."

A snarl tore from Jace's throat before he could stop himself.

Robert took a step toward him. "Don't try to kid yourself, Jace. You know it's true. I know you can see the resemblance."

Jace stepped back. "I don't give a shit whether we look similar or not, you're not my damn brother. It's not possible." Jace couldn't hear this. He couldn't. Not another damn word of it.

Robert made a tsking noise, then sighed. "Explain to me how it's not possible, brother. How many times did our father stumble home drunk after he'd spent the night fucking countless whores? Tell me. Tell me how many times he tossed your mother aside to sheath himself inside some nameless slu—"

"Shut up!" Jace roared. Was it really true? And if it was, how the hell had Shane missed that bit of information? He fired another round into Robert's torso.

Robert's body jerked with the hit, but he didn't fall. Laughing hysterically, he stared Jace down with the same fucked-up look Tom had always given him. "When our father finally left you, he shacked up with *my* mother. But unlike you, dear old Dad took me under his wing. He told me all about you. How you were weak, not man enough to follow in his footsteps. But I was stronger. So much stronger." He gestured to his chest and pulled his shirt open to show the bullet emerging from his body and the skin healing over, as if to demonstrate his superiority. "He taught me how to kill, how to live. I knew I was a berserker. I *knew*."

Jace's breath caught. "You killed him so you could come into your full power."

Robert smiled. "Unfortunately, no. By the time I went to the otherworld and learned I needed to kill our father to become a true Berserker, he was long dead. After all that time, can you believe the lucky old bastard died in his sleep? A heart attack from old age. Such a normal, boring way to go, don't you think? Especially for someone who spent a hundred and fifty years on this earth."

He flipped his knife around in his hand, admiring the gleam of light on the bloody blade. "I traveled the world for a while, perfecting my technique before I came home again. It started out as nothing but good fun—killing the women here in Rochester. The occasional wolf. But it became so much more than that."

Robert gazed down at the knife blade. "I realized I could use them to lure you to me. I realized I didn't need to kill our father to gain my abilities." He met Jace's eyes. "I just needed to kill you."

Before Jace could react, Robert threw his knife. The blade hit Jace's shoulder, lodging in his flesh with a sickening sound. Pain shot through him, and he fell to his knees. Blood gushed down his arm. His grip weakened and he dropped the gun, which skidded across the floor. The knife must have nicked an artery.

The old man died of a heart attack. His heart stopped. His heart stopped. Jace's thoughts screamed the truth at him. *Robert's not into his full power—yet. We're both berserkers.*

He scrambled for the knife. If he could stab it through Robert's heart, he might have a chance. He ripped the blade from his shoulder and launched himself at the other man. At his brother.

FRANKIE'S HEART STOPPED when she saw Robert throw the knife at Jace.

"No!" she screamed.

Her heart kicked into high gear when the blade lodged in Jace's shoulder. His blood poured out, but thank goodness the hit hadn't killed him. She would never forgive herself if he died. Damn it. She was a fool. She couldn't lose him.

"Frankie," David said, shaking the bars to get her attention. "This isn't working. Take this." He handed her the lock pick he'd been using. "Keep working at it. I need to get to Allyson, get her out of here, and hand her over to Shane. She's losing too much blood. She—"

"David, it's all right. Robert is busy with Jace. It's your only chance. Go."

He threw her a grateful look and said, "When you get out, go to Shane. He's waiting outside. Don't try to fight Robert." Then he left and made his way to Allyson's side as stealthily as possible and began working at her handcuffs.

Frankie's eyes darted to the other side of the room, where Jace was rolling on the ground with Robert, in a tangle of punches and kicks. Forcing herself to look away, she shoved the lock pick into the keyhole, feeling around for the tumblers.

Come on. Come on. Come on.

She continued working at the lock. To hell with David's instructions. She needed to help Jace. She would be damned if she was going to abandon him when he needed her most. Damned if she wouldn't avenge her parents, herself, Allyson.

There was a thud as Allyson's shackles opened and she fell to the floor. She tried to get up and toppled into David's arms. He hoisted her onto his shoulder and half-ran, half-limped awkwardly toward the rear exit. Thank God for that at least.

She kept working the lock.

Damn it.

The thing wouldn't budge.

She kept at it frantically, and just as she felt a small shifting as the lock yielded to her efforts, a loud bang echoed through the warehouse as the front doors burst open, revealing the three other members of the Rogue Brotherhood.

Coming to the aid of their friend.

JACE SLAMMED HIS fist into Robert's jaw with a sickening crack. Bone crunched beneath his hand, but he knew it would heal in a matter of minutes. Robert slashed at him with the silver knife, which he'd managed to wrest back. Warm blood covered his body, flowing from multiple wounds on his chest, shoulders, and arms. Heat burned through him, rushing to his wounds. He felt the skin knit together and regrow seconds after the wound had been made.

An equal playing field. It all came down to sheer ability.

To his belief in himself and skills gleaned over years of being a hunter.

With a massive shove, Robert pushed Jace off him. Jace fell back onto the floor, and Robert was on him in seconds. He slammed the knife down toward Jace's chest. Jace grabbed his wrist and struggled to hold back Robert's arm.

A tingling sensation ignited beneath his skin, and he was faintly aware of the glowing blue markings covering his body and shining through his clothes. Electricity pumped through him. He felt stronger, faster.

But Robert retaliated, quickly channeling his own energy. Energy that was more practiced, more refined than Jace's. The knife shifted down an inch, closer to plunging into his chest.

Fuck. He was going to lose this fight. He couldn't lose. He *couldn't.*

The image of Frankie's face clouded his mind. If he had one wish, it was to see her gorgeous smile one last time.

In an instant Robert was ripped off him and the

bloodied knife skidded across the floor as Jace's fellow hunters attacked the bastard. Damon's fists collided with Robert's face in an angry frenzy.

Jace grabbed the knife and jumped to his feet, prepared to fight.

As he lunged forward, a surge of power pumped through his body. Without warning, he grabbed Robert by the back of his neck and ripped him away from Damon's fists, then stabbed the knife straight into the fucker's side.

"Damon, get the girls out!" Jace yelled. He ripped the knife from Robert's flesh and stabbed him again.

Robert threw a wild punch, his fist slamming backward into Jace's kneecap, and Jace crumpled to the ground right alongside him. The bastard was indestructible. There was no way he could manage to stab him in the heart. Jace scrambled to his feet, but Robert slammed into him again, pinning him to the ground. His nails dug into Jace's wrists, and Jace could tell he was channeling all his strength in order to hold him down.

"Just let me kill you, Jace. Give up and I'll leave your bitch and her friend in peace."

Jace spat into Robert's face and snarled. "Not a chance, you murdering motherfucker."

"Don't make this harder on yourself than it has to be, Jace. I have you trapped. You have no way out."

Jace growled. Robert was right. He had him pinned. The other hunters were trying to get Frankie out safely. They couldn't help him before Robert made his move. The bastard could strip him of the knife any time he wanted, and once he did it would be inside Jace's heart within seconds.

"It's too bad it had to be this way, brother," Robert went on patronizingly. "You would have made an excellent berserker if you weren't such a bleeding heart, so weak."

Jace ground his teeth together. Weak? No. He was a lot of things: a stubborn, hardheaded chain-smoking asshole who sometimes drowned himself in alcohol. But he was *not* weak. If he had his way, he would rip out Robert's throat with his...

Jace's eyes widened. With his teeth. He would rip Robert's throat out with his teeth.

Robert's fingers dug into the flesh of Jace's hand, and Jace felt the knife begin to slip from his grasp. He ignored that and focused on Robert's disgusting face. He thought of all the women he'd hurt, all the women he *would* hurt if no one could stop him. He thought of his dickhead of a father, who'd created the monster before him. His inner beast stirred, and he pushed all his energy into his chest, straining beneath Robert's grip.

He wasn't like his father. Like Robert. He never would be, and he was going to prove it.

In one massive push, Jace lunged forward, his body contorting and shifting as fur sprouted from beneath his skin.

Robert recoiled, the knife in his hand falling. He raised his arm, but not quickly enough.

Jace's muzzle collided with Robert's neck, and he sank his canines into the meaty flesh of Robert's throat as he ripped through the bastard's jugular.

Blood spurted from the wound, and Robert's body convulsed several times, thick red spittle pouring from his mouth.

Within seconds Jace's fur folded in on itself and he lost his shift, but it didn't matter. He glanced down at his body as the claws retracted back into his hands. His shirt hung off him in shreds. He'd only managed to shift the upper half of his body, but he'd done what he'd needed to.

His gaze shot to Robert, and he realized the fucker still wasn't dead. He stared at the bloodied mangled mess that he was ashamed to call his brother. Already the skin of Robert's neck was beginning to knit together.

Grabbing the knife, Jace loomed over the killer and let out a low growl. "Say hi to Dad for me." He stabbed the blade straight into Robert's heart, and scarlet arterial blood spurted from Robert's chest.

In one last attempt to save his own life, Robert reached for Jace, going straight for his neck, but Jace simply twisted the knife. Robert's eyes widened, and he gurgled on his own blood. The other man's body continued to twitch for several moments until finally he fell limp. Jace's breath caught.

Dead. Robert was finally dead.

He let go of the knife and leaned back. The intricate blue designs pulsated on his skin, then quickly faded. Energy trickled out of him as if he were a drained battery. Black dots swam in front of his eyes.

"Jace? Jace!" Frankie cried.

It was the last thing he heard, the sound of his mate's voice.

But strangely, Jace was at peace with that.

So long as she loved him.

And as he faded from consciousness, for once, he had the strange thought that he just might deserve her.

EPILOGUE

It'd been three days. Three days since Jace had been awake, and still he hadn't come to see her. Upon waking, fully healed, he'd kissed her, told her he loved her and that he always would, but then he'd told her he needed some space.

To take care of a few things, he said.

Before he'd promised to come back to her.

Frankie had agreed, of course somewhat unwillingly, but she hadn't been able to voice her protests. Not when he'd both shown and told her exactly how much he loved her. Not when she knew he'd return to her once he was ready. They had the rest of their long lives ahead of them after all, and into the otherworld beyond. He was a part of her now, and she a part of him.

They always would be.

Frankie closed the door to the old studio, saying her goodbyes to the young woman who'd come to tour the inside. She was human, young, fresh out of dance school, but full of a wonder and determination, exactly like Frankie had wanted her to be. The perfect buyer.

The door to the studio open and closed again, and Frankie glanced up, only to find her mate now standing there. She smiled, and the ache in her chest eased instantly. She'd missed the sight of him, the heat of him over the past few days, and all she felt now was relief. The tension in her shoulders released. Relief that they'd made it through everything that'd been thrown at them, that they'd reached the other side of the conflict that'd caused them to meet.

No doubt they'd face other, different challenges in the future, but for now, she wouldn't even consider anything but feeling happy that he was back here with her.

"I thought you wanted to keep this place?" he said, hitching a thumb over his shoulder to indicate the human girl who'd she'd been speaking with a few moments before. "Something for yourself. To remind yourself you're more than a packmaster," he continued.

Frankie smiled to herself, glancing about the studio to where she'd painted over the graffiti on the walls within the past few days. "That's where you're wrong, mate."

She wasted no more time then, moving to join his side.

She wrapped herself around him, reveling in his embrace. "When I first became packmaster, those words probably would have been true, but not long after, things changed. I came to see that the weight of the responsibility placed on my shoulders wasn't a burden, but a gift." She snuggled close to him, placing her head on his chest. "For a long time, I felt guilty about ever having wanted that gift to have been given to someone else. This place was a reminder of that guilt. A safeguard so I wouldn't ever turn away from my pack, so I would remember."

Gently, he cupped her chin in his hand, tipping her head up toward him. "And now?"

She smiled at him. "Now, it's an acceptance, a memory of

all the different parts of myself. It was even before I met you, but these days…" She cupped his face again, like she had before the first time he'd told her he loved her. "Now I don't need it. Now I have you to remind me."

Jace smiled at her, full and wide in a way he rarely had before. "I'll gladly serve as that reminder every day. More, if you need it."

Frankie stood up on her tiptoes, drawing into kiss him. Soft, loving, deep. "What's kept you away?" she whispered against him.

"Tying up loose ends, and other business."

She lifted a brow, pulling away only enough to look at him.

"Somehow, Damon managed to convince Headquarters to let me go, to stop hunting me. Apparently, he told them having a warrior from an ancient bloodline as an enemy wouldn't benefit them, and continuing to search me out was a waste of resources, so it's all the Rogue Brotherhood for me from here on out."

Frankie huffed an amused laugh. "I'm glad for you. If that's what you wanted."

Though they'd have to find a way to explain the rogue brotherhood and what they stood for to the pack. But she was happy for him, really. She saw the good in him, in what he could do in his position now more than ever.

"It is." Jace nodded. "For now. While we work to weed out the bad actors in the organization. Once we do, then and only then will I walk away." His gaze hardened slightly, the only outward sign she could see of his pain at what the Execution Underground had become. "Damon was right. We started this. Now it's our responsibility to finish it."

There was an honor in that, in seeing it through to the end.

Whatever challenges he may face.

Frankie nodded, understanding in her own way. "I know a thing or two about responsibility, if you can believe it." She grinned.

"And I've been thinking about that over the past few days, about you too," Jace's eyes glimmered with something that looked dangerously like hope, "about what claiming me as your mate meant for you, what you and your pack had to sacrifice, and Frankie, I have to be honest, I don't want that for you."

"Jace—" She started to protest, but he placed a single finger to her lips.

"Shhh, mate. Let me finish."

She smiled, then playfully bit his finger, sucking it into her mouth.

A low growl tore through him, and his arousal pushed against her belly in an instant.

"If you shush me again, it'll be more than me who tears into you," she teased, nipping at his neck now. "The pack won't stand for it. But go on, my mate."

Jace's grin as he looked at her was pure rogue it was so wicked. "I think you'll find they'll be more protective of me than you think once you give them this." He stepped away from her momentarily, only long enough to remove a folded paper document from his pocket.

"What's this?" Frankie lifted a brow.

"Another gift," Jace's smiled broadened. "One of the conditions I asked Damon and the others to negotiate before they agreed to return to the Execution Underground."

She unrolled the paper, reading the header at the top and stared at it. It read:

THE NORTH AMERICAN INDEPENDENT PACK AGREEMENT.

"I made a few calls. Might owe a few favors to some friends out west who had contact with the Grey Wolves to see how it was done."

Frankie stared down at the paper, wanting, but unable to read the fine print from the tears welling in her eyes. She could hardly breathe. "What does this mean?"

Jace cast her that familiar wry grin. "This means that the Execution Underground, and by clandestine association, the U.S government, will now recognize independent packs like yours, as fully separate entities from larger packs like the Grey Wolves, among others. You don't have to strike any sort of deal with Amarok that you don't want to. Not on my watch."

Frankie couldn't bring herself to speak. She was too overwhelmed, too full with all the love she held for him. His acceptance not only of her, but of her pack, and most importantly, of himself. She could see that newfound determination in his eyes, in all their strength.

It would be a long, hard road for him to get there fully, to move past all the years he'd spent in self-hate, but she had no doubt they would be able to get there—together. Given time.

"Please say something," he whispered.

"Jace, you have no idea what this means to me," she breathed. "Thank you."

"I have plenty more gifts where that came from, Princess. One of my life goals is to spoil you. What can I say? It does something for me." He shrugged, still grinning.

She kissed him then, fully, totally, completely.

Neither of them holding any part of themselves back.

"Just promise one thing for me," Jace whispered again once she'd come up for air again.

Frankie nodded, feathering kisses over the edge of his stubbled jaw. "Anything."

"Promise me that in the future, each time I buy you lingerie, there'll be no complaints when I rip it off you." He growled against her skin. "With you, it's kind of my thing."

She chuckled. "But what if I want to be a brat about it?" she pouted.

"Don't worry," he purred, his gaze sparking with heat, as he slapped a playful hand over her ass. "I'll take care of that." She yelped, before giggling, but she fell silent quickly, entranced as he gripped the heat of her in his hands and he pulled her closer.

A sinful smirk twisted his lips, and she knew exactly what that would mean.

She grinned, both her body and mind filled with heat in an instant, heady with the resolve that while they were no longer enemies, for her he'd be as devilish and wicked as one, whenever and wherever she needed him to be.

David and Allyson's story is next...

Grab your copy of *Cold Demon Hunter* now!

ABOUT THE AUTHOR

Kait Ballenger is the award-winning author of the Seven Range Shifter and Rogue Brotherhood paranormal romance series, where she weaves captivating tales filled with dark, sexy alpha heroes and the independent women who bring them to their knees.

When Kait's not preoccupied writing "intense and riveting" paranormal plots or "high-voltage" love scenes that make even seasoned romance readers blush, she can usually be found spending time with her family or with her nose buried in a good book. She lives in Florida with her husband and two sons.

Readers can visit Kait's website and sign up for her newsletter at www.kaitballenger.com.

For right inquiries, contact Nicole Resciniti at The Seymour Agency: nicole@theseymouragency.com

ACKNOWLEDGMENTS

Foremost thanks to my friend and agent, Nicole Resciniti, for giving me a chance way back when I was a debut author. Nic, you changed my life with a single phone call, and there is no way I could ever express my gratitude. Thank you.

To my previous HQN editor who edited this book's original edition, Leslie Wainger, thank you for believing in this series from the start.

To my friends, Mara Wells, for the brainstorming, and Abigail Owen, for the first read, I am so grateful for your friendship.

To my mom and dad, thank you for investing both time and money in the future of my writing career before it could even be called a career. You believed in me, even in the face of initial rejection. Thank you. I love you.

Lastly, thank you to my amazing husband, Jon. Writing the first draft of this book while we were dating (over a decade ago) was a challenge, but you were the best kind of distraction. You influenced Jace's original character in so many ways, but you also influenced this updated (and better) version of him. He's grown and become an even more impressive man in the same ways I've witnessed you grow and change for the better in the years we've been together. I love you—now, and always.

Hunters of the paranormal, the Rogue Brotherhood are an elite group tasked with protecting humanity, but at what price?

As an exorcist, David Aronowitz grew up the target of demonic assassins. Now he's a member of the Rogue Brotherhood and hellspawn everywhere fear his name. But when a demon slips into the seductive body of the only woman he's ever loved, David must confront the heartbreak of their past to save her...

ALSO BY KAIT BALLENGER

Seven Range Shifters

Cowboy Wolf Trouble

Cowboy in Wolf's Clothing

Wicked Cowboy Wolf

Fierce Cowboy Wolf

Wild Cowboy Wolf

Cowboy Wolf Outlaw